The Trial of Jenny Sykes

Hebe Weenolsen

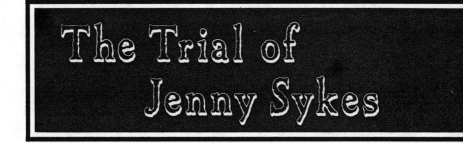

The Trial of Jenny Sykes

ST MARTIN'S PRESS NEW YORK

Design by Judith A. Stagnitto

Quality Printing and Binding By:
ARCATA GRAPHICS/KINGSPORT
Press and Roller Streets
Kingsport, TN 37662   U.S.A.

To the Reader

This story is based upon the seventeenth-century discovery, later to become one of the basic tests in legal medicine, that the lungs of the deadborn infant would sink in water, (as opposed to the floating of the lungs of the live-born infant, which had breathed). This phenomenon, first observed by the anatomists Bartholinus (1663) and Swammerdam (1667), was introduced into the courtroom in 1682 by Jan Schreyer of Zeitz, Saxony, in his successful defense of a peasant girl accused of infanticide, the sinking of the fetal lungs securing acquittal.

The following story, *The Trial of Jenny Sykes,* is set three years later in England, where medical jurisprudence had as yet scarcely begun to be recognized.

The Trial of
Jenny Sykes

One

The hill was deserted now, an empty solitude of gorse and heather. But it had not always been so. In ages past, men had fought and died for Yeggor Dun.

Little was known of those who first claimed the mighty fastness as their home, but primitive rites ending in sexual orgies had likely been rooted in their religion. For when, in time, they were driven from Yeggor Dun, they left behind the phallic figure of their god, a colossal form hewn out of sarsen stone, his penis jutting, the lewdness of his grin accentuated by patches of black lichen on his cheeks.

The centuries passed, unrecorded, and the hilltop stood forsaken by all save the mountain fox and the plover. No human foot trod the lofty fastness of the forgotten granite god, no sound that bespoke man's presence mingled with the sighing of the wind in the heather. Then the Celtic hordes crossed over into Britain, and one of their tribes, the fierce, red-haired Durotriges, took possession of Yeggor Dun, bringing to it their own dark faith, worshiping the dead and the powers of fertility that recreated life in each new generation and spring. To ensure fertility in themselves and their cattle they gathered around the phallic figure on certain nights of the year to perform their own mysterious rites, sacrificing a fair young man to the deity in the belief that the youth's sexual vigor would be transmitted to the aging god and renew his life-giving energies. The festivities that followed through the night, the wild ritualistic incantations, the frenzied dancing, the potent brews that roused them to an urgency of desire, the final orgiastic sexual excesses were an intrinsic part of their religion. And when the conquering Roman legions marched over The Downs and Vespasian planted the Eagle atop Yeggor Dun, those Durotriges who escaped the slaughter slipped away, down a hidden track cut in the hillside, to perpetuate their race and their cult in the caves and demon-haunted valleys below.

Sixteen centuries had passed since then and now. A Stuart king sat on the English throne. Yet still, for the simple villagers of Little Liscombe, at the foot of Yeggor Dun, the lofty hilltop held a fascination as powerful as it was strange. The Reverend Jude Sykes scolded from his pulpit, chiding them for sins too vague for his own mind to identify. But though they listened to their tight-faced, puritanical, London-bred minister, they still felt the pull of Yeggor Dun when the moon was full; they still reverted to the customs that had continued through the ages, still felt the stirring of the older blood, the compulsion of the older, darker faith. Though the name of the god their ancestors worshiped was long forgotten, as were the fertility precepts that had struck so deeply into the core of their beliefs, the rituals themselves endured in the folklore and superstition of the local people, and on certain nights of the year they assembled on the hilltop to perform strange rites under the white-faced moon. The chants and incantations, the fire ceremonials in which traces of human sacrifice were unmistakable, the wild dancing that showed, in its primitive character, its pagan origin, the drinks that induced unchecked sexuality—all appealed to the darker natures and unsated urges of the rustic population. And on such nights the Old God once again assumed his ancient power, until dawn broke in the east, driving the villagers home.

One evening in September of the year 1685, the Reverend Jude Sykes was riding slowly homeward along the country road leading to Little Liscombe. A serene crescent moon was rising over Yeggor Dun, but the vicar eyed it with rankling displeasure. He had just come from the bedside of young Tom Dutt, who was dying of gangrene and who, for all his agony, had made it clear that he would face Glory the easier for being relieved of the strain of the vicar's presence. Well, a wise shepherd expected no gratitude from his sheep, the vicar reflected. After ten years of preaching Christ Crucified to these contemptible sinners, they still remained as stubbornly inaccessible to him in death as they did in life.

Tall, gaunt, and dark, ascetic in his mode of life, Jude Sykes was not a man to recognize his own faults. Cynical and supercilious, it never occurred to him that he might be lacking in Christian charity. He never recognized that as a boy he did not have a friend, that he had grown friendless into manhood. At Cambridge, with lack of funds as his excuse, he lived a solitary existence. He had little in common with the other reading men, and when they showed no desire to cultivate him it was, in his view, because they saw his rectitude as a rebuke to their own hedonistic lives.

At his ordination he was presented with a small incumbency in Dorsetshire, entering upon his office with a pretty bride and high hopes of preferment. But a few years later those hopes perished in an eddy of whispers, and his transfer was hastily arranged. His second incumbency was even less harmonious than his first, and after yet another transfer the Reverend Jude Sykes found himself in this ministerial dunghill of Little Liscombe. His new parishioners, mostly stolid, unread farmers, were antipathetic from the start, and with the flow of time, when his wife ran off with some itinerant theatrical performer, they seemed actually to condone her behavior. The vicar bore his wife's departure with unemotional detachment, but he had no intention of allowing so unfit a woman to raise their five-year-old daughter, Jenny. When he located the adulterous pair and fetched the child home, his parishioners, with the characteristic blind stupidity of their class, deplored the separation of mother and child and created an embarrassing state of things by refraining, in a body, from attending services. In the weeks that followed, the vicar found himself preaching to an almost empty church. But after a while, as old parishioners died, their kin were forced to come, hat in hand, to the vicarage to arrange for burial. Thus, out of mutual need, was a grudging truce rough-hewn between the unforgiving vicar and his unwilling flock.

Twelve years had passed since his wife's departure. Jenny was seventeen now. She kept house for him tolerably well, but the two had little to say to each other at mealtimes and nothing to say in between. In these years at Little Liscombe he had held her tightly in rein, never allowing her to venture beyond the church and the vicarage. He thwarted attempts by the neighborhood women to reach out to Jenny by going himself to the village to buy their provisions. Nor had he ever permitted any friendliness to develop between Jenny and the husky young rustics who ogled her on Sundays during divine service. When they called at the vicarage later, in Sunday breeches and cap in hand, he took the precaution of sending Jenny to her room before admitting them. He never allowed himself to forget the nature of her mother's sin, or the preferment it had cost him.

The moon was high over the hilltop now and Little Liscombe lay just beyond the bend. There was no wind. From the deep quiet of the woods that fringed the road came the occasional whisper of a falling leaf. A white owl ghosted above the fern brakes.

Then, from the darkness of Squire Haynes's woods, he caught a gleam of light. A single flash, and it was gone. He reined in, sitting tense and aware, focusing his eyes upon the underbrush. So the night poachers were at work again, netting and strangling the squire's deer. Well, for all their pious denials, he was going to catch his parishioners red-handed tonight.

He dismounted and tethered his horse. Then he started into the woods, moving with the stealth of a nocturnal animal. He expected to hear the crackling rush of startled deer, the curses of throttling poachers. But all was still. Even the light was gone.

Halting, he glanced around. Then he saw the light again. It was burning steadily now, coming from a short way off where an open patch of turf broke the underwood.

Cautiously he approached and saw a lantern standing on a boulder. Its light burnished the low black ceiling of foliage, and within its small encircled space four men kneeled, grouped around a hole they were making in the ground, scooping out the loose clods with their bare hands. As the vicar watched, the men stopped scooping, and Joe Roos, the blacksmith, raised the lantern and held it over the hole. Then, still kneeling, the men leaned forward and stared down, in silent awe, at the thing they had uncovered.

The vicar's curiosity surged. If they were not out poaching tonight, they were certainly engaged in some other mischief. He waited. The men were whispering among themselves now, too low for him to catch what they said. Noiselessly he edged closer. Then from the shadows came the low growl of a hunting dog and the four men turned in unison, startled, peering out into the interspaces of leafy gloom until they made out the black-garbed figure of their vicar.

Unabashed at being caught eavesdropping, the vicar walked toward the kneeling men.

His tone was sarcastic. "Praying?" he asked.

No one answered. The men remained upon their knees, the flickering light of the lantern playing on their upturned faces, so the vicar stepped to the brink of the hole and peered down and saw, partially enshrouded in a woman's blue shawl, the body of a newborn infant.

"Holy Lord in His heaven!"

Slowly he dropped to his knees beside the others, staring down at the tiny naked male creature with its oversized head and puny body. Its hair was fine and dark, its scalp still swollen from the recent process of birth. Its tiny fists were clenched. Its forehead was as furrowed as that of an old man. Twelve inches of the navel-string remained attached to its belly.

The vicar's voice was barbed with suspicion. "How did you men know this was here?"

"Us didn't, Rev'rend," replied Luke Grimes, the thatcher, the dialect heavy on his lips. "T'was yonder pup found it. Him ain't used to night work yit and started running off by hisself, yammering and scratching up. So us flashed the lantern down and saw the loose sods and figured so'thing must be hid here."

"It is a bastard, of course," the vicar declared, "—some unmarried woman who killed her child and secretly buried it to conceal her immorality. Well, I will leave the body in the church overnight and hand it over to the constable in the morning."

He reached down and replaced the shawl about the dead infant, making neat angles at head and toe, tucking them under, and the men watched, uneasily at first, then with bewildered concern as their minds began to grapple with the terrible implications of his action.

At last, when he lifted the small bundle in his arms and rose to go, Luke Grimes spoke quickly, in a shocked tone.

"Rev'rend, did 'ee not know?"

"Know what, Luke?"

" 'Bout yer girl, Jenny?"

"What about Jenny?"

"That pore scrap of child 'ee got in yer arms—it be her'n."

The vicar frowned, fighting the hard knot of comprehension behind his eyes, and the four men continued to kneel there, staring dumbly up at him. The silence dragged. When a hazelnut dropped from its cup it seemed to fill all the woods with sound, tap-tapping on branch and twig as it fell.

At last Luke stumbled to his feet, a short, thickset man with a bush of graying hair.

" 'Tis true, Rev'rend," he said gently. "Do 'ee not rec'nize yer own girl's shawl? Us all has knowed fer months that her was with it."

"With it?"

"With a young'un."

The vicar's voice was strained. "And how could men like you have presumed to know a thing like that about my daughter?"

" 'Tweren't us, Rev'rend. 'Twere midwife Effie espied it—saw how yer girl was filling out her Sunday dress and all. After that, the whole village took to watching her every Sunday—jest out of meddlesomeness at first, but later 'cos us got to feeling mortal afeared fer the pore young thing, seeing how wild-eyed and poorly her looked. Did 'ee not see it too, Rev'rend? Did 'ee niver know her was with it? Did yer own girl niver tell 'ee?"

For the moment the vicar had control of his surging rage. He answered so quietly that even the slight vibration in his voice gave no indication of the suppressed passion behind it.

"No," he said. "I had no idea. She did not tell me."

"Well, no matter," said Luke, laying a gnarled, compassionate hand on the vicar's arm. "Don' 'ee be grieving, Rev'rend. Ain't no harm coming to yer girl. Us'll fix it."

"Aye, us'll fix it," Joe Roos agreed, getting to his feet. "Now best thing is fer 'ee to turn yer back on all this and go on home—'ee being the vicar and all. Then us four can do what needs be done."

"And us'll do it right, Rev'rend," Luke promised. "Us'll take the little creature off somewheres and bury it proper, where no one 'ull ever find it. So no need to go calling in the constable and gitting yer own girl put in jail—'specially her having niver had no mother to tell her, like. Us all be sorry fer that pore young thing, Rev'rend. Us don' want no harm coming to her."

At that the vicar's rage broke. Roughly he shook off Luke's hand and stood, inflexible, derisive.

"You are a fool, Luke Grimes, to think you can dissuade me from my duty. 'Whoso sheddeth man's blood, by man shall his blood be shed.' "

"All same, Rev'rend, it prob'ly were not the girl's fault. Musta happened some night on Yeggor Dun. When our boys git worked up, Rev'rend, ain't no girl kin stop 'em."

But the stern-faced preacher was motivated by something more compelling than the demands of a tyrannical conscience, though the impulse to destroy his own daughter was cloaked in elaborate disguise.

"Will God excuse the commission of this crime?—the murder of this innocent?" he cried. "Will He excuse the shameful abominations of the flesh that went before? Do you men know your Bible?" And now the vicar's voice rang with a curious note of conscious joy. " 'Then they shall bring out the damsel to the door of her father's house, and the men of her city shall stone her with stones that she die, because she hath wrought folly in Israel, to play the whore in her father's house.' Those words, men, come from the Holy Scriptures. Yet you are asking me—a minister of the Lord—to deny them by shielding a whore from justice because she is my daughter. 'The adulteress shall surely be put to death,' says the Bible. Amen. Amen!"

With that he wheeled, the blue bundle still in his arms, and strode off in the direction of the road, his black coat flapping behind him. He moved swiftly, heading straight through a patch of thickly clustering brambles, yet seemingly insensible to the thorns that tore his hose and clawed at his flesh till the blood ran down to his shoes.

Staring after him, the men were aware that their vicar was driven by a strange and complex mass of forces outside their comprehension.

"Don' that Rev'rend un'erstand?" Luke asked, rumpling his graying hair in puzzlement. "Don' 'ee know what him's gonna do to that pore girl? Don' 'e know child murder is a hanging crime? Jesus Lord! That Rev'rend's gonna git his own girl hung."

Young Doctor Toller had been a nameless, homeless waif of some six years when old Doctor Toller found him crouching under a bush, frozen and starving, at the close of a cold autumn day and, being a childless widower, took him to his heart that night and gave him both a home and a name. From then on they lived together in careless bachelor fashion, man and boy, doing for each other; though, the doctor being a zealous patron of the city pothouses, it was mostly the boy who did for the man, bedding him down when he came reeling home, roaring, cursing by all the devils in his rich and variegated vocabulary. On occasion, in a senseless rage, he would reach for a strap and come after the boy. But for young John, survival had so long been the sum total of life's experience that his legs were as nimble as his wits. In the morning the doctor would remember nothing of their cat-and-mouse antics of the night before. And young John never told him. For drunk or sober, he loved the kindly, capricious, obscene-tongued old man, so their relationship was a satisfying and rewarding one for both.

The doctor was delighted when young John showed an interest in medicine. "Like father, like son," he would declare proudly, quite forgetting—at eighty-two—that his late-blooming fatherhood was accidental rather than biological. Then, for the first time in his life, he tried to remember to collect his fees, though always with the apology, "Young John must enter on the study of medicine, you see."

John was thirteen when old Doctor Toller died, leaving behind a staggering accumulation of debts and an abiding reputation for benevolence. What fees he had taken from the houses of the rich he would, for all his avowed attempts at thrift, often leave in the houses of the poor, making the act of feeling the pulse a cover for slipping money into a needy patient's hand. On Sundays the poor flocked to him from every part of the county, since on Sundays it was his custom to see all comers free.

Doctor Toller's death seemed to have put an end to young John's dream of following him in the medical profession. But again fate stepped in when another kindly doctor, the illustrious Thomas Sydenham, made possible the completion of his education, and John was graduated as an M.D. at Pembroke Hall, Cambridge. Now in his twenty-eighth year (more or less, for he never knew his true age), "young" Doctor Toller still found that walking in his foster father's shoes was no easy task. For almost two centuries there had been a Doctor Toller in that part of Dorset—father, son, grandson, great-grandson—so that, when young John completed his internship in London and returned to the only home he had ever known, he quickly found, in a loose sense, he had inherited the peculiar Toller reputation and with it what was left of the Toller medical practice.

It was a far-spread heterogeneous practice, partly urban, which was remunerative, largely rural, which was not. Ofttimes he would find himself riding thirty miles to attend a patient who could give him nothing for his services but a boiled turnip and a cup of goat's milk. Or his horse would be halted along the way in some emergency and "young Doctor John" would dismount to stop a hemorrhage, or tend a farmhand stunned by a fall, or, watched by a hoard of screaming, delighted urchins, extract an iron splinter from a beggar's eye with a magnet. He had married young. The union was disastrous from the start and ended when their second child was killed as mysteriously as their first and his wife was dragged, clawing and screaming, to the county madhouse. Since then the only women in his life had been those he paid for in the elite establishments of Dorncaster and, occasionally, in a few less-elite waterfront brothels when, discouraged and lonely, he rode over to the ancient seaport of Poole. Then, by chance, he met the woman in the cottage by the river.

Now, two days after the discovery of the Sykes baby in Squire Haynes's woods, Doctor John was awakened at dawn by a loud knocking on the door of his two-room cottage.

"Doc, they be wanting 'ee at coroner's inquest," the foot bailiff shouted through a crack in the boards. "Said to tell 'ee the body's i' the deadhouse."

Doctor John shook himself out of a deep sleep. "The body? What body?"

"Some wench gone and kill't her bastard."

"God's ears! All right, then. When is the inquest?"

"This morning, Doc—eleven o' the clock sharp."

"Thank you, Benny."

John Toller swung his long legs off the bed. No need to dress, thank God! He had come home toward dawn, having worked futilely to save the life of a tired young mother who had attempted an abortion on herself with a bodkin. It seemed only an hour since he had dropped, supperless and fully clothed, onto his unmade bed.

Hurriedly he pulled on his boots, then went out to the backyard and put his head under the pump. The water was cold. It roused him. His mare heard him moving about and began stamping in her shed.

"Whoa! Iris. Quiet down. I have not forgotten you."

Iris blew lovingly at the sound of his voice, then kept blowing until he went into her shed with fresh water and began tossing her some feed.

"Eat up, girl," he said briskly. "No dawdling today. We have to get to the hospital early if I am to fit in my morning rounds."

Iris disliked being hurried so early in the day and put up her customary protest, turning her head and gazing at him reproachfully, her nostrils flared, her ears pricked at him.

"Come on, girl," he said, "no time for sulks. You know the city pays me the tall sum of eight pounds a year to play physician to the poor of this town—and this town's poor are as numerous as sparrows. Besides, we must get to the coroner's inquest by eleven o'clock, and you know as well as I do that Sir Mark's lust for punctuality frets him like a prurient itch. So eat up, my lovely. Come in when you are ready. And do not keep me waiting."

Iris was still not mollified, so he slid a gentle hand along the arch of her neck and continued to talk to her. Her ears twitched to his voice. After a moment she turned, snuffled at his coat, then lowered her head and began obediently to eat.

Back in the cottage he took only a moment to straighten his rumpled clothes and pull a comb through his hair. From the cupboard he took cheese and a loaf of bread and cut a thick slice off each, chewing them hurriedly and washing them down with a pot of ale.

By the time he finished, Iris had left her stall and, since there was no other exit from the tiny yard, had paced slowly through the parlor of the two-room cottage and was standing by the front door, waiting to be saddled. A few moments later he was mounted and riding through the narrow cobbled streets.

The rising sun cast a crimson light on the rooftops, and already the city's merchants and journeymen were out about their business. The pounding of Iris's hooves on the cobbles caused them to turn quickly, a sudden apprehension on their faces. For these were evil times, and Englishmen walked in fear. Spies were everywhere. No man knew when a body of the King's special cavalry patrols would swoop down and drag him off to jail, to rot forgotten in the bowels of the earth or be handed over to the hangman on a trumped-up charge of high treason. After a rule of only seven months, James the Second had already shown himself to be a lawless king.

The great-grandson of Mary Queen of Scots, James brooded on the fact that Mary had been beheaded by order of her kinswoman, Queen Elizabeth of England. Now that he ruled England, his hot brain nurtured thoughts of vengeance, combined with the conviction that he was

King by divine right. The precious freedoms Englishmen had won under the Magna Charta were odious to him. When Parliament, weighing his arrogance and Catholicism, refused to permit his coronation until he pledged to preserve both the Church of England and the traditional rights and liberties of the English people, James had so pledged. But it was a pledge he never meant to keep. Once crowned, he showed himself to be fanatical in his resolve to outlaw the Church of England and force his staunchly Protestant subjects to embrace Roman Catholicism. Henceforth only Catholics would hold the highest offices of state and the principal dignities of the universities. The royal army was being quietly officered by Catholics in an effort to convert it into a force that could be used to uproot the Protestant religion.

A rebellious mood swept the country. The loyalty of the nation wavered as Englishmen began to ponder ways to limit the King's arbitrary power. When the young Duke of Somerset refused to carry out a royal command on the grounds that to do so would be against the law, James cried angrily, "Do you not know I am above the law?" To which the Duke replied, "Your Majesty may be, but I am not," and was straightway dismissed from Court. Thereafter James claimed the right by his royal prerogative to suspend the laws of England at will and seemed incapable of understanding the conception of the supremacy of law, the principle that law was above the King.

Perhaps it was the revelation of this overriding lust for arbitrary power that first aroused suspicion, causing his subjects to question whether James's sudden accession to the throne might not have been brought about by some agency less recondite than the will of God.

This suspicion grew out of the curious circumstances surrounding the death of his predecessor, King Charles the Second. Charles, for all his illegitimate offspring, had no legitimate issue by his queen, so his younger brother James was regarded as his heir. Charles enjoyed a robust constitution and was expected to have a long life. But the previous February he had suddenly become ill. His personal physician being out of town, he was tended by a certain Doctor King who, chancing to be in the palace, and chancing to have his lancet in his pocket, proceeded to bleed him. The treatment was ineffective. The King began fainting. They purged him. They let blood from both jugulars. Soon he was exhibiting symptoms of epilepsy, shrieking and falling to the floor, his face purple, saliva pouring from his mouth. He was purged again. More blood was let. He began to vomit. As he struggled for breath, they drew another twelve ounces of blood. He died the next day. The cause of death was officially given as an apoplectic fit. If certain of his courtiers had doubts concerning the strange affair, they were silenced by the knowledge that the new king, James the Second, was a cruel and a vengeful man.

That was the alarming state of the country when, at midsummer, the Duke of Monmouth, the illegitimate son of the deceased king, sought to snatch his father's crown from James. Landing in Dorset, Monmouth proclaimed himself King of England and defender of English Protestantism. The gentry held aloof from his cause, but the humbler classes, largely Puritans who had long suffered religious persecution, flocked to his standard in the mistaken belief that the worthless Monmouth would champion religious toleration. But it was to be a broken hope. The campaign ended with the Battle of Sedgemoor, where these peaceful farmers and miners, armed mostly with pitchforks and mining picks, faced the cannon fire of the royalist army. When Monmouth saw the battle go against him, he secretly fled the field, leaving the brave rustics who had espoused his cause to pay the ghastly price of high treason.

Nine days later Monmouth was found cowering in a ditch and lost his cowardly head on Tower Hill. But a more terrible fate awaited the men he had abandoned. It was known that most of Monmouth's scratch army came from Dorset and Devon, so the King's cavalry had only to overtake the battle-weary survivors as they tried to make their way home on foot. The savage vengeance taken on them was stimulated by orders from the King, who sent down Chief Justice Jeffreys, a man known for his insane lust for cruelty, to earn the seals by a series of judicial murders which, for the widespread horror they generated, became known as the Bloody Assizes. Sufficient to convict was a forced confession, or an injury resembling a battle wound, or even a suspicion that the accused had recently been absent from home.

The terrible vengeance James took on these simplehearted rebels of Dorset and Devon left his name a byword for cruelty.

John Toller, heading for the hospital, gave Iris a gentle nudge and turned her into the Market Place, a route he took these days only when he was pressed for time. As a doctor he thought he had become inured to the manifold perversions of human nature, yet he was sickened by the sight of scores of human heads, trunks, legs, and arms in varying degrees of putrefaction. The trials under Chief Justice Jeffreys were still in progress, and day after day the condemned rebels were being dragged to the Market Place, where the infamous London executioner, Jack Ketch, and his assistant, Pascher Rose, did the gruesome work of slaughter.

Each man was first hanged until almost dead, then he was cut down and his bowels and genitals burned before his eyes. He was then dismembered, his severed limbs boiled in brine and tarred, and exposed on iron spikes throughout the city. The tarred heads were treated like trophies, set high on every steeple and chimney pot to blister and blacken in the sun till they looked like a grotesque flock of roosting crows. The roadsides leading out of town were lined with long rows of tarred and gibbeted rebels.

John Toller drew a hard breath. Many of those poor human remnants had been known to him in life. Many had been his patients. He had known them in the flesh, those blackened heads with open mouths and empty eye sockets. *Pax vobiscum.* He had saved as many as he could. At times a doctor found ways to exploit his professional privileges. He could come and go through the ancient city gates at will, by day or night, even under the suspicious, watchful eyes of the King's own henchman, Colonel Kirke, and his savage band of troopers known derisively as "Kirke's Lambs." By now Kirke and his "Lambs" recognized him as he rode through on Iris. They no longer stopped and questioned him. But he knew the risks. He, too, would be butchered by Ketch and Pascher Rose if ever it became known how many nights he had spent searching the countryside for Sedgemoor stragglers, how many pike and musket wounds he had closed, how many brave but misguided rustics he had already smuggled back to their homes by one ruse or another.

He leaned forward and patted Iris's neck. "You and I have our secrets, eh, girl?"

A few moments later he had reached the hospital, a massive ivied structure which, before the dissolution of the monasteries, had been a Benedictine house. Turning into the courtyard, he gave Iris into the care of the stableman, then he took the steps three at a time and entered the hospital through the side door.

A boy of about eight years was waiting in the lobby. He was slight and frail-looking, with flaxen hair and large, anxious eyes. He got quickly to his feet when he saw John.

"Good morning, Noah."

The boy did not answer, only gave a shy smile, but his large blue eyes seemed to be saying something which, being a deaf-mute, his lips could not express.

John read the question.

"I cannot tell you that yet, Noah," he said. "We will have to see how he is feeling today. But you can come with me, if you wish. We will go up to his room together."

The boy reached confidently for John's outstretched hand, and side by side they climbed the stairs and headed straight for the Men's Ward on the second floor. John motioned the boy to wait at the door, then, passing swiftly between the rows of beds, he made his way to a bed at the far end of the room, separated from the rest by a curtain.

He slowed his pace as he entered the small cubicle.

"Father? Father Dominic, are you awake?"

The patient, a priest in his seventies, recognized John's voice and opened his eyes.

His smile seemed to come with an effort. "I thought you had forgotten me this morning, my son."

"So you have been waiting? Are you in pain, then?"

"I am resting comfortably, my son."

"No pain at all?"

"I have told you—I am resting comfortably."

John pretended to believe him. "Well, now, let me see how things are with you today."

He pulled down the covers and his hands moved skillfully until his groping fingers found the mass. He scarcely needed to examine it. He knew this growing thing would be there. He knew what he would find today, and tomorrow, and the next day, until death took the life of this humble priest with the gentle, scholarly mind.

"Well, John?" Father Dominic asked.

John was carefully blank-faced. "Not much change today, Father."

He reached for the old man's wrist and stood a moment pretending to take his pulse, but his eyes were carefully scrutinizing the cadaverous face with its ashen skin, the compressed lips, the telltale shadowed eyes. Large beads of sweat gathering on the priest's forehead betrayed his determination to suffer this growing agony in silence. One frail hand, white-knuckled with pressure now, clutched at a small black cross on which hung the image of the crucified Christ.

John was filled with quick anger. Goddamn! By what right did the Church permit men to suffer martyrdom in emulation of the sufferings of Jesus? The toleration of martyrdom brought the Church into direct conflict with medicine. To the physician, martyrdom was self-destruction no less than the slow suicide of the ascetic. Where a patient could not be healed, the physician saw it as his moral obligation to ease his dying. Had not Hippocrates, the Master, "the Divine," taught that it was within the scope of the physician "to remove the suffering of the patient, or at least alleviate these sufferings"? John sighed irritably. I care not one damn for the doctrines of the Church, he thought. Medicine is my religion.

Aloud he said quietly, "I am going to change your treatment today, Father."

"Why, my son?"

"I want to try something new."

He opened his bag and took out a vial and mixed a small amount of liquid in water. Then he raised the priest's head and put the cup to his lips.

"Drink," he said.

The priest hesitated as a suspicion crossed his mind.

"You know, do you not, my son, that whatever pain He sends me I will gladly bear for His sake."

"I know that, Father."

"What is this new medicine, then?"

John forced himself to smile reassuringly. The bond of trust and affection between Father Dominic and himself reached back into his childhood. He had always been too proud to lie to Father Dominic. He felt uncomfortable lying to him now. Even the knowledge that his old teacher would probably die without ever realizing his deception did not mute the small outraged thing crying out inside him.

"It is something new," he found himself saying, "—something that is being tried out in London hospitals in cases like yours. Come, Father, I am making you my guinea pig. If it helps you, it will help others, so let us try it with that in mind. Now, drink, please."

"But, John, you still have not told me—"

"God's ears!" John burst out. "Have you no trust in me at all?"

Father Dominic stared, shocked by the suggestion. Then obediently he put his lips to the cup and emptied it.

He grimaced at the bitter taste and wiped his mouth on his sleeve. "And I have asked you, John, not to use profanity in my presence."

"Profanity, Father?" John grinned, relieved by the change of subject. Opium, tears of the poppy, symbol of Morpheus, heavy-eyed god of dreams. Opium, whose origin was lost in the mists of antiquity. The "nepenthe" of Homer. Galen's "potent destroyer of pain." "Why, Father," he said very gently, "in your presence I am as choosy of my words as when I am called to treat Her Grace at the castle."

Father Dominic lay back and closed his eyes and John pulled up a chair and quietly sat there, saying nothing, watching the old man's face, carefully noting how the frail hand slowly relaxed its grip on the crucifix as the opium began to blunt his pain.

But presently Father Dominic spoke again, softly, more peacefully now.

"My son, why must you always talk so lightly of God? Have you no religion anymore?"

John gave a low laugh. "Perhaps I would have, Father, if I had time for it."

"Do you never go to church?"

"And give up my Sunday? The only day I have to lie in bed?"

The priest shook his head disapprovingly. "You were not always so irreligious, John."

John was suddenly serious. "In these past years I have seen a lot."

"As a doctor?"

"Aye, as a doctor."

The old man's eyes seemed to be probing John's thoughts. "And now," he prompted, "finding the world drowning in human misery, you take issue with that misery by questioning the existence of God?"

"I did not say I question the existence of God."

"Nay?" The priest was silent for a moment, waiting. Then he added softly, "You did not always find it so difficult to confide in me."

"It is not confidence that is lacking, Father Dom."

"By that I take you to mean that you do not wish to distress me— that you are troubled, perhaps, by the usual intermittent doubts."

John shifted his gaze to the floor. "I am troubled more by the fact that there is no material for an answer."

"An answer? To the question of God's existence? John, down through the ages man has suffered martyrdom and death for his religious beliefs. Does not the persistence of such faith *prove* that God exists?"

"Not to me, Father. To me it proves only man's pathetic need to rely on someone outside his own puny self, to rely on some power greater than his own."

"You talk like a man who has lost faith, my son. Is that it? Have you lost faith?"

"To me, Father, faith has become an illusion—a belief that something exists without adequate proof to support that conviction. I am a scientist, Father Dom. I ask questions. I search for answers."

"And do you not sometimes get answers in unlooked-for ways? In these busy days of healing and saving lives, do you not sometimes feel that God in His love walks beside you?"

"Such a thought would fill me with despair."

"Despair? Why, my son?"

"To think that the dear God of my childhood could walk with me into some of these hovels and not be moved to compassion by the misery there, by the herding and filth that spread contagion, by infants born stunted and diseased, whose eyes will never see the sun's light, by scabby children growing daily more crooked of limb and dull-witted with hunger—"

"Enough, my son! Enough! God's reasons are beyond our poor comprehension."

John shook his head. "So I have heard. I have just never heard what those reasons are."

The old priest lifted his brows. There was deep concern in his eyes. "And with your loss of faith, my son, have you also ceased to pray?"

"The all-knowing, all-seeing God you pray to, Father, would turn away His face from this black sinner."

"Nonsense! What sins of yours could be so black? Tell me, my son. Let me be the judge."

The suggestion amused John. He gave a broad grin. "The sins you would hear from me these days, Father Dom, might burn your ears off."

"After a lifetime of hearing confessions I may be more worldly than you think."

Father Dominic waited, gazing affectionately at John's down-bent head. But already he knew he would get no further revelations from this disillusioned young man.

Delicately he changed direction. "John, how long have I known you?"

John looked up at that. He smiled. The question roused up treasured childhood memories.

"Since I was about six. Since the day Doctor Toller took me by the hand and dragged me to your presbytery—a wild and ignorant whelp fresh off the wild heath—and begged you, for a penny a week in Saint Anthony's poor box—to teach me my manners, my sums, and my letters."

"And do you not think, my son, that in all these years I have come to know you?"

Again John grinned. "My better side, perhaps—the only side I let you see."

"You are wrong there, John. I know both sides—the saint and the sinner."

John gave a brief chuckle. "The saint you speak of is a stranger to me, Father. It is the sinner I know well."

"You judge yourself too harshly, my son. But, there! How can I convince you? You always were strong-willed and independent. And wild? Yes, you were wild, so wild that the first day in my classroom you would not even answer to your own name."

"Answer to it? How could I? I did not yet know it. It was only that very morning that Doctor Toller decided to name me 'John' after himself, but though he informed you, he forgot to inform me. I do not think I ever had a name before that." Suddenly his voice dropped to an undertone. He seemed to be speaking to himself. "My mother never called me anything but 'Child.' "

"Your mother?" The priest's voice expressed surprise. "My son, in all these years this is the first time I have heard you speak of your mother. Tell me about her. I would like to hear."

But John did not answer. Instead, he got to his feet and crossed to the window and stood looking out over the city, sunk suddenly in his own thoughts.

Father Dominic, sensing the other's sudden withdrawal, twisted around to keep him in view. As long as he had known John, there had been moments like this, moments when a chance word or action had seemed to snatch him up and precipitate him back into his own private past. Now was such a moment. The old priest had long come to realize that there had been more to John's story than any of them had guessed, some tragedy, perhaps, that had seared itself on the young child's memory. But in all these years John could never be brought to speak of it. In all these years the terrible secrets of John's life before he met Doctor

Toller on that bitter autumn night twenty-odd years ago had remained locked deep inside him, too deep for anyone to reach.

Now, vaguely troubled, the priest lay there, wondering if perhaps there was more they could have done. Then, slowly, as though with suddenly refined and heightened senses, he became aware of something new in the atmosphere, some intuitive truth that seemed to be reaching him, ghostlike, across the years, the aura of a love so tender and binding and strong that it communicated itself to him.

He said gently, "Your mother must have loved you, for you to feel the way you do."

John answered without turning. "Aye, she loved me. And she loved my father . . ."

He said no more. And Father Dominic did not press him.

Instead, presently, he said, "My son, you and I have not talked of it, but we both know I will be leaving you soon. No, please do not deny it. I am ready to face my God. But it would grieve me to know that I am leaving you like this—with your soul tormented by doubts. You must find your way back to God, my son. God is forgiving. Believe that! It is told that Saint Francis of Assisi, while at prayer one night, heard a voice saying, 'Francis, there is no sinner in the world whom, if he be converted, God will not pardon.' Now I am going to ask you to do something. There is a little chapel down the hall. On your way out, will you step in there and say a prayer? One prayer, John? Just one prayer?"

John turned quickly.

"Father Dominic! You cannot be serious. Spend my time praying? Now? With thirty patients waiting, and an infant's body in the morgue, and Sir Mark Hardwick expecting me to testify at his eleven-o'clock inquest?"

"Even so, my son. Please! For the love of Jesus?"

John caught the pleading note in the priest's voice. One prayer. Suddenly he was fighting a thickness in his throat. This was perhaps the last request his old teacher would ever make of him.

"Very well, Father. I will say this prayer. Not for love of Jesus, though—for love of you."

The priest sighed. "Thank you, my son."

John averted his face. He busied himself with his bag. It was a moment before he could make his voice sound natural. "And, Father, Noah is here. Do you feel well enough now to give him his lesson?"

The scholarly priest uttered a little cry of joy. "Does he want me to?"

John turned. He managed a smile. "He is out by the door, waiting."

"Then let him come in, John. Let him come in. I have not had so exceptional a pupil since you were a lad."

"How is he progressing?"

"He is learning fast—much faster than I thought possible. And he is changed from the morose boy you first brought me." Then suddenly the joy left the old man's voice. He sounded bereft. "But who will teach him, John, when I am gone?"

"Sister Teresa, over at the nunnery, knows the deaf-mute signs, Father. I have already spoken to her. She has promised to carry on your work."

"Good, my son. Good. But tell me, how did Sister Teresa learn the signs?"

"She has a younger sister, Alice, who was born a deaf-mute. Their father is an intelligent man, a solicitor. I told him about Doctor Delgarno of Aberdeen, who has been doing remarkable work in this field. Doctor Delgarno agreed to accept Alice as a live-in student for two years, providing another family member would take instruction at the same time, then in turn instruct their parents and siblings so that Alice would be drawn into family life. Teresa was selected to accompany Alice to Aberdeen."

Father Dominic looked troubled. "But did you know, John, that there are at least two forms of sign language?"

"So I discovered. But the form Doctor Delgarno uses, and which he taught Teresa, is the same double-handed alphabet you are teaching Noah."

"Extraordinary! God is very good."

"Now Sister Teresa has started teaching the signs to Noah's mother. In time mother and son will be able to communicate. The boy will no longer live in isolation."

Father Dominic gazed steadily at John for a moment.

At last he said thoughtfully, "You may not know it now, John, but Almighty God has blessed you in one unique way. Always remember that. Remember it when I am gone."

John smiled ruefully. Such a thought was disquieting. He had long since ceased to be a Grail-seeker. He picked up his bag.

"Medical science has improved since the days when such children were destroyed, or left to carry on an animal existence, or looked on as a family embarrassment and hidden from the world in some neglected county asylum. Now we know better. Hippocrates was right. 'The art of medicine is the most beautiful and noble of all the arts.' Amen." Then, as he turned to leave: "May I tell Noah to come in now, Father?"

John hurried through his rounds that morning, lingering by a bedside only where an emergency demanded his immediate attention. Despite his haste, it was almost midmorning by the time he had made his promised stop at the chapel and was free to go bounding down the long dark steps leading into the subterranean bowels of the ancient stone building.

A long tomblike passage led to an oaken door heavily banded with iron. Beyond this lay the hospital deadhouse. As John pushed the door open, the sudden rush of air caused the lanterns to flicker, casting strange shadows on the whitewashed walls with their array of scalpels, curved bistouries, and other instruments. In the center of the room several long tables stood in a row. On them lay the naked bodies of two men. John glanced at them as he passed. One had been almost eviscerated in a brawl. The head of the other seemed to loll drunkenly. His neck had been broken.

Andrew Barnes, the chirurgeon, was working at the far end of the room. He looked around.

"Over here, Doctor," he said.

John Toller hurriedly discarded his coat and waistcoat and rolled up his shirt sleeves. Then he came and stood looking down at the tiny naked body laid out for his inspection.

It was small, weighing under six pounds. The creases of the skin still bore a few faint smears of blood from the process of labor. The livid swelling at the back of the skull suggested to the medical eye that the mother was young and this her first pregnancy. The pupils of the eyes were natural. John opened one tiny fist. The nails were fully formed. There appeared to have been no bleeding from the untied cord, so umbilical hemorrhage had not been the cause of death. Traces of *vernix caseosa* clung like a fatty film to the folds of the axillary region and the crotch. The testicles had descended into the scrotum, so the birth had occurred at or near the full term. From the medical viewpoint, then, it had been a viable child. There were no overt signs of injury, but that meant little. The murder of a bastard infant took many ingenious forms.

Suddenly he asked, "Did you wash this child, Andy?"

"No, sir. You have always warned me not to disturb anything."

"Well, someone washed it. I wonder why?—if they were planning to destroy it. Curious!"

He began his examination, his large strong hands moving first over the skull, parting the hair with his fingers as he searched for fractures or contusions. Sometimes, to escape detection, midwives were known to murder unwanted infants by thrusting a fine, sharp wire into the brain by the fontanels. He searched for puncture holes.

"Has the coroner viewed the body yet?" he asked as he worked.

"He came early this morning, sir."

"And the jury?"

"He brought them along, too."

"And what do you know of this case, Andy? The foot bailiff said only that some girl had murdered her bastard. Have they identified the girl yet?"

"Her name is Jenny Sykes, sir."

"Jenny Sykes? And who is Jenny Sykes?"

"Her father is the vicar of Little Liscombe."

"Oh! That tall, thin man who looks like a cadaver? I ofttimes see him as I ride through. So the girl they accuse of murdering this infant is the vicar's daughter. That should create a spicy scandal around Little Liscombe."

"And here in the city, too, Doctor. This morning, in Dorncaster, that is all folks are talking about."

"Already? And this poor little creature hardly cold? A vicar's daughter should have known better."

"They say she has no mother, sir."

John shrugged cynically. "I have never heard that that mattered. Have they learned yet who the father is?"

"No—and that is what has folks mystified."

"Why?"

"Because no one took her for a trollop. She never went into the village. The vicar even did the shopping. On Sundays she would sit apart from the parishioners, listening quietly to her father's sermons. If any young man ogled her, she did not seem to notice. She showed no interest in the neighborhood boys."

"Well," John said dryly, "we all know how girls get babies, so she managed to make contact somehow."

"Aye. And she did live at the foot of Yeggor Dun."

After a thoughtful moment John asked, "Did you know Jenny Sykes, Andy?"

"No, sir!" Andy answered quickly.

"Then how did you come by so much information?"

"From my cousin, Jim Barnes. I met him this morning on the way to the hospital. Jim has just been made petty constable, you know."

"So he is in position to cry the latest news."

"Well," Andy said awkwardly, "you know how folks are."

"Mmmmm," John answered.

He had been examining the baby's mouth and nostrils. Now his hands moved on, searching for marks of pressure around the throat, then down to the chest and abdomen. He studied the free extremity of the cord. Usually it was cut smoothly with a sharp instrument. This one, from its ragged appearance, had been torn across with the hand.

"Where have they got the girl now, Andy?"

"Here in Dorncaster, in the county jail."

"Quite an embarrassment for the vicar, I imagine."

"I doubt that, Doctor. 'Twas the vicar himself reported the discovery of the body to the constable."

"God's thighs and shin bones! The girl's own father!"

"Folks do find it odd."

"Did he know it was his daughter's baby when he reported it?"

"Aye, he knew it. But Jim says the vicar is quite rabid. He preaches that all men are lewd in the eyes of an angry God. Hellfire alone can purify them. He shouts terrible warnings from the pulpit till you can smell the sulfur and brimstone. Jim says some of his parishioners are afraid to 'tend his services. 'Times his church is near empty."

"Small wonder the girl was afraid to go to him. Did she have no one she could talk to—a friend, perhaps?"

"Jim says she had no one. Seems she thought she was keeping her plight a secret. But Effie Connor, the neighborhood midwife, recognized it in church one Sunday."

John Toller was silent for a moment.

"It will go hard with her in court," he said thoughtfully. "This is not an immature fetus that miscarried. This is a mature child. They will use that against her and charge her accordingly."

"Even with no violence showing on the body?"

"I incline to think it was stillborn, but unfortunately the law is harsh in cases like this. The law makes cruel presumptions against the unwed mother." He crossed to the basin and washed his hands, then hurriedly put on his waistcoat and coat. "At least I have the necessary facts for the inquest. It starts at eleven."

Andy gave a broad grin. "It is more than that now, sir."

Three

By the time John arrived at the Shire Hall the inquest was already in progress. The jury had been sworn, the charges had been read, and the last of the four poachers who discovered the body had just finished his testimony.

Sir Mark Hardwick presided as coroner, a proud and ancient office that dated back to the reign of Alfred the Great, the name "à Coroner" having been derived from the fact that the coroner formerly kept the pleas of the Crown. Since the office was judicial in nature, it was generally held by a qualified legal practitioner, but always by one who held the required land in fee.

Sir Mark interrupted the proceedings as John entered. He motioned him to approach the bench.

"Kind of you to come, Doctor," he said sourly. He looked pointedly at his larum watch. "But did you not receive word to be here by eleven o'clock?"

John gave a slight bow.

"I beg the court's pardon," he said. "It is not out of lack of respect that I am late. There were emergencies at the hospital. I was only able to complete examination of the infant's body a few moments ago."

Sir Mark studied John in crushing silence, his disapproving gaze moving coldly from his unruly hair and unshaven face down over the shabby brown coat that hung rumpled and weather-beaten from his tall lean frame.

"And," he added, "I mislike having medical witnesses come unkempt into my courtroom."

"Again I beg the court's pardon. But by the time I got to bed, the cocks were crowing."

Sir Mark raised a critical brow. "So it seemed rational, perhaps, to sleep in your clothes."

John smiled. "Entirely rational, sir, since at that hour there was little point in removing them. But once more, I beg the court's pardon."

John was still smiling and Sir Mark scowled back at him. He had a mind to censure this exasperatingly unconventional young man. On this particular morning Sir Mark had breakfasted badly. The herring had been too salty, the ale too warm, and seeing John Toller come disheveled before the bench made him want to deliver a public ranting for his unprofessional mode of dress and his disrespect for the court. But he knew it would be futile. A rebuke would slip off John Toller's back like an eel slipping off a bab. And John Toller was not only his personal friend, but also his personal physician. He was the most respected medical practitioner in Dorset. Only last year John had pulled him and his family through the epidemic of diphtheria that carried off thousands in the city and the surrounding countryside, so it seemed unmeet to berate him. Besides, it was said that John Toller had only two suits, one of which he wore constantly, rain or shine, the other being his churchgoing suit, which, since he never went to church, he had few occasions to wear. And in an age when a successful physician proclaimed his prosperity to the world by wearing rich silk or velvet robes and hiring a footboy to run behind his horse carrying his medical instruments, John Toller chose to ride alone, his instruments in a weather-beaten bag hanging from his saddle. It seemed that John Toller cared not one whit how he appeared in other men's eyes. It was the mysteries and miracles of medicine, not the outer semblance of personal success, that interested John Toller.

Sir Mark heaved a resigned breath. He adjusted his periwig so that its long curls framed his face and hung in graceful dignity down over his shoulders.

"Well, be seated, Doctor," he said. Then, to the clerk: "Pray continue."

"Vicar Sykes, please step forward," the clerk called.

As the vicar arose and moved toward the witness-box, John found himself craning for a better view.

He had often passed the vicar as he rode through Little Liscombe on his way to visit some patient, but the vicar's austere manner seemed to discourage even a friendly nod. Sitting straight-backed on his horse, his gaze fixed on the distance, he gave the impression of being indifferent to the company of others. His cadaverous face suggested the ascetic, the scholar, and it was easy to picture him living amid a priceless collection of classics acquired, perhaps, by the self-deprivations of a lifetime. A man of educated tastes, as the vicar obviously was, should have enjoyed routine promotion by the Church, and John found himself wondering what other personal shortcomings, real or suspected, had caused his superiors to waste him in a backwater like Little Liscombe.

A physician became adept at reading men's faces, and now John began to study the vicar more closely. There was about him much that was difficult to read. He was outwardly composed, but John sensed that an ominous turbulence moved just below the surface. His eyes were dark and cool, but their vaguely haunted look suggested that strange and uncontrollable forces were locked deep within him. And there was something else, something remote and elusive, something that seemed to be carefully hidden behind the refined and cultured exterior.

Then John turned to look at the girl. She sat in the prisoner's dock, shackled at wrist and ankle. Her fair hair fell in two long braids over her shoulders. He could not see her face, for her head was bowed, but her form was slight and she looked pathetically young. Her hands were clasped tightly in her lap and he had the impression that she was trying, as a young girl might, to sustain her present courage by fixing her thoughts on happier things outside the courtroom.

John frowned. He would be an unwilling witness at this inquest.

Sir Mark was addressing the vicar.

"Sir, would you look at the prisoner, Jenny Sykes, and tell me if she is your daughter?"

The vicar gave a brief, reluctant sideways glance. "Unfortunately she is, sir."

"And it was you, I believe, who took the infant's body from the poachers and delivered it to the constable?"

"It was."

"Were you aware, at the time, that it was your daughter's child?"

"I was, sir."

"How did you know?"

"It was wrapped in my daughter's shawl."

"Had you no other reason for believing the infant was your daughter's child?"

"No, sir."

"You had not known your daughter was pregnant?"

"I had not."

"Even though she lived under the vicarage roof?"

The vicar was obviously irked by the question. "I can assure you, sir, that at no time did it cross my mind that my daughter might be pregnant."

"Then she did not confide the fact of her pregnancy to you?"

"It was not my daughter's custom to confide in me at all, sir."

At that one of the spectators burst into a whinny. But the coroner glanced in his direction and he quickly covered his mouth with his hand.

"And," the coroner continued, "in these past few months you noticed nothing unusual in your daughter's behavior?"

"No, sir."

"You did not notice a natural change in her appearance—I should perhaps say, in her contours?"

"No."

"Nothing to suggest to you that she was carrying a child?"

"Nothing at all."

"Did her gentlemen friends never call at the vicarage?"

The vicar's voice was resonant with anger. "At no time, sir, was I aware that my daughter had any gentlemen friends. She managed to deceive me on that point, too."

"Then, prior to the discovery of the body in Squire Haynes's woods, you had no inkling that she was about to give birth?"

"Certainly not."

The coroner looked down at his papers for a moment. "Thank you, Vicar," he said. "That will be all. The court commends you for what must have been a most painful duty."

The vicar made no reply, only turned and strode back to his seat. To reach it he had to pass directly in front of his daughter, but he did not glance at her. Nor, though she must have known he was there, did she look up.

"Midwife Hetty Crome," the clerk called.

Hetty Crome's name caused a stir among the spectators, for they knew she would be required to answer questions of an intimate nature concerning the young female prisoner. The jurors, too, leaned forward, eager to catch every word of the midwife's testimony.

Well up in her sixties, with rheumy eyes and bristled chin, she was paid by the city to attend the lying-in of female prisoners in the jail and workhouse.

She approached the witness-box slowly, a moving bulk dressed in filthy, shapeless black.

"Midwife Crome," Sir Mark said, after the preliminaries, "would you kindly look at the prisoner, Jenny Sykes, and tell me if you have ever seen her before?"

"I see'd her yisterday, sir."

"Under what circumstances?"

"I was tole to 'zamine her fer signs of recent deliv'ry."

"And did you examine her?"

"I did, sir."

"And what did you find?"

"That her recen'ly give birth to a child."

"How did you arrive at that opinion?"

"First, I 'zamined the skin of the belly and found a thin brown line from the pit of the stomach to the center of the sharebone. I found that the belly had folds and rimples in it—"

"I do not understand," Sir Mark interrupted. "What do folds and rimples signify in this instance?"

"They mean the slack of the womb after birth of a child, sir. That be one of the signs of recent deliv'ry."

"Go on."

" 'Zamining further, I found the forebirth bloody with a new rent at its entrance. It were loose and sore and her was tore along the stretch—"

"The what?"

"The stretch, sir."

Sir Mark frowned and turned helplessly to John Toller.

"It is a common term for the perineum, sir," John explained. "In the female, loosely the part between the anus and the vagina."

"Thank you, Doctor." Sir Mark turned back to the midwife. "And what would this last indicate?"

"That it had bin a diff'cult labor. Firstborns oft tear the mother, 'specially if the head be large."

"Go on."

"With me finger I 'zamined inside o' her. There was fresh bleeding. Her had more tears 'long the birth canal. Her had the fluids, like them that plagues a woman after deliv'ry."

"And these fluids, do they occur exclusively after childbirth?"

"Them kind do, sir."

"How long do they last?"

"Anywheres from two to four weeks."

"Well within the period of our inquiry."

"Aye, sir."

"Anything else?"

"Her still had the afterpains."

"And are all these generally considered to be signs of recent delivery?"

"Aye, sir."

"So you can say the conclusion is infallible that Jenny Sykes, the prisoner you examined yesterday, recently gave birth?"

"There be no doubting her give birth, sir—an' to a ripe child, mos' likely."

"By 'ripe' I take you to mean mature?"

"Aye, sir."

"How long ago, in your opinion, was her child born?"

"In the past two days, I reckon."

Sir Mark turned to the jury. "Gentlemen, any questions?"

A juror raised his hand. "Sir, I would like to ask if the midwife could tell if the child was deadborn? I mean—or how else could it have died? Was it murdered?"

"I tend on'y women's ailments, Ephraim," Mrs. Crome replied. "That other's so'thing 'ee has to ask the Doc here."

"Well, I thank you for your testimony, Midwife Crome," Sir Mark said. "You may step down."

"Doctor Toller," the clerk called.

"Doctor," Sir Mark began, after John had been sworn, "I requested that you examine the body of the infant found buried in Squire Haynes's woods. Have you done so?"

"Yes, sir."

"And were you able to form an opinion as to when the infant was born?"

"Roughly within the past forty-eight hours."

"On what do you base that opinion?"

"On the general condition of the body. There are certain physical signs and conditions to be looked for."

"Such as?"

"Evidence of the color of the skin, the presence or absence of the *caput succedaneum.*"

"The *caput succ* . . . what is that, Doctor?"

"It is the swelling formed on the presenting parts of the child during labor. In the case of a head presentation, the swelling would be on the head."

"And this infant you examined, could it in any way be described as a nonviable fetus?"

"No, it was fully matured."

"How could you determine that it was fully matured?"

"By its length—it measured nineteen inches; by its weight—just under six pounds; by the fact that its finger- and toe-nails had grown beyond the tips of its fingers and toes; by the fact that, this being a male child, its testicles had descended into the scrotum. All these signify a mature infant."

"Thank you, Doctor." Sir Mark spent a few moments studying the papers before him. "Now, Doctor, it is the purpose of this inquiry to determine the real mother of the infant in the deadhouse. The law holds that the best method of proving the relation between the dead infant and a suspected mother is by comparing the date of the woman's delivery with the apparent date of the child's birth. You have heard Midwife Crome testify that her examinations revealed that the prisoner, Jenny Sykes, was delivered of a child within the past two days. From your own testimony the estimated time of birth of the dead infant was within the past forty-eight hours. The two coincide. Do you agree with the court, then, that the conclusion is irresible that Jenny Sykes is the mother of the dead infant?"

"Medically, it appears possible."

"It is, in fact, more than possible. It is fairly proven, is it not?"

"It is possible, sir."

The coroner frowned in annoyance. "Can you tell us, then, how the infant died?"

"An external examination does not always reveal the cause of death."

"Were there no signs of violence on the body?"

"None."

"No wounds of any kind?"

"None."

"No signs of strangulation?"

"Strangulation would have left marks. There were no marks of pressure on the neck."

"Suffocation? Contusions?"

"No."

"Was it alive when it was buried?"

"There was no earth in mouth or nostrils."

"That does not mean it was not buried alive," Sir Mark said sharply. "After all, it was wrapped in its mother's shawl."

"Sir, it hardly seems likely that a woman intent upon the gruesome task of burying her child alive would be so motivated by tenderness as to first bathe it and wrap it in her shawl."

Again Sir Mark frowned. He misliked having witnesses dispute him in his own courtroom.

"That is conjecture, Doctor," he snapped. "Had the umbilical cord been tied?"

"No."

"No? Come, Doctor, are you not overlooking important evidence of a possible case of child-murder? Is it not a fact that omitting to tie the umbilical cord always proves fatal to the newborn?"

"In this case failure to tie the cord was not the cause of death."

"And how can you know that?"

"Because umbilical hemorrhage would have left the body in a blanched and bloodless state. This was not the case."

"But is it not a fact, Doctor, that failure to tie the umbilical cord is a form of passive infanticide?"

John looked thoughtfully across at the girl for a moment.

"Not always," he answered at last. "Where the mother is young, inexperienced, and unassisted, she may not know what should be done. In any case, this infant did not die by omission to tie the cord. The body was not in a blanched and bloodless state."

"Then, if not to violence, to what do you attribute the infant's death?"

"Possibly to reasons not revealed by the examination."

"Such as?"

"Midwife Crome has testified to the severity of the prisoner's birth injuries. This infant, if it was already weak, might have died by consequence of an exhausting and protracted labor."

"Is that possible?"

"It is a common cause of infant death—especially in a primipara."

"A primipara? What is that?"

"A woman giving birth for the first time."

"But you did testify, Doctor, that the cord was severed?"

"Yes."

"But that it had been left untied?"

"Yes."

"And, I repeat, is not an untied cord commonly viewed as a form of passive infanticide?"

"Commonly, yes."

"Because without the knot the child would be left to bleed to death?"

"Yes."

"So that in this instance, even if the untied cord was not the actual cause of death, it clearly suggests intent to murder on the mother's part."

"Not necessarily, sir. It might have been left untied out of ignorance."

"Ignorance? Are you suggesting that this woman giving birth for the first time—this primipara—was knowledgeable enough to sever the cord, but too ignorant to tie it?"

"I am suggesting that it is possible."

"Doctor, that sounds to me like a case of ignorance and knowledge going conveniently hand in hand."

"Ignorance in such an instance is to be expected in the young, sir. As for knowledge—well, most of us have seen how a bitch, having whelped, presses the cords of her puppies with her teeth, as if masticating. This is instinct. I think the human female possesses no less instinct in such matters as the lower animals. Once her child is born and she sees that long cord joining her to her child, she would know instinctively that it must be severed."

"Well," Sir Mark said dryly, "fortunately the question of murder is not fundamental to this inquiry. It would appear we already have sufficient evidence to hold the prisoner for trial on the charges. Doctor, I thank you for your testimony."

The clerk looked toward the dock. "Will the prisoner, Jenny Sykes, take the witness-box."

The girl was still sitting with head bowed, hands clasped tightly in her lap. When she did not stir, a warder leaned forward and nudged her and a hush of curiosity fell as she struggled to her feet and started across the floor. She moved slowly, looking down, hindered by the iron shackles on her ankles, which dragged and clanked as she walked. The outlines of her form were lost under the loose dress of cheap gray material, ill-fitting and visibly homemade. Coarse black stockings covered her legs. Her boots appeared to be too large, as if someone else had bought them for her with concern for price rather than size.

She reached the witness-box at last and climbed the steps awkwardly, the chains clanking with every dragging step. At the top she halted and stood, her head hanging, eyes on the floor, as though the shame of these public revelations concerning the most intimate regions of her person had been more than she could bear.

"Are you Jenny Sykes?" Sir Mark asked.

Her lips moved, but her reply was scarcely audible.

"Speak up, girl! I cannot hear you. Are you Jenny Sykes?"

She heaved a hard breath. "Yes, sir."

"And you are seventeen?"

"I am eighteen, sir." She hesitated, then added softly, "Today, I think, is my birthday."

"God!" John said under his breath. "What a way to spend it."

"Did I hear you say you were eighteen?" The coroner was clearly irritated. "I still can hardly hear you, girl. Look up! There is nothing to see on the floor. Look up! Let the court hear what you have to say for yourself."

Obediently she looked up, and with a sense of mild surprise John Toller saw her face.

In a countryside where Yeggor Dun continued to exert its arcanal allure, many an unwed mother killed her newborn in an effort to conceal her promiscuity. Many a reputed virgin was glimpsed at dusk darting down some alley to buy a potion whose mysterious ingredients would put an end to her temporary embarrassment. John Toller himself was no seraph. In his wild youth he had known every cesspool of vice in the city, including Mr. Oglethorpe's brothel in the cockloft of the jailhouse. He became more discriminating as maturity changed him, but in the rough-and-tumble of his life he still encountered many a trollop and he recognized at once that Jenny Sykes did not fit the pattern. And now some deep insight made him wonder if there was not something more to her story than they all knew or suspected.

Suddenly curious, he leaned forward and began to study her with thoughtful, diagnostic eyes.

There was a look of innocence in her face that was puzzling in the circumstances. There could be no doubt that she had recently given birth. It was evidenced by the swelling of the mammae and the secretion of a serous fluid from the nipples, which had already left two wet circles on her dress. She was not pretty in the way other girls were pretty. Indeed, she was scarcely pretty at all. There were too many contradictions in her face. Yet there was about her a strange and elusive beauty that had nothing to do with facial features, but which touched him in some curious, indefinable way. She was frightened. Her eyes looked enormous in her pale face. But he sensed in her an unexpected strength and suddenly he wondered if even the threats of a biased and sometimes abusive court would succeed in prying from this girl any secret she did not choose to tell.

"Jenny Sykes," Sir Mark was saying, "you are charged with concealment of birth and presumption of infanticide. As you have heard, the purpose of this inquest is to determine if you should be held for trial. Do you understand?"

"Yes, sir."

"I will explain the law to you. If you go to trial, it will not be necessary for the prosecution to prove you murdered your child. Cases of concealment do not come under the ordinary rules of evidence. The law takes the position that when an unmarried woman conceals the birth of her bastard, that fact alone affords presumptive evidence that she concealed the birth for the purpose of later killing her bastard. Do you follow that?"

The girl said nothing, only hung her head.

"Speak up, girl! You must defend yourself. The law makes no provision for legal representation."

Still the girl did not speak, only nodded.

"The law takes the position that, even in cases where the infant's body cannot be found, the court is required only to prove signs of recent delivery on the person of the suspected unwed woman to charge her with concealment of birth. Is that clear?"

Again the girl nodded, her eyes on the floor.

"Now, you have heard the midwife's testimony. It is the court's view that scrupulous care has been taken in determining signs of recent delivery on your person. Having heard the evidence against you, then, have you anything to say in your own defense?"

The girl spoke softly. "No, sir."

"Come, think carefully. Your life may hinge on it."

When the girl again stood silent, Sir Mark grew impatient.

"Girl, I have just told you that we have evidence of concealment of birth against you. Are you aware of the penalty for concealment?"

"No, sir."

"Concealment on the part of an unmarried woman is a capital crime. The penalty for concealment is the same as for child-murder. The penalty is hanging."

A slight tremor passed through the girl's body, but she said nothing.

"You are unmarried, is that correct?"

"Yes, sir."

"Then how did you get pregnant?"

The girl only hung her head.

"Were you raped?"

Still the girl said nothing. Only by the rapid rise and fall of her bosom did she show the strain she was under.

"Did it happen on Yeggor Dun?"

The girl remained silent, her gaze still fixed on the floor.

"You have a lover, then. Who is he?"

Sir Mark allowed another moment of silence to go by.

"Girl!" he said sharply, "do you not understand? I am trying to help you. This court has proved you guilty of the charge. If you have proof to the contrary, it must be clearly shown. Do you have such proof?"

"I do not know what proof you want, sir."

"Well, did you kill your child?"

She looked up quickly at that. "No, sir."

"Then how did it die?"

"I do not know, sir."

"Was it alive at birth?"

"It did not seem to be."

"Did it breathe—cry out?"

"No, sir."

"Then it was stillborn?"

"I cannot say, sir."

Sir Mark gave this a moment's thought. "Well," he said at last, "the law allows the court to accept a plea of stillbirth if there is at least one reliable corroborating witness. Do you have such a witness?"

"No, sir."

"Come, girl, surely you have a witness."

"I do not, sir."

"You need only *one*."

The girl looked down at her feet, but stood mute.

"Did you confide the fact that you were pregnant to anyone?"

"No, sir."

"Did you consult a midwife?"

"No, sir."

"Did you confide in your mother? Your siblings?"

"I have neither, sir."

"Your lover?"

The girl was silent.

"Where was the child born?"

"At home—in my room."

"At the vicarage?"

"Yes, sir."

"And when you found yourself in labor, did no one hear you cry out?"

Again the girl stood silent.

"Is there no housekeeper at the vicarage?"

"No, sir."

"Where was your father?"

The girl hung her head, but said nothing.

"You delivered the child alone—in solitude?"

"Yes, sir."

"Now think carefully before you answer. You say you delivered the child in solitude. Was there not even *one* witness to corroborate your pretension that the child was stillborn?"

"No, sir."

"That is unfortunate. In cases of concealment, the onus of proof of stillbirth is on the mother. You can understand the reason for that, can you not?"

"No, sir."

"Well, the law is based on the premise that only those unwed mothers who are planning infanticide will deliberately conceal their pregnancy and fail to seek assistance when parturition becomes imminent. That is why, to disprove the charge of concealment of birth with its presumption of child-murder, you need at least one witness of good repute to attest that the child was stillborn."

"But I have no witness, sir."

"Did no one see the child before you buried it?"

"No, sir."

"And had you previously tried to rouse it? To induce respiration?"

"Yes, sir."

"In what way?"

"I washed it in warm water—"

"Yes?"

"—and wrapped it in my shawl to keep it warm. I held it in my arms awhile, but it still did not move. In a few hours it was . . . and I knew it was dead. . . ."

"Go on."

The girl was openly struggling now to hold back her tears.

". . . So I took it into Squire Haynes's woods and buried it."

"And did it not once cross your mind that all these actions were against the law?"

"No, sir."

"You say you wrapped the baby in your shawl. Why did you use your shawl? Did you have no swaddling clouts?"

"No, sir."

"You had prepared none."

"No, sir."

"Then if you did not prepare swaddling clouts, you were clearly not expecting the child to live. What does that tell us, girl?"

"I do not know, sir."

Sir Mark frowned. "Well, there seems to be nothing more this court can do. Lacking a single witness, we can find no grounds for a plea of stillbirth. We must therefore proceed. As I have stated, the purpose of this inquest—its sole purpose—was to determine three points: whether you were recently delivered of a child, whether the body found in the woods is that of your child, and whether said child was delivered in secret. All these questions have now been resolved in the affirmative." He turned inquiringly to the jury box. But since the facts were not in dispute, it took only a brief conference among themselves for the jury to reach a verdict.

"Jenny Sykes," Sir Mark announced, "in view of the evidence presented against you, this court has no option but to commit you for trial on the charge of concealment of birth." He turned to the warders. "You may return the prisoner to jail." Then he got to his feet and swept from the room.

A short while later John caught up with Sir Mark in his chambers on the top floor of the Shire Hall.

He dropped angrily into a chair, stretching out his long legs. "Mark, the law cannot hang this girl. She did not murder her child."

Sir Mark did not answer immediately. He had pulled off his periwig and now was arranging it carefully on its stand. He spent a thoughtful moment easing his itching scalp. Then he loosened his lace-edged cravat and sat comfortably back in his chair, his cropped hair sprouting around his head like a battered halo.

He said, "I am in agreement with you, John."

"Then what are you going to do about it?"

"The matter is out of my hands."

"Out of your hands? Good Jesus! You are talking of hanging a girl who is probably innocent of any real crime."

"John, you fail to understand the complexity of the law. The question here is not whether or not Sykes murdered her newborn. The courts are no longer required to determine that point. The question here is whether or not Sykes is guilty of the crime of concealment of birth. The answer to that is clearly yes, and by law concealment is punishable by hanging."

"That term is a legal trap, Mark, and you lawyers know it. And think how many innocent girls have fallen into your trap. Last year there was that poorhouse girl over in Carven. Only after they hanged her did they learn she had given birth to her child right there in the poorhouse. The body they found was that of another woman's child. And that farm girl up in the Winterborne area. After they hurriedly strung her up they discovered her unborn child was still inside her. The examining midwife had been drunk. And those two Bridport girls. The child of one had accidentally strangled on its cord during delivery, the second suffocated at birth on a portion of the membranes that covered its face. Both girls were accused of concealment. Both were rushed to the gallows. Later, quite by chance, the truth became known. Mark, through a deficiency in the law, these cases are never sifted. The facts are never diligently brought to light. Yet the girls are summarily hanged in due observance of the law. God's death! there is something lawless in that—lawless in the most profound sense."

Sir Mark's eyes had a sudden angry glint.

"John, you see things through a doctor's eyes. What we lawyers have had to grapple with is a succession of unwed mothers who outwit the law by contriving ingenious, at times grisly ways of disposing of the bodies of their murdered newborns. Before the concealment law was introduced, if a search failed to discover the infant's body, the guilty woman escaped the gallows. Now, however, the courts are no longer required to furnish proof of infanticide to bring the woman to justice. Instead, by making it a crime for an unwed woman to conceal the birth of a child, the law enables the court to prove concealment of birth in a way which even the suspect cannot refute—by signs of recent delivery on her own person. Yes, a suspect may still kill her newborn and hide its body, but she rarely escapes the law. She is still sent to the gallows, but on a charge of concealment of birth."

"But what has that to do with Jenny Sykes? Sykes did not murder her infant. It was probably stillborn. Yet the court will apply the same oppressive law in her case as it applies in cases of child-murder. Where is the justice there?"

"I suspect there is more to the Sykes case than that, John. We know she is hiding something, but that is beside the point. However you and I may feel about the case, the trial judge may not view Sykes as a hapless innocent. He may view the secret disposition of her bastard child as an attempt to conceal her guilt."

"I suspect she concealed the body for reasons other than guilt."

"What other reasons could she have?"

"I do not know, but I agree with you that she is carefully hiding something, that there is a great deal more behind all this than she is willing to tell the court."

"Then what do you want me to do? Order a postmortem?"

"That would not help in this instance."

"Why not?"

"Because, while a postmortem can prove certain forms of death by violence, stillbirth remains a medical mystery. Except in certain specific cases, there is at present no way to determine stillbirth after the fact."

"That is precisely why the law places the burden of proof on the mother, John. It is simple logic. Nonetheless, lawyers like myself are troubled by this law."

"Then why have not lawyers like yourself acted to repeal the law?"

"Because it has stood for more than sixty years and in some respects has proved a very good law. It has saved many a newborn's life, since most unwed girls would rather face the terror of exposure than risk hanging. But yes, it's true. A great many hapless girls do get trapped. Perhaps in time the law will be changed—but not in time to save Jenny Sykes."

"Is there no likelihood that grounds can be found for dismissal of the charge?"

"So far her answers have provided no such grounds—not even a single witness. I hope that when she comes to trial she will be more helpful. You know as well as I that, unless stillbirth can be proved, the law obliges the jury to convict upon presumptive evidence, which consists merely of proof of concealment."

"And how soon will she go to trial?"

"The assizes are presently in session. First the Sedgemoor rebels must be dealt with, then the regular jail delivery will commence. For Sykes, probably a matter of weeks."

"And after that?"

"If you are asking me how soon after trial she will go to her hanging, the law prescribes that execution shall be on the day next but one after trial and sentencing, 'unless it be Sunday, in that case on the Monday following.'" Sir Mark paused, staring at John with a curious expression. Now he asked, "What is all this to you, John? Have you a special interest in this girl?"

John gave a surprised laugh. "I never set eyes on her until this morning in your courtroom."

"I am relieved to hear it. We can all be more objective when we are dealing with strangers." Then, as John rose to his feet: "Tell me, how is Amy?"

"No better, unhappily."

"Does she still not recognize you?"

"No. To her, I am not her husband. I am a stranger."

"But you had begun to see some improvement."

"That, I think, was more airy expectation than reality. At present she is sunk deeper than ever in her own strange madness."

"Is there no hope?"

"After four years? It seems unlikely."

"Where is she now?"

"I transferred her. I placed her in the Bethlehem Asylum. Their treatment of the insane is more humane, but there is still very little they can do. Sometimes she will sit for hours huddled in a corner in a strange state of catalepsy. Then suddenly she will explode into a fit of rage and attack anyone at hand with all the fury in her poor skinny body, even stripping off her clothing and tearing it to pieces. Ofttimes, when I ride over to visit, I find her sitting in her room shouting with wild frenzy of grotesque happenings. If I try to quiet her she goes right on shouting, completely self-absorbed."

"Does she still refuse to eat?"

"Yes, but they have learned to cope with that by first tying her wrists and ankles, then forcing her lips apart. Still, by now her bones are visible through her flesh."

"Is she allowed any freedom at all within the asylum?"

"Very little. There is no way to anticipate her moods. During her fits of violence it takes four of them to tie her to her bed. And she has developed a curious cunning. Now they hardly dare walk her in the garden without two attendants for fear of what she will do."

Sir Mark slowly shook his head. "I am sorry, John. It is all most unfortunate. A man like you deserves a loving wife and children of his own."

John's eyes examined the floor beams for a moment.

"Well, I have given it all a great deal of thought, Mark, and I have to acknowledge that I was not always a good husband. I was not always faithful. Nor, indeed, was I always sober. Sometimes I think I am only getting what I deserve."

"Nonsense! I know you better." Suddenly Sir Mark reached over and put a hand on John's arm. "Why not ride over tonight and have supper with Philippa and me? She always enjoys your company. And my children love you. Will you do that, John? Will you come?"

"Tonight? Thank you, Mark, but I have patients to see."

"There is danger in letting patients substitute for friends. Come, change your mind. Ride over to Cawood Court tonight and share my family with me—that is, if it would not be too painful."

John smiled. "Another night, Mark."

"Very well. But feel free to come any time the mood takes you. Only yesterday Philippa was asking if we all have to get sick before you come to visit. You are always welcome to share our meal, John, and a glass of good wine. Will you bear that in mind?"

"I will. And thank you, Mark."

"And about the Sykes girl—it is true that in her case there appears to be injustice in our mode of justice. The girl might well be innocent of any real crime. But recall the ancient dictum, John, that compassion is an indulgence few professional men can afford. I should not have to remind you of that. You know that sooner or later we must become inured to all things. Self-involvement in a hopeless case leads only to frustration and heartbreak." He paused, then added in a lighter tone, "Come, John, how can I persuade you? Philippa has a pretty young cousin visiting us whom you would find most diverting."

"Thank you, Mark, but unfortunately I will not have time tonight."

Sir Mark's eyebrows lifted in sudden curiosity. "A woman, John?"

John only laughed and turned toward the door.

"Because I have often wondered," Sir Mark continued, "since reports have it you have given up the bawdy life."

"Do they, indeed?"

"Surely a man like you does not live for four years without a woman in his life. Yet never a whisper. Why?"

"Maybe," John grinned, "because there *is* no woman in my life."

And Mark's chuckle of disbelief followed him down the stairs.

But after dark John rode out of the city, heading north, riding by discreet byways until he came to a twisting lane leading down to the cottage by the river.

He had met the woman three springs ago, when he was riding by and found a four-year-old boy sitting in the middle of the highway, lost and crying, a great gash in one knee. He dismounted and picked up the child and quieted him, then looked around for the mother. No living figure was in sight, not even a house, only empty fields, but he reasoned that so small a child could not have strayed far from home, and when he sighted a twisting lane leading off downhill, he followed it. In a little while, he was knocking on the door of the cottage by the river for the first time.

It was opened by a young mother, a nursing baby at her breast. She had not even missed the boy and was dismayed to see the still-wet tears on his cheeks and the bleeding gash on his knee. John explained that there was no cause for alarm, that he was a doctor and if she would permit him to enter he would clean and dress the wound.

At first she was word-bound before the tall stranger, but seeing how gentle he was with the boy, and how the boy was without fear of him, she lost her reticence and presently, encouraged by his kind concern, she found herself telling him of her husband, who had been a charcoal burner in the nearby Ticknor Woods: of how one day last summer, when she went to take him his midday meal, she found him dead beside his burning pit, his skull crushed, his bags of charcoal gone. Since then she had lived as best she could, off woods and river mostly, fishing, gathering berries. And John, seeing the want in which she and her children existed, left some silver coins on the kitchen table for her to find later. After that he went by frequently to drop off food left on his doorstep by some of his grateful but nonpaying patients, chickens, eggs, vegetables. That was how they came to know one another, she a young widow lonely for companionship, he with a wife in an asylum. One day she asked him to return after dark and spend the night.

None of the countryfolk around had any suspicion that Minnie Jackson had a lover. Even her children rarely saw him. He arrived noiselessly after dark, leading Iris by the bridle along the grassy border of the path, and was gone as noiselessly by sunup. He was tender and understood a woman's needs, but she knew he did not love her. She knew that for him their relationship was a simple one. For her it was more complex. She had come to love him. Yet she knew enough never to let him know it. Nor, whenever she conceived by him, did she let him know that, either. She was familiar with the herbs her grandmother and great-grandmother had used as an abortifacient, so she placed no constraints upon him. He came when the mood took him, shared her bed for a few hours, and was gone by morning, leaving the silver coins on the kitchen table.

Now, arriving at the cottage on this particular evening, he stabled Iris in the lean-to, then crossed the yard and knocked softly. Minnie peered out the window, then quickly opened the door. She welcomed him, smiling. She crossed the kitchen and quietly shut the children's door, then came and slid her arms up around his neck. She was somewhere in her middle twenties, with a face that was plain, yet with an inviting earthiness and a body that was curved along voluptuous lines. Her thick, jet-black hair was piled on top of her head and shone in the lamplight like a blackbird's wing. After a moment she pulled away from his arms and put out the lamp. Then they went together into the bedroom.

It was not their way to do much talking. Minnie was quite unschooled, so they had never held a real conversation. But their lovemaking had little need for words, excepting for such endearments as their moments of passion called for. In an instant she had slipped out of her dress and petticoats. She loosed her hair so it hung about her, long and dark, and stood naked before him, limned in silver moonlight. He gazed at her, breathing in the sight of her as he dropped his clothing hurriedly to the floor. Then he came to her, feeling the swift thudding of her heart under his hand as he touched her breasts, cupping them a moment before moving slowly, sensuously, down over her hips to the swell of her buttocks.

She made a low, contented sound, then she twined her arms around his neck and raised her face to his, her lips waiting. He bent and put his mouth on hers, a long, slow kiss, gentle at first, then with the surging, powerful drive she had come to know as he pressed her body against him, caressing her with hands made expert by intimate knowledge. After a moment he picked her up and carried her to the bed.

He laid her down in a pool of moonlight, her arms still twined about his neck. "Eh! but I has hankered for 'ee," she breathed, her passion for him shafted by the warmth of his naked body pressing down upon her, flesh upon flesh. "Aye, girl—" And he thrust his hands into her long black hair, holding her face up to his as he kissed her lips, her throat, her bare shoulders. She held her breath, expectant, clinging to him now as his hand began its knowing motion downward, exquisitely tantalizing, touching and seeking till it came at last to the waiting core of her.

Sometime later he awakened, disquieted by something lingering in the back of his mind. Minnie still slept beside him, spent with loving, her breathing heavy and slow, the covers fallen away to expose her belly and wanton thighs. She felt him stir and turned, half-drugged with sleep. She murmured, "Eh! but lie still the while. 'Tis no ways near to dawn yit." And she edged closer to him, thinking he would take her again in his arms. But now his wakeful mind was busy with other concerns, with Sir Mark's gloomy appraisal of the outcome of the Sykes trial, with the image of a girl dragging her chains across the courtroom floor, with his own sharp sense of surprise when, in obedience to Sir Mark's command, she looked up and for the first time he had seen her face.

Suddenly he was anxious to be gone. Already Minnie had lapsed back into sleep, so he leaned over and kissed her shoulder. Then he arose and crossed to where his clothing lay in a pile upon the floor and started hurriedly to dress.

The moon was low over the hills when he left the cottage. He led Iris noiselessly up the lane to the highway, then mounted up and turned her head toward Dorncaster.

The night was windless, the distances so startlingly clear that each lonely farmhouse seemed within hand's reach, time-bound in its ancient earth, its farmlands outspread in a patchwork of fallow and tilth. The sounds of night were all around: the deep, long-drawn hoot of the brown owl, the banshee-like wail of a distressed vixen searching for her strayed cub, the call of curlew and whimbrel, the sound of mallard on the wing. The bracken growing in the shelter of the woods still was green, and from it the ghost moths rose up to dance in the moon's pale light. Above a patch of swampy ground, the marshlights ran and flickered.

He frowned.

Why could he not forget her face? Why had the image of a girl seen briefly in a courtroom remained so clearly etched upon his memory? Even now it was as if she were standing just an arm's length away in the frond-scented moonlight, her eyes enormous in her pale face. If she were a beautiful woman he could understand such an obsession. But that was hardly the case with Jenny Sykes. No, it must be something else—something he recognized without as yet being able to define.

Her caprices, by all accounts, had led her down reckless and forbidden paths. Strange, then, that no suggestion of that wantonness seemed to reflect upon her face. Standing there in the witness-box, responding carefully to the coroner's questions, she seemed somehow untouched by scandal, a lonely, friendless girl accused of an unspeakable crime, yet in some mysterious way wrapped in the grace of innocence that clung to her like an illusive light.

It was said that something of the secret self was written on each human face. What, then, had he read on the face of Jenny Sykes that caused these ceaseless intrusions upon his thoughts?

What was there about her face that haunted him?

Four

John thought about the girl next morning, as he tended his patients at the hospital, and later, as he made his country rounds. He thought about her as he rode slowly homeward through the falling twilight. He thought about her as he ate his lonely supper. His last thought was of her as he dropped off to sleep.

Early next morning he rode over to the jail. He stopped at the office of Mr. Oglethorpe, the jailer, and asked to see the prisoner Jenny Sykes. Most jails were the income-producing property of private owners, with the unsalaried jailer living off whatever fees he could extort, by starvation and other forms of coercion, from the wretched inmates, their relatives, or friends. A few coins had to change hands, therefore, before Mr. Oglethorpe led John to the top of the stone steps leading to the dungeons and shouted his orders to the turnkey.

The turnkey, too, had to be bribed before he would lift the lantern off the wall and lead John down the vaulted corridor to the cell in which the girl was being held. Unlocking the heavy door, he took cudgel in hand, then stepped inside and raised his lantern to shed its light on the dense huddle of filthy, starving prisoners within.

The dungeon was windowless and reeked of excrements combined with the feral stench of unwashed bodies. As they stepped inside, a blast of fetid air seemed to spring at them like a caged beast. The turnkey swung his lantern around, scattering the rats, lighting up a sea of pallid faces with their hopeless, staring eyes. Most were naked, for the custom of garnish—"pay or strip"—was enforced, the prisoners' clothing being sold to pay the required two-shilling admission fee to jail. There was no separation of the sexes, but starvation served to curb promiscuity, for charitable donations for the purchase of food were apt to shrink as they passed through Mr. Oglethorpe's grasping hands. The prisoners were lucky if they got a bowl of bread-slop once a day.

So men and women were crowded together, the sick and the well, lunatics, aging prostitutes, rapists, murderers, some driven to fits of savagery by their galled flesh, for irons were a prime source of revenue to

Mr. Oglethorpe. A prisoner's light purse meant heavy irons, a heavy purse meant light irons or no irons at all, or an even wider ambit of liberty such as admission to the upstairs brothel, or to the taproom where an obliging tapster would make a man drunk for a penny, dead drunk for twopence, and would give him straw to lie upon to recover free.

But here in the lower regions, whether tried or untried, those who could not pay were left to sicken in the damp and cold, until in time they conveniently died. One madman, abandoned by his kin and forgotten even by the courts, was chained to the wall like a brute, his skeletal body covered with rat bites and black with moving vermin. The sudden flash of light wrenched him back out of half-conscious nightmare into conscious horror and now, driven by some mysterious inner compulsion, he raised his head like a wolf and began to howl.

John passed hurriedly on until, with relief, he sighted Jenny Sykes. She was crouched by the far wall, her eyes closed, her head laid against the stone. They had garnished her dress, boots, and stockings. Now she was clad only in her shift.

He stepped over the sprawling bodies and made his way toward her.

"Jenny?" he said. "Jenny Sykes?"

She did not move. She was so still she appeared to be lifeless.

Alarmed, he went down on one knee and gently shook her shoulder. "Jenny?" he said again, louder.

She came to with a start and raised her head, a look of sudden terror in her eyes. She recoiled when she saw him, shrinking back along the wall as though trying to melt right into the stone.

"No, do not be afraid," he told her quickly. "I am a doctor. I have come to see if I can help you."

She stared silently up at him. Her eyes had a vague, feverish look. Despite the cold, her forehead glistened with sweat and he knew he must waste no time getting her out of this overcrowded fever-ridden dungeon.

But for the moment he just waited, not daring to move, until she had stopped recoiling and had gone as far from him as the narrow space would allow. Huddled back against the wall, she licked dry lips and stayed mute, watching him with fear in her eyes.

"Jenny," he said gently, "I came to find out how you are, but I can see you are ailing. You probably need the services of a midwife. I will send one over this afternoon from the hospital. Have they given you anything to eat?"

She did not answer and he glanced down at her wrists and ankles. Already they were raw and bleeding from the irons.

"Those must be painful," he said. "Before I leave I will speak to the jailer, Mr. Oglethorpe. I will arrange to have the irons removed."

Still she continued to crouch there, staring silently up at him. But now her gaze was moving slowly over his face, studying it in a thoughtful, searching, questioning way, and to this he submitted patiently, letting her take her own unhurried time inspecting him.

She saw a tall man, lean and hard-bodied. He seemed at the first glance younger, at the second older, than his twenty-eight or so years. He wore no periwig. His own thick, dark hair reached to his shoulders and had been carelessly barbered, being longer on the one side than on the other, as though he had become impatient of sitting overlong and had abruptly ended the session. A jagged scar cut across one cheek. His skin was bronzed from exposure to every sort of weather. His mouth was strong and kind, set in a solid jaw. His eyes were warm and very blue, half-humorous, half-sad, as though they had looked on things other men had not seen, things beyond sorrow or hope or despair. But now they seemed to be smiling as he waited, submitting willingly to her intense inspection.

Slowly her fear of him began to ebb. After a moment, she said softly, "Who are you?"

"I am Doctor Toller, Jenny." Then, reading the sudden question, he added, "Do not be alarmed. I did not come at your father's request."

Some of her tenseness seemed to drain away at that. But still she continued to inspect him in a quiet, questioning way.

"Then if my father did not send you," she asked, after a moment, "why did you come?"

"I would like to help you, if I can."

"But why?"

"Because I am concerned about you."

She frowned at that, puzzled. "Was it you in the courtroom yesterday . . ." Her words drifted off.

"I was there, yes."

"You said—"

He waited, but again she did not complete her sentence.

"Jenny," he said, "I am going to have you moved upstairs to the women's quarters. There is sunlight up there—and open windows. I will have your clothing returned. And I will see that you get three good meals a day, but I want you to promise me you will eat them."

She shook her head listlessly. "I am not hungry."

"That is because today you are a little feverish. But tomorrow, if you feel better, I want you to try to eat. And now I must go. I have patients waiting at the hospital. First, though, I will go up and talk to the jailer. I will be back to see you tomorrow."

It cost him two pounds to make the necessary arrangements with Mr. Oglethorpe. But prisoner Sykes would be transferred within the hour, her irons struck off, her clothing returned, she would have clean straw to lie upon and three meals a day sent in from the tavern.

"And you had better see that it is done," John added in threatening tones, incensed anew by the greed and inhumanity of the prison system. "And better stay within the law this time, Oglethorpe, or I will ride over and have a little talk with Lord Mallington about you."

John was thoughtful as he left the jailhouse, troubled by the extreme harshness and cruelty of the law in dealing with the unwed mother. He was disquieted by the knowledge that, in an age that was witnessing the dawn of scientific liberty, when the flourishing of new ideas was moving legitimate medicine out of the dark ages of ignorance and superstition into the light of pure science, the medical community was still without an answer to so basic a question as stillbirth after the fact.

Already the seventeenth century had produced giants in the field of scientific endeavor. Willis had discovered the characteristic sweetish taste of diabetic urine; Sydenham had roused the medical world by calling for fresh air in sickrooms and had written his treatise on gout; Needham had shown that the fetus was nourished by the placenta; Hooke had demonstrated the true function of the lungs by artificial respiration, and the great William Harvey had discovered the phenomenon of the circulation of the blood. Intravenous injection of drugs and transfusion of alien blood had their scientific origins in the seventeenth century.

Yet despite these remarkable experimental trends in English medicine, a sluggish medical community still held stubbornly to its sterile formulas and texts without taking heed of its great contemporary thinkers and scholars. While there was an emergence of scientific physicians, there was as yet no established scientific medicine. Ancient doctrines were too deeply rooted, innovations too poorly tolerated. Although seventeenth-century medicine was witnessing a florescence of individual genius, its popular medicine was in a period of stagnation. The 1677 *London Pharmacopoeia* listed compounds containing the viscera, bones, claws, teeth, hooves, horns, sexual organs, and excreta of animals of all sorts, cast-off snake's skin, human perspiration, saliva of a fasting man, and "the triangular Wormian bone from the juncture of the sagittal and lambdoid sutures of the skull of an executed criminal."

From the scientific viewpoint, John reflected, the seventeenth century was an age of contrasts, an age of the best and the worst in English medicine.

By the time he reached the hospital, the clinic was already full. The line of patients extended out to the courtyard.

"Well, Jacob," he said as he seated himself at his desk and watched a farmer from south of Rockwych come limping toward him, "what happened to your leg?"

Jacob was nervous. His face wore the defensive, reconnoitering expression that John had come to recognize when a patient was getting ready to lie to him.

"A pitchfork, Doc. I fell on't."

"Did you, now? And when did this happen?"

"Yisterday."

"Up on the table, then, and let me look at it."

John had become aware of the odor of suppurating tissue and crusty, pus-filled rags the moment Jacob entered the room. Now, as he cut away the bandages, the odor became concentrated, more foul.

He bent over to examine the exposed wound. It was discolored and swollen. A yellowish opaque matter was oozing from it.

"A pitchfork, you say? Well, Jacob, the tines of a pitchfork do not make this kind of wound. A slashing sword did this."

"No, Doc, I swear to 'ee—"

"Save yourself the trouble, Jacob. This wound is long, straight, knifelike. And you did not receive it yesterday. This wound is two months old. It has been festering for weeks. Now what do you suppose all that tells me?"

Jacob looked away and John quickly opened the wound and began to clean it. Jacob writhed, clenching his fists to choke back any unmanly groans.

But presently, when the pain eased, Jacob said humbly, "I did not want to lie to 'ee, Doc, but Kate said I should not tell 'ee the truth. Kate said they 'ud hang me if ever they found I was at Sedgemoor. Kate said they 'ud likely hang 'ee, too, if they caught 'ee tending a sword wound." "Yes, they likely would. We are required to report it, you know." He finished cleaning the wound and began applying a dressing. "You came a long way with this leg," he said. "How did you travel?"

"Kate drove me in the haycart—me lying down behind. But me pore Kate come near to jumping from the cart and running for her life at the sight of all them tarred trunks and quarters hanging in the Market Place. And blood everywheres. Smells like a slaughterhouse on a hog farm, it do."

"You were foolish to come," John told him. "Lucky you were not searched for wounds. Be careful as you leave. A woman holding the reins suggests her man is ailing. However much it hurts, sit up and drive till you are safely out of town. And make a show of farm supplies in your haycart to suggest a reason for your coming."

Jacob gave a nervous smile. " 'Ee be thinking I could still be strung up?"

"By tomorrow—if they catch you today."

But Jacob shook his head with the inborn stubbornness of his breed.

"I still say us did right. 'Tis said this Catholic king aims to Romanize all England. Even a small farmer like me 'ull not be told how to worship. Like all them pore tarred things hanging in the Market Place, I was fighting for the Protestant duke—for freedom of religion."

John was silent. Sometimes it was puzzling to reflect that, while in general staunchly loyal to their king, there was one institution most Englishmen loved more than hereditary monarchy, and that was the Church of England. Yet the Englishman's love of the Church was not based on intimate knowledge. Few among them could give any reason, drawn from Scripture or ecclesiastical history, for adhering to her doctrines. Nor were they, in general, strict observers of that code of morality which was common to all Christian sects. Yet this inherent tendency was not peculiar to the English. Throughout known history man had demonstrated a curious readiness to fight to the death, or to persecute without pity, for a religion he did not fully understand and whose precepts he habitually disobeyed.

Now John said, "You will not be able to work your fields for a while, Jacob. Let the boys do the plowing. They are old enough for that. I will have to dress this wound again, but do not risk coming into Dorncaster. One evening, after dark, I will drop by the farm."

Jacob was limping away when, through the open doorway, John caught sight of a woman, the local saddler's wife, standing in the middle of the waiting room. A strange, fixed expression was on her face. Her tears were coming soundlessly. In her arms she clutched a small girl.

John felt his body go tense. He hurried into the waiting room and looked searchingly into the child's face. It was purplish, contorted with some terrible exertion. Her small fists weakly flailed the air. She was not breathing, only struggling desperately to breathe. From her throat came an occasional hard croak.

He wrenched the child from her mother's grip and raced with her back to the examining room. On the table, he forced her mouth open and looked inside. Her throat was blocked by a rough false membrane that extended murderously into the larynx. He put his ear to her chest.

"Mrs. Colley!"

The nurse came running in.

"Diptheria," he said. "No time to find Mr. Barnes. You will have to help me. My tray, please."

Mrs. Colley looked startled, but nodded, her eyes round with fright. Like other nurses of her time, she had no scientific training and only such practical nursing experience as she had learned by working in sickrooms.

With trembling hands she picked up the tray and brought it to him.

He snatched up a scalpel and began working fast, making an incision low on the child's throat. She was almost unconscious, almost beyond feeling, but still her small body was suddenly convulsed with feeble agony.

"Hold her! Hold her still!"

The blood ran dark and swift, obscuring the field of operation. John swabbed. His next incision was deeper, keeping carefully to the middle line. Again the child writhed. Her terrible croaking filled the room. He glanced anxiously into her face. She was still struggling to breathe, but now her lips had taken on an ominous bluish tinge.

He could feel the tension gather. He knew he must soon bring air to her gasping lungs and a sense of feverish urgency filled him. He parted the tissue with bloody fingers and found the trachea. Holding it steady with one hand, he swabbed again lest she drown in her own blood and mucus after he made the opening, then, snatching up his scalpel, he started to cut down upon it between the first and second rings. He was racing frantically against her ebbing strength and he knew it. The child was almost gone.

Then suddenly the croaking stopped.

John looked up, staring with hard concentration into the child's face. She had ceased to struggle. Even her small fists had dropped limply to the table.

She lay quite still.

A terrible grief filled him. He had watched over this child ever since, weighing barely five pounds, she had come prematurely into this world. She had always been small and frail, but he had pulled her through measles and whooping cough, scarlatina, chicken pox—

"Oh, Lord!" he whispered, more out of habit than in prayer. "Oh, Lord! Do not let me lose her—please!"

Sweat burst out on his forehead, running down almost to blind him. Roughly he brushed it away with his sleeve.

A sense of desperation flowed over him. He was still holding the trachea. Now he cut transversely across the front. Instantly a stream of bloody mucus came bubbling out of the opening. He swabbed it, and swabbed again, cleaning away all the foul secretions, then he quickly thrust a silver cannula into the tracheal opening and held it in place.

A gasp came from the child. Her chest gave a convulsive heave.

"Breathe, little Lucy!" His voice shook with anguish. "Breathe!— Breathe!"

He waited, listening with spent emotions to the low whistle of air rushing through the cannula and down into the child's suffocating lungs. For a moment her chest continued to heave spasmodically, then slowly settled into a normal rhythm.

After a moment the blue faded from her lips. She began to move, to return to life. Hastily, before she came to, he swabbed her throat clean of blood and put in a few stitches to close the wound and hold the cannula. Then he tied the tube in place and dressed her throat with clean linen.

By the time he finished, Lucy had opened her large blue eyes and was gazing wonderingly up at him.

"Good girl, Lucy," he said. "Good, brave girl."

For a moment she continued to stare up at him, as though trying to remember what had happened.

Then suddenly she recognized him and gave a shy smile.

He bent over her. "You have been sick, little Lucy, but I think you will be all right now. I am going to keep you here in the hospital for a few days, though. You will not mind that, will you?"

Again she gave him her shy smile and he stood there smiling back at her, struggling to contain the almost unbearable joy that flooded his being. Father Dominic's words came back to him: "In these busy days of healing and saving lives, do you not sometimes feel that God in His love walks beside you?"

"Sometimes . . . perhaps . . ." he murmured.

But a moment later it was all forgotten as he plunged back into work: a palsy of the lower limbs, three small brothers with diarrhea and vomiting, a man with the sweating sickness, a woman whose arm had been fractured by a sadistic husband.

"Better watch that temper of yours, Nick Brown," John said angrily to the husband, as he applied the neck bandage. "And no use coming in here lying to me. Fell out of a tree picking apples, indeed! I know what is afoot at your place. Next time I hear of you beating your wife—or your children, by God!—I will have you hauled up before the City Council and sentenced to the pillory, then whipped at the cart's tail for every Jack to laugh at. Carry that thought back with you to your hovel."

It was almost sundown. The waiting room was empty at last. And he had not yet set out on his rounds.

"You may go, Mrs. Colley. And thank you. You are going to be a very good nurse."

The clatter of hoofbeats on the cobbles of the courtyard below drew him to the window. A horseman was just flinging himself off his steaming mount and was running for the hospital steps.

John leaned out. "Grimes, what is it? What has happened?"

The horseman halted and looked up.

"They sent me t' fetch 'ee, Doc," he shouted breathlessly. "They said 'ee wuz to cum—no matter what. It be real bad this time."

A few moments later John was riding at top speed along the country road leading to the Bethlehem Asylum. He had sensed that something terrible had occurred, but Grimes could give him no particulars.

Now, as he rode, the lurking specters of those remembered years with Amy filled his anguished mind and crowded out the present.

She had been so young and pretty, the only child of Reggie Clay, the miller. Her mother had died when she was small, and she and her father lived in the roundhouse on the ground floor of the mill just outside the town. Her father, after an accident that paralyzed one arm, wanted to sell the mill and move away. But Amy wept at the thought. The mill seemed to exert upon her an unnatural fascination. From childhood she had felt drawn by it—by the steep ladderlike stairs leading up to the dark chambers above, by the shadows forever lurking behind gear wheel and shafting, by the secretive nighttime whispers of the louvers on the sails, by the furtive movements of the great central post braced against its struts. Hers! All hers! Yet still her father talked of selling. Then one day, when he was working upstairs in the mill head, he was caught and crushed to death in the great cogwheels. Amy was distraught, but refused to postpone the wedding. Tearfully, she pleaded with John to come and live in the roundhouse after the ceremony.

The roundhouse was small and cozy. Even the stone piers and sack hoist and the now rusting chains and pulley added to its charm. The newlyweds were happy. But soon he found himself watching her, aware that something was wrong, and was disturbed by her changing moods and long periods of brooding secretiveness without ever being able to learn the cause.

Within a year their first child was born. But the roundhouse lacked space for a child. A nearby cottage fell vacant and John talked of buying it. But before a decision could be made, the infant was killed. At the time it was assumed to have been a freakish accident. Something had jarred loose one of the millstones on the upper floors and it rolled to the open shaft of the sack hoist. The infant's crib happened to be directly under the shaft when the millstone fell, crushing the infant. John tried to persuade the grieving Amy to leave the mill now, to let him take a house in town. When she refused, and over her very vocal objections, he brought in a millwright to secure all the machinery on the upper floors. Then he hired a carpenter to block up the stairs and gaping sack hoist with heavy oaken beams.

Their second son was born the following year. The infant was only three weeks old when John, chancing to be riding up a nearby country road on an emergency call one afternoon, looked up and saw the great sails of the mill rounding against the sky. He reined in and stared in amazement. The millwright had secured the sails. All the gear wheels and cogs, the millstones, the spindle and bevel gears had been put out of use. Something terrible stirred in his mind. With a jerk, he swung Iris off the road and urged her at top speed up the rough hillside toward the mill.

He leapt from the saddle even before Iris had time to come to a halt. A single bound took him to the door. He flung it open. Amy was sitting in the middle of the room in a rocking chair, quietly rocking back and forth. She seemed to be waiting, snakelike, every nerve stretched taut. Her lips were twisted into a horrible smile of chilling cunning. The infant's crib had been pulled over and placed directly under the sack hoist. But now the shaft of the hoist was open and Amy's eyes were fixed upon it with tight expectancy. And as she watched, she rocked back and forth and waited, rocked and waited, rocked and waited—

He took in the scene from the doorway. "Amy!"

She leapt up and rounded on him. A brutalized change came over her, a transformation that twisted her features and brought a gleam of fierce hatred into her eyes. A pothook hung by the fireplace. She reached for it and swung it upward as she leapt toward him, shrieking obscenities he had not known she knew. But above her shrieking his ears had already caught the ominous sound somewhere upstairs of rusty gears getting into motion. The hoist had started its descent. His first desperate thought was to reach the crib, to push it away from the open shaft before it was too late. He was barely aware, as he leapt past her, of the pothook swinging down on him. It caught him on the side of the face, hooking solidly into the flesh of his cheek. Then, with mind-numbing malevolence and triumphant rage, she began tugging on the long iron handle, tearing the flesh mercilessly as she dragged him backward.

He struggled to break free, but the hook held fast. The child! Ignoring the streaming blood and cruel pain, he suddenly turned on her. He had never before struck her. Now he raised a clenched fist and sent it smashing into her face. She gasped and stumbled backward, yet still kept her grip on the handle of the pothook. But now, as her breath came harshly like tearing cloth, she played more warily, using the long iron handle to hold him off at a distance, while at the same time keeping him hooked to prevent him from reaching the crib. There was something diabolical in her cunning, in her almost supernatural strength, in the inhuman venom with which she watched him, artfully waiting for what she knew was about to happen, her eyes glittering with insane glee.

The noise of their scuffling had awakened the child. Its whimpering filled the roundhouse. The hoist! A kind of blind panic seized John. With a terrible wrench he tore out the hook, heedless of the flesh that came with it. Then, as she sprang at him, clawing at his eyes in a frenzy to blind him, he jerked quickly backward, raised one booted foot, and lashed a kick that took her full in the stomach. She grunted and fell back, mouth agape, then rolled over and crouched, retching. He did not even spare her a glance. He whirled and leapt toward the crib.

"God! Oh, God!"

His broken, grief-stricken cry filled the roundhouse as the millstone fell, crushing their second son as it had crushed their first.

Now, as he rode toward the asylum, he tried to banish from his thoughts the terrible memories of that day. But after four years the images still were fresh, always there, at times just beyond the level of conscious thought, but always there. He sighed. Would he ever be able to forget? Would he ever feel anything but bitterness and loathing whenever he visited her? Would he ever feel any grief for what had become of her?

Would he ever find it in his heart to forgive?

The asylum was coming into view now. Even from a distance it presented a forbidding aspect, set apart on rising, brushless ground, its windows peering like barred eyes over the high spiked wall. The porter recognized horse and rider from a distance and opened the gates to let them go speeding through. An instant later John was knocking loudly on the front door.

The superintendent hurried to meet him in the entrance hall.

"A terrible thing, Doctor," he began, "a terrible thing! But we cannot be held responsible, you know. She did it herself—"

John was impatient. "Did what? What happened?"

"She made herself into a living torch. Somehow she procured fire —a lighted candle, maybe—I do not know, she is very cunning. She dragged her mattress into the middle of the floor of her cell, sat down on it, and set it on fire—"

John did not wait for the rest. He took the stairs three at a time. The corridor leading to Amy's cell was crowded with asylum attendants who were standing in awed silence before the open door. The air of the corridor was rank with the odor of roasted human flesh.

John pushed roughly through the group and entered the cell.

Amy was sitting contentedly on her charred mattress, cross-legged, singing softly to herself. Her face was black with smoke and scorched flesh, her hair was singed to the scalp and standing up around her head in crisp black spikes. Her clothing hung from her blackened lower body in ribbons so brittle they fell to dust when she tried to move. Her arms were raw and bleeding. Her legs had received the onset of the flames and now, unrecognizable as legs, they were black and shriveled.

Yet strangely, she appeared to feel no pain.

Harrowed by the sight, he moved toward her and went down on his knees.

"Amy?" he said softly. "Amy, do you hear me?"

She stopped singing and looked up at him, mild and calm. For a moment her eyes roved with tranquil disinterest over his face.

"Who are you?" she asked.

"I am John. My name is John."

She thought about that, her eyes still on his face. Then she shook her head, uncomprehending, and dismissed it.

"Did you see it?" she asked. "It was pretty—all those colors—"

"Amy," he said, "does it hurt?"

"Hurt?"

"Are you in pain?"

She frowned, puzzled by the question, but she did not let it concern her for long.

"Did you see the fire?" she asked. "It was pretty—all those colors —I will do it again—"

She paused, for now she was having trouble breathing. Heavy perspiration was breaking on her forehead, running down with bits of charred skin and ash to obscure her vision. She tried to raise a hand to brush it away, but her lower arms were useless, so he reached for his own handkerchief and gently wiped the sweat from her eyes.

He turned to the attendants still crowding the doorway. His voice was harsh.

"A basin of cool water and a cloth—at once!"

The water was quickly brought and he began to bathe her face, down over her throat, dabbing lightly with the cloth, avoiding those raw areas that were already blistering and exuding serum. For once she was compliant, like an obedient child, sitting cross-legged as he had found

her. The cooling water soothed her. She submitted without her customary wild and excited outbursts.

But now some troubling thoughts were beginning to intrude, some
disjointed, confused images washed by the dark currents of her mind.

She turned her head and looked up at him, inquiringly, searchingly.
"Was it you?" she asked. "Was it you who did it?"

"Did what, Amy?"

"Was it you who took my children?"

His throat tightened. It was the first time she had even half-remembered. It was the first time she had linked him to her life.

He said, "No, Amy, I did not take your children."

"Then who took them? I want them back. Will you bring them
back to me?"

He stopped sponging and looked deeply into her face. There was a
vestige of awareness in her eyes. There was a strange pleading quality in
her voice. She was on the brink of remembering. But he knew she was
dying. She could not last till dawn.

A great compassion welled inside him. He said gently, "They will
be back, Amy. The children will be back."

"Will they?"

"Aye."

"Are you sure?"

"I am sure."

"When? When will they be back?"

"In a little while."

"By suppertime?"

"Aye—surely by suppertime."

She lapsed into reverie at that. But presently she said wistfully,
"You know, it is strange. I cannot remember what they looked like. I
know there were two of them, two little boys—two little boys—two
little boys—" Her voice was rising, reaching the anguished pitch of a
recently bereaved mother. "Two little boys—two little boys—two little
boys—"

"No, Amy. Ah, no." Quickly he moved closer and put his arms
around her. "There, Amy. It is all right now. Hush! Everything is all
right."

She made no effort to pull away, but stayed willingly within his
comforting embrace, silent suddenly, her head against his breast. It was
so quiet in the cell that he could hear each rasping breath as it came

from her tortured lungs. After a while he heard a faint gurgle as the blood welled up in her throat and trickled from her mouth to fall in droplets on his wrist.

Then he was aware only of a deep silence.

He looked down. She was staring up at him, a vacant, unseeing stare. For a moment he stayed there, holding her, looking down into her face. Then he raised a hand and gently slid the lids over the sightless eyes.

There was no way he could lay her on the bed. The bones of her charred legs were fused with the ashes of her mattress to the floor. He could only leave her sitting there, cross-legged, statue-like. Slowly he arose and moved toward the door, turned once and looked back.

Then he went out and locked the door and put the key in his pocket.

Down in the entrance hall the superintendent was waiting.

John's face was unrevealing. "My wife just died. I locked the cell door. Please give strict orders that no one is to enter. I will send you final instructions."

Then he mounted Iris and rode slowly away.

The night was dark, the racing cloud rack so thick that not even a star was visible. Soon it began to drizzle. Yet still he did not turn toward home. Instead, he rode with bowed head, loosing his hold on the reins so they lay slack on the mare's neck, leaving her free to go whither her vagrant fancy took her.

Unguided, the mare slowed her pace. Once she halted, listening, her flesh quivering, but the phantasmal company of ghostly footsteps following along behind resolved into a single lonely bullock, its hooves brushing the long grasses. Presently John raised his head and saw, looming dark through the shrouding mist, the great prehistoric earthwork of Maiden Castle—the Mai-Dun or Hill of Strength—lost now in the sleep of the millennia on The Downs just off the ancient Roman Way. He contemplated it. This deserted place of the Old Ones, this lofty solitude of forgotten barrows and ancient ramparts and labyrinthine passages he had loved and explored since he was a boy. For some reason the sight of it now, reassuring in its permanence, eased the deep sadness that tonight seemed to fill his soul and envelop the world.

It seemed quite by chance, then, that he found himself on the country road just below the mill. He reined in and sat staring up at the tall, dark, silent shape, held by something unidentifiable, something buried deep, some compelling primal awareness beyond memory or human understanding, but there nonetheless. For a long time he sat gazing up, musing on the incomprehensible, while the drizzle turned to rain and the blowing wind chilled him under his wet clothing so he hunched his shoulders against it.

The mare was growing restless, out of temper. She was hungry. It was past her bedtime, so suddenly, of her own volition, she turned about and started for home.

He halted the mare and eased her gently in the opposite direction. Then he leaned forward and patted her neck.

"Bear with me tonight, girl," he said. "I know you are tired. I know you are thinking of home and fodder. But bear with me. It is not a lonely cottage I want tonight. Tonight, it is a welcoming fireside and friendly talk. So let us ride out and see if the lamps still are lit at Wynford Eagle. You know you always get good stabling there. And good fodder, too."

Wynford Eagle.

Even now, the name had the power to bring comfort to John's troubled spirit. It was still so vivid in his memory, his youthful trepidation as he ventured down the dark tunnel of trees and saw, at the tunnel's end, the great mansion standing on its grassy plat, its many-casemented windows brilliantly lit, the proud stone eagle perched, wings outspread, on its roof. For a long time he had stood there, an orphan boy of thirteen, gazing up at the great manor house, awed by it, ignoring the first sprinklings of the summer thunderstorm that threatened momentarily to drench him and the grinding hunger in his stomach that had lured him here. That was how he had first come to Wynford Eagle, almost fifteen years ago, three days after old Doctor Toller died.

That kindly eccentric old man had always given away nearly as much as he took in, so that at his death his financial affairs, for a busy and successful doctor, were confounding. He probably never knew that he was in fact bankrupt. His cottage, even his horse and medical instruments, were in pledge to the local usurers. He owed every merchant in town. His patronage was no longer welcomed at his favorite pothouses. John's grammar-school bill was almost a year overdue. At thirteen, therefore, half-educated, penniless, and once again homeless, John knew that his bright dream of following in his beloved mentor's footsteps were shattered.

He could now never be a doctor.

It was late afternoon on the day of Doctor Toller's funeral, and John, a small bundle in his hand, was trudging northward, heading for the farming country up beyond the Medburys. He had slipped out of Dorncaster that afternoon, nimbly evading the orphanage spotters, and had already traveled a distance of some seven miles. The apple and piece of bread he had in his pocket when he started out were long since gone, but he still remembered the lessons of his early childhood. It would not be the first time he had found his supper in wild places or slept comfortably out of the wind hard by a hedge-bank.

Suddenly, as he trudged along, he heard a horse coming up behind him. After a quick glance to make sure it was not the orphanage spotters, he looked straight ahead, for they had buried Doctor Toller only that morning, and just a short while ago, finding himself alone in open country, he had finally given way to his grief and wept.

He squeezed to one side of the road as the horse passed. The rider was a man in his middle years, with an aristocratic bearing and a periwig that was fashionably long and curled. His hat was of fine plum-colored felt. His dress was rich: dove-gray breeches and pearl-gray coat, beneath which was a shirt of fine white cambric liberally edged with lace.

As the rider passed the trudging boy, he turned and gave him a long, searching look. Then, a few yards up the road, he reined in and turned to wait for John to catch up with him.

"Are you not Doctor Toller's lad?" he asked.

"I am Doctor Toller's adopted son, sir," the boy replied.

"That is what I meant—and proud he was of you, I hear. I saw you at the funeral. Your name is John too, I hear."

"It is, sir."

"Yes, yes, for generations the Tollers have named their eldest son John. And all of them were doctors. John Toller has been a proud name in these parts. Remember that."

"I have always treated it with respect, sir."

The gentleman gazed quietly down at the boy. He pretended not to see the telltale redness of the swollen eyes, for he had heard in town that the boy loved the drunken old man and had cared for him like a baby in his last helpless year. The same uncritical gaze seemed to pass, unseeing, over the small bundle of worldly goods wrapped up in a cloth.

"Well, John," he said at last, "what are you doing so far from home?"

"I am heading up into farming country, sir."

"What for?"

"To become a farmhand."

"Why a farmhand?"

"Because I would make a good farmhand, sir. I am tall for my age, and strong."

"Oh! I doubt none of that. But were you not in the grammar school?"

"Aye, sir."

"And doing well?"

"Aye, sir."

"And preparing for Oxford or Cambridge?"

"Aye, sir."

The gentleman waited. But the boy offered no explanation for what, on the surface, appeared to be either an aberration or an outrageous form of childish rebellion. And looking into the boy's intelligent and self-reliant face, it was hard to believe that young John Toller was capable of either.

"Well, now," the gentleman said, "it seems you have walked a far distance this afternoon. Where were you planning to get supper and a bed?"

"I expect I will manage, sir."

The gentleman smiled at that.

"Yes, I expect you will. But let me introduce myself. I am Thomas Sydenham. I grew up hereabouts. Doctor Toller and I were good friends when we were both much younger men and, like Doctor Toller, I am a medical doctor. Now I practice in London." He raised his riding whip and indicated a mansion standing some distance off, its gables rising behind some ancient trees. "That is my house yonder. It is called Wynford Eagle. I am down from London on one of my brief visits, but this time I am alone. My family stayed in London. I mislike being alone,

John. I would be complimented if you would stop on your way and sup with me this evening."

The boy stood there, lost in awe before the great man.

Doctor Toller had often spoken of Doctor Sydenham, and always in terms bordering on veneration, for it had been Sydenham, the innovator and plain dealer, who had struggled to bring English medicine back to clinical observation and personal experience. The title "the English Hippocrates" had been bestowed on him by his contemporaries, and in such high esteem was he held that his busy London practice included royalty and nobility. Now, gazing up at him, the boy felt more than admiration. He felt strangely drawn to this brilliant and kindly man. But still he hesitated. He looked back down the road. It was not yet dusk, and as yet there was no sign of pursuit. But he knew he must be many miles from Dorncaster before the orphanage spotters realized he had decamped. All they ever did with a thirteen-year-old was apprentice him to a baker, a bricklayer, or, worse still—a butcher. He would never allow himself to be apprenticed to a butcher!

He must move all night and be safe in the Medburys by tomorrow's dawn.

"You are very kind, Doctor," he answered, "and I thank you. But I must be on my way."

"Very well, John," Doctor Sydenham said. "But if you should change your mind, just come up to the house. We will be having steak and kidney pie. Do you like that? And mashed potatoes to take up the gravy. And Mrs. D'Oyley, my housekeeper, has made a gooseberry tart with Devonshire cream for dessert. She is an excellent cook, Mrs. D'Oyley. So do try to come. And do not bother ringing the doorbell. The door is always unlatched. I take my evening meal at seven." He was about to ride off when suddenly he looked back. "And remember, John, I mislike supping alone. If you would change your mind and join me, I would look upon it as a very special favor."

Dusk was falling by the time John passed the great iron gateway leading to Wynford Eagle. Beyond it, a few humble cottages hugged the road, then fields widened out again. He began to look around. He must hurry and find a bed, for a summer thunderstorm was brewing on the horizon. But the first thing was supper. Hunger was doing strange things to his head.

He glanced speculatively at the cottages as he passed. He could of course knock on some door and beg for food, but his pride was too unyielding for that. He could dig up some roots and take them into the woods to roast them. For someone as adept as he was that would be easy enough. The trouble was that his youthful imagination had already been seduced. His senses were tantalized by the image of steak and kidney pie, "and mashed potatoes to take up the gravy." After that would come Mrs. D'Oyley's gooseberry tart with Devonshire cream. . . .

And, he thought with something bordering on alarm, it must be almost seven o'clock. . . .

He glanced quickly at the sky. The thunderclouds were scudding low. Already lightning was flashing beyond the hills. He could hear the thunder. He could smell the imminent rain. Those orphanage spotters would not still be on the move under threat of a downpour. They were probably already holed up in some tavern. That would give him time to sup with Doctor Sydenham and be on his way again before they even settled their accounts.

Almost before he knew it he had turned around and was running back in the direction of Wynford Eagle.

Doctor Sydenham was just sitting down to his meal. He looked up and smiled as the boy pushed open the dining-room door, then hesitated, panting, on the threshold.

"Ah, John, I was hoping you would come." He indicated a place set for him, then turned to the maidservant. "Kathleen, my young friend is giving me the pleasure of supping with me."

After the boy was served, the doctor proceeded, in his easy manner, to discourse at length on the history of Dorset, particularly of Dorncaster and its prehistoric beginnings, giving the boy a chance to consume, with polite restraint, his first large helping of meat pie with its golden crust and rich gravy. After that the boy's energy returned with surprising rapidity and he began to exhibit his usual keen interest in his surroundings.

"Do you often visit Dorset, sir?" he asked presently.

"Dorset is my home, John."

"But your practice is in London."

"True, but I was born here at Wynford Eagle—right in the very bed in which I now sleep. I return here frequently during the year. I have always loved Wynford Eagle. My family has held it for generations. Have you noticed the fireplace?"

John turned. Above the handsome overmantel was a carved shield with heraldic devices.

"The coat of arms of the Sydenhams," the doctor explained. "But before my family acquired this place, it was held by the barony of Aquila, or the Eagle, in Sussex. That is how it got its name."

"I had not realized the place was so ancient."

"Some parts are assumed to be Saxon, but other parts are not ancient at all. Alterations have been made over the centuries. One of my ancestors married a Catholic lady, so we even have a priest's hole, built at a time when the celebration of the Mass was strictly forbidden. The King's soldiers broke in and searched the house, but, though they wrecked a great deal of paneling, they never found the priest's hole. Other secret passages exist to this day within the walls. And hiding places for treasure. And secret staircases you would never guess at. This is an interesting house, John, with a long and interesting history, which is why I very much regret that my sons do not care for Wynford Eagle —or indeed for Dorset. They never come here anymore. They prefer the London life."

Something had come into the doctor's face as he spoke about his sons, something John took to be disappointment, even bitterness. He quickly sought to introduce a happier note.

"But Mrs. Sydenham must enjoy Wynford Eagle?"

"She used to, John. She always accompanied me on my visits. Now she is buried in the family plot here on the manor grounds."

"Oh! I am sorry, sir. I did not know—"

"That is quite all right, my boy. I appreciate your interest. But now tell me about yourself. What did you like to do after school?"

"Mostly I enjoyed helping Doctor Toller with his patients. His office was in our cottage, so after school and on Sundays—his clinic was free to the poor on Sundays, so we were always crowded on that day— he let me assist, doing the bandaging, extracting foreign bodies, swabbing wounds—though only with boiled water, or water mixed with wine."

The doctor turned and looked keenly at the boy. "And you enjoyed that?"

"Oh, yes, sir, very much. Doctor Toller taught me the different methods of stopping hemorrhage, even how to ligate arteries. And that was lucky because one evening, when he was out on his rounds, a man stumbled into the cottage hemorrhaging from a knife wound. I was afraid the man would die if I waited for Doctor Toller to return, so I ligated the vessels and closed the wound. After that the doctor let me do most of his sewing-up. I learned to do all minor work. But sometimes during an emergency, in the typhus epidemic, for instance, I did major work as well. Sir, do you hold with the general opinion that the work of surgery is only for the uneducated, for barber-surgeons?"

"Well, that is hard to say. There are exceptions, of course—Richard Wiseman, Alexander Read. But yes, it is true that the abyss separating the physician from the surgeon is considerable. It is mostly a matter of education. For the physician, we have the universities of Oxford and Cambridge, and great hospitals like St. Bart's. But for the young man who, lacking the means to become a physician, decides to become a surgeon, there is little competent instruction available. He has to learn his craft by trial and error on the battlefield or seek apprenticeship with a practicing surgeon who himself has only learned his craft experimentally, without the aid of science."

"But that is not right, is it, sir?—that surgery is only for the uneducated, I mean?"

"Why do you think it is not right?"

"Because Hippocrates practiced surgery. Hippocrates taught that surgery was a noble art."

The doctor turned, surprised. "That is true," he said. "But where did you learn about Hippocrates?"

"From the medical books at the hospital."

"You have a questing spirit, John—a spirit of inquiry. Have you ever thought of becoming a physician?"

There was a passionate note in the boy's voice. "Oh, sir, that is all I ever wanted to be!"

"Yet now you are setting out to be a farmer?"

For the first time that day the boy dropped his gaze. But again he offered no explanation.

He said quietly, "That is true, sir."

Thomas Sydenham studied the boy thoughtfully, noting the sensitive face topped by a shock of dark unmanageable hair. A handsome lad, the doctor reflected, big for his age and coltish still, but with fine aristocratic features and a forceful chin and mouth. Idly he wondered about his parentage. It was said in Dorncaster that the boy was a foundling. But something nudged the doctor's memory . . . The Great Hall at Dunheved Castle . . . a young man sitting on a great black stallion. The young man had died shortly after that portrait was painted and the great stallion died with him. But that was how this coltish boy would look a dozen years from now, like the young man on the stallion, the same blue searching eyes, the same look about the face, proud, spirited, independent. A startling family resemblance.

Yes, indeed, a family resemblance. There was no other way to explain such a likeness. But then, what was the rest of the story? Did the boy know anything of his beginnings? Probably not.

After supper the doctor said, "Come, John, I want to show you my latest acquisition."

He led the boy down a passage to the rear of the house and ushered him into a large white room filled with white cases and bottles and instruments with curious shapes.

"This is my laboratory," he explained. He crossed to a table on which stood an object covered with black cloth. Carefully he removed the cloth. "Look at that, John. Do you know what it is?"

John approached, puzzled. "No, sir."

"I am not surprised. I just received it from Holland. It is a microscope."

He noticed the quick intake of breath, the sudden flash of excitement as the boy moved closer to the instrument, seemingly drawn to it by some irresistible force.

"A microscope? They did not have one at the hospital. They could not afford one. But I have read that microscopes can enlarge small objects so that an ordinary housefly looks as big as a sheep. Is that possible, sir?"

The doctor smiled. "Well, John, why not examine an ordinary housefly and judge for yourself."

He stepped to a window and picked up a dead fly from the sill. He brought it to the microscope, dropped it on the plate and adjusted the screws and lamp. Then he motioned the boy to place his eyes close to the lens.

The boy gasped. "It is true, sir! It actually does look as big as a sheep. And it is covered with hair. The housefly is covered with hair! And it has angular joints. That is extraordinary, sir! It is quite extraordinary!"

The boy was trembling with excitement now, clasping both hands tightly around the instrument, peering through the lens with such absorption that his cheeks flushed pink and moisture burst out on his forehead.

"There are plenty of other wonders to be seen through a microscope, John," the doctor said after a moment. "One can finally understand what Leeuwenhoek means by his 'little animals.' One can study the blood vessels, or examine the structure of the muscles and observe their fibers and their increased size in contraction. And you would be amazed to follow Kircher's experiments upon the nature of putrefaction, to see how maggots and other living creatures develop in decaying matter—maggots not perceptible to the naked eye."

The boy had looked up and now stood listening intently. He said nothing. But his eyes were shining. He seemed to be breathing in the doctor's words like the air he drew into his lungs.

"At the moment, John, microscopists are studying the respiratory organs of insects and their vascular circulation. They are even studying the structure of the optic nerve of fishes and the effect on animals of the deprivation of blood. Can you imagine what such study will eventually mean for the study of man himself? There is no telling—"

He looked up as running footfalls were heard coming down the passage. An instant later Kathleen burst into the laboratory.

"Doctor, there be two men asking to see 'ee. They be from St. Joseph's Orphanage i' Dorncaster."

John's instant leap for the window was intercepted by the doctor, who put a firm restraining hand on his shoulder.

"That is all right, Kathleen. Tell the gentlemen I am working in my laboratory, but that I will be with them shortly."

"An', sir"—Kathleen's eyes shifted, round and accusing, to John. "They say they be looking for a Dorncaster boy name o' John Toller. They say they found tracks on your driveway and wonder if he be here."

"In that case, Kathleen, show the gentlemen into the library and offer them each a glass of my good canary. But be sure to answer no questions. That is a strict order." The doctor still had his grip on John's shoulder and after Kathleen had left he looked down, an amused twinkle in his eyes. "They came sooner than you expected, did they not, John?"

"Aye, sir—and if you will excuse me, I will—"

"Easy, my boy! As I told you, there are many ways out of this old house, and all of them lead in different directions. I suspect my ancestors had good reason to occasionally speed their leave-taking, just as you are about to do now. The Medburys, you say? Come, I will show you a deer run through my private woods known only to me and the poachers."

A few moments later they were heading through heavy woods,

following a series of zigzag deer runs screened by thickets. The thunderstorm had passed. The air smelled sweet and earthy. Small creatures scampered from their path.

Presently the doctor halted and pointed in a northerly direction.

"You cannot lose your way now, John. Cross the stream by the stepping-stones. They will lead to a trail which will carry you right up to the Medburys. I have a friend up there who farms a few nice acres. His name is Jeremy Scopes. He will be needing good hands for the harvest. Go and see him. Tell him you are a friend of mine."

"Thank you, sir. I will do that."

"I had better go back to the spotters now, looking properly helpful, but craftily making evasion sound like truth—something at which we doctors become regrettably proficient."

John took the doctor's outstretched hand and clasped it warmly.

"I am very grateful to you, sir. Thank you for supper. And thank you for helping me evade the spotters."

At that the doctor gave a low chuckle.

"I will share a secret with you, John. I have not felt so delightfully devilish since I was a lad and sneaked out of the house at night to steal Squire Chumway's apples."

Two weeks later Doctor Sydenham rode up to the Medburys to look for John. He found him in Farmer Scopes's wheat field, stripped to the waist and glistening with sweat, helping harvest the grain. He waited till the noonday meal was brought, then man and boy sat in the shade of a wagon and talked.

"John, do you still want to be a doctor?"

"No, sir."

"Why not? Because you lack money for your education? The reason I rode up here today is to tell you that I would very much like to make that education possible."

A quick anger stirred in the boy. The slow flush colored his face right to the hairline. "Sir, I have changed my mind."

"You could never convince me of that, John. Your single consuming aspiration is to become a doctor. I recognized that at supper when we talked of medicine and microscopy and Hippocrates. It was the truth you told me then. You said that being a doctor was all you ever wanted. Now you are placing an obstacle in your own path."

The boy turned. "An obstacle?"

"Your pride, John. Your infernal pride. The feelings you have at this moment that you could not bear to be beholden to me for your education."

"How can you know what I feel?"

"It is written on your face."

The boy looked out to where the poppies splashed the harvest with scarlet. "I do not think that is wrong. My pride is what I have in life."

The doctor's voice instantly softened. "No, it is not wrong, John. But it is not enough for a boy like you—for the man you are going to become. Pride, as it relates to self-respect, is important to us all. Pride alone can get a man through the rough of life, but a doctor needs those qualities which, according to the Hippocratic concept, cannot be separated from love for the sick."

"But I have told you, sir, I am no longer planning to become a doctor."

"Then are you planning to squander everything you already know? Everything Doctor Toller taught you? Will you go through life stumbling on your own rigid pride because you cannot bring yourself to accept help from others? John, I am a rich man. I have already educated my own two boys. It would mean nothing to me to educate a third. If you want to finish at the Dorncaster Grammar School, you can board there until you graduate. You can receive your doctorate in medicine at Oxford or Cambridge. You might even choose the University of Padua. The great Harvey got his M.D. there. With the remarkable promise you show, your horizon is unlimited."

"Thank you, sir, but I could not accept—"

The doctor broke in angrily. "Do not make the mistake I made, John. Like you, I dreamed of becoming a doctor, and, like you, I allowed obstacles to stand in my way. By the time I came to my senses and started working for my M.D. at Cambridge, my eldest son was already an undergraduate there. I still regret those lost years. Do not build up the same regrets. We are all human, John. We all need others sometime in our lives—even you."

The boy's face expressed surprise. "Did you ever need others?"

"All through my life, though I did not always know it. I needed my parents, but they died before I knew I loved them. I needed my wife; now she is gone, too. I needed my sons; now they are strangers. One thing remains, though. I am still a doctor. My life is rich because of that one fact. So you see, John, being a doctor is what *I* have in life. You can have that too, if you choose."

The other harvestmen had finished their noonday meal and now were drifting back to work.

"I must go," the boy said.

He got to his feet. The doctor rose with him, but the boy did not leave. Instead, they stood together, side by side, looking out across the half-reaped field, watching the rooks glide in and dive and settle on the stubble, picking the fallen grain.

At last the boy said, "You have given me much to think about, sir."

"That was my purpose."

"It is a hard decision. And I promised Mr. Scopes I would stay till the end of harvest. That should be another ten days."

"Let me know what you decide. I will not be returning to London for two weeks yet. The choice is yours, John—to become a doctor or not. But you must want it badly enough to sacrifice for it."

"To sacrifice, sir? Sacrifice what?"

"Your pride, my boy. A small part of that unbending pride."

Iris broke into a full gallop as she turned into the tree tunnel at Wynford Eagle and knew that feed and a comfortable stall lay just ahead. John took her directly to the stables and roused the sleeping groom. But he himself took off her saddle and watered her and tipped some feed. Then, talking in his usual caressing tones, he began to curry her.

"She has had a hard day," he said, when the groom, still in his nightshirt, appeared in the doorway. "Finish currying her, then let her rest. I will be back to look at her later."

He found Doctor Sydenham in the paneled library, clad in a dressing gown, reading and sipping his port. He had removed his periwig and now wore a comfortable nightcap to keep his cropped head warm. One foot, sheathed in a slipper, was raised upon a footstool.

"Ah, I thought I recognized Iris's hoofbeats," the doctor said, as John entered. "I am glad to see you, my boy."

John touched him fondly on the shoulder as he passed. "How is the gout, Tom?"

"No better, I am afraid. It still has me hobbled. John, you look tired."

"Yes, I am tired."

John flung himself into his accustomed armchair on the opposite side of the fireplace and wearily closed his eyes and Sydenham watched him, studying the bronzed face with its strong features and firm jaw. The leaping flames seemed to magnify the jagged scar left by Amy's pothook. But tonight Sydenham detected something new, a hint of convulsed emotions, a shattering sadness in the drawn face. And there were some drops of dried blood on his hand which, since John appeared to have no corresponding wound, could not be his own.

Sydenham was curious, but asked no questions. Instead, he rose to his feet and limped over to the decanter, returning with a glass of port. "Drink this, my boy," he said. "Have you supped?"

"Thank you, Tom, but I am not hungry."

They sat there, not speaking. There was no need to speak. They were accustomed to their comfortable silences.

Fifteen years had passed since their conversation in the wheat field and in that time Sydenham had come to love John Toller as he had loved his own sons. It was more than a mutual passion for medicine that drew them together. It was a bond of trust and friendship. Sydenham could not help but be gratified at the part he had played in John's young life. But he asked nothing of him. Once, after John had completed his internship at St. Bart's in London, Sydenham suggested that John join him in his London practice. When John expressed a desire to return to his native Dorset, Sydenham, though disappointed, made no effort to dissuade him. Sydenham was as proud of John's independent nature as he was of John's expanding reputation and glittering accomplishments. And though it saddened him to know he must be content to play an ever dwindling part in the younger physician's concerns, he drew comfort from the realization that always, in moments of crisis in his life, it was to Wynford Eagle that John came.

He sensed that something of that nature had brought him there tonight.

After a while John said, "Amy died a while ago."

"I am sorry—truly sorry, John. What happened?"

"Somehow she obtained the means to set her mattress on fire."

Sydenham's face expressed no surprise. "My God. John, I am sorry. But it's a mistake to grieve for her. She might have lived another fifty years, alone as only the mad can be alone, suffering mental torments the rest of us can only guess at. For the past four years she had been alive only in the sense that she had breathed."

"Aye, 'tis true."

"Did she die immediately?"

"Of her lower body little more than the half-charred bones were left, but the upper body lived on for an hour or more. She was able to talk—was almost sane. It has me puzzled, Tom, this extraordinary lack of perception to pain."

"It is part of an age-old mystery. The more humane physicians who visit the Bedlams are now accepting the theory that those women who were burned alive for witchcraft, and who actually sang and laughed as their flesh was being consumed by the flames, were not witches at all, but were afflicted by a singular form of madness which, because it affects the body as well as the mind, actually made them insensible to pain."

"And you think that is what happened to Amy?"

"It is possible. But, John, you seem unduly distressed. Did you still love her, then?"

"Amy has been outside my life for so long now that the sorrow I feel is hardly personal."

"Then why has her death been so harrowing for you?"

"It is not her death so much as the *manner* of her death. It is the fact that in the end she came so close to the borderline that separates the sane from the mad, so close to remembering. She cried out to know about the children. She called piteously for her 'two little boys.' For the first time in years she seemed almost to recognize me—to link me to her life. Tom, I found myself hoping death would come swiftly, before her memory cleared and those last terrible scenes at the mill flashed back to her."

"Well, there is nothing more you can do for Amy, John. It is time to think about yourself. At last you are free. Now you can find yourself a good woman who will give you children. Every man needs a home and children, especially a doctor. Is there any woman in your life at the moment?"

"No woman I would choose to marry."

Sydenham reflected on this a moment.

"In that case, maybe the time has come for you to try a new place. As you know, I am pestered by this gout. It is getting hard for me to make my rounds. John, you know I have always hoped you would join me in my practice. Why not come back to London. Eventually, of course, I would turn the practice over to you. I would feel comfortable, knowing my patients were in your hands. They pay well. They are mostly royalty and noblemen. You could look forward to becoming wealthy in time."

John smiled. The affection he felt for Sydenham showed in his eyes.

"Thank you, Tom, but I still feel the way I did when I started out. I have everything I want here. I am a Dorsetman. This is my home. These people are my people. They trust me."

Sydenham nodded. "I understand."

He said no more, only sat and listened to a blackbird in the poplar outside singing his autumn sub-song, a lovely, idle song, muted, under his breath.

Presently he asked, "Are the executions still proceeding in Dorncaster?"

"From sunup to sundown. The stench of the slaughter is sickening. There is general horror and disgust at the sight of the king's vindictiveness."

"Did you know, then, that some of the rebels are being spared? I had a dispatch from London this morning saying that Admiral Penn's son, William Penn, a Quaker who refuses to remove his hat in court, has begged twenty rebels off the King?"

"Did he get them?"

"For gold. The King thought he was selling them into slavery, but rumor circulates that Penn is sending them off to the Americas, where he has a free colony called Pennsylvania."

"Will they be allowed to take wives and children?"

"That was one of Penn's conditions. In London there is angry talk of deposing James for his savagery toward these religionist rebels. Are people murmuring against the King in Dorset?"

"They are too busy murmuring against the Lord Chief Justice of England who, since arriving from London to open his assize, has shown such diabolical pleasure in carrying out the King's orders that already it is being called 'the Bloody Assize.' Today, in passing Town Hall, I stepped into Jeffreys's courtroom to see for myself and found him sitting on the dais more drunk than sober, the fumes of liquor so thick around him I feared for our old timber building. He is clearly racked by disease, the stone, I suspect. He is a proper tool for a sadistic king—a blasphemous, foul-mouthed bully with an insane lust for cruelty. He, with four other judges, had three hundred rebels to try. The King gave them five days in which to complete the trials and Jeffreys seems bent on earning the Great Seal of England by satisfying the King in this."

"Five days?" Sydenham exclaimed. "It will take five months to try three hundred rebels."

"Normally, yes. But Jeffreys must have calculated he would sit in judgment till the spring assizes if he gave each man a fair trial, so he found a way to pass sentence of death on ninety-eight rebels at one and the same time."

"How did he do that? England's common law does not permit the use of torture to extract confessions."

"No, but he maneuvered to put an end to the need for trials by letting it be known that the only chance of obtaining pardon was by pleading guilty, then, after these ninety-eight had fallen into the trap and confessed, they were promptly sentenced and hustled off to the gallows, where Jack Ketch and Pascher Rose, already up to their elbows in blood, were waiting to butcher them."

Sydenham thoughtfully sipped his port. "Tell me, John, is the vicar's young daughter likely to be brought up before Jeffreys?"

"Jenny Sykes? I hope not. There are still some two hundred rebels to be tried, but Jeffreys must leave in three days to carry his commission to Devon and Somerset. Within that time he will probably try, unsuccessfully I hope, to get the rest of the rebels consigned to the hangman. But since these rebel trials have delayed the regular jail delivery, Jeffreys will be forced to leave behind at least one judge to preside over the leftover rebel trials as well as the delayed case list with its accumulation of murder, witchcraft, blasphemy, and general crime. I am hoping he will designate Sir William Montague for this. Montague has sat in Dorncaster before. He is a patient, fair-minded judge who will listen to any new facts presented at the trial of Jenny Sykes."

Sydenham looked surprised. "New facts in the Sykes trial? But from what I hear there is no way the girl can escape the gallows. The evidence against her is conclusive. Mrs. D'Oyley says she even admits the baby was hers."

"I am still hoping she will not be hanged."

"That is a futile hope, John. You know the law. Concealment of the birth of a child which, if born alive, would have been a bastard, is to be accounted satisfactory proof of murder against the mother."

"But the law continues on, stipulating that the evidence of one witness at least is required to establish the fact of such a child having been born dead."

"Well?"

"Well, I intend to ride over and have a talk with the vicar."

"My boy, you will get no help from the vicar."

"How can you be sure?"

"Because I know his mind. Because he abhors the nature of his daughter's offense. The vicar holds physical passion to be sinful."

"Then how did he himself beget a daughter?"

"There is more to it than that, John."

"You know him personally?"

"I met him once under strange and odious circumstances."

John was quick to read something into that statement that Sydenham had not meant to reveal.

"As a patient, Tom?"

There was a long pause. "Yes, as a patient."

John waited. "Are you going to tell me?"

Sydenham hesitated. "Only because it might serve to guide your actions. But it would have to be in the strictest professional confidence."

"Of course."

Still Sydenham hesitated, reluctant to begin.

"It happened about three years ago," he said at last. "I was working late one night in my study, writing. The weather was warm. I had the French doors open. Suddenly I heard a faint rustle outside, the crunching of leaves under a furtive foot. I listened. After a moment I heard it again. I called out, 'Who is there?' Then the vicar stumbled in through the French doors. His face was ashen and glistening with sweat. His eyes were staring. His clothes were disheveled. His breeches were covered with blood that seemed to be dripping from his groin down his thighs. I helped him into the laboratory and examined him. The vicar had attempted self-castration."

"Good God! The man must be plagued by mystic ecstasies. Was he successful?"

"No, he had incised his scrotum with the intention of removing the testicles, but apparently his courage failed before he completed the procedure. After I sewed him up I asked him why he had done it. He replied angrily that he wanted to be rid of sexual desire—that all carnal pleasure was bestial and sinful in the eyes of the Lord."

"Is he still your patient?"

"Fortunately, no. I see him only when we pass as strangers in the village. But now you can see how futile it would be to appeal to the vicar —even to save his daughter's life. Besides, Mrs. D'Oyley, who goes to his church, since it is just down the road, tells me it was the vicar himself who turned over the infant's body to the constable."

"Men sometimes come to regret their hasty actions. Men sometimes wish to make amends."

"Not this man. I suspect that in his actions toward his daughter the vicar is taking full and terrible revenge on his runaway wife."

"Is that what happened to Jenny's mother? She ran away?"

"With an actor—one of a company of roving players. She took the child with her. But apparently he tracked down the lovers and wrenched the child out of her mother's arms."

"How old was Jenny at the time?"

"About five years."

John was silent for a moment, gazing intently into the fire. Then he said thoughtfully, "I wonder how much of all this Jenny remembers."

Sydenham said nothing. He was struck by something in John's manner and now he sat quite still, studying the younger man with puzzled, questioning eyes.

Presently John said, "Tom, a year or two ago, there was a case tried in a German court. It was similar to the Sykes case—an unmarried girl accused of infanticide. Do you know anything about it?"

"No, my boy, I do not. Where did you hear of it?"

"From Doctor Van Roonhuyse, my medical correspondent in Amsterdam."

"I thought old Hendrik was dead."

"I am speaking of his son, Rogier, who has taken over his practice. Doctor Rogier, too, practices obstetrics. He said this particular case created considerable interest because the defense introduced in evidence a test based upon work by the Dutch microscopist Swammerdam."

"Swammerdam's extraordinary work is universally recognized. But what was this particular test?"

"He said only that it was a water test."

"Has the validity of the test been confirmed?"

"By several medical faculties."

"And how was it made available for purposes of justice?"

"A Doctor Schreyer, of Zeitz, in Saxony, first had actual recourse to it in the legal proceedings against the girl. The test proved to the satisfaction of the court that she could not have murdered her child."

"And you are thinking, perhaps, that this test might be useful in the Sykes case?"

"It might prove what is presently not provable."

"What are you going to do?"

"I have already dispatched a courier to Amsterdam requesting details of the test from Van Roonhuyse. I asked him to let my man bring me the information with all speed, since the assize is already in progress and the girl will go on trial shortly."

"But how sure are you of the girl's innocence? Of still greater import, John, how sure are you that by using this test you will not be tightening the noose around the girl's neck?"

"I am certain her baby was stillborn."

"You examined the body?"

"At the coroner's request. There were no marks of violence to indicate infanticide; no signs of smothering, no fractures, no contusions, no concealed puncture wounds, no marks of pressure on the neck. But that examination revealed one compelling fact, a fact which has stayed with me and vexed my thoughts ever since. That tiny creature had been carefully washed before it was buried."

"And why should that be so compelling?"

"Because it is inconsistent with human nature that a mother who has so tenderly washed her baby should have murdered it."

There was a long pause. Sydenham was still studying John with his puzzled, penetrating look.

Suddenly he said, "John, do you mind if I ask you a question? Why is this Sykes case so important to you?"

"Because I believe in the girl's innocence."

"Yet it is evident to all that she is hiding something. Unless this is another Immaculate Conception, there is a lover somewhere in the background."

"I bear that in mind."

"A lover whose name she is refusing to tell the court."

"I bear that in mind, too."

"Therefore, a lover she is protecting."

"Aye, that too."

"And as you know, where there is something to conceal, there is also a mind troubled by guilt."

"So one might argue."

"And knowing all this, knowing the girl is pursuing a deliberate course of concealment, how can you still believe in her innocence?"

"Because I know in my heart that she is innocent."

Sydenham frowned. Distress and anxiety showed on his face. "John, this is not like you. One thing I have always been sure of is your rationality. Yet now, despite all indications of her guilt, you are basing your belief in this girl's innocence on something you 'know in your heart.' My boy, a test accepted in the German courts will not necessarily be accepted here. So why are you letting yourself be drawn into a case whose probable end will be the gallows? Why this sudden unreasoning obsession? Explain it to me, John. Explain!"

John seemed unprepared for the question. He stared back at Sydenham for a moment, then got quickly to his feet and began moving in agitation about the library, pausing here and there to read a title or pull a book from the shelf and riffle through its pages. But he moved like a man detached from his surroundings, like a man absorbed in some more immediate matter that perplexed and absorbed his mind.

Sydenham, sitting back in his chair, watched him anxiously, patient and troubled.

Then suddenly John turned.

"Tom," he said, "I know you are right in most of your suspicions. I know there is something she is not telling—not even to save her own life. I know there is more to her story than any of us have guessed, more perhaps than any of us can conceive. But I sense that whatever it is she is hiding, it is not her own guilt. And I still say that whatever the proof against her, though she is guilty before the law of concealment of birth, she is innocent of crime."

Sydenham was silent for a moment as his fond, perceptive eyes searched the younger man's face.

"Is that really all there is, John?" he asked at last. "Is that the only reason for your concern?"

John stood looking down, puzzled. "What are you asking, Tom?"

"Come, my boy," Sydenham said. "Think again. Are you being entirely honest about this? Can it be you feel more for this girl than you have yet been willing to admit to yourself?"

John gave a surprised laugh. "That notion is absurd."

It was barely dawn when John, having slept at Wynford Eagle, returned to his cottage in the city. There, waiting on the doorstep, was a messenger from Dunheved Castle.

"Doc, the sight o' 'ee be a load off m' mind. His Lordship sent me to fetch 'ee, sir. His Lordship begs 'ee to cum at once. It be urgent, him says—mos' urgent, sir."

"What happened, Baines?"

"His Lordship did no' say, Doc. But I reckon it be so'thing terr'ble. His Lordship be clearly beside hisself. Him begs 'ee to cum 'thout no delay, sir."

"Very well," John answered. "But I have to stop first at the hospital. There is a patient I must see. You ride ahead and tell his Lordship I will be there shortly."

John had developed a curious aversion to his visits to Dunheved. The sight of its distant towers engendered a strong urge to turn back. He always rode away from it depressed in spirit, torn by the secret knowledge of a ghostly link between the castle and his own dimly remembered beginnings.

He had become aware of that link four years ago when he was first called to the castle to attend Lord Tremoigne's son. On that occasion, while passing through the Great Hall hung with ancestral portraits, he had chanced to notice the painting of a tall young man on a black stallion. The sight of the portrait shocked his memory, forcing it back to the time when, as a child of perhaps five years, perhaps six, he had been in the habit of waiting for the tall young man, who he knew was his father, to come riding to the place where he and his mother, Chérie, lived in a secret world of their own, hidden deep in a deer forest. He remembered his fear of the horse, a huge black beast so powerful and unruly that, in his child's mind, it was some kind of Evil One. But his father always laughed at his fears and, bending down, would swoop him up and set him before him in the saddle, then they would go riding up to the High Moor where the great black brute, stretching out his legs, seemed to fly over the rugged turf like a fiend bent on outstripping the wind. But if the black horse was the Evil One, Chérie was the Angel of Love in both their lives. Mostly John and Chérie lived alone in their· beautiful forest world. But sometimes, when his father came, the three of them would walk through the forest, his father's arm around Chérie's waist. His father and Chérie would stop from time to time to kiss, or speak together in low tones, while he, the small child, chased butterflies and waited till they had time for him again.

All these things John remembered, but through the long years he had kept them buried deep inside him. Dim as they were, his memories still were wreathed in sadness, in a sharp awareness of loss, in hurt confusion and a sense of cruel betrayal. For he never knew why, one day, his father came no more. And he never knew why Chérie awakened him one night and fled with him through the darkness up into the High Moor, hiding in the most desolate places. And he never knew why, with a searching party fanning out below, Chérie made him run to his secret hiding place in the pit of a denuded dolmen, forbidding him to come out till the searchers were gone.

Squatting there, trembling with fear, he peeped above the rim of the pit and saw Chérie break into the open and run. Chérie knew the High Moor better than the searchers. She would escape, then return under cover of night to fetch him. He waited in the pit all night, all next day. But Chérie never came for him. He kept telling himself, "Chérie loves me. Chérie would not leave me." But he never saw Chérie again. For a week he waited, subsisting upon the last of his mother's small store of dried leveret until, driven by hunger and the November cold, he ventured down from the heights and was found, half-frozen and starving, by Doctor Toller. But though he deliberately thrust them from his mind, the old questions lingered, never ceased to puzzle him, tugged him back. Only now, having seen his father's portrait in the Great Hall, he faced the conviction that, if he still wanted to scourge himself with answers, they were to be found at Dunheved Castle.

Dunheved was set upon a hill, its lofty towers rising above the treetops of its spacious park. Most of the massive structure dated from the thirteenth century, but a defensive tower was said to have preceded it, built by Oesc, son of Hengist, and certainly a palisaded fortress stood there in the tenth century, in which, according to legend, the beautiful but infamous Elfrida found refuge after treacherously murdering her stepson, King Edward the Martyr, at nearby Corfe.

Many other stories—romantic, heroic, or bloody—had been told of Dunheved through the centuries. Even now the countrymen, many of whom were in the habit of supplying their own larders by poaching Dunheved game, swore that as they were prowling his Lordship's chase at dusk they sometimes sighted a ghostly figure walking the castle battlements, a man (they thought), cloaked and hooded, who, when he turned and they glimpsed his face, was as white as chalk in the twilight. This rumor persisted in varying forms, but when someone laughingly recounted it to Lord Tremoigne, his Lordship first looked alarmed, then abruptly turned and hurried away.

But if some people spread such rumors, to others it seemed natural that the great quadrangular, four-towered castle should be the subject of neighborhood gossip, the more so since Lord Tremoigne now lived there in lonely seclusion. Lady Tremoigne, the romantic love of his youth, had died giving birth to their only child, a son, James. Lord Tremoigne never remarried. Some years ago James, by then a grown youth of eighteen, had reportedly set out to travel in Africa. He never returned. Nor did Lord Tremoigne ever speak of him. The neighborhood folk, who remembered James as self-willed and hot-tempered, whispered that his voice had been heard raised in a violent quarrel with his father and that his bones were likely buried in the castle's dungeons. In any case, most of the servants had now been dismissed. Only the older, more faithful ones remained, and they had become singularly close-mouthed. Guests were no longer welcomed at Dunheved, so the atmosphere of brooding secretiveness that surrounded it only fed the curiosity of the gossipy country folk.

Lord Tremoigne was waiting for John at the front door. Despite his efforts to appear composed, it was evident that he was in a state of extreme agitation. He hurried forward as John gave Iris into the care of the waiting groom and ran up the steps.

"My dear John, thank you for coming so quickly. Something terrible has happened."

"James?"

"Yes. Come, I will take you to him." Then suddenly he turned back, abandoning all effort now to hide his anguish. "John, I do not think I could bear to be present this time. Would you mind seeing him alone?"

John followed Lord Tremoigne through the Great Hall hung with its collection of ancestral portraits, then on through many sumptuous rooms hung with silks and tapestries, until they reached the West Tower. This they ascended by means of a flight of worn stone steps within the thickness of the wall. On the third floor was a heavy door studded and banded with iron.

Lord Tremoigne knocked on the door. A hoarse reply came from within and he pushed open the door, then stood aside to let John enter.

The odor given off by the single occupant of the tower filled the air with foulness. James had been standing in the middle of the room, but now he limped painfully away, moving backward, as though mindful of the infectiousness of his own ulcerating flesh. The leprous process had covered his face with blanched patches, leaving it milk-white, and his features were so distorted they no longer seemed to be those of a man. There was nothing left to show that he was now only twenty-five years. His limbs were crooked with destruction of his bones and joints. His hair was gone, his bald scalp covered with oozing vesicles that had spread down his neck and covered every visible part of him. The thickening of the mucous membranes of his nose and mouth had twisted his neck and affected his larynx, causing his hoarseness. Only his intelligent, darkly glittering eyes showed him to be human, and they were filled, not with resignation of his tragic affliction, but with rage and fear.

John approached, but did not touch him.

"Well, James, your father tells me you have another problem. What has happened?"

With a succession of croaking noises the youth struggled to explain, but his state of pure terror made most of what he said unintelligible. At last he held up a hand from which the middle finger was missing. He pointed to the table.

"The . . . just . . . dropped off. . . ."

John looked. On the table lay a human finger.

He turned back to the frightened youth. He spoke in quiet, gentle tones.

"I have already explained to you, James, that this is to be expected. Other fingers will drop off—toes, as well. This loss is caused by deep ulceration and necrosis. You must be ready for it to happen at any time and not be frightened by it. Will you remember that?"

The youth stared up at John, horror in his eyes. "You knew . . . drop off?"

"Yes, I knew. And I warned you about it. And now I am trying to impress upon you that it may happen again. I do not want you to be frightened if it does. Now, let me see the stump."

Still without touching, he examined the mutilated hand.

"You see, James, by the time the finger dropped off, the stump was already healed. That, too, is to be expected. You will never experience the pain of a raw stump the way other people would. Knowing that should at least ease some of your apprehensions. You do not feel any pain now, do you?"

James shook his head, his intense, horror-filled eyes still on John's face.

"But I do not . . . lose . . . . my fingers. I do not want . . . leprosy. I want . . . you . . . heal me. Why do you not heal me? Why cannot . . . heal me?"

"Because there is no cure for leprosy. Leprosy is incurable. The best we can do is keep you as comfortable as possible. I explained all that to you before, too. Do you not remember?"

"Yes . . . but that . . . last year. I thought . . . now . . . this year . . . you could . . . heal. . . ."

Slowly John shook his head. "Nothing has changed since last year, James. There is still no cure for leprosy. Someday, perhaps—"

"But why must . . . live alone . . . up here . . . the tower?"

"Because your father has no choice. The isolation of lepers is strictly enforced by law."

"Then I will . . . go away from here. I will . . . leave Dunheved . . . go from here . . . from this prison . . . tell my father . . . I want to leave."

John considered this.

Lucas Tremoigne's love for his son was protective and tender, but it was also weak and indulgent. He had always quailed before the need to tell James any wrenching truth, preferring to leave the transmission of all such truths to John. And now, lacking any understanding of the leper's life in the outside world, James was talking of leaving Dunheved. The truth here was particularly harsh. The law condemned the leper to symbolic death.

Again he spoke with extreme gentleness.

"James, if you were to leave Dunheved, where would you go? Leprosy, once so prevalent, has all but died out in England. The lazar houses have been abolished. And you would not be allowed to wander, as lepers once did. Leprosy is infectious. The leper's outcast state is enforced by law. But if your mind is made up, perhaps we could find a lazar house for you in Scotland. Or you could go to join the colony of lepers who live along the riverbank between Delft and The Hague in Holland, dwelling in huts on the brink of the water, receiving provisions by means of a floating box which they cast out. In Africa, too, the disease still exists, as unfortunately you know. But consider your decision with care, because here at Dunheved you not only have all the comforts your affliction will allow, but you are under the protection of a father who loves you. So do you really want to go far from home into some strange country, James? Is that what you want?"

James stared, shattered. He began to tremble.

"No!" he cried out. "No! That is not what I want . . . I want . . . like I used to . . . ride a horse . . . sometimes . . . with other people . . . with my friends. Oh! sometimes I long to . . . sometimes I long . . . but I am always here . . . the tower . . . alone. I do not want to be a leper . . . to always be alone . . . I want. . . ." And then all the pent-up anguish and despair, the rebelliousness and wild bitterness seemed to burst like a torrent inside him and, overwhelmed by the monstrous horror of his life, he dropped his leprous face into his leprous hands and sobbed.

John stood there, overcome by pity, filled with an angry awareness of his own professional limitations, of his ultimate impotence to help this young man whose suffering would end only with his death. For once he was silent, finding nothing to say. Then, because he could give the leper no words of hope, nor even extend a sympathetic hand to touch him, he went to the window and stayed there with him in the tower room until his paroxysm had passed.

Lord Tremoigne was waiting for him downstairs. He appeared to have regained his composure.

"John, you have probably not had time for breakfast. Mine is about to be served on the terrace. Will you not join me?"

John started to refuse, but changed his mind. Looking into Lucas Tremoigne's face, he had the feeling that the lord of Dunheved was troubled by something besides the condition of his leper son.

"Only if it is fast, Lucas. There is a sick girl I must see at the jail. Then I must get to the hospital."

From the terrace the land sloped steeply, providing a wide view of the park with its turfy glades, breezy hilltops, and wandering woodlands filled with game. Below the terrace, surrounded by flower beds, stood one dead tree, its roots still in the earth, its giant limbs leafless, its trunk lovingly supported by a post and chain. This dead skeleton was the venerable Dunheved wych-elm under which court had been held in ancient times for the settlement of local feuds. To the north, the shoulders of the High Moor were clad in purple ling. Dark on the distant horizon lay the deer forest.

"John," Lord Tremoigne began, after they had been served, "did you explain to James?"

"I did."

"How did he take it?"

"He is brave, Lucas. You can be proud of him."

"And there is still no hope of curing him?"

Regretfully John shook his head. "None at all, I am afraid."

"How long will he live?"

"That is hard to say. Lepers have been known to linger on for years."

Tremoigne looked about him, letting his sad and thoughtful gaze pass slowly up over the towers rising against the sky, each crowned with a projecting octagonal and machicolated turret, then turning to survey his domain.

"What a pity!" he murmured. "And James was heir to all this."

"It will still not pass out of your family, Lucas."

"That is true. At my death, all lands and titles will pass to the nearest male heir."

"And you have a first cousin up in Oxfordshire."

Tremoigne reacted as though John had struck him across the face with a whip. His eyes snapped. His aristocratic mouth curved into an expression of supreme contempt.

"Sidney Tremoigne? My cousin Sidney? Already that crafty, cold-blooded schemer is closing in on me with the tenacity of a bloodhound hot on the scent. His agents must have been nosing in the neighborhood, for his suspicions are aroused. He has started writing me frequently, suddenly solicitous of my health—most especially of James's health, asking if the boy returned safely from Africa. He is eager to see me, he writes, and begs to be invited to Dunheved without delay. God Almighty! He has only one thing in mind—to see James and me dead so he can have my lands and titles for himself and his sons. My cousin Sidney! I detest him as much today as I did when we were children."

John stared, amazed at the violence of Tremoigne's feelings. He looked deep into Tremoigne's face and saw a man who was bitter and proud and aged beyond his years, a lonely man, grief-stricken, who drank too much port. A man without hope for tomorrow.

He reasoned, "Lucas, the matter is out of your hands. If Sidney is the eldest male in the next degree of consanguinity, he and his sons will inherit in the natural order of things. But if you want to frustrate his ambitions, there is a simple way. You can remarry and have other sons of your own."

"Ah, yes," Tremoigne murmured.

They talked of many things after that and Tremoigne seemed to have forgotten the unpleasant matter of his cousin Sidney. But at the end of the meal, when John rose to hurry off, Tremoigne placed a restraining hand on his arm.

"Come, John," he said, "there is something I want to show you."

He led John back through the sumptuous rooms, through the magnificent old presence chamber with its painted and gilded ceiling, its armorial windows displaying the arms of Tremoigne impaling those of Delamere, Mortain, Hungerford, Farleigh, and Montacute. Soon they turned into the Great Hall, moving down past the long lines of ancestral portraits, and John, still impatient to be off, found himself wondering what Lucas had in mind. His curiosity deepened when they halted before the portrait of the young man on the black stallion.

For a few moments the two men stood together in silence, side by side, gazing up at the portrait, their mutual attention centered not on the majestic black beast, but on the rider. He must have been about twenty-four at the time the portrait was painted. His face was sensitive but strong, intelligent and self-reliant, his tall frame perfectly proportioned. His hair was dark and cropped at the shoulder, his coat of gold-colored fabric braided and tagged around the slender waist. There were slashes in his sleeves, showing the exquisite lace-trimmed shirt beneath. His cloak, thrown carelessly back, was of emerald-green, richly trimmed with marten's fur.

At last Tremoigne spoke. "John, have you ever seen that man? Look at him well."

But John did not need to look well. He remembered every lineament of his father's face as clearly as he remembered those of Chérie with her laughing eyes and springtime beauty. . . .

"Well, John?"

Still John did not answer the question. Instead, he asked quietly, "Who was he, Lucas?"

"He was my brother."

"What was his name?"

"Adam Ambrose Charles Tremoigne."

John was thoughtful for a moment. He seemed suddenly far away. "What happened to him?"

"He was killed—in an accident."

"What kind of accident?"

Lucas hesitated for an instant. Then he answered vaguely, "A hunting accident."

"How long ago was that?"

"Oh, many years now—while our father was still alive. It killed the old man, losing Adam. He doted on him. Adam could do nothing wrong. But you have not answered my question. I asked if you had ever seen him."

Still John did not answer. "Why do you ask?"

"I just thought it possible. You are obviously not without interest in the portrait. Sometimes, when you pass through the Great Hall alone, I have seen you stop and stand here, gazing up at it."

"Well?"

"And there is no denying that, when you look at this portrait of Adam, you might be looking at yourself in the mirror—the same eyes, the same shape of face and jaw, the same unruly hair."

John turned and faced Tremoigne. "Lucas, if you are searching for an heir to displace your cousin, he would need to be legitimate."

"Of course."

"And from what little I know of my background, I doubt that I would fill that requirement."

"Are you sure of that, John?"

"No, I am not sure, Lucas. But you are asking me about things of which I know almost nothing."

"Have you always supposed you were illegitimate?"

"I have never had reason to suppose I was not."

Lucas was looking at him now with a queer expression. His eyes seemed to probe for an instant. "Was not your mother Margaret Bemis?"

"I have never heard of Margaret Bemis. Who was she?"

"Margaret Bemis was Adam's wife."

"Ah, so that was it." John turned back to the portrait, gazing thoughtfully up at it. "So that was the problem," he murmured, as though speaking to himself. "He had a wife. And her name was Margaret Bemis."

Lucas was getting impatient. "You still have not answered my question."

"You asked if I had seen him? Yes, I have seen him," John admitted slowly. "He was my father. He and my mother were very much in love—a pair of romantic lovers living out their idyll in the forest."

"You remember your parents, then?"

"Very well."

"Did he ever call her Margaret?"

"Not to my knowledge. We both called her Chérie."

"But that probably was not her name, John. 'Chérie' is a French term of endearment. It means 'darling.' "

John's face expressed astonishment. "You are thinking Chérie and Margaret Bemis might have been the same woman?"

"I thought you might know the answer to that."

John glanced quickly around at the portraits of family members and their ladies down through the centuries.

"Is there a portrait of Margaret Bemis?"

"Unfortunately her portrait was never painted."

"Why was that?"

"Because none of us ever saw Margaret Bemis."

"You never met your brother's wife?"

"John, we did not know Adam was married."

"A secret marriage?"

Again Lucas hesitated. Then he stumbled hurriedly into a reply. "I do not think that is what Adam intended. You see, our father was very ill at the time. He was suffering from apoplexy. He outlived Adam by only a few days. I think in not telling him, Adam was trying to spare him, to avoid an argument, because Father was trying to force him into a marriage with one of the Cudleigh girls. Then Adam was killed. It was suspected at the time that there was a woman in Adam's secret life. But no one seemed to know for sure."

During most of this explanation John had become increasingly aware of his own misgivings, of a succession of curious responses. Now he was suddenly on guard. He could feel the nape of his neck prickle. He was conscious of the pumping of his heart.

"Then where did you get the name 'Margaret Bemis'?"

For an instant Lucas looked startled, then his eyes began darting uneasily about, moving rapidly over various objects. In his medical practice John had come to read the faces of men, to know when they were telling the truth, when they were preparing their minds to lie to him.

Lucas was about to lie.

Now, with a wave of his hands, Lucas brushed aside John's question as trivial. "Local gossip, I suppose," he said, "—probably just guesswork on the part of prying people. I have always discounted such common talk, John. But recently I have been struck by your likeness to Adam, which is why it has all come to mind once again. I was hoping you might know something of your parentage."

John pretended not to have noticed Lucas's moment of discomposure.

"No, Lucas, I am afraid I can be of little help. I do not know where I was born. I do not know my birth date. If I had a baptismal name, I do not know that, either. My parents called me simply 'child.' But now I must go. I have to get to the jail, then on to the hospital." He looked back as he was walking away. "If James should need me, just send me word."

He was thoughtful as he rode back to Dorncaster.

Though it was commonly believed that Dunheved held its secrets, today's revelation still surprised him. He was certain now that Lucas had facts at his disposal that he had withheld all these years and which he was willing to reveal at last only out of his long hatred for his cousin Sidney. But Lucas knew that to unseat his cousin he would need to present incontrovertible proof of the legitimacy of any prior claimant. Did he have such proof? If so, why had he remained silent until now, until it appeared certain he would die without issue and Sidney would succeed him? Certainly his half-truths, his calculated disclosures, suggested that he knew more than he was willing to reveal at this point in the game. But if that was true, did he also know more about Chérie? Did he know about the searching party that had crept up on their cottage in the night? Did he know who tracked them up to the High Moor? Did he have knowledge of Chérie's disappearance? Did he know her fate?

Did he know what happened twenty-odd years ago to destroy so many lives?

John was still deep in thought as he reined in before the jail. Mr.

Oglethorpe had earned his bribe by moving Jenny to a room on the third floor, with windows onto the street, which she shared with a dozen accommodating prostitutes and other privileged prisoners.

She was lying on the floor, on a straw pallet, her face turned toward the wall. One of the prostitutes had covered her with an old coat, and beneath it she looked so young, curled up, so very small. John was struck again by the curious pallor of her skin. What kind of life had kept her, he wondered vaguely, where the sunlight never reached her?

He dropped to one knee beside the pallet. "Jenny?" he said softly. "Jenny?"

His voice seemed to reach her down an endless black void and she roused herself to turn her head and gaze up at him, her eyes dull with fever. Then something—almost a smile—stirred in their fevered depths.

"Jenny," he said, "I am Doctor Toller. I came to see you yesterday —downstairs. Do you remember?"

Silently she nodded. Today she was not afraid of him. Today she did not shrink from him.

He said, "How are you feeling?"

She did not answer, only continued to gaze silently up at him, searching his face in her quiet, concerned way, feature by feature, coming to rest thoughtfully on the cheek with its jagged scar. Then slowly, almost imperceptibly, a new expression gathered in her eyes and she seemed to be trying to speak, to convey something he could not fathom, but whose vague message left him perplexed and troubled.

He bent over her. "What is it, Jenny? What do you want to say to me?"

She seemed to be gathering her strength, but no words came. Yet her urgent gaze never left his face. After a moment, when he reached out a hand to her, she put her hand in his. Then her eyelids fluttered and she slipped away from him again into unconsciousness, her hand still in his.

John caught his breath as a chilling realization filled him.

Jenny had a puerperal fever.

Without medical care Jenny would die.

By now all the prostitutes were crowding about, their curiosity aroused by the magnitude of his concern. Quickly he got to his feet and looked around. He knew each one of them—which ones had records, which were guilty of criminal abortion, which had abandoned unwanted infants on the convent steps. He knew all their sins, all their secrets. All had appealed for his help at one time or another.

"You, Nellie," he said, "how long has she been like this?"

"Ever since they brung her in here, Doc."

"When was that?"

"Yesterday—'bout noon."

"I sent a midwife from the hospital. Did she call?"

"Her come last night. Her cleaned the girl up a bit, but said there were nothing more her could do. Her said the rest be up to 'ee, Doc. Her said her 'ud see 'ee at the ho'pital."

"Well," John said, "the patient's name is Jenny. If she should come to and want water, will you give it to her, Nellie? All she wants."

"Like 'ee says, Doc."

"Thank you, Nellie. Girls, help Nellie take good care of my patient. I will be back later in the day."

He hurried down the stairs and across the street, heading for a small building a short distance from the jailhouse. Here, on the second floor, he entered the law offices of Pollexfen & Moss.

The clerk at the desk looked up, startled, at his precipitous entrance.

"Lenny, is Henry in?"

"He is working on a brief at the moment, Doctor. But I am sure he will see you if it is urgent."

"It is—very."

"Just a moment, please."

Henry Pollexfen put aside his work as John entered. He motioned to a chair.

"What is it, John?" he asked. "My clerk said it is urgent. No trouble, I hope."

"I want you to help me, Henry. There is a girl in jail who I suspect is dying of puerperal fever. I want you to get an order to move her immediately—today!"

"Move her? Where to?"

"To St. Mary's Lying-In Charity."

Henry's forehead creased in a frown. "Well, now, that all depends. What is the charge?"

"Concealment of birth."

"Concealment! You are not talking of the Sykes girl, are you?"

"I am."

"John, you must be mad."

"No, Henry, I am not mad. I am trying to save an innocent life."

"Innocent? The Sykes girl?"

"If she is left in jail, she will be dead before the week is out. Will you get her transferred?"

"Supposing I do and she escapes?"

"How can she escape? She is barely conscious."

Henry Pollexfen's circumspect gaze was suddenly tinged with curiosity. He and John had been to school together. They had been firm friends most of their lives.

"John," he said quietly, "have you given this matter proper consideration? You know, do you not, that if you interfere in this girl's case, people will talk."

"People always talk, Henry. I, especially, am no stranger to that."

"But in this instance they will question the selflessness of your motives."

"I am a doctor. My concern is medical."

"But the Sykes case has created quite a stir. Everyone is curious about this shadowy girl and the brutal nature of her crime. The mouths of the gossips are in full cry. Many questions are asked, most go unanswered, including the most baffling question of all—the identity of her lover. Who is he? Why has he abandoned her? Is he a married man who fears scandal? Will the girl's loyalty collapse under the coming strain and will she finally blurt out his name? Or will she walk tight-lipped to the gallows without ever revealing his identity? The questions are endless. And still the girl remains inscrutable."

"Inscrutability is no crime under the law. The crime would be in hanging a girl for the presumed murder of a stillborn child."

"Can you prove in court that the child was stillborn?"

"Damn it! Henry, you know that is impossible. You know there is no way to prove stillbirth after the fact."

Henry gave an almost painful smile. His cool green eyes were shadowed with regret.

"Precisely my point, John. There is no way to prove stillbirth after the fact. That is why the girl's trial will be brief—a mere formality. Her sentence is mandatory. Jenny Sykes will go to the gallows."

John slouched back in his chair, putting the tips of his long, strong fingers together and gazing thoughtfully down at them.

"You are a good lawyer, Henry," he said, "and you argue effectively. But I think you are wrong in this. We may yet save Jenny Sykes from the gallows."

Henry raised a quizzical eyebrow. " 'We?' "

"I will need your help, Henry."

"Legal help?"

"Of course."

"John, this girl is already on charity for her halfpenny-worth of bread-slop. Who is going to pay her legal fee?"

"I will—since her father will not."

"You? When you know there is a lover out there cowering somewhere in a corner? When you know the girl is protecting him? Why, John? Why?"

"Dear Christ! Henry, I do not know. Instinct, perhaps."

"Instinct may suffice for a doctor," Henry snapped with scornful disapproval. "A lawyer needs a rational premise he can argue in court."

John made no answer to that and an angry silence filled the room. From below the window came the noises of the street: the measured clump-clump of a donkey on the cobbles, his market basket filled with cackling geese; a peddler crying his bright ribands; the singsong of a knife grinder as he turned his stone. Other city noises, mixed and varied —the voices of hucksters of fish and cloth and fruit, a boy whistling, the clear laughter of children.

But after a while Pollexfen looked up. John still had not stirred. He still slouched in his chair, gazing thoughtfully down at his long, gabled fingers.

"You are an obstinate, free-going rebel, John Toller," he said. "You always were. You will never change. And in this Sykes matter you are lamentably devoid of logical reasoning."

John ignored the continued disapproval. "Can I count on you to get the girl transferred?"

"You can count on me to try. I had better not go to Judge Simmons, though. He is too well-informed on neighborhood gossip."

"Sir Colin Petre, then. A bit baffle-headed, yes, but a judge with a conscience."

"Conscience or no, I could only persuade Sir Colin to allow the girl to be hospitalized if I deliberately withhold the facts."

"Well?"

"Hmmmm—yes. And Jailer Oglethorpe. If he is to be dissuaded

from running to Petre with all the hearsay, he will expect his usual douceur."

"Damn the man! The weight of his moneybags will sink this island in the sea."

Pollexfen gave a broad grin. "It is still fortunate we have him, John. There is not a lawyer anywhere around who would want to see him lose his office."

"Thanks for your help, Henry," John said. "Will you send Lenny over to the hospital as soon as you have news? I will be anxious." He got up and was moving toward the door, when Pollexfen called him back.

"Do not be in such a hurry, John. I have been wanting to talk to you."

John turned. "What about?"

"Are you not Lord Tremoigne's doctor?"

"I am."

"Well, it seems there is something strange going on at Dunheved."

"Oh? And even if that were true, how does it concern you?"

"It concerns each man of us if it is against the law."

John came back and reseated himself. "Go on," he said.

"I heard a curious tale from a former servant at the castle—a temporary man who was dismissed for prying."

"What was the man's name?"

"Tinker. Alan Tinker."

"What did he tell you?"

"He said that once, during last winter's influenza epidemic, when many of the castle servants were stricken and unable to work, he was given a tray of food and told to carry it up to the West Tower and leave it in front of a certain tower room. Later, he was sent to remove the tray. It was empty. He made the natural assumption that a person was being held up there—a sick person, maybe. After that, being curious, he made a point of looking up at the window from the garden. On several occasions he saw a face at the window—a white, white face—a strange moonlike face—inhuman, he said—horrific!"

John had been looking directly at Henry, but aside from a suggestion of courteous interest his face was expressionless.

"It would seem," he said, "that Lord Tremoigne had good reason for dismissing so fanciful and indiscreet a servant."

Pollexfen was sensitive to the gentle reproach.

He said, "I am thinking solely as a lawyer, John. You know as well as I do that it is against the law to conceal persons with certain communicable disease—for the public good, I mean."

"So it is."

Pollexfen spoke slowly, phrasing his question with utmost care. "Would you consider it to be so in this instance?"

John's gaze never left Pollexfen's face. His eyes gave no clue to his thoughts. "That would depend," he said, "on the nature of the disease."

"I mean, supposing he was concealing a case of consumption, for instance—or syphillus—diseases which by law must be reported and isolated in special hospitals."

John's still eyes never wavered. "Are you asking me that question with reference to Lord Tremoigne or in purely hypothetical terms?"

Pollexfen shifted his feet uneasily. "In hypothetical terms, of course."

"Then you are correct. Certain diseases must, by law, be reported and isolated for the common good."

Pollexfen gave this a moment's thought, slowly bringing order to the papers on his desk, then impatiently throwing them into disorder again. He opened his mouth to ask another question, but seemed to change his mind.

Then suddenly he looked up and grinned. "It is no use at all asking what's afoot at Dunheved, is it, John?"

John grinned back at him. "No use, at all, Henry."

John slowed his steps as he passed through the ward and approached Father Dominic's cubicle. These days he was increasingly troubled by a sense of guilt. He was still surreptitiously administering opium when the priest himself had made clear his desire to suffer whatever pain He sent in emulation of Christ's sufferings on the Cross. By what right, John constantly asked himself, did a doctor deny a patient's dying wish? Such self-doubts were disturbing. They left him questioning whether his own state of irreligion had influenced his medical judgment.

But this morning, as he drew near the cubicle, he was surprised to hear the old priest chuckle. Then he glimpsed a small shadow move behind the curtain and, upon entering, found Noah, the deaf-mute, sitting happily on Father Dominic's bed, the two of them communicating by signs made with the fingers in what, to the uninitiated, would have appeared to be some form of mysterious rite.

John felt the tension and self-doubt drain from him. He found himself smiling. "And what are you two gossiping about?"

Father Dominic chuckled again. "Noah was telling me how he and his brother, who has learned a few signs, were able to escape from a bully the other day by organizing their strategy through sign language."

John playfully ruffled the boy's flaxen hair. "That was clever, Noah," he said. "Very clever."

The boy sensed John's approval and smiled up at him. Then he slipped off the bed and stood respectfully aside, his intelligent, questioning eyes on John's face.

John nodded, answering the unspoken question. "Yes, please, Noah. For just a few moments." As the boy left the cubicle, John turned to the priest. "Now, let me see how things are today, Father Dom."

The daily examination had become an unnecessary formality. It revealed nothing that John did not expect to find, but it provided an excuse to administer the pain-soothing drug as part of the routine treatment.

By now Father Dominic was accustomed to the bitter taste and drained the cup without protest. Then John seated himself and prepared to remain on watch. He had just increased the dosage and wanted to be sure his deception would pass unnoticed.

"And how is Noah progressing, Father?" he asked.

"The boy is quite remarkable, my son. He is learning faster than I would ever have thought possible. Did you know that yesterday his mother came to see me?"

"No, I had not heard. What did you talk about?"

The old priest's face lighted up. "You know that Sister Teresa has been teaching her the signs. Now she tells me that already she and Noah can converse in simple terms."

"That must have made you very happy."

"Ah, my son, God is good." Then the old priest's face clouded over. "But there is one thing that troubles me, John. All goes well with the boy for now, he is only eight. But what will become of him later? His mother is a poor widow who supports her children by going out to clean the school. What will become of Noah when he must support himself? Who will employ a lad who is deaf and can only speak in signs? How will such a one fit into the wider world where spoken orders are given and must be executed?"

John spoke in soothing tones.

"Now, Father Dom, do not trouble yourself about the boy's future. I have already spoken to one of my patients, a wealthy man. He has agreed to send Noah up to Doctor Delgarno in Aberdeen. He has agreed to pay all Noah's expenses, even in the event that the boy wants to continue under Doctor Delgarno to train as a teacher of other deaf-mutes. As a teacher, he can lead a happy and useful life."

"There is no doubt of that, my son. But what if Noah should prefer some other calling?"

"My wealthy patient has thought of that. He has a vast estate and has promised to employ Noah as a gardener or gamekeeper, or in whatever other capacity the boy is suited for. But as you yourself have said, Noah is only eight. Why not let the matter rest for now? In another few years we can put the question of his future to Noah directly and let him decide for himself."

The old priest nodded, satisfied. "I can see, my son, that I shall be leaving Noah in good hands. I won't worry anymore. Thank you, John. Thank you, my dear son."

The aged face was relaxing now. The pain was receding. The opium was taking effect.

John rose to go. "Do you feel like continuing the lesson, Father?" he asked. "Shall I tell Noah to come in now?"

"Please do, my son. The boy is a great comfort to me."

By the time John had finished in the wards, the morning was half gone. As he hurried down the stairs leading to the clinic he caught sight of the blacksmith, Saul Perkins, sitting uneasily on the bench.

He stopped short. "What is it this time, Saul?"

"It be one o' me boys, Doc. Young Mikey. Walking down the street, him wuz. Got hisself in a fight. Got hisself in a fistfight with 'nuther boy."

John did not wait for Saul to concoct the rest of the story. He turned and strode into the examining room.

The chirurgeon, Andrew Barnes, already had the boy on the table.
"It is bad," Andy said, as he stepped aside to let John take over.

The boy was about ten years, thin and frail. Andrew had removed
his shirt, revealing a mass of welts and bruises that were beginning to
darken. John examined his scalp. He had a gash on the left side and the
oozing blood was matting his hair. There was another gash on his forehead, at the hairline. One eye had begun to blacken. Blood was oozing
from a broken nose. He was unconscious.

Swiftly John cut the hair from around the scalp wounds. He
cleansed and bandaged the head, working slowly down to face and torso.
When he came to the boy's small, delicate hands, he felt the cold anger
charge through him. He bent closer and examined the boy's knuckles.
They were without a mark.

He stepped to the door. "Saul Perkins, come in here."

Saul came in, his expression already showing defiance. He was a
massive man, with dark curly hair and a face pale from days spent
indoors at the forge and evenings at the pothouse. His small, sickly wife
kept giving birth to small, sickly children. Ten of them had survived so
far. He was a tyrant of a man, proud of his brute strength, proud of the
fact that most other men were afraid of him. His large decaying front
teeth jutted out. At the moment they showed in an insolent grin.

John said, "Now, Saul Perkins, tell me what happened."

"I a'ready tole 'ee. Mikey got hisself in a fistfight wi' 'nuther boy."

John knew Saul was lying. He made no effort to conceal it. "What
other boy?"

"Some peddler's boy passing through."

"Aye—a boy who has left town already and cannot be questioned."
He held up one of Mikey's hands, palms down. "Saul, there is not a
mark on Mikey's knuckles. Mikey was not in a fistfight. Now, what
happened? The truth, this time."

"I a'ready tole 'ee twice. The boy got in a fight wi' a strange boy.
Got hisself hurt. That be all."

"You did not beat him?"

"Course not."

"I want to see your fists."

Defiantly the blacksmith brought his hands up for inspection.
There were traces of blood on his maul-like fists. John reached for a
cloth and wiped them. The blood came off on the cloth. The flesh
beneath, horny from work at anvil and forge, was unbroken.

John looked up. "That was not your blood I just wiped off. That was Mikey's blood. Saul Perkins, you beat Mikey. You are a liar—a cowardly, callous liar!"

Saul stepped up so close that his foul breath fanned John's face. " 'Ee calls me names agin, 'ee Toller bastard, an' I 'ull smash yer face."

John ignored the threat. His eyes were cold and calculating. "If Mikey dies, that will be the second son you'll have killed."

"I a'ready tole 'ee—I did not kill Colin. Colin caught hisself wi' me hammer."

"Don't be stupid, Saul Perkins. A puny boy like Colin could not crush his own throat with a blacksmith's hammer. Only a man could do that—a violent man."

Saul thought a moment, then drew off. "Anyway, that be long gone by. That be forgot."

"Murder is never 'long gone by.' Murder is never forgotten."

"Then if 'ee thought I done murder, why did 'ee not haul me into court long ago?"

"You know why. Because courts demand proof. Because you had bullied your wife and children into lying for you. But we are watching you, Saul Perkins. We will catch you yet. You will end up in jail—if not on the gallows. Now, get out of here. Get out—quick!"

"Not without me boy. I be taking Mikey wi' me."

"No, you're not. I'm keeping Mikey here. There is still a chance we can save his life. Now go!"

Saul hesitated. His fists still hung, clenched and ready, by his side. He glanced quickly at the boy stretched out on the table just a few feet away, then at the tall craggy figure of John Toller deliberately positioned between him and his son. Suddenly the defiance seemed to drain from Saul. He left the room, mumbling threats under his breath.

John turned to Andrew Barnes. "Andy, get Mikey upstairs. Let me know if he shows signs of coming to. And, Andy, give orders that under no circumstances is Saul to visit him."

His anger swiftly dissipated as he turned to face the next patient, a plain but wholesome young woman, the wife of Constable Hurley. Her face was anxious. She carried an infant in her arms.

"Him will not stop, Doc," she gasped.

"Will not stop what? Hiccuping?"

" 'Ee hear it, then?"

"Of course I hear it. But I do not think there is any cause for alarm, Maria. Put him on the table and let me take a look at him."

John examined the baby. He was about ten months, fat and healthy, clean, well-clothed.

"You are a fine mother, Maria," he said. "I wish all our young mothers were like you. Now, what have you done for the hiccups so far?"

"Mostly, I been tickling his nose with a feather."

John looked quickly down at the infant so Maria would not catch his smile. Not bad, he thought, for country folk who still passed children, stripped naked, through a cleft ash tree as a cure for rupture or rickets, or believed in birthtrees, or decorated their houses with holly because its red berries and evergreen prickly leaves were supposed to repel witches.

Aloud he said, "Well, I can find no reason to be concerned at the moment, Maria. Hiccuping is normal with babies."

"Ain't nuthing I kin do?"

"Generally nothing need be done. Just stop tickling his nose for now. Let him fall asleep if he can. Come back if he has not stopped by evening." Then suddenly he looked at her closely. "You are expecting again, are you not, Maria?"

She smiled shyly up at him. "Aye, Doc."

"How long has it been? About three months?"

"That be what midwife says."

"Good! I will have another fine, healthy baby to take care of. My congratulations to you and Jim."

An endless stream followed, the poor of the county for whose care he was paid his eight pounds a year, some in ragged clothing, their feet shoeless or clad in rotting leather, but for the most part proud and clean. He knew them all, remembered their ailments, their births and deaths, their sorrows and joys. These were his people. This was his world.

By the time the clinic doors closed, John had still received no word from Henry Pollexfen, so he walked down the street to the law offices of Pollexfen & Moss. Henry was out, so he told Lenny that he would be at the Mermaid Tavern and asked that word be sent to him there.

He had just started on a dish of hare pie when Henry himself appeared. He slid into a chair opposite John and called for a pot of ale.

"Lenny said I would find you here," he began. Then he lowered his voice. "Everything is settled. The patient has already been transferred."

"Transferred already? That was quick. How did you manage it?"

"I impressed Sir Colin with the urgency of the case—the matter of a young girl's life or death. He is a good fellow, old Sir Colin, a bit baffle-headed, as you said—but a good fellow. He wrote out the transfer order right away."

"Was he familiar with the facts of the case?"

"Just as you guessed, he was not. He even asked me how to spell the prisoner's name."

"And Oglethorpe? How did you handle that?"

Henry grinned. "I thought I had better make sure the transfer had been brought to a happy issue before some little bird whispered in Sir Colin's good ear, so I showed up at the jail with the transfer order and a hired coach. Oglethorpe looked surprised. I do not know if he would have dared question the order, but after a few coins changed hands he was all willingness to help. He ended by sending two brawny turnkeys to carry the prisoner to the coach."

"And where is Jenny now? At the Lying-In Charity?"

Henry nodded. "When I told Reverend Mother that Sykes was your patient, she set to work at once to find a bed for her."

"Thank you, Henry. I am very grateful to you."

Henry flashed his brazen grin. "Not too grateful, I hope, John. You are going to pay for it, you know."

John grinned back at him. "I always do. But I am still grateful. You have never failed me yet."

Henry sat a moment staring down into his pint pot. "And now," he said, "there is another matter I want to talk to you about. The old mill of yours out on the Charnminster Road."

"What about the mill?"

"I have a client who wants to buy it."

John's jaw tightened. He bent his head and quietly resumed eating, but a succession of terrible images flashed across his mind, leaving him cold and sick. He thought of Amy's father, the one-armed Reggie Clay, so mysteriously crushed to death in the great cogwheel. He thought of his first small son killed by a falling millstone. He thought of Amy's final murderous attack upon him as he tried to save their second son. After that last tragedy it had been generally assumed that Amy lost her reason as the result of the second infant's death, and John never corrected that assumption. The truth he had kept to himself. The law dealt harshly with murderers—even with the insane.

Now he answered coldly, "The mill is not for sale."

Henry raised his eyebrows in surprise. "Do you mean to live there again?"

"No."

"Then, with Amy gone, why would you want to hold it?"

"I did not say I want to hold it. I said it is not for sale."

Henry was puzzled. "Neither hold nor sell? What else is there? That is valuable property now, John—close to town, very salable, yet you have left it sitting for four years now—all but derelict. Be practical. Sell it and get the money in hand."

"I have said the mill is not for sale."

"Then what will you do with it? Come on, John, do not be a mule. Name a price and I will try to get my client to meet it."

"I have got plans for that mill, Henry."

"Oh?" Henry was interested. "Plans you would like to tell me about?"

"No."

But Pollexfen was insistent. He rephrased the question. "Well, plans like what, for instance?"

John got to his feet and threw some coins on the table. He said roughly, "Plans like tearing the damn thing down."

A half hour later John was riding out in the direction of St. Mary's Lying-In Charity. The convent had risen painfully out of the ruins of a nunnery destroyed in the Dissolution and was located just south of the city, its precincts bounded by a wall whose falling boulders had scarred the green symmetry of moss and lichen. He dismounted at the wicket and pulled the raveled bellpull. After a few moments a girl of about fourteen opened it. She wore the striped pinafore of the orphans of St. Mary's.

She curtsied when she recognized John. "Good day, Doctor," she said shyly.

"Well, Tillie, and how are you feeling? How is your knee today?"

"Mostly better, Doctor. I kin move 'bout easy now."

"And how is your little brother? Is he out of bed yet?"

"Sister Elizabeth let him git up yisterday an' play i' the garden."

"Splendid! And now would you run and ask Reverend Mother if I may speak to her a moment?"

The Reverend Mother received him warmly. "You have come about the new patient?" she asked.

"Yes, but I also want to apologize for sending her without first having received your permission. I am grateful to you for accepting her."

"I understand, Doctor. This was an emergency. The girl is gravely ill—close to death, Sister Brigit tells me. I take it this is a hardship case, that her child was illegitimate. Where is the child now? And who is the girl?"

"The child, I believe, was stillborn. The girl's name is Jenny Sykes."

"The vicar's daughter?" The Reverend Mother's face clouded over with alarm. "Then she must have come directly from the jail. That is why Mr. Pollexfen asked that she be isolated. Surely, Doctor, the girl does not have a form of pestilence?"

John smiled reassuringly. "Reverend Mother, when I saw her this morning she showed no sign of pestilence, or I would not have sent her to you. The reason for her transfer is that she seems to have puerperal fever. She needs medical care or she will die."

The Reverend Mother's tone held gentle reproof. "Many of those jailhouse inmates will die, Doctor. They are not all transferred here."

"This is a special case."

"Oh?"

She waited, but John evaded her implicit question. "With your permission, Reverend Mother, I will see her now."

"Of course, Doctor. You know your way to Lying-In. You will find Sister Brigit there. And afterward, if you have time, would you take a look at Baby Dennis? He was ailing this morning."

The Lying-In was situated beyond the Infirmary, on the second floor of the ancient building. As he made his way down the long stone corridor, flanked by saints in their niches, the extreme poverty of the convent was apparent through the open doors of the sickrooms—the whitewashed walls, the tall undraped windows, the plain sparse furnishings and bare floors. The sisters smiled at him as they went about their business, some carrying infants to their mothers to be nursed, some washing the sick or tending fretful children. Yet if poverty was everywhere evident, the pall of poverty was not, for from the east wing across the courtyard came the shrieks and laughter of the fifty or so orphans whom the convent housed, clothed, fed, and schooled. The convent was sustained by donations. It had become John's yearly custom to assemble a party of his richer patients to pay a Christmas visit to the convent in the somewhat pragmatic view that those who gave publicly were apt to give more generously.

He found Sister Brigit in the Isolation Room, bending over Jenny's bed. The nun looked around as he entered.

"How is she, Sister?" he asked.

Sister Brigit shook her head. She was an aging nun, her face brown and wrinkled as a walnut shell, her body wiry and active still. She had tended the patients in Lying-In most of her life.

"She is just about as sick as any I have ever seen, Doctor," she answered.

John crossed to the bed and stood looking down at Jenny. She appeared to be sleeping, but he knew it was something deeper than that. They had washed her and braided her hair again in two long pigtails. She looked like a child, vulnerable, strangely remote, and again he was struck by the look of innocence so puzzling in a girl with her dark history. In the courtroom, covered as she had been with jailhouse filth, he still had perceived the delicate sensitivity of her face, and now he gazed thoughtfully down at it, moved again by something that disturbed him, something whose deep mystery he still could not penetrate.

He asked, "Has there been any vomiting?"

"Not so far, Doctor."

"Has she not yet recovered consciousness?"

"She was unconscious when they brought her in. I tried to revive her, but she has not opened her eyes or spoken one word. I have the feeling she is resisting it—that she does not want to wake up. What ails her, Doctor? Is it puerperal?"

"I am afraid so."

"And the baby? Did it die?"

"Yes."

"Is she grieving for it, do you think? Is grieving part of her illness?"

"Yes, Sister, she is grieving. But I think there is something else. I think there is something here beyond grief." He looked across the bed into the nun's soft and melting eyes. "More than anything else, she needs compassion, Sister Brigit. That is why I wanted her to come to you."

The nun nodded understandingly. "Has she no kin?"

"None, I think, who would care if she lives or dies."

"Poor little one! Is she likely to recover?"

"Perhaps—with your help. Now tell me what you have done for her so far."

"We immediately washed her and burned her clothing. Since we could not revive her, we treated her fever with cold spongings. That seems to have reduced it somewhat."

"Have you examined her?"

"Only superficially. In her present condition it is impossible to judge the degree of pain or abdominal tenderness. But we did find a significant discharge."

"Yes," he said, "I was afraid of that." He pulled up a chair and sat down beside the bed. He placed his fingers on Jenny's wrist. Her pulse rate was rapid.

He shook her gently by the shoulder. "Jenny," he said softly. "Jenny."

Once again his voice seemed to reach her in the confused borderland between oblivion and actuality. Slowly she opened her eyes and looked about the room as though searching for him. At last they came to rest on his face, startled, staring wide, and she just lay there, gazing fixedly up at him. It was a strangely haunted gaze, unfathomable, filled with the dark shadows of the past. He thought absently, she is too young to have known such horror.

"Jenny," he said gently, "I am Doctor Toller. I came to see you in jail. Do you remember?"

For a moment she continued to stare up at him. Then she nodded. She whispered, "And it was you in the courtroom—"

"Yes, I was in the courtroom. You still remember that, do you?"

Again she nodded. She drew a painful breath. She seemed to be deep in thought. "You said my baby did not . . . did not die . . . because I left the cord—"

"That is right, Jenny. I said that."

"You . . . you?"

"Yes, I believe it. I saw your baby, Jenny. I examined it. I believe it was deadborn, in which case there was nothing you could have done to save it."

At that a low sob broke from her and she closed her eyes and seemed to drift off again into unconsciousness. He bent anxiously over her, taking her hands in his and holding them.

"No, Jenny! Jenny! I want to talk to you. I want you to listen to me. I want you to open your eyes."

Again she responded to his voice. She turned her head and looked up at him.

"Listen to me, Jenny. You are not in jail now. You have been transferred. You are in a convent infirmary and this is Sister Brigit. I want you to remember her. I want you to do as Sister Brigit tells you. Will you promise me that? Will you, Jenny?"

Her eyes were fixed on his face in her curiously reflective way. Then slowly she nodded her head.

"And you will take the broth and milk she brings you?"

Her voice was barely audible. "Yes."

"You promise me?"

"Yes."

He put his hand on her forehead. It was cooler now than it had been that morning in the jail. He glanced at the bedside table. A cup and spoon lay there.

"Sister, what have we here?"

"It is broth, Doctor. I had hoped she— But now it is cold."

"That will not matter. Bring it nearer."

He slipped one arm around Jenny and raised her, cradling her head against his shoulder.

"Now," he said, "show me what you can do with this."

He spooned up the broth and raised it to her lips, letting it dribble slowly down her throat. She swallowed it, unresisting, and he continued to sit there, patiently feeding her, encouraging her in low tones.

But the effort soon left her exhausted. Her eyes closed. Her head fell back. Sister Brigit quickly began to sponge her forehead with cool water in an effort to revive her. But John motioned her to stop.

"Let her go, Sister," he said. "She has had enough broth for the moment. What she needs now is sleep."

He laid her gently back on the pillow and covered her again with the blanket. Then he rose to his feet and stood looking down at her.

"She might come out of it, Sister," he said thoughtfully. "When she awakens, if she has abdominal pain, give her Sydenham's Drops through the night. Continue to feed her broth, milk, thin gruel—plenty of cool water." He looked across the bed into the nun's kindly face. "She is in your good hands now, Sister. Take care of her."

It was after midnight when he finished his last call and approached the cottage by the river. The place seemed wrapped in sleep. The kitchen window was dark. No plume of smoke curled up from the chimney. He stabled Iris in the lean-to, then went around to the side of the cottage and tapped lightly on the bedroom window.

Minnie awakened and ran and opened the door. She put her arms up around his neck and he bent and kissed her, but absent mindedly, like a man musing on other things. "Eh!" she said, "but is't on'y half of 'ee I be having tonight?" But he only smiled and followed her into the bedroom.

He dropped his clothing to the floor and flung himself down on the bed, more weary and apart than she had ever seen him. She came and kneeled beside him, stroking his hair, looking into his face as though to read it. For a while he lay with closed eyes, eased by her caresses. But presently he took her hand and kissed it. "Come to bed," he said. And as his arms reached out and drew her to him, she thought the strange new mood had passed.

But a few hours later something roused her. She turned her head on the pillow to find he had awakened and now lay on his back, his eyes open and fixed on the square of moonlight formed by the window. A sudden gust of wind rattled the shutters and stirred ghostly shadows on the wall. He did not notice. She whispered, "Wha' ails 'ee, luv?" He did not seem to hear. He lay without stirring, withdrawn into himself. She wondered silently what strange new seeds were springing in his mind to keep his thoughts from her.

But something inside her made her fear to ask.

It was mid-afternoon the next day when John left the clinic and rode out to Little Liscombe. He wondered vaguely how the vicar would receive him. He had glimpsed him in town only once since the inquest, but the vicar, recognizing him, had turned his back and hurried off down the West High Street. Perhaps he felt resentment of John's testimony. Or perhaps the vicar was beginning to feel a certain shame and remorse at what he had done. If that was so, an opportunity for him to repair the damage might present itself before Jenny's upcoming trial.

Little Liscombe lay just beyond Yeggor Dun. Remembering the continuing speculation concerning Jenny, John glanced thoughtfully up at the hill as he passed.

There was always an eerie stillness about the place, the disturbing sense of a watchful, waiting presence that made the country people fear to venture up there alone. Only on those special nights of the year, when the moon was full and the sound of chanting, dim, muffled, insistent, was borne to them on the evening wind, did they drop their work and, obeying the chant's arcanal allure, converge upon the hill, climbing up beyond the standing stones, beyond the lonely barrows of the long, long dead to gather around the figure of a god inconceivably remote from them in time and spirit, for the performance of pagan rituals old beyond all power of probing.

John knew that intoxication of the kind that induced their disordered, flushed appearance, widely dilated pupils, and shameless sexual excesses was almost certainly the result of potions mixed with leaves or berries of belladonna or henbane, plants that grew wild in the surrounding woods and waste places. It was not generally known who prepared these potions, of which all freely partook, for they were offered by masked figures. But to the hard-working country people, burdened by the dullness of their daily lives, there was something magical in the frenzied sexual orgies accompanied by vivid hallucinations that left them hardly aware that the moon had waned and gray day dawned.

The vicarage lay in the shadow of Yeggor Dun. John pulled Iris to a halt and threw her reins over the picket fence. The house had a strangely empty look. He raised the knocker and tapped on the door. No one answered. He turned and looked around. Then, from the church, came the sound of the vicar's sonorous voice and he crossed the graveyard to the church porch and pushed the door open.

It was a somber little church, with a worn red-cushioned pulpit, a tiny altar under a trio of colored-glass windows, an ancient baptismal font, ancient pews. The high-pitched roof was supported by weathered black oak beams carved with the cheerless faces of angels. At the west end was a choir loft approached by a ladderlike stair. To one side were a dozen hardwood seats for the poor.

A wedding ceremony was in progress and John stood unobtrusively within the shadows of the choir loft. For the moment the vicar's attention was focused on the ceremony. His tall form seemed to tower above the bridal couple, his great voice filling the small church, reverberating among the stone walls and blackened rafters. He paused an instant to permit the groom to answer "I will." Then he turned to the bride.

"Wilt thou have this man to thy wedded husband, to live together according to God's ordin—"

He broke off in the middle of the word as he caught sight of John watching from the rear. For an instant he hesitated, staring at John with startled eyes. Then his demeanor underwent a curious change. He appeared to forget the wedding ceremony and, standing there at the foot of the altar steps, he began to deliver a sermon, preached with vehemence and ecstatic fervor, and filled with hellish imagery, haranguing the bride, groom, and wedding guests on the irredeemable sin of fornication.

"O, ye sinners in the hands of an angry God," he cried with passion, "give not thy strength unto women. For the Bible teaches that such is the way of the whore that she eateth, and wipeth her mouth, and saith, 'I have done no wickedness.' Therefore lust not after the whore's beauty, for her lips are as the honeycomb, and her words are smoother than oil, but her end is bitter as wormwood, sharp as the two-edged sword. Listen, all ye fornicators, I tell you that stolen waters are sweet, and bread eaten in secret is pleasant. But the whoremonger knoweth not that the tormented souls of the whore's dead guests are with him in the whore's bed. So harken well to the words of my mouth. The whore's house is the pathway to hell where devils wait amid the putridity and hideous rottenness of quivering souls which can never quite die. All ye fornicators are evil in the sight of God. He will smite off your offending member as He would smite off the wings of a bird that hath offended Him, or tear out the tongue of an adder. Fear Him, then! Fear this merciless God. For ye, too, shall know His wrath. He shall make your living souls to writhe in the lake that burneth with fire—"

Again, he broke off suddenly. Then he turned, his vestments fluttering behind him, and strode to the vestry, passed inside and slammed the door.

The bride and groom were still standing where he had left them, looking uncertainly at one another, not knowing if they were married or not. The wedding guests began to murmur. John walked to the vestry. When he found it empty he went out through the vestry door and recrossed the graveyard to the vicarage.

He was not expecting an answer to his knock. When none came, he tried the door and to his surprise found it unlocked. In the entrance hall he looked about. The doors on either side stood open and signs of extreme poverty were everywhere. The well-scrubbed floors were bare. The parlor was sparsely furnished with four sagging chairs and a settee covered with black horsehair. The dining room had only a large kitchen table flanked by two kitchen chairs. Farther on, toward the back of the house, was a third door. It was shut. A glimmer of light showed beneath it.

He approached the door and knocked. "Vicar?" he called. "Vicar?" Not a sound came from within. But he had the feeling that someone was in there, waiting.

He opened the door and entered.

Even though he had been expecting it, he was nonetheless surprised at the sanctum in which he found himself. At the inquest he had taken Vicar Sykes to be a man of scholarly pursuits. Now this earlier assessment was confirmed by a single glance around this magnificent room.

The sight of so much extravagant luxury chased away his intended apology for the intrusion and he found himself instead moving past bookcases paneled in oak that lined the room to the ceiling, his eyes moving with admiration over the finely tooled bindings, the Greek and Latin classics—works of Euripides, Aristotle, Homer, Herodotus, Seneca, Tacitus. He suspected that many of these volumes had come by illicit means into the vicar's collection from the dusty shelves of monastic libraries, for some still bore the marks of their chains. . . .

"Well?"

The single word had a razor edge. John turned. The vicar was standing across the room, his back to the fireplace, his dark, glittering, hostile eyes fixed on John's face.

"Please forgive me," John said, anxious to temper the vicar's hostility, "but this treasury of books has left me quite overwhelmed. Some of these volumes are seen only on the shelves of great libraries. Vicar, I stand amazed at your collection."

"And I, sir, stand amazed at your insolence in so rudely trespassing my home."

"Vicar, the door was unlocked—"

"The lock, sir, is broken. My superiors are too penurious to repair it."

John did not reply to that. He let his gaze drop to the rich Kurdistan carpet with its field of beautiful springtime wildflowers as he deliberated how best to approach the difficult matter he had come to discuss. "Again I apologize," he said gently. "I did not intend to presume upon your privacy. But your daughter is gravely ill. She has puerperal fever and may die. I was riding up here to the Grimage farm and thought it only right to advise you."

"What you thought does not concern me at all, sir. Please leave my house."

"Vicar, I need to point out—"

"The Bible says of the adulteress, 'Because thy filthiness was poured out, and thy nakedness discovered through thy whoredoms with thy lovers—' "

"But Jesus said, 'Judge not, and ye shall not be judged; condemn not, and ye shall not be condemned; forgive, and ye shall be forgiven.' "

The vicar stared. "You are a fool, sir, if you think yourself qualified to dispute the Bible with me."

John smiled at that. "I have neither the inclination, Vicar, nor the time. I have patients waiting. But I thought that you, as a man of God, would be sufficiently familiar with Christ's teachings on love and forgiveness to now find it in your heart to bestow love and forgiveness on your own child."

"If that is what you came here to say, Doctor, then you have said it. Good day to you."

"No, Vicar, there is more. The body of Jenny's dead infant still lies unclaimed in the hospital morgue. This morning I received a court order requiring me to surrender it for burial in Potter's Field."

"Well?"

"If Jenny lives, she will be brought to trial in about two weeks, as soon as the trials of the Sedgemoor rebels are concluded. You were present at the coroner's inquest. You heard how harshly the law deals with unwed mothers whose infants have died. Vicar, I examined Jenny's infant for the court. I am certain it was stillborn. In England we have no medical test to prove stillbirth, so innocent girls are being sent to the gallows. But now, in Europe, a test for stillbirth has been developed. About two years ago, in a court trial, it won dismissal of alleged infanticide against the defendant. Since then it has been applied in other European courts of law where infanticide was suspected and has saved the lives of other innocent girls. I would like the opportunity to use this test to prove stillbirth in the case of Jenny's child."

"You are at liberty to do as you please in the matter, sir."

"But I will need your help, Vicar. I have already dispatched a rider to Amsterdam to collect the necessary data. But to prove stillbirth in court it will be necessary for us to have the infant's body available. That is why I have come to ask you, as the infant's nearest relative, to block the Potter's Field burial by claiming the body yourself, after which you will have the authority to permit us to hold it in the mortuary until the trial."

"Sir, what is done with the infant's body is no concern of mine."

"On the contrary, Vicar, it is very clearly your concern. This is your grandchild. You are the only known family member in position to claim it."

"The child was a bastard. Under no circumstances would I acknowledge it as my grandchild."

"Vicar, perhaps my point eludes you. I am suggesting a possible way to save Jenny from the gallows."

"You are suggesting more than that, sir. You are suggesting that I conspire with you to circumvent the law."

"If that is what you think," John said patiently, "then again you misunderstand me. Any new evidence would be presented in court by a practitioner legally qualified to—"

"Sir, what makes this your business?"

"Sir, I am paid eight pounds a year to serve the city's indigent. At the moment your daughter is numbered among those indigent."

The vicar flinched at that, for his self-esteem had been wounded. But he was not a man to be easily swayed, and the eyes he flashed at John were filled with venom.

"It is intolerable," he said, "when a gentleman must vacate his own library to rid himself of an intruder."

And he turned and strode past John, out through the library door and up the stairs.

As John made his rounds of the nearby farmhouses he found it hard to blot from his mind the image of the vicar's cadaverous face with his blazing eyes and self-tormented mouth. His extreme emaciation suggested that hunger was a continuing fact at the vicarage. Pollexfen had said that Jenny was never seen in the village, that the vicar went himself to shop for whatever was needed. The treasure-filled library explained why he was desperately pressed to make ends meet, and why Jenny looked emaciated and wore shabby clothes and outsized boots.

There was something darkly sinister about the vicar. What horrifying mental images evoked the biblical foulness that poured from his lips? What monsters haunted the dark nights of his soul? What repressing forces had driven him to attempt self-castration? There was no doubt that the man endured great suffering. But why had he turned on Jenny? Could it be that he was so crippled by hatred for his runaway wife that handing their daughter over to the hangman was a full and terrible revenge for her unfaithfulness?

Or was there more?

Something vague, coming like the yapping of distant dogs, seemed to be warning that there was more.

It was dusk by the time John reached the Grimage farm, a ramshackle cabin set in a few acres of hard-worked hillside.

Mrs. Grimage received him anxiously. "Her's bin bad today, Doctor John—real bad. I was hoping 'ee 'ud come by."

The relief in her voice troubled him.

"Molly, whether I come by or not will make no difference in the end. You *must* understand that. You *must* understand that there is nothing I can do for Cathy anymore."

She stared up at him, willfully resisting the truth. "But the med'cine 'ee left. That bin he'ping her. It he'ps a lot."

"That is only temporary help, Molly. It is the only help I can give Cathy now. Do you understand what I am saying?"

Something flickered behind her eyes. Then, as though impelled by inner pressures, she began bustling about the kitchen, talking rapidly of crops and the weather. John watched her as she poured fresh water into the trough for him to wash his hands and found him a clean rag to dry them. Then, still unyielding, she put a mug of home-brewed ale on the table and a plate of potatoes and turnips hot from the hearth.

"Eat up, Doctor John, 'fore 'ee go in to her," she urged. "Eat up! 'Ee be looking deathly tired today and us don' want to lose 'ee, or who 'ull be doctoring us country folk? I declare, 'ee be jest like yer pa, riding far and wide like 'ee do, niver forgitting us. Eat up, now! And don' be worrying yer head 'bout Iris. Giles and the boys 'ull be coming in from the fields directly. Them 'ull feed and water her in the barn with the cow—"

"Molly," John interrupted, "I want you to stop chattering and answer my question. Do you understand what I have been telling you for weeks now—that there is nothing more I can do for Cathy? Do you understand that, Molly?"

She turned evasively from him and threw more wood on the fire, then began slowly blowing it up with the bellows. "I un'erstand what 'ee bin saying, Doctor John," she answered into the fireplace. "I jest know it ain't true, that be all."

"But it *is* true, Molly."

At that she stopped working the bellows and stayed quite still, stooped there over the ashes. Then she cast the bellows aside and turned and faced him. There was a hard stubbornness in her eyes.

"Doctor John, 'ee kin not let Cathy die. Cathy's on'y a little girl. Her's on'y nine. I know there be so'thing 'ee kin do, so'thing 'ee ain't thoughted on yit, so'thing 'ee 'ull think on now that it be needed. 'Ee a'ways bin able to do so'thing. Like the time Giles got a poisoned foot and us all thoughted it 'ud have to come off. And the time Danny ate them berries and come close to dying—"

"Those were medical problems for which there were medical solutions. But it is different with Cathy. For Cathy there is no cure. You must prepare yourself, Molly. You must understand that Cathy will die. Cathy will die very soon now. And there is nothing I can do."

She stood there staring up at him, frightened now. Then she went and sat down in the rocker by the fire and began silently to rock, her worn face suddenly sallow as boxwood, her lips tight and bloodless and set in hard, defiant lines.

He finished drying his hands and sat down at the table. He picked up a piece of turnip and tried to swallow it, but could not. The home-made ale was watery and bitter to the tongue, but he gratefully drained the mug.

After a moment he got to his feet. He went over to Molly and put a hand on her thin shoulder. "I am sorry," he said, "but you must not go on foolishly hoping, Molly. You must think of Giles and the other children now. Do not turn your back on them. They need you."

Then he went quietly into Cathy's room.

The child roused herself to open her eyes when she heard John enter. He stood by her bed and forced a smile.

"Well, Cathy?"

Out of her huge pain she struggled to smile back at him. In the lamplight her face was white and delicate as frost. "I was hoping 'ee 'ud come by tonight, Doctor John."

"Were you, Cathy? Why?"

She looked down, twisting the corner of her coverlet. " 'Cos tonight I be scared."

"Scared? Why are you scared?"

" 'Cos it be near, now."

"What is near, Cathy?"

" 'Ee know—"

John frowned. He said, "Cathy, have you asked your mother about this?"

"Aye, but Mam 'ull not talk 'bout it. Mam on'y makes like it ain't gonna happen a'tall. Me pa, me brothers—no one 'ull talk 'bout it, Doctor John. When Mam turns 'way and goes back to the kitchen, I git more scared. I know it be coming—and I be all alone—and I be scared."

John bent over and looked searchingly into the child's face. Then a cold chill ran through him. It was strange how certain patients knew. Somehow Cathy knew. She had only a few hours to live.

He sat down on the chair beside her bed. Religion was something he matter-of-factly left to the clergy. But now he found himself saying things he rarely ever thought of.

"Cathy, do you believe in God?"

"Aye, Doctor John."

"Deep down inside?"

"Aye."

"Do you believe He loves you?"

"Aye."

"Then you must believe He wants you to go to Him."

"I do, on'y sometimes I think 'bout Mam. I don' want to leave her. Mam niver cries. But I know her 'ull cry when I go."

"But time is short, Cathy. It only seems long to a little girl. Soon God will want to take your mother, too. He will take your father, your brothers. Soon you will all be together again."

She looked up at him uncertainly, shy of revealing to another human being still one more of her secret fears. "But 'ee see, Doctor John, the thing that scares me most is the—the leaving."

"The leaving? Why?"

" 'Cos it 'ull be like going out alone into the dark."

"Is that what you think it will be like? Going out alone into the dark?"

"Aye."

"I do not think that is the way it will be, Cathy."

"Why not?"

"Because of what one of my patients, a little girl with the same sickness you have, once told me. She said that two angels would come to fetch her and put a garland of flowers on her hair, then they would take her up through the blue starry sky. She said God would be there to take her into His arms and heal her of her sickness, and all about Him would be beauty and light."

"Kin it really be like that, Doctor John?"

"I cannot say for sure, Cathy. But this was an intelligent little girl. She had given much thought to it. So think it over, too. But now I must go. I only stopped to leave you some more medicine. Iris gets ill-tempered if I keep her out too late."

At that Cathy reached out impulsively and gripped his hand.

"Nay, do not leave me, Doctor John," she begged in weak, desperate, terror-stricken undertones. "Nay! Not now! Please, Doctor John! Do not leave me all alone—"

"But, Cathy, you are not all alone. Your parents are here—"

"Aye, but they 'ull ne'er stay with me—not now! They be scared, too! Oh, please, Doctor John, do not leave me. I 'ull be alone! Oh, please!" And she clung to his hand, looking up pleadingly, overwhelmed at the thought of what to her would be total abandonment. "He'p me, Doctor John! Please he'p me! I be scared—so awful scared—"

John stood gazing down at her with troubled eyes. For a moment he was silent. Then he said quietly, "Cathy, have you had your medicine tonight?"

"Aye, Doctor John, but it do not—"

"I know, Cathy. But now I am going to give you a little more. It will help you to sleep."

She nodded wordlessly and he mixed the medicine and watched while she drank it.

"Now," he said gently, "there is nothing for you to be scared of any more because I will not leave you, Cathy. I am going to stay here with you while you sleep. But I want you to close your eyes and lie still. Will you do that for me, Cathy?"

"Aye, Doctor John."

"Make yourself comfortable then. And remember, I will be sitting right here beside your bed."

She settled herself, then turned her head and gave him her brave, tortured smile. Then obediently she closed her eyes and John leaned back in the chair, listening to her harsh breathing grow quieter and more even as the draft he had given her eased her into sleep. Through the open doorway he heard Giles and the boys come in from the fields and go to the trough and wash themselves. He heard Giles tiptoe timorously to the doorway and stand there looking in, then turn and go away again. He heard the soft hum of the family as they started hungrily on their potatoes and turnips, talking in quiet, concerned tones. Listening to them brought to mind the murmur of the congregation in Father Dominic's chapel when he was a boy. He had sung in the choir then, a hundred years ago, it seemed—"Kyrie eleison. Christe eleison. Kyrie eleison"—a hundred years ago—a hundred years—

He awakened with a start some hours later, instantly aware of a strange, compelling stillness. He turned and looked at Cathy. She appeared to be sleeping, her eyes peacefully closed. He leaned over and placed his fingers on her throat.

He felt no pulsation.

After a moment he got up and went out to the kitchen. The boys had long since climbed to their beds in the loft. Giles had fallen asleep in front of the kitchen fire. But Molly was sitting in a straight-backed chair facing the doorway. He could see the whites of her eyes in the gloom as she sat, still and intense, waiting for him to come out.

She arose noiselessly and went to the hearth and brought him a bowl of porridge. He gulped down part of it. Then he beckoned her and together they stepped out into the graying dawn.

He stood a moment looking out over the bones of the hills misted with approaching rain, trying to find the will to tell her. But when he turned and looked down into her face he saw there was no need. She already knew.

"I am sorry, Molly," he said.

She gave him a sad, comforting smile. "Thank 'ee, Doctor John, fer staying. Her thoughted a lot o' 'ee, Cathy did. I know 'ee made it easier."

He put his hand on her cheek, dried and wrinkled before its time. Then he stooped and kissed it. He said softly, "I wish I had the power to change things."

" 'Ee do change things, Doctor John," she answered. "Howe'er bad things git, 'ee makes 'em better. I 'ull go now an' wake Giles. Him 'ull git Iris out o' the barn an' saddle her for 'ee."

"Let Giles sleep, Molly. I can saddle Iris."

He mounted up and started through the massed trees toward the road. Iris was cantankerous, displeased at the interruption in her sleep. She moved slowly, heading for home at a leisurely pace, and John did not hurry her.

Poor Molly! They were strong, these Dorsetshire women. Molly would weep for Cathy. But not until she had got her man and boys properly breakfasted and off to the fields. Then she would withdraw into the darkest corner of her kitchen and there, alone, she would weep for the child she had come to love the most because she was weak and ailing, the one whom, despite her fierce resistance to the truth, she had always known she would lose.

But for the physician, too, the loss of a child patient was emotionally convulsive and John was aware of a deep and settled grief. He remembered Tom during his first year at St. Bart's: "A doctor must learn to distance himself from his patients, to ensure his own survival by becoming inured to pain and death, to so change his nature that he will come to think of each patient not as a person, not as an individual with a face and name, but as a case." Yet how was it possible to think of Cathy as a "case"? To think of Father Dominic as a "case"? To think of poor tormented James Tremoigne, alone in his tower room, as a "case"?

It was raining hard now. Dorncaster was in sight, and on all sides he caught the odor of fresh tar. The grayness of the gray dawn cast its somber light over the town. The rooftops outlined against the lesser gloom looked like so many infernal Christmas trees hung with grisly black objects that were the tarred heads of men. The sight oppressed him. He closed his eyes and let his chin rest upon his breast.

Margaret Bemis . . .

Who were you, Margaret Bemis?

Were you Chérie?

Were you my dear Chérie?

. . . The vicarage with its curiously malevolent atmosphere. "Sir, what is done with the infant's body is no concern of mine. . . . The child was a bastard. . . ."

Well, regardless of the vicar's refusal to cooperate, the infant's body would not conclude its brief journey, naked and coffinless, in Potter's Field, thrown into a common grave with criminals. If Jenny died, then he himself would find a way to have the little thing interred in the unconsecrated section of some churchyard. If Jenny lived and was put on trial, he must then find a way to hold off burial for some few weeks. He would need the tiny body if he was to provide Pollexfen with the necessary legal defense.

He wondered suddenly how Jenny would receive their efforts to save her life. He supposed she would welcome them. Yet it was a point he found it hard to judge. She had been remarkably self-contained that day in court, unwilling to lie to save herself, yet unwilling to divulge the truth, silent on the most crucial points of concern to the court.

These days he found his thoughts constantly turning to her, lingering on her even while he was tending his patients, wondering about her, what her life at the vicarage had been, how she had passed her days. From the deathly paleness of her skin he surmised she had been kept indoors. Had she only been allowed out on Sunday, then, allowed only to cross the graveyard to the church, then back again, and always with her father's hawklike eye upon her?

There were rumors, Andy said, that occasionally one of the young men who saw her in church got up the courage to call at the vicarage, but was received in the chilly parlor only by the vicar. His daughter never appeared. Nor did the vicar seem to expect her to. Living so cloistered a life, then, how had she found a lover? True, the vicarage was at the foot of Yeggor Dun. Could there be any truth to the gossip that Jenny had sometimes escaped at night to climb the hill with the rest? No, he could not believe that. Not Jenny. A girl like Jenny would have needed to fall in love.

He was still thinking about her when he reached home.

He thought about her as he ate the meat pie one of his patients had left on his doorstep.

He thought about her as he threw himself onto his bed and lay staring up into the darkness of the timbered ceiling.

He went to sleep thinking of her.

Nine

Mother Ridley was in her garden hanging out some freshly washed linen. She looked around when she heard Iris's hooves pounding the dirt lane.

"Well, now, Doctor John," she called, "I was jest thinking 'bout 'ee. Jill Snyder was telling me on'y yisterday that 'ee took little Mikey from that shameless Saul Perkins and 'ull not let the big bully have him back."

John dismounted and tossed the reins over a nearby bush. Then he came and began picking up the wet linen from the basket and handing it to her to hang.

"That is not quite how the story goes, Mother Ridley," he answered. "But there is enough truth to it."

"And a good thing, I say. It be time folks did so'thing 'bout that Saul Perkins."

"It is not always easy, Mother. Sometimes we know very well what the trouble is, but we cannot get proof."

"You mean his chil'len still ain't telling on their pa? Not even when one of 'em gits kill't?"

"You must forgive the children. They have reason to be afraid."

The old woman smacked her lips in disgust. "Well, I would not wait fer proof if I was 'ee, Doctor John. There be more of them chil'len going to follow pore Colin to the grave. If I was 'ee I 'ud up and take that bully and clap him in jail." Then suddenly she turned. "Oh, 'ee be wanting yer shirts? I ain't got 'em ironed yit, but I kin do 'em right away if 'ee be needing 'em."

"No, Mother, there is no hurry for my shirts. That is not why I came. I want to talk to you about something else."

"So'thing else, is't? Well, now, that washing's all hung out. Come inside, then, Doctor John, and have a bowl o' porridge with me."

John always liked sitting in Mother Ridley's kitchen. The atmosphere was one of tranquillity, the peaceful atmosphere of an old woman who had learned long years ago to reconcile herself to her griefs. He dropped into his accustomed chair by the fire and stretched out his long legs, letting the flames toast boots that still were damp from last night's drenching.

Mother Ridley kept up a steady stream of gossip as she set down a saucer of milk for her mewing cat. A pot was simmering over the coals. She ladled some porridge into a bowl and covered it generously with honey before bringing it to John. Then she fetched a mug of home-brewed ale and set it down at his elbow.

"Now," she said, taking her own bowl and seating herself on the opposite side of the fireplace, "what wuz it 'ee be wanting to talk 'bout?"

"Mother Ridley, through the years you have had the goodness to claim the bodies of numberless abandoned children in order to save them from burial in Potter's Field."

She looked up and for a moment her quiet brown eyes studied John's face.

"Do 'ee have such a one now, Doctor John?"

"Yes, an infant. Yesterday I received an order to surrender the body to the city for burial. I have been trying to find some relative who will claim it, but without success. If it continues to go unclaimed, the body is scheduled to be picked up today for burial in the common grave."

Mother Ridley turned her head and now sat staring into the flames as a flood of painful memories came rushing back.

She had been a young woman when the plague swept England in 1646 and was among the first of its victims. While she was lying helpless and unaware in the almshouse, her young husband was stricken. He fell down in the street and, in the general terror and chaos of the time, was carted off and tumbled into the common grave in Potter's Field. Her four children followed their father. When she had recovered she went to Potter's Field and searched futilely for the place where the five were buried. Then, because she was alone, and because the plague had not yet subsided, she stayed on at the almshouse and assisted in the children's ward. Many children died there, some with no surviving family member to bury them. And young Ellen Ridley, grieving over the loss of her own children, began to claim these unclaimed ones so that they, too, would not be carted off and stripped of their clothing and tumbled haphazard into the terrible common grave. These children, at least, would be buried in some churchyard with a cross and a name to mark each grave. That had been forty years ago. Since then Mother Ridley had claimed and buried scores of abandoned children.

Now she asked, "Do it have a name, this little one? Has it been baptized? I 'ull need to know if it kin be buried in holy ground."

"I doubt it was baptized. But I will try to find out."

"And 'ee say there be no family to claim it?"

"No."

"Who be the mother?"

"Her name is Jenny Sykes."

"The vicar's daughter? The girl they be gossiping 'bout?"

"Yes."

Her eyes widened in surprise. " 'Ee don' say! But the vicar—surely —I mean, this be his gran'child, eh?"

John evaded the question. "These are things, Mother Ridley, that we sometimes find it hard to understand. I only know that at the moment the infant's body is waiting in the hospital deadhouse. Unless I can make some other arrangement, it will be picked up this morning for burial in Potter's Field."

"This morning, Doctor John? That be mickle soon."

"I am sorry. This is a complicated case."

"What time do 'ee 'spect 'em to come fer it?"

"They usually make their calls about mid-morning."

"Means I should leave right 'way. But, Doctor John, how 'ull I git to town so quick?"

"I will arrange for that. I will pass by Tom Dillon's on my way and tell him to pick you up in a coach. There is just one thing, though, Mother Ridley. I do not want you to remove the body just yet. I want you to give me permission to hold it in the deadhouse for the next few weeks."

"Eh? And why so, Doctor John?"

"It is a legal as well as a medical matter. We expect to need the body when Jenny Sykes is brought to trial." He got to his feet and touched her gratefully on the shoulder. "Thank you, Mother. I appreciate your help. I will be waiting for you at the clinic, then. Look for me there when you arrive."

As the doctor turned into the hospital courtyard, he heard the sounds of a brawl. It was coming from the clinic, yells and curses from the men, screams from the frightened women. In an instant John had leapt off Iris's back and was running up the steps and through the clinic door.

Saul Perkins was fighting his way up the stairs to the second-floor ward as Andrew Barnes struggled to restrain him. Andy had leapt on Saul's back and now was clinging there as precariously as a man riding an angry bull. Two patients, Joe Colney and Cliff Brice, had answered Andy's cry for help and were dragging on Saul's legs, trying to haul him backward. But the three were no match for Saul. Even encumbered as he was, the gigantic blacksmith had already pushed halfway up the stairs. The acrid, wet-dog smell of sweat was strong on the air and his shirt clung damply to his body, outlining the bulge of ropelike muscles beneath. Each straining movement was coupled with an animal-like grunt and a spasmodic heave of his hairy chest.

"Bastards!" he was yelling, his face red with fury. "I 'ull kill 'ee all. Out of me way! I want to fetch me son. Mikey be coming home with me. So off me, scum! Off me—"

Suddenly, with a tremendous heave, he crashed Andrew Barnes against the wall. As Andy's grip loosened and he started to fall, Saul dealt him a blow to the head with his clenched fist that stunned him and sent him tumbling down the stairs. Colney and Brice were still dragging on Saul's legs, struggling to pull him backward. But now Saul spun around and, again with a clenched fist, sent Colney reeling. Then he stooped, picked Brice up in his thick-muscled arms, raised him above his head and, with a string of curses, prepared to hurl him down over the banister into the waiting room.

By now John had pushed through the crowd and came leaping up the stairs. He passed by Saul and positioned himself two steps above the blacksmith, blocking his path.

"That is enough, Saul Perkins," he said quietly. "Put that man down on his feet. Do it gently and do it now. At once!"

Saul Perkins swung around, his head jerking up, a gleam of surprise in his eyes. Still balancing the struggling Brice in midair, he scowled up at John from beneath his bushy black eyebrows. His breath rasped, short and hard, making the air about him reek with its foulness.

"Eh! 'tis the doc," he panted. "Well, I come to fetch me boy. I come to fetch Mikey. I be taking him home with me. Yer hear that? I be taking Mikey home with me, so 'ee kin jest git outta me way."

John's face was tight and angry. He laid a powerful grip on Saul's wrist. "Put that man down."

"Take yer hand off me!"

But John's brutal grip only tightened. "Put that man down at once —and do it gently."

Something made Saul hesitate. For a moment the two men stared into one another's eyes, watching each other with the wariness of two dogs readying for a fight.

Then suddenly Saul grinned. Slowly, with exaggerated care, he lowered the struggling Brice and set him on his feet.

"There, Doc, I done what 'ee wanted. Now git out of me way 'fore I clod 'ee one. 'Ee may be big enough to thrash most folks, but not me, so don' go trying. Now, outta me way! I be going up to fetch Mikey, and I be warning 'ee. Don' go trying. Jest don' 'ee try."

There was a dangerous note in John's voice.

"Saul Perkins, you are not taking Mikey out of this hospital. You have done Mikey enough harm. The boy has been unconscious since you brought him in here. If he lives, it will be a miracle. If he dies, he will be the second of your sons to die violently within the year. That will be reason enough, I think, to re-examine the cause of Colin's death."

"Pish! 'Ee cain't prove nothing 'bout me and Colin."

"Maybe not. But then, a man does not need to be responsible for two violent deaths. One is enough to hang him."

"Hang 'im?"

Saul gaped in amazement tinged with fear. His fists had been clenched. Now he unclenched them. He became aware of some male nurses collecting on the landing, watching. He looked down at the crowd staring silently up at him.

Saul's brain was hard at work. John Toller was a large man—good with his fists if pressed to use them. To thrash him in an open fight would not be easy. But there were other ways. Not here, though. Not in the hospital with witnesses to the scabby tricks a man would need to use to get quit of John Toller. Suddenly something flickered behind Saul's eyes as his mind adjusted to successive possibilities.

He backed off down the stairs.

"Well," he said pleasantly. "I 'ull be back in a coupla days to see that Mikey. But I be warning 'ee, Doc. 'Ee had best took good care of me little lad. I jest be warning 'ee, like any good pa should, is all."

Then, smiling, hoisting his sagging breeches; he turned and made a leisurely way down the stairs, pushed through the crowd and strode out to the street.

They seemed to be all in the clinic today: those suffering from the "love sickness" who had already exhausted their old wives' remedies and now were seeking from the clinic cures that medical science had not yet devised; the brave and the fearful; the young, the old, the dying; an oozing carbuncle, a case of apoplexy, scurvey, bloody dysentery, ulcers, dropsy, an old woman stooped double with arthritis, a newborn with pneumonia.

A young man, once robust, now stood weak in the legs, with severe tremors of the muscles and chattering teeth. His bearded face was pale, with dark circles under tortured eyes. His features were pinched and sharp with disease.

John motioned to a chair, then arose to take his pulse. It was hard and quick. He examined the scarred and calloused hands. The fingers were dead-white, the nails blue.

"Well, Harry," he said, resuming his seat, "you have not been in to see me for three months. I had been hoping that meant you were improving."

There was desperation in the pitch of Harry's voice.

"Doctor John, it be gitting so me last hope be to die soon. From when I was a small lad I dreamed of owning a farm. All I ever wanted was that—to own a farm. Now that I own it I cain't work it. This fever lays me low more days than I kin work. Mostly I shiver and sweat and so much weakness runs through me I kin on'y lie abed. It be but a year since I scraped the money and bought me farm. Now me fair fields be on'y a tangle o' weeds. Doctor John, I got no money left. Unless 'ee kin help me—unless I kin work me land, I be all done in."

"You are not married, are you, Harry?"

"No, Doc. I was looking for a wife—till all this."

"Then who takes care of you on your bad days?"

"I does fer meself, sir."

John sat back and studied Harry with his accustomed circumspection. The small quantity of cinchona bark (with its alkaloid quinine) that he had stored away was recently being applied with good effect to the treatment of malarial fever. But it was rare and costly. It came from

Peru and had to be paid for out of exorbitant fees he charged his rich patients. While he dispensed it gratis to the needy poor of the clinic, he did so sparingly, a treasure not to be heedlessly dissipated.

And here came Harry Cammin.

Until a year ago, when he bought his farm, Harry Cammin had known but one home, the Dorncaster Orphanage. At thirteen he had been apprenticed to a saddler. But young Harry had had a fixed idea—that someday he would own a farm, a hopeless dream for an orphan boy with no prospects and not a farthing to his name.

Six months into his apprenticeship Harry had decamped and found his way to the nearby seaport of Poole, where smugglers in worsted caps swore in many tongues and jingled gold pieces in their pockets. Here, amid the intricate waterways of the seven-mile estuary, he found a master more to his liking, one who would give him a share of the spoils, the notorious smuggler Peter Thorpe. For five years Harry sailed with Thorpe in the *Black Cat*, learning to handle the helm, learning the tricks of cargo-running, of moving a ship unseen through the hidden creeks of the lagoon with its bush-covered islets; getting to know the best hiding places for smuggled goods, the innkeepers who, for a consideration, would develop a "blind eye." When Thorpe met his death at the hands of the law, Harry steered the *Black Cat* up a maze of reedy waterways and hid her under a lattice of branches. Then, on a chill November day, when the sky was overcast and fog shrouded everything that stirred, he threaded the little ship through the snaky channels and slimy pools to the open sea.

From then on the coast of France belonged to Harry. From Calais to La Rochelle he could come and go at will. The fishermen along the slumberous French quays professed to know nothing of him, for he paid them generously for running his kegs and bales of contraband goods. To the French authorities, however, he had become a source of frustration and embarrassment. They set many a trap from which, apparently with prior knowledge, he easily escaped, so they had never even glimpsed him and knew him only by the French contraction of what was thought to be his English name, " 'Arricam." But through it all Harry held close to his dream. By the time he was twenty-five, when he had saved enough gold to buy his farm, he gave the *Black Cat* over to his shipmates and returned to Dorncaster, shivering with swamp fever, tall and broad, bearded, showing a curious reluctance to talk of the years between now and the time he had been a puny saddler's lad. Then one day he came to the clinic seeking treatment for his swamp fever. That was when John recognized the elusive wanted smuggler " 'Arricam."

But he had said nothing.

Three months had passed since them. Now, after a moment of reflection, John arose and went to his locked cabinet and checked his precious store of rare cinchona bark. Lady Camworth must be left to suffer her chills and fever until the next shipment arrived. So must Major Raleigh-Coates. And the Earl of Carrisborough.

The time had come for 'Arricam to work his farm.

"Well, Harry," he said, "today I have something to help you. I will give you a powder which you will take in water. Can you read?"

"Enough."

"Good! Instructions are written on the package. I want you to take it twice a day and come back to see me in a few weeks."

Harry accepted the package and rose unsteadily to his feet.

"I be purely grateful to 'ee, Doc. 'By, then."

And John answered softly, "Good-by, 'Arricam."

Harry Cammin swung around. There was astonishment on his face. But there was fear, too, fear of discovery, fear of the law.

He asked, his voice gone suddenly harsh, " 'Ee knows?"

"I knew the last time you were here."

" 'Ee said nothing to me."

"No."

"And afterward. . . .Who did 'ee tell?"

"I told no one."

"And now?"

"Now?"

"Who 'ull 'ee tell now?"

"Again, I will tell no one. 'Arricam is wanted only for smuggling, not for any felonious crime."

For a moment the two men stood looking at one another. Then Harry Cammin sighed as the tension left him.

"Thank 'ee," he said, Then: "But I still cain't see how 'ee knew."

"It was not hard. You and I had a fistfight once, with the other lads standing around goading us on. Remember? When we were boys? You called me 'Toller's bastard'?"

Harry stared. "The lad who come to the shop with the raggedly saddle to be stitched. The high-headed boy in the red cap? That was 'ee?"

John chuckled. "It was. You left me with some bruised ribs that kept me out of school for the next two days. And I left you with a token across your knuckles which you have to this day."

Harry glanced down at his right hand. The knuckles showed where the gaping flesh had knit together in the form of some grotesque convoluted growth.

"But this," he said thoughtfully, "on'y tells 'ee I was the lad in the saddler's shop. It don' tell 'ee I was . . . that other."

"No, but I have a patient who lives a few miles outside Poole. Usually he rides into the city to see me. On this occasion—about two years ago—he was too ill to leave his bed. I visited him at his home; then, it being late, I decided to spend the night in Poole. I had supper at the Anchor Inn, then went around to the courtyard to make sure my mare was comfortably stabled."

"The Anchor Inn? That were a safe house fer me contraband. 'Ee saw me there?"

"Quite by chance. The courtyard was dark, except for a single lantern, but I saw you. You were not bearded then, and you had changed from the lad whose fists had bruised me up. I looked at your knuckles, then I knew. You were directing some seamen as they carried in kegs of French wine and stowed them down in the cellar. One of them—a Frenchman—carelessly addressed you as 'Arricam."

"Damn fool! Him could ha' blowed the gaff."

"Anyway, you had better keep that beard until the hue and cry dies down."

Harry Cammin looked down at the floor. "It be strange, though. I feel a weight lifted off of me. I bin feeling badly—me secret being so heavy, I mean. Now—with 'ee knowing and not letting on—it somehow ain't that heavy."

Again John chuckled. "A little like the confessional—a relief to share your secret with someone, just so long as that someone keeps your secret."

Harry Cammin nodded and smiled. Then, still clutching his precious package of cinchona bark, he turned and limped away.

Next was a young mother with her two-year-old son. By now, John instinctively braced himself whenever Cassie brought little Bertie to the clinic. The child was dying and, as he had with Molly Grimage, he had told Cassie there was nothing medical science could do to help him. But some mothers, he had found, would not accept finality. Some mothers had unshakable faith. They refused to surrender hope. So it had been with Cassie. John had been troubled. He had made a point of stopping at the stall where her husband worked to tell Bert that his young wife would need all his love and care when the time came.

"Well, Cassie," he said now, "which one is the patient today?"

"It be still little Bertie, Doc. I have not bin in these last months. I was afeared to come."

John gave her a searching look. "Afraid? Why?"

She made no reply, only stood there smiling an odd, secretive little smile, clutching her baby to her breast. Then, still without a word, she placed him in John's arms.

He sensed that something strange was about to happen, but he said matter-of-factly, "Come, then, Little Bertie. Let me take a look at you."

He sat Bertie on the examining table and waited while Cassie removed his clothing. Then, as he had a dozen times in the past six months, he commenced the examination.

He knew what to look for, the large tumor in the abdomen, malignant, growing tenaciously, spreading, slowly killing the child. But now as his hands explored, he found nothing. No trace of the tumor. He frowned, puzzled. It was the first time within his medical practice that he had come upon something for which he had no scientific explanation. He explored a second time.

At last he straightened up and turned to the young mother.

"Cassie, I do not understand. What happened here? You knew when you brought him in that the tumor had disappeared."

"I seen it gitting smaller this past month, Doctor John."

"Now it has completely disappeared. There is no trace of it."

"Do that mean little Bertie 'ull live?"

"I believe so. It is extraordinary! Quite extraordinary! Do not ask me to explain it, Cassie. I cannot. I have no explanation."

She was still smiling her happy, secretive smile.

"I kin 'splain it, though, Doctor John. It be a miracle. I bin praying. Every day I went to church and took the child and laid him at the Virgin's feet. I prayed to her. I prayed hard. Her done it, Doctor John. Mother Mary worked a miracle."

A flicker of irritation crossed John's features. Miracles mocked the known laws of nature. Miracles, therefore, like the supposed curative powers of the "shrew-ash" and the "witch-bar," were at odds with medical science.

Still, he was moved. He watched with a sense of wonderment as Cassie dressed the child, working tenderly, kissing him intermittently, talking to him in a language his infant mind seemed to comprehend. He thought, some things, too, like mother love—who could say? Human understanding did not reach that far . . .

"I will want to see him again, Cassie, so bring him back in a month." Then, as she lifted the child and prepared to leave, he laid a hand on her arm. "I am happy for you, Cassie. And for Bert. Something strange and rare and wonderful seems to have come into your lives."

The matter of little Bertie's seemingly miraculous recovery stayed with him as he rode out to St. Mary's Lying-In to see Jenny.

He, like most medical men, rejected the possibility of miracles and knew there had to be some logical reason behind every such recovery, something that transcended man's understanding of the known laws of nature, that lay beyond the scope of medical knowledge, but which existed in the natural world nonetheless. The phenomena known as "spontaneous cures" were not unknown. There were records of them in medical history. But they were rare.

A doctor was only a man—a humble man. He might know more than the great majority of other men. He might have mastered the vast store of medical science accumulated through the centuries, might be familiar with the writings of Paracelsus, of Versalius and Fallopius and Harvey, even back to Avicenna and the Aphorisms. Yet he was still only a man. His understanding was still only a man's understanding. Human understanding. But the phenomena of "spontaneous cures" were inexplicable in terms of human understanding. They were something beyond man.

At the Lying-In he headed for the Isolation Room. He met Sister Brigit in the corridor.

"Oh, Doctor, I am relieved to see you. I am so worried about that poor girl."

John's heart gave an unprofessional thump. "Jenny? She is growing worse, then?"

"No, it is not that. This morning she is awake and alert. But she is very troubled—in fact, I would say quite distraught."

"Jenny Sykes has many things to trouble her, Sister. What in particular is it at the moment?"

"I do not know. I asked her, but she will not tell me. I think it is you she wants to talk to. She keeps asking when you will be here."

"Has she been taking any nourishment?"

"Sister Catherine fed her milk and broth three times during the night. This morning she swallowed some gruel and a soft egg. But she does it unwillingly—only when I remind her of your orders. She does not want to eat." Sister Brigit lowered her voice. "Doctor John, God forgive me, but I do not think that girl wants to get well. I do not think she wants to live."

"Small wonder," John answered shortly. "She is beginning to remember. I will go in and talk to her right away."

When he entered the room her eyes were closed. He drew up beside her bed and spoke softly. "Well, Jenny, how are you feeling today?"

She must indeed have been waiting for him because at the sound of his voice her eyes sprang open. Quickly she dragged herself up on one elbow and reached out and grasped his hand. Her eyes were wide and filled with intense pain.

"Oh, tell me—please—what have they done with it? Where is my baby now? Please tell me—"

He sat down on the chair beside her. "Is that what has been troubling you, Jenny?"

"Oh, yes—I have been thinking—they will not care—no one will care . . ."

He spoke quickly, solicitous to relieve her anguish. "Jenny, do not let that trouble you any longer. I have the body safe in my care at the hospital. No one will take it unless I say they may."

She lay back at that, relief flooding her face. She was thoughtful for a moment. Then she said more quietly, "But still, it must be . . ."

"Yes, I have arranged for that. There is a good woman, Mother Ridley, who lost her own four children in the Great Plague many years ago. Now, if you agree, she would like to bury your baby. It will be done in a churchyard. She will see that it has a small cross with its name on it."

"But it never . . ." Her voice trailed off.

"It never had a name? In that case, would you like her to write simply 'Baby Sykes'? You should let her write something. You will want to be able to find it later on."

"Oh, yes—thank you—" The emotional effort had drained her strength and she fell back against the pillows and closed her eyes again.

He placed his fingers on her wrist. Today her pulse was noticeably stronger. She was doing better than he had dared to hope.

But he could see that a new thought was troubling her. There was still something she wanted to say. She was struggling to gather the courage to say it.

He leaned forward. "What is it, Jenny?"

She looked up at him again and now he found himself chilled by the stark terror in her eyes.

"But I will never be able to find it, you know. Because they are going to . . . they are going to . . ." Again she broke off.

"Send you to the gallows?"

"Yes."

"I hope not, Jenny. That is what we are now working to prevent."

She lay quiet at that. Then, after a moment, she asked, "But how can you prevent it? The coroner said they do not need to prove infanticide. They can hang me for concealment of birth."

"That is true. But the coroner was citing the law in cases where the mother is unable to prove stillbirth."

"But that fits my case."

"I do not think so."

"But he said that there must be at least one witness to stillbirth. I have no witness."

"We may find another way to prove stillbirth, Jenny. That is what we are now exploring. There is a barrister working on your case. His name is Henry Pollexfen. Henry is an able criminal lawyer who has agreed to defend you when you come up for trial."

"Why will he defend me?"

"Because he believes you are innocent of the charge."

"Why does he believe that? Did you tell him I am innocent?"

"I did."

She looked up at him gravely. "Why do you believe it? Why should you believe I am innocent?"

He chose his words with care. "Innocent of child-murder? I have no doubt of that at all."

"But how can you not have doubts? I am a stranger to you."

John smiled. "What now, Jenny? Are you trying to prove me wrong? Come, we have talked enough for today. The rest can wait a day or two. Then, if you feel strong enough, you can ask me some more questions. But I would also like to ask you some questions. Would you mind that?"

"No."

"Will you answer them?"

"Yes."

"And now I want you to think only about getting well. I want you to do everything Sisters Brigit and Catherine tell you. I do not want you to lie here worrying. I want you to leave all these unsettling matters to me. Will you do that for me, Jenny?"

He had not meant his voice to sound so tender. But she caught the unbidden note. She nodded in response to his question, then her wondering gaze moved over his face, unhurried, in the same thoughtful, searching, questioning way to which he had submitted in the dungeon cell.

For the first time he saw her smile. It was almost indiscernible at first, coming slowly, with a strange melting wistfulness, lifting the corners of her mouth and changing her face in some mysterious way. Unaccountably he found himself thinking of the sun breaking out over the gray, storm-swept flanks of the High Moor.

There was something about that smile that haunted him as he mounted Iris and rode away. Despite Henry's continued skepticism, his own belief in her remained unshaken. There was still much about her case that puzzled him, much he knew she was holding back. Some of these questions he would begin to probe now that she was recuperating, some of them he would deliberately refrain from probing. He would leave her to explain in her own time, if ever she so chose.

Suddenly he frowned, staring hard into the distance. He realized that the rebel trials were drawing to a close. The daily executions were still turning the inner city into a slaughterhouse. But soon the last of the rebels would have been dealt with and the regular jail delivery would commence. He was hoping Jenny would not regain full strength too soon, since then, if they so demanded, he would have no excuse for refusing to return her to jail. Her trial would come up in only one or two weeks now and he was troubled by the fact that his courier, Jason Smith, had not yet returned from Amsterdam with Doctor Van Roonhuyse's documents. He would need time to study those documents himself before the trial, time to brief Henry on the test and the purpose to which it was applied. Henry had become increasingly uneasy as he realized that the outcome of this case would rest upon a procedure novel to him, a test which, while already accepted by European courts of law, had not yet been applied in a legal case in any English court.

John was secretly troubled too on that point. He did not yet know enough about the test to be convinced of its validity. But even if he himself could be satisfied, what of judge and jury? Could they be convinced? Would they, untrained in pathology, understand that an important step in this new-fledged science of legal medicine was the proper recognition of infanticide?

Yet there might be no other way to save Jenny's life.

He wondered suddenly how he had ever thought her unpretty. Not that he set great store by a pretty face. He knew too much about women for that. But there was about Jenny something rare, something that moved him more than he cared to recognize. He had thought that after a time her strangely haunting face would cease to invade his daily life. But no, it was always there, on the edge of every thought—as he worked in the clinic, or rode the countryside, or sat alone at night by his own fireside. He found himself deeply touched by the fact that this girl, so bruised by life, so isolated and therefore so strangely self-contained, had come to trust him. That trust had shown just now in her smile, for he knew instinctively that growing up as she had in a cold, impersonal home, remote from kindness and human love, she did not smile easily.

And yet, he reflected, with a saddening sense of loss, she must have smiled in just such a way at her lover. . . .

Ten

John knocked on the door of Saul Perkins's hovel. After a lengthy wait it was opened just a crack by a small, half-naked girl who peeped out timorously.

"Good day, Millie. Is your father home?"

Millie gaped up at him, but stood silent and undecided. Then two small boys squeezed through the crack, their clothing torn and filthy, their faces covered with scabbed sores. They, too, just gaped, their minds reacting slowly to their visitor. Then suddenly one of them raised his head like an excited hound and shrieked, "Mam!"

A shuffle of slow feet and Mrs. Perkins appeared, as thin and frail and filthy as her brood, her unwashed hair clinging to her scrawny neck, her lips sagging into spaces once occupied by three front teeth knocked out by Saul in the first year of their marriage.

"Cally," John said, "I apologize for calling so early, but I must get to the hospital. I need to speak to you and Saul for just a moment. May I come in?"

Mrs. Perkins hesitated, then poked her head outside the door cautiously and looked down the street. Then she turned and looked up the street.

"Ain't no sign o' Saul," she answered.

"Is he not inside the house?"

"Saul ain't come home yit. Seems like Saul's bin gone all night."

"Well," John said, "may I come in anyway? I would like to speak to you, then you can give my message to Saul."

She made no reply, only opened the door for him to step inside.

It was dark in the two-room hovel. He stumbled over a sleeping child, tangling his feet in the straw of the mattress. He circumvented a pair of ten-year-old twins fighting a dog for possession of a gnawed meat bone. Other children seemed to see in the dark and scrambled out of his way. The air was foul with the sour odor of crowding animal bodies. He took one breath, then stepped to a window and threw open a shutter to admit a rush of air and light. Then, avoiding the underfoot herd, he crossed and stood with his back to the empty fireplace.

"I have told you before, Cally, you must keep more light and air in here."

She said nothing, only stared stonily up at him.

"Cally," he said, "I have brought you sad news. Little Mikey died yesterday."

Still she said nothing. Her eyes never left his face.

"We did everything possible to save him, but there was very little we could do. He died without regaining consciousness."

Her voice was expressionless. "What'd him die of?"

He answered her astonishing question with gentle reproof. "Cally, do you not know?"

At that her pale eyes dropped to the floor. She answered defensively, "How 'ud I know?"

"Because when Mikey was brought to the hospital he had massive head injuries, a broken nose, and multiple cuts on face and body. He was bleeding from internal injuries, the full extent of which we do not yet know." He looked down at her searchingly. "Cally, would you care to tell me how Mikey received those injuries?"

Her eyes were still on the floor. "How 'ud I know?" she said again.

"You would know because Mikey appears to have died of extreme physical violence, just as Colin did."

She remained silent, her lips set and hard.

"Cally," he asked after a moment, "do you never weep for your dead children?"

She looked up sharply at that. "Folks that live in a deadhouse cain't weep fer each dead child."

John was stunned by the insight implicit in her response. It was the first indication he had that this seemingly apathetic woman viewed the tragedy of her life with grief and despair.

"Then why do you protect Saul? Why not tell the truth? Look around you. There is not a child in this room whose body does not bear the telltale marks of Saul's brutality. Cally, they would shelter you and your children at the workhouse if you would let them."

For an instant a flash of hope brightened her dull face. Then quickly it died away. "Him 'ud on'y come to fetch us. Him 'ud on'y—"

She broke off as heavy stumbling footsteps were heard on the stoop outside. At the familiar sound the children scattered, disappearing like figments. The door was thrown open and Saul burst in, his face flushed and furious.

He stopped short at the sight of John. "Now, what 'ud 'ee be doing in my place?"

"I came looking for you, Saul. I came to tell you that Mikey died yesterday."

"Well, now 'ee tole me. Now git out."

But as John turned to go, Saul laid a savage grip on his arm. "I 'ull come fer the body betimes."

"No, Saul, we cannot release the body yet."

"Eh? Why not?"

"We will need to perform an autopsy."

Saul glared at him suspiciously. "Now what tricks 'ee be playing?"

"It is a matter of law. You claimed that Colin crushed his own throat with your blacksmith's hammer. Improbable, perhaps. But lacking evidence to the contrary, his death was ruled accidental. Now Mikey appears to have died of internal injuries. You claim these injuries were inflicted in a street fight with a passing peddler's boy. You will be required to testify to that at the inquest. In a street fight there are always witnesses. You will be required to produce those witnesses. If you cannot, you can perhaps explain to the coroner how, without any witnesses, and without any signs of a fight on Mikey's fists, he was embroiled in a street fight. Whether or not you are then bound over will be up to the coroner. You see? It is a matter of law."

Then he shook off Saul's restraining hand and left.

He was still cold with anger when he reached the hospital. He made his rounds of the wards and spent a few quiet moments chatting with Father Dominic. By the time he came downstairs, the clinic waiting room was crowded.

His anger flared anew as he examined his first patient, a bricklayer with a family of young children.

"I told you two days ago, Simon, this foot is gangrenous. It is mortifying. It will have to come off."

"And I tole 'ee, Doc, I cain't do 'thout me foot."

John almost shouted at him. "Would you rather die?"

Simon was a brave man, but he had begun to sweat. " 'Ee don' un'erstand, Doc. I cain't lay bricks 'thout me foot. Bricklayers needs two feet."

"And you cannot lay bricks if you are dead, man, so do not continue to argue. If you delay any longer, you will risk losing your leg as well as your foot. Now, Mr. Barnes is in the hospital somewhere. Shall I send and ask him to perform the amputation this morning?"

Simon looked aghast. "Well—Doc—"

"Come on, Simon. You no longer have a choice, you know."

"Well, Doc—if the thing must come off, I 'ud take it kindly if 'ee 'ud do the thing yerself."

"I am not a chirurgeon, Simon. You know Mr. Barnes does our surgery."

Simon was almost weeping now. "But 'thout me foot, how'm I going to—Doc, I 'ull be out of work for good."

John's voice was suddenly filled with compassion that no roughness of tone could quite disguise.

"No, Simon, you will have no excuse for being out of work. You will work just as before. You will have a false member, which in your case will take the form of a raised leather boot to replace the foot. These boots are comfortable and practical. I have a patient who has worn one now for four years, a farmer up by Cerne Abbas, who farms his land as well now as he ever did before his accident. I will speak to the saddler myself and explain just how I want your boot to be made. You should be able to resume bricklaying within a very short time once the stump has healed. Now, shall I send word to Mr. Barnes?"

"And if I say yea, Doctor John, will 'ee stand by while him's adoing it?"

John hesitated, thinking of his crowded waiting room.

"All right, Simon, I will stand by. I will come as soon as Mr. Barnes is ready."

Mrs. Lake, a tired mother with a ten-year-old son, was waiting for him. There was a hint of nervous sadness in her eyes. Her clothes were shabby. Her shoes were worn and covered with dust. She looked as though she had walked a long way to get there.

"You have never visited our clinic before, have you, Mrs. Lake?"

"No, Doctor."

"And what brings you here today?"

"It is the boy—as you can see."

"Ah, yes."

He beckoned the boy to come and sit near his desk. As the boy got to his feet and crossed the room, John had time to observe the involuntary twitching of the muscles throughout his entire body—the sudden upward jerk of the shoulder, the trunk twisting about, the dragging of one leg, the mouth working as the tongue lashed in and out. He had been quieter as he sat beside his mother on the bench, but now anxiety and self-consciousness were intensifying his distress and making this a moment of extreme agony.

John waited till the boy was seated. Then he said gently, "Son, what is your name?"

The boy had to bring his tongue under control before he could answer. "Tim, sir."

"Well, Tim, have you ever been to a doctor before?"

"No, sir."

"I hope you did not mind coming to see me."

"No, sir."

"You know I am going to try to help you, do you not?"

"Aye, sir. My mother told me."

"And would you mind if I were to put you on the table to examine you?"

"No, sir."

"Come with me, then."

He dropped behind as the boy moved toward the table, observing again the convulsive muscular movements, the face jerking sideways and distorted into grimaces, the marked alternation of gait, now halting, now leaping. The boy almost tripped himself as one foot flung itself in front of the other. The medical term "insanity of the muscles" flashed through John's mind.

He assisted Tim up the step, then helped him to remove his shirt.

The boy was thin and frail, almost girllike, worn out by the disease that had impaired his general health and was causing increased difficulty in eating, since much of his food was lost on its way to his mouth. But now, as John examined him, his apprehension seemed to wane. His jerks and grimaces became less pronounced. He obeyed each instruction carefully, looking up at John with wide blue eyes that were suddenly trusting.

"And you are ten years old, is that it, Tim?"

"Aye, sir."

"How long have you had this problem?"

"Seems like ages and ages, sir."

"Do you go to school?"

"I go to the free school up my way."

"Do you have trouble with the other boys?"

"Aye, sir."

"What kind of trouble?"

"They laugh at me . . . they mock me."

"And that bothers you?"

"Aye, sir."

At last John straightened up and put a hand on the boy's thin shoulder.

"Tim, would it make you happy if I were to tell you that I think we may be able to correct this problem of yours?"

A smile flitted over the boy's pale face. "That would make me very happy sir."

"Come, then, let us go back to your mother and talk about it."

The boy followed along confidently after John and resumed his seat beside John's desk.

"Mrs. Lake," John said, "you heard my conversation with Tim just now. Tim appears to be suffering from a disorder of the nervous system known as Sydenham's chorea, after our own Doctor Sydenham of Wynford Eagle, who has made an extensive study of the disease. The chorea is essentially an ailment of the young. It generally afflicts children between the ages of nine and twelve."

"But you said you might be able to correct this problem. Is that really possible, Doctor?"

"Entirely possible, Mrs. Lake. For his London patients Doctor Sydenham devised a regimen which has resulted in complete recovery in the great majority of his cases, considerable improvement in the rest. We will follow that same regimen. I am going to give you a medicinal remedy which I want Tim to take morning and night. In time it should control these convulsive muscular movements."

He crossed to his cabinet and began mixing the medication. Again Tim followed along and stood there, on twisted legs, watching him.

"Sir, what you said—does that mean I am going to be like other boys?"

"That is what I am expecting, Tim."

"And I will not do all this jerking anymore?"

"Within a few months that should all have disappeared. But there is more to your treatment than medication, Tim."

"What, sir?"

"For one thing, I will want you to stay home from school for a while."

"Why, sir?"

"Because you say the other boys mock you. You see, this twitching and jerking is aggravated by strong emotions such as you feel when you know people are watching you, or when other boys make thoughtless remarks."

"You mean like when I want to cry, but do not?"

"That is just what I mean. Then there are other things I want you to do. Does your father farm his land?"

"Aye, sir."

"Then I want you to go out there and help him. I want you to stay out in the fresh air, to avoid excitement or anything that overtires you. I want you to eat well and go to bed early. In one month I want you to come back here so I can watch your improvement. Then, if you like, we will talk about returning to school." He suddenly looked around.

"Where are you from, Mrs. Lake? You are not from around Dorn-caster."

"We are from out Saltfox way. The Totten farm. Before my marriage I was Marcy Totten."

"Then you do not know that, since this clinic is free, it services only residents of Dorncaster and a small surrounding area? No, do not let that trouble you. I did not tell you that to keep you from coming. I said it only so that, when you learn our rules, you will know that Tim is an exception and is welcome here. I like my new patient. I will want to see him again." He returned and handed her the bottle. "But Saltfox is far away. How did you get here?"

"We walked, mostly. We slept in a field last night. When we got near the city, a farmer let us ride in his wagon."

"Well, you are not likely to reach home tonight. And the sharp autumn air would make sleeping in a field uncomfortable. But there is a farm along your way, Theo Crunch's place, just off the Silesby Road. He is a good man, Theo Crunch, and a patient of mine. He will give you supper and a warm bed in his barn if you knock on his door. Tell him I sent you. He will understand. And now, good-bye. Good-bye, Tim. I will expect to see you back here in a month."

He saw a man with diabetes after that, treated various children's diseases; a case of pulmonary consumption, to be isolated and reported; an old woman with dropsy; a "bleeder"; a youth with cerebral palsy. They came in a seemingly endless stream.

It was almost three o'clock by the time Simon's gangrenous foot had been amputated. John was just washing his hands when word was brought that a courier was over at the Mermaid asking for him.

"Is it Jason?" he asked quickly.

"No, Doc, it be Ken Smith. Him jest cum in by stagecoach."

"By stagecoach!"

"Aye, Doc—on 'count o' him be hurt an' bleeding."

"Did he say what happened?"

"No—on'y that him's got news 'ee bin waiting for."

John hurriedly put on his coat. If Ken Smith sent for him under such circumstances, the news must be bad. Ken was the cousin of Jason Smith, the courier he had sent to Doctor Van Roonhuyse in Amsterdam for details of the new test for stillbirth. Both cousins were couriers. John employed them regularly.

He hurried over to the innyard and found Ken Smith in the

crowded stables, lying exhausted on a pile of straw, covered with mud and sweat.

He pushed through and dropped to one knee. He took a quick look at Ken's wounds. They had been tended by a chirurgeon along the way and could bide awhile.

"Now," he said, "what happened?"

"Jason's down, Doc."

"Tell me."

Ken's eyes swept the hostlers, the stage coachmen, the waiting stagecoach passengers crowding around, listening, absorbed and curious. He whispered, "I gotta speak to 'ee alone, Doc. I got things to say—private things."

John looked up. "Please, folks, all of you, out into the courtyard to oblige me." Then, when they had drifted out of earshot, he turned back to Ken.

"Now, what happened?"

"Well, Doc, Jason and me chanced to meet on the packet boat crossing back from Holland, him from Amsterdam, me from Delft, both heading home by way of London. Seemed like a lucky meet at first, the roads being that dangerous these days—"

"Yes, yes, Ken, what happened?"

"Us made it to London and was jest passing through, aiming to fetch up on the Salisbury Road. But seems there had bin a public hanging that very morning and the streets was crowded with folks come out to watch. Soon, in the crush, Jason got a bit ahead of me and suddenly I see'd his horse being stopped by a body of the King's cavalry patrols. They laid rough hands on his bridle, giving out they was arresting him fer carrying papers plotting high treason. Jason argues that him was jest a peaceful merchant, but him knowed they 'ud soon be at his satchel, so him turns around and gives me the sign, then slips it off the other side of his horse, back of a fish stall. With all eyes on the scuffle, I goes up fast and lays holt of that satchel. But next thing, I look up and see Jason being pulled off his horse and hustled down the street like a common cutpurse. I could tell, though, that the patrol had not see'd I was with him, so I was able to follow along at a distance to watch where they took him. I see'd 'em drag him into a prison—Newgate, I was tole by a man standing alongside me on the street. The gates was shut. That was the last I see'd of Jason."

"What did you do?"

"I asked the man next to me—Job was his name—when they 'ud likely let him out. Job on'y shrugged. 'Ain't likely a'tall,' him tells me. 'With the patrol laying hands on him, chances are 'ee 'ull niver see yer friend no more. Chances are him 'ull be dead 'fore nightfall.' That be what Job tole me, Doc."

"But why did the patrol suspect him? Have you any idea?"

"That be what I hung 'round to find out. That be why I did not hie outta the city right off. I had questions. So I takes this man Job to the pothouse and buy him a pint. Him begun talking, with me all ears, and soon one pint becomes two, then more. After a while Job be pretty well fuddled, talking freely of things him should not be telling, things 'ud git him throwed into Newgate hisself jest fer knowing."

John frowned. "What kind of things?"

"Like, folks 'ull not stand fer a king that holds with all this butchery of the rebels. Like, there be a plot afoot in London to put James off the throne and bring over Mary—his daughter that be married to the Dutchman. Seems the King got wind of that plot. Now his spies is watching fer couriers crossing from Holland, seizing their satchels. One courier, Job said, got hisself caught with a satchelful of papers. They took him to Newgate and tortured him till him named all of them that was in the plot—some high-up men, too, dukes and earls, Job said. All was arrested fer high treason and got took to the scaffold. Seems the King be in a panic of fear with so many plots agin him."

"But Jason's satchel, Ken?"

Ken looked sheepish. "I be coming to that, Doc. I had to cast it off."

"To the cavalry patrol?"

"Aye."

"Why? What happened?"

"Doc, it were not me fault. When me talky friend in the pothouse was far gone in drink, I left him hanging over the table and I took off, thinking to git outta London fast. I got out all right, and be riding along the Salisbury Road like one of the Devil's own when, on'y ten miles out, I heard some horsemen coming up behind. Doc, that patrol could on'y have knowed I was taking the Salisbury Road if Jason had tole 'em. That means pore Jason be dead. Pore Jason was tortured beyond what him could bear, else him 'ud niver have tole 'em. Goddamn their souls fer what they done to Jason. Goddamn—"

"The satchel, Ken? What of the satchel?"

"Aye—so I done me best to outride 'em, Doc, but them patrols has fast horses. So when they was closing in, I flung the satchel on the road and kept going at full speed. They followed a ways, firing shots. That be how I got these bullet holes in me. I on'y got away 'cos I took a wild ride over the hills. But I be real sorry 'bout yer papers, Doc. Was they important?"

"Most important. I was hoping they would save a young girl's life."

He rewarded Ken for his services, tended his wounds, and sent him home stretched out in a wagon. Then, his rounds forgotten, he started to walk the streets aimlessly, racked by the knowledge that his efforts to save Jenny Sykes's life had failed. It would be impossible to recover the papers. Yet without them there would be no hope of proving Jenny's baby stillborn.

Suddenly he swore an angry oath. He had to find a way. He *must* find a way.

But how?

The rebel trials were proceeding with such reckless speed that they had become in fact nothing more than a series of judicial murders. The regular jail delivery would commence soon, possibly next week.

Would there be time enough?

Would there be time?

By now he had left the town behind and was walking along the riverbank. He pulled up at a footbridge spanning the river. This had always been a peaceful spot, filled with the reflections of trees and the whisperings of swampy ronds and osier beds. Now its atmosphere was unsettling. Now spikes had been raised the length of the bridge, topped by the tarred heads of rebels set there by order of the King. The tyranny of this Stuart knew no bounds. His new justices of the peace were being established all over the land, men of small repute and still less learning, for James recked little how they discharged their office as long as they were popish. Popish judges, too, were slowly filling the courts, judges chosen in haste, often ignorant of the law, frequently perverting it, so furiously did James drive against the Protestant Church of England.

These days a sense of despair filled the hearts of Englishmen. News of James's latest acts of tyranny was spread only by the slow process of word-of-mouth, for censorship had now become so rigid that no book, pamphlet, or newssheet could be legally printed without a license from the authorities. Brave men still struggled for freedom of the printed word, but as fast as their secret presses were set up in some London garret, they were informed against by the King's spies and savagely dealt with. The effect of Monmouth's rebellion had been to goad James on to fresh tyranny, even to the point of wreaking his vengeance on women. Elizabeth Gaunt of Bayford, whose only crime was the charity of harboring a wounded rebel, was burned at the stake. And Alice Lisle, a woman of seventy years, was sent to the block in Winchester for the same act of compassion. Scores of other women guilty of concealing rebels were hunted down and scourged from market town to market town. In such an atmosphere, unless Henry could offer strong testimony of her innocence, what hope was there for Jenny Sykes at the hands of a Jeffreys court?

Yet perhaps there was a way.

Aye—and Jesus God! Distasteful as it would be, he would take it.

He turned and hurried back to town, moving swiftly through the cobbled streets, too absorbed in his new plan to notice nods and greetings. He headed straight for the shabby part of town, where many a red curtain proclaimed the occupant's unblushing commerce and gutters ran with ordure tossed carelessly from windows. The streets here had long been robbed of their cobbles. Now pigs rooted in the swill, chickens pecked and fluttered underfoot, and draggle-tail women quarreled over eggs laid casually in potholes. John sidestepped the hazards. He paused to ask directions, then halted before the door of a run-down cottage and knocked, waiting while a pair of savage dogs inside threatened to tear him apart if they could break down the boards and get to him.

Presently he heard heavy footfalls approaching. The door swung open and a man stood there, removing the dogs with a large-booted kick that sent them spinning.

He was a burly man, with coarse features and insolent, calculating eyes. His face and arms bore the scars of many a savage brawl, and it was said his fists could crack a man's skull as easily as a walnut. He gave the impression of boldness untinged by fear, yet the pull of local superstition was evidenced by the jointed hare's foot strung on a greasy leather thong around his neck, a symbolic link between himself and the terrifying demon-haunted unseen world.

Now his scarred face expressed surprise to see John Toller standing on his doorstep.

"Bugger me!" he exclaimed. "What we got here? The doc hisself come to call? Him that 'ull not so much as reck'nize me other times.

Well, well, Doc. And what 'ud 'ee want with the likes o' me this fine day?"

"That, Joe Fox, is a matter to be discussed inside."

"Well, whether 'tis or no, I don' care a turd." And Joe Fox went to slam the door.

But John Toller's shoulder was already in place. "It might be worth your while to listen," he said.

Joe Fox's belligerent face reappeared. "Eh? Worth what?"

"Ten golden guineas."

Only by the flicker of an eyelid did Joe Fox show his astonishment at the sum named. He turned and shouted obscenities at the dogs, then he let the door swing open and motioned John to enter.

It was the usual two-room cottage of the working class, but John was instantly struck by its singular cleanliness: the dishes washed and stacked, posnets ranged in sizes on the wall, the scanty furniture dusted. Some potatoes were cooking near the glowing ashes of the open hearth. A pair of partridges were roasting on their long spits, sending out a delectable aroma. They had certainly been poached from some private estate. John discreetly averted his eyes.

The door to the other room was open. He could see the neatly made bed, a child's truckle bed beside it. Some woman's clothing hung on a row of wooden pegs by the window. Beside them hung the clothes of a small girl. It had been more than two years since Joe Fox's wife and child had disappeared. Folks said they were likely buried in the dirt of his floor. Others said they had likely run away. The clothing suggested he was still waiting for them to return.

"Well?"

Joe Fox had lighted a candle. Now he was standing there, glowering at John. The dogs, too, were crouched, watchful, their eyes alert. At a word from their master they would leap at his throat.

John said, "Are you disposed to carry a dispatch to Amsterdam?"

In the flickering candlelight it seemed that every cunning line of Joe Fox's face showed. "Amsterdam?" he repeated. "Folks is a'ready talking of what happ'ed to pore Jason Smith."

"Folks always talk."

"But Amsterdam? That be a dangerous go."

"For some, perhaps."

"Reckon 'ee could git no other courier to make the ride."

"I have not approached another courier."

" 'Ee come to me first?"

"I did."

Joe Fox spat into the glowing coals and stood there watching it sizzle.

"Ain't hard to figger why. Them others is all rabbit-hearted." Then he turned back, a thin, contemptuous smile on his lips. "So 'ee had to come to me, eh, John Toller? 'Ee had to come to Joe Fox! Well, well! Jest to think! Jest to think on that one!"

John held his temper. It had cost him a great deal in humbled pride and the compromising of his ethical principles to come here. If anyone could make the ride within the restricted time, that man was Joe Fox. He was known to be the fastest, most audacious courier in all the southern counties, but he was also known to be unscrupulous and cruel, especially to his mounts. Many a good horse had been pushed till it dropped dead under him. And it was rumored that on such occasions Joe Fox did not hesitate to waylay and murder some other rider to satisfy his pressing need of a mount. Yet for all his crimes, suspected or imagined, he was known to have one single virtue, that of a safe hand.

And for Jenny Sykes, life or death might turn upon the rider's speed and resourcefulness.

Now he said, "Joe Fox, you and I may not like each other, but money sweetens all things."

"Of what use be money if I git meself kill't on some chancy ride?"

"The times are chancy. So what else will you do? Become a farmer? Raise sheep?"

A quick look of revulsion crossed the other's dark features. "Still'n' all, Jason Smith 'ull niver ride agin."

"Jason Smith was careless. He took the London run."

"Eh? And what else 'ee got in mind?"

"That you should make the crossing from one of the Kentish ports. I have no doubt you know them all, Joe Fox. I have no doubt you are a practiced hand at evading patrols, at finding a shipmaster who knows how to wrap the truth in an untruth and turn a blind eye for a price."

Joe Fox's calculating gaze was fixed on John's face, seeking to penetrate the workings of his mind. Amsterdam? Now why was the doc looking to Amsterdam? What business could he have there? He had offered ten golden guineas. That signified. Leastways, it told something. It told that the doc set great store by this ride, so he must stand to gain handsomely. And since his mind seemed bent on it, could he be gulled into a higher price? How much higher would he go? But Joe Fox searched in vain for answers. John Toller's face told him nothing.

"What 'ull I be carrying?" he probed.

"Papers."

"And bringing back?"

"Papers."

"On'y papers?"

"Yes."

"No gold? No jew'lry—or the like?"

"No."

Joe Fox was forced to rearrange his thoughts. Only papers? Nothing of value?

They were starting to haggle now, getting ready to negotiate the final terms. Joe Fox proceeded cautiously.

"But that way, crossing over from Kent—like 'ee want—it 'ud be a long, breakneck ride to Amsterdam. A long, breakneck ride."

John said nothing.

"And dangerous. Bloody dangerous."

Still John said nothing.

"And these days I could 'spect to be halted here and there all the length of the run."

"You are saying you will need bribe money."

"Aye—else be clapped hands on and took in."

"You will have bribe money."

Still Joe Fox pretended indecision. "Bribe money ain't a'ways enough," he said. "Times all's I kin count on to save me scut is me own sharp wits."

John was silent, waiting.

"Pish!" Joe Fox burst out with seeming disgust. "Amsterdam, is't? A bad gamble, make no doubt. A losing throw! And fer on'y ten golden guineas. I dunno. I jest dunno. Risking me life—and fer on'y ten golden guineas."

"And ten more," John said, "if you bring me the papers in less than seven days."

"Seven days? Eh! but that be narrow! That be bloody narrow!"

John turned to go. "I will find another rider," he said.

But abruptly the smoldering animosity evanesced from Joe Fox's manner. "When do 'ee want me to leave?" he asked.

"Within the hour," John said. "I will be back before then to complete our arrangements."

He returned a short while later, dogged by strong misgivings. He was a fool to trust Joe Fox. The man was a known rascal. Could he be trusted to even attempt the ride? Yet for Jenny there was no other way. With a few last instructions he placed the letter and the gold in Joe Fox's hands, then he hurried down to the Mermaid for a quick meal of beef and cabbage. As he was leaving he sighted Joe Fox in the stable-yard, dressed for travel, saddling his horse. Their glances met but, as usual, they appeared not to know each other. But some of John's gloom lifted. At least Joe Fox was on his way.

It was not until the next day that he was able to ride out to St. Mary's Lying-In to see Jenny.

He found her sitting in a chair by the window. She did not hear him enter and remained very still, looking out over the empty yellowing sheepwalks. There was about her an air of such intense private grief that for a moment he hesitated to intrude upon it.

"Jenny?"

She turned quickly. "Oh!" Her cheeks were streaked with tears. She hastily brushed them away and seemed to withdraw into herself. Yet something in her manner told him she was pleased to see him.

He drew up a chair on the opposite side of the window, then he leaned forward and looked searchingly into her face.

It had been two days since he had seen her. It was the first time he had seen her in full daylight. Her hair had been freshly washed and shone like mellow gold in the soft September sunlight. Her skin was delicate and milky smooth. Her eyes were gray, limpid as rainwater, the irises rimmed with black. There was some quality in their quiet, thoughtful depths that always had the power to move him.

He said, "What is it, Jenny? What thoughts were making you sad today?"

"I was only thinking," she said evasively.

"That I know. My question was, what thoughts were making you sad?"

She took her time considering this. In the comparative solitude of her life at the vicarage she was unaccustomed to sharing her thoughts with another human being. Now she seemed to shrink from abandoning a habit forced upon her by need and inured from early childhood. After a moment she turned silently away and looked back over the empty sheepwalks.

He continued to watch her, carefully gauging the direction of her thoughts.

No, it was not for her lover she had just been weeping.

"The baby, Jenny?"

Again she seemed about to leave the question unanswered. But then she turned back to him. "Yes," she said in a low voice.

"Your grief comes sweeping back over you, is that it?"

Again she hesitated, as though finding it hard to speak of her inmost feelings. "It is the question," she said at last.

"The question? The question of why the baby died?"

"Yes."

"You must not grieve over that, Jenny. It was not your fault. You did nothing to cause your baby's death. You did nothing to harm it."

"Then why did it die?"

"I cannot answer that. I do not know why it died. Many babies are stillborn. Their mothers always ask why they died. Most of the time we doctors cannot answer. We simply do not know. But you will find that presently, after a little time has passed, the pain you feel now will begin to recede. Today that may sound like a banality, Jenny, but it is a profound banality."

There was a long silence as she thought about that. Then she shook her head. "What I feel now will never recede. I can never forget. I think I will always see its little face. Always."

He fell silent at that, deeply troubled, feeling himself without any valid words of comfort for Jenny. In his practice he had rarely found it difficult to comfort the mother of a stillborn child, speaking to her of her young husband's love, of hope for the future, of other children yet to come who would fill her life. But now that his whole being strained toward this girl with an ever-deepening, painful, almost piercing love, now that he yearned to comfort and console her, he was restrained by the knowledge that any promise of a bright and fulfilled future would only sound fatuous. He knew that for Jenny there was at present no certainty of hope, no certainty even of a future. Nor could he bring himself to utter false and hollow words to this friendless and hauntingly lovely girl who had come to trust him.

Sensing the reason for his troubled silence, Jenny moved instinctively away from the cause of it. She asked, "Did you always want to be a doctor?"

He was surprised by the question. "It is the one thing my heart was set upon."

"Like Aesculapius."

"So? What do you know of Aesculapius?"

A sad little smile touched her lips at his amazement. She answered:

> "A gentle craftsman who drove pain away
> Soother of cruel pangs, a joy to men,
> Bringing them golden health."

"Your father's library," he said. "I should have known."

"And do you, too, think 'thoughts too great for man'?"

He laughed. "I am afraid not, Jenny. My thoughts are mostly pedestrian. But I can see you have read a great deal."

"All the time—the moment my household duties were done."

He was relieved that their conversation had turned to the commonplace. It gave him an opportunity to learn something about her.

"What kind of duties did you have?"

"I swept the church and got it ready for services. I kept house and washed and cooked. I tried to grow a few flowers once, but my father got angry and made me stay indoors. That left me plenty of time for reading."

"You must have gone to school to learn to read."

"No, I never went to school. My father taught me to read and write when I was little—before things became too difficult between us. He wanted me to make copies of his sermons and look up his quotations. Like many brilliant scholars, he could not read his own writing."

"He actually allowed you to use his library?"

"Not at first. That only came later."

"Then how did you come to read about a mythological figure like Aesculapius?"

"One day I decided to run away. He caught me as I was slipping out of the house."

"Why were you running away?"

She hesitated. "To look for my mother."

"Did you know where to find her?"

"No, but I was only ten at the time. I thought the first person I asked would know where Elizabeth Sykes lived."

"And that was when your father gave you permission to use his library?"

"Yes."

"A bribe, in a sense."

"I never thought of it that way. I only thought of the exciting world of books I could now explore."

"What did you read?"

"Everything—Ovid, Cicero, Virgil, Marlowe, Plautus, Petrarch, Spenser. I have read all my father's books at least twice. My favorites, Shakespeare and Seneca, I have read many times."

"But those were not all in English, surely?"

"My father taught me to read Latin."

"That is most unusual, Jenny."

She looked surprised. "Is it? Why?"

"Because there is strong prejudice against learned females. Most men hold the view that an education tends to make a woman impudent and vain."

She frowned, mystified. "Then girls are never educated?"

"Occasionally—where the father is a scholar. But in general even the daughters of the aristocracy have only a modest education—music, French, dancing, and the homely skills, with an emphasis on needlework and graciousness."

He paused, looking down at her, asking himself again by what combination of related circumstances in the pitiful tangle of human affairs had such a girl as this been brought to the very foot of the gallows.

He said, "And after your father caught you at the front door that day, did you ever try to run away again?"

"As I grew older I knew I had nowhere to run to."

"Have you no relatives?"

"None that my father ever told me about."

"Has your mother never tried to see you?"

She shook her head. "Never. My father told me later that it was no use looking for her. She was dead."

"Did you believe that?"

"No."

"Do you remember her?"

"Yes."

"Did you love her?"

"Yes—very much."

"And your father?"

"I do not really know my father. We are strangers."

"Has he ever been cruel to you?"

"No."

"Did you and he talk easily to one another?"

"We no longer talked at all, except when it was necessary. For the most part we lived at the vicarage in silence."

"You must have found it very lonely."

"You see, I had all those books."

"And now this world outside the vicarage must seem very strange to you."

"I found it terrifying at first, until the day you came down into the dungeon to see me. After that I was not so afraid."

"Why not?"

She looked down at her hands, searching in her quiet, self-communing way to find an answer to his question.

"Perhaps," she said at last, "because your face was strong and kind."

He stared down at her bowed head, touched and surprised.

"I was concerned about you," he said, scarcely able to keep the disturbing protective note out of his voice. "I am still concerned about you. Pollexfen and I will use every legal and medical means in your defense. We are working for your acquittal. I want you to remember that when you are alone, Jenny. Remember it and don't be afraid."

As he rode away he looked thoughtfully out over the undulating country, the stripped fields and isolated hamlets, the lonely farms nestled against the hillsides, the orchards where windfall apples dotted the grass with topaz and ruby. Far in the distance, barely visible between a gap in the hills, rose the gabled roof and tall stone chimneys of Aethelthorpe Manor. What, he wondered, would he find there? He had received a cryptic message that morning from Lady Coningsby asking him to come. "And do not let yourself be turned back at the door."

"Stop dawdling, Iris," he said. "Come on, girl! We have work to do, you and I."

Perhaps, he reflected, his thoughts reverting to Jenny, he was wrong to give her hope. Perhaps there would be no way to save her. Yet how could he let her go on, day after day, sitting alone in black despair, facing the horror of her own thoughts? No matter what the eventual outcome, for the while at least she must be given a glimmer of hope—something to hold to.

Suddenly he frowned. Despite Jenny's willingness today to answer his questions, he had not asked her that one question which, from the day of the inquest, had so puzzled and intrigued him—the identity of her lover. Who was this man who had fathered her child? And under what circumstances? Had Jenny truly loved him? Did she love him still? How had she, isolated by her father at the vicarage, found the opportunity to meet him? And where? Was he a married man who could ill afford the scandal? Or some young member of the county gentry willing enough to seduce an innocent girl, but looking to make a more lucrative match when it came to marriage? Powerful families had powerful influence in the county. By coming forward he might, with the help of a skillful lawyer, have used the one convenient lie to fit the requirements of the law and save Jenny's life. Why, then, had he abandoned her? All these questions had plagued his mind even as he had been talking to her, but he had resisted the temptation to touch upon them. This, he told himself with firm resolve, was one area of Jenny's life into which he had no right to pry.

He was so deep in thought that he seemed to arrive all too soon at Aethelthorpe Manor. As he exited from the tree-lined driveway a groom ran forward and, with his usual greeting, took Iris by the bridle and led her away.

Then something made John turn and look about him. Today a curious stillness hung over Aethelthorpe. Even the rooks seemed to feel the pall. Usually at this hour the great black birds could be seen at their aerial tricks, rising to meet the strong winds from the sea, wheeling and diving and rolling, flying upside down in their stunting, raucous and joyful, their large bodies dark against the sky. But today for some reason the rooks had gone early to roost and now were perched on the uppermost branches of the elms, silent and watchful. The treetops were black with their numbers.

Something swept over John's skin like a chilling draft as he recalled Lady Coningsby's strange warning. "And do not let yourself be turned back at the door."

He swung on his heel and ran up the steps.

A footman appeared in answer to his knock. His bow of recognition was tinged with embarrassment to see John standing there.

"Good day, Doctor," he replied in answer to John's greeting. "I will inform Lord Coningsby of your arrival."

"No need, Bradley. It is Lady Coningsby I was called to see."

Bradley hesitated, looking carefully down at his shoes. "I will inform his lordship of your arrival," he said again. "Please come in, Doctor."

It was only a moment before Bradley returned and led John into the Music Room.

"Doctor Toller, m'lord," the footman announced, then hurriedly withdrew, closing the door after him.

Lord Coningsby was seated at the spinet, playing. He nodded as Bradley made his announcement, but made no move to interrupt his music.

John stood there, waiting. Then, recognizing the intentional affront, his quick temper flared. He turned to go.

At that Lord Coningsby leapt angrily to his feet.

"Sir, you will not leave until I say you may."

"Sir," John answered sharply, "I shall leave when I choose."

"But not until I have told you that your services are no longer required. You are dismissed."

John stared in anger tinged with contempt. He had little admiration for men of this sort. He had never cared for Coningsby in particular. He was a haughty man, with cold eyes and an aristocratic nose. His periwig was extravagantly large, its curls falling well below the shoulder. In dress he was stylish: a cravat of priceless lace, a blue satin coat reaching to his thighs and cut wide to show the long-skirted waistcoat beneath. His yellow breeches were edged with a deep lace frill and rosetted at the knee. His narrow elongated shoes were squared at the toe and buckled. Like many fashionable men, he wore an onyx earring in one ear.

"Coningsby," John said, "I would be remiss in my duty as Lady Coningsby's physician if I were to fail to respond to her summons. I received an urgent message to attend her only this morning."

Lord Coningsby raised his eyebrows. "An urgent message? And who brought this message, may I ask?"

"One of Lady Coningsby's maidservants. She came looking for me at the hospital."

Coningsby's keen eyes seemed suddenly to gather interest. "Which maidservant, sir?"

John demurred. So the maidservant Maggie was mixed up in this. "I do not recall which maidservant, sir. And now, please excuse me."

As he turned away, Lord Coningsby shouted at his back. "Doctor Toller! This is my house—" But John passed, unheeding, out through the Music Room door and shut it behind him.

Bradley was loitering in the entrance hall. As John passed he looked up with a crooked, apologetic smile. But he made no move to halt him or inquire where he was going. Nor did John need to ask direction. He had attended Lady Coningsby before her marriage at her family home of Foxdrift Hall. For the past six months he had attended her here at Aethelthorpe. He took the grand staircase three stairs at a time, then turned down the corridor in the direction of Lady Coningsby's apartments.

He regretted now that he was always so inattentive to county gossip. He knew that Lord Coningsby had been a childless fifty-eight-year-old widower when, last spring, he had married the eighteen-year-old Agatha Hammond. It was said the young bride wept through the ceremony. And little wonder, for Lord Coningsby was an unfeeling, arrogant man. But he was known to be enormously wealthy, and the financial difficulties that had plagued Agatha's father had vanished abruptly after the wedding. Even within the first months of their marriage there had been whisperings of some sort of scandal, but in John's busy life he had little time for flying rumor.

He halted at the door of Lady Coningsby's boudoir and knocked. It was opened by a frightened maidservant.

"How is she, Maggie?"

"Her be bad, Doctor—real bad."

Maggie glanced down the empty corridor before closing the door. Then she led John through the boudoir to Lady Coningsby's bedroom.

John crossed quickly to the bed. Lady Coningsby was in obvious pain, groaning intermittently. Her face was flushed and damp. John looked into her eyes. Then he stripped down the covers and began to examine her. When he reached the swollen abdomen she writhed at his touch.

"Maggie," he asked, "what have you been feeding her ladyship?"

"Whatever her 'ull take, Doctor, and that be gitting less and less—soup, milk, an egg—"

"How do you get her food?"

"It be sent up from the kitchen."

"Who prepares it?"

"Cook do, sir."

"Does her ladyship complain of excessive thirst?"

"Her keeps asking fer water."

"When last did the midwife see her?"

"That 'ud be yisterday, sir."

"Has she been worse since the midwife's visit?"

"Much worse, sir."

"How long has she been pregnant?"

Maggie hesitated. "A few months, sir."

"Who is her midwife?"

"I cain't say no more, sir."

"Why not?"

" 'Coz midwife's bin changed. His lordship chased off the last one and got this new one."

"And you do not know her name?"

"I ain't even see'd her, sir. I be a'ways chased off when midwife's here."

"How long has this been going on?"

"Since the new midwife come. 'Bout a week."

"I see." John turned back to the bed. "Agatha? Can you hear me, Agatha?"

Lady Coningsby opened her eyes. They were dim with pain. Her voice was a whisper. "Ah, Doctor Toller, you came, then . . . you got my message. . . .Help me! Doctor Toller . . . please help me. . . ."

"I want you to answer some questions, Agatha. Now tell me, when did these abdominal pains commence?"

"Oh, . . . days . . . days ago. . . ."

"After you changed your midwife?"

"Yes . . . after the new midwife came. . . ."

"Did you ask to change your midwife?"

"No."

"Do you know of any reason why your husband changed her?"

"No . . . please, Doctor Toller . . . I am frightened. . . ."

"Now, Agatha," John said reassuringly, "something will be done about those abdominal pains, but I want you to follow my instructions closely. I will return in an hour. Until then you are to eat nothing. You are to drink only the water Maggie gives you. Do you understand?" He waited for Lady Coningsby to nod her head, then he turned to Maggie. "Go now and fetch fresh water directly from the well. Bring it back here, then stay with your lady until I return. She is to have no food or drink other than the water you yourself have fetched from the well. Those are strict instructions, Maggie."

Maggie looked even more frightened than she had before.

"But supposing his lordship tells me off?"

"Then explain to him that you are simply obeying my instructions. In any case, I will have a talk with Lord Coningsby on my way out—"

"There will be no need, Doctor Toller. I have already said everything to you that I intend saying."

John swung around. Lord Coningsby had come noiselessly through the boudoir and now stood listening in the doorway.

"But I have not, Coningsby," John replied angrily. "There is something more I have to say—and to save you embarrassment it had best be said in private."

Down in the library, John had to fight to keep his anger under control.

"Coningsby, your wife is being given drugs which are unlawful in England since their sole purpose is to excite the uterus to expel its contents. Apparently Agatha is unaware that she is ingesting abortifacients. But if this is being done on your instructions, and if harm should come to her, or to her unborn child, you will be held personally accountable."

Something dangerous flickered behind Lord Coningsby's eyes. "What the devil do you mean by that?"

"My meaning is very clear. Abortion, whether induced by drugs or by mechanical means, is a crime in England."

"Now you are making bizarre assumptions, sir. My wife is having a hard time carrying her child, that is all."

"That is not all, Coningsby, and I suspect that you are well aware of it. If this continues, she will lose her child. She may even lose her life."

Coningsby appeared startled by that and there was a long pause. Then he said, "You are suggesting that Agatha may die? It is as serious as that?"

"Aye, it is as serious as that."

Lord Coningsby took a slow turn around the library, pausing here and there to touch some exquisite object. When he returned, his momentary irresolution had left him. His customary arrogance had returned. He stood regarding John with a scornful drooping of the eyelids and a shrewd, self-satisfied air.

"If, as you say, my wife's life is in danger," he said, "I had better send for Doctor Booth, who practices up in Sherborne. Only recently he saved the lives of Lady Chatham and her child. There will, of course, be no need for you to trouble yourself further with this case. You have already been dismissed. And one thing more, Doctor Toller. This time you were able to force your way into my house on the excuse that you received a call from my wife. But there will be no more such calls. No maidservant will come to fetch you, so if you try to force your way in again, you will be refused admittance. Good day to you, Doctor."

John was filled with frustrated anger as he mounted Iris and started down the driveway. He glanced up at the elms. The rooks were still behaving strangely, roosting in the topmost branches in large numbers, black, silent, watchful. It was as if they understood that, unknown to the expectant mother, a tiny unborn human creature was slowly being destroyed in there.

He left Iris with the groom at the hospital, then he hurried across the street to the law offices of Pollexfen & Moss.

"Henry," he began, "what is the going gossip on Aethelthorpe?"

"That," Henry answered cautiously, "would depend on what you mean by 'going gossip.' "

"Do not fence, Henry. Tell me why Lord Coningsby, who until his recent marriage was a rich but childless widower, would be procuring the abortion of a child who is his wished-for heir?"

"Have you considered," Henry answered, "that Coningsby might not view this matter in quite that light?"

"What are you telling me?"

"I am telling you nothing. I am asking the question. In any case, what concern is this of yours? Is Agatha Coningsby your patient?"

"She has been my patient since before her marriage."

"And?"

"This afternoon, at her request, I called on her. During the course of that call two things occurred. I discovered that, unknown to Agatha, she is being treated with abortifacients. And Lord Coningsby dismissed me as his wife's physician."

"What else would he do? You are an ethical physician and he is in the process of suborning a crime."

"That part I know."

"Then forget that you know it. An Englishman's house is still his castle—most particularly when his home is Aethelthorpe Manor."

"But why is Coningsby destroying his own child?"

Henry seemed to give this point a moment's thought.

"John, why have you come to me? You know your professional position in this, so it is not legal advice you want."

"I want you to find out the name of Lady Coningsby's new mid-wife."

"Ah! And even if I did, there is nothing you can do about it."

"Maybe there is."

"You mean something foolish, like calling on the woman to threaten her with exposure and jail if she does not immediately cease and desist? Useless! Coningsby would only hire another compliant mid-wife, even if he had to import one from London. Besides, there is another side to the argument."

"What other side?"

"There are those who might argue that Coningsby is well within his rights in this."

"Now what are you talking about?"

Henry leaned back in his chair and leveled his shrewd green eyes on John.

"I sometimes think," he observed, "that you spend entirely too much time in your medical world and not enough time outside it. Though I know you hold it in contempt, there is much to be said for listening to county gossip."

John gave an amused laugh. "Why waste my time, Henry? If it is county gossip I want, I need only come to you."

Henry grinned. "It is my business to know things."

"Then tell me what you know about the Coningsbys that might relate to all of this."

"Such as tidbits of their personal lives? Well, before her marriage Agatha Hammond was in love with young Roger Chaworth. There was no money there, so Agatha was virtually sold to Coningsby. But after her marriage Agatha continued to meet young Chaworth with the connivance of her maid Maggie. One might assume that if this is Chaworth's child, Coningsby knows it. Does that suggest a reason why Coningsby might fail to view this fetus with the doting eyes of a father for his longed-for heir?"

John was silent for a moment. "All your points are well made, Henry. You have an admirably logical head. I am still troubled, though, by the knowledge that if these drugs continue to be administered, Agatha may die."

"That would be unfortunate."

"It is hard for a doctor to just stand by."

"Granted. But do not make the mistake of looking for ways to interfere. You have a tendency to become too passionate in the care of your patients, John, too protective of them. Now that Coningsby has dismissed you, be glad. Responsibility for the state of his wife's health is turning into a risky business. If she should die, the reasons for her death will become the business of the law. You are happily out of it."

John was still frowning as he rose to go.

"I wish I could feel as happily out of it as you suggest, but I do not. Coningsby is a proud and unyielding man." Then, as he reached the door, he turned. "I have a premonition that tragedy lies ahead and that, whether I want it or not, I will somehow be drawn in."

Eleven

It was barely dawn next morning when John was awakened by a vigorous pounding on his cottage door.

"God's belly!" he shouted, "can a man never get a full night's sleep?"

" 'Ee be wanted at the jail, Doc," an apologetic voice called through the cracks. "Seems like so'thing awful has broke out there."

John leapt out of bed. Angrily he threw open his front door and stood there, nightshirted, barefooted.

"Damn it! What the devil do you mean by—Oh, it is you, Benny. Well, what is it?"

"Sorry, Doc, but Mr. Oglethorpe says to tell 'ee there be prisoners awful sick below. Looks like some of 'em be dead, even. 'Ee said to tell 'ee to come quick, please."

A half hour later John burst into Oglethorpe's office. "Now, what is this all about?"

"Dungeon Two," Oglethorpe replied. "Niver see'd nothing like it —not in *my* jail. Musta started days ago."

"Then why was I not called days ago?"

"Thought it 'ud blow over."

"You are a negligent fool, Oglethorpe." A moment later John was racing down the dark stairs to the subterranean world below.

Even before he reached the bottom he recognized the distinctive odor. No other disease smelled quite like it.

Jail fever!

The turnkey was sitting apprehensively on a stool, waiting.

"It be in here, Doc," he said. "Dungeon Two."

He lifted the lantern off the wall and handed it to John, then he unlocked a door strongly clouted with iron and gave it a cautious push, standing aside to let John pass, unwilling to enter the contaminated cell himself. John took a few steps inside the doorway. He was met by a putrid stream of miasma that almost made him retch. He held his breath, then he raised the lantern above his head and looked around.

They lay on every side, men and women sprawled out wherever there was space. Some were already dead, their nostrils crusted with dried blood, sores about their lips, their lolling tongues fissured transversely and coated with brown fur. Others, still alive, breathed stertorously, their muscles twitching. One young man was in convulsions, his cheeks flushed a bright red, blood oozing in thin rivulets from his nose and down his cheeks to the floor. A woman gaped with unseeing eyes at the ceiling. In her delirium she had torn off her rags, exposing a chest and abdomen cropped with rose-colored spots. Now and then she let out a thin wail. Her agony would soon be over. No less than sixty prisoners were crowded together in this small dungeon. And above them all, in a still and noxious cloud, hung the stench of cadaver and vomit and green dejecta.

As John stood there, someone moved. A crazed man, anticipating death, raised himself slowly from the floor and stood a moment swaying on emaciated legs. His long gray hair falling in disorder about him gave him a wild look, but the expression on his pallid face was sad and calm and gentle. His glazing eyes were fixed on John as he started unsteadily toward him, as though in this vision of a man appearing suddenly in the doorway, with a concerned face and the light flowing down on him from above, he perceived his longed-for Saviour.

John spoke to him in quiet tones. "Not just yet, friend. Go back. I will come for you presently."

Then he backed out of the cell and motioned the turnkey to lock the door.

"I had better take a look at Dungeon One," he said.

The turnkey expressed surprise. "There be nothing wrong in there, Doc. I was on'y tole to show 'ee Number Two. Mr. Oglethorpe ain't said nothing 'bout—"

John's face tightened. "I want to see Number One, Leo. Unlock the door, please."

The turnkey hesitated, then shrugged and did as he was told. But this time he stepped inside and held the lantern high.

"There! 'Ee see?"

Unspeakably foul as the cell was, the disease had not yet crossed the passage. John took the lantern from the turnkey's hand and spilled its light around. Here, too, the atmosphere was tainted with the stench of excrement, for the tubs substituting for sewers were emptied only once a week, if the scavengers felt so inclined. Men and women were crammed one upon the other, clothed only in rags, infested with vermin, their skeletal bodies scaly and full of sores, their hungry eyes glittering in the lantern light. One pauper lunatic, who was chained with wrist- and leg-bolts to an iron rod, his neck padlocked to the floor, was screaming in frenzy at the rats that had already disfigured his face and mortifying limbs, but against which his chains made him helpless to defend himself.

John's moving gaze was arrested suddenly. In the far corner a boy of ten squatted against the wall. A look of hope had come into the boy's face on seeing John enter, for he had been a patient at the clinic. But now, as their eyes met, John only stared back at him without apparent recognition. Then his gaze moved on, passing right over the boy as though he were not there, and the boy sank back, despairing, against the wall.

But a moment later John turned to the turnkey. "Leo, go fetch Oglethorpe down here."

Leo stared. "Mr. Oglethorpe, Doc? 'E don' niver come down here."

"Then tell him I said Dungeon Two is a pesthole and the fever will soon spread to Dungeon One. Tell him that if he does not come at once, I will feel free, as jail physician, to loose any healthy prisoners from One out onto the street. Now, go!"

He waited only until Leo's hurrying footsteps had died away above before he beckoned the boy out into the passage.

"Billy," he whispered, "what are you doing here?"

"They put me in, Doc."

"What for?"

"I stoled a pound of bacon, sir."

"Bacon? Why?"

"We was all hungry at home, sir. Pa niver did come back from the fighting. Mam says him prob'ly got hisself kill't."

"Does your mam know you are in here?"

"No, sir. Her prob'ly thinks I be off somewheres."

"How long have you been in here?"

"They brung me in last night."

"Good! Then you are still strong enough to run if you have to. How long are you in for?"

"Till I go to the gallows, sir."

"The gallows! For a pound of bacon?" For a moment he looked thoughtfully down at the boy. Then he glanced around. Some spare sanitation tubs were stacked against the wall. "Billy, I am going to get you out of here. I want you to crouch down behind those tubs and wait. Understand?"

An instant later Leo reappeared. Behind him, slowed by his massive bulk, came Oglethorpe.

The jailer came and stood before John, confronting him so belligerently that the thick black hair on his arms and chest seemed to bristle. His face was flaming with rage and the cords of his throat stood out as if he were being choked with a rope. The stale sweat exuded by his body was offensive even in this tainted atmosphere.

"What the hell do 'ee mean, sending me messages, threatening me—"

John cut him short. "I meant what I said, Oglethorpe. There is an outbreak of jail fever in Two. Most of the prisoners in there are dead or dying. Only a few will survive. Unless you get the prisoners out of One and upstairs where the air is fresh, they are likely to catch it, too."

"Well, I don' give a damn—"

"You had better give a damn, or the turnkeys and scavengers will come down with it. They will spread it outside the jail and we will have an epidemic. You had better waste no time getting all the prisoners from One stripped and washed and transferred. You will need to bring in fresh air by driving a shaft down through the wall from the outside, then have the place cleaned. Once that is done, you can clean any surviving prisoners in the contaminated cell and transfer them over here to One."

Oglethorpe had been staring in utter amazement. His manner was insolent, defiant.

"Well, Doc, 'ee kin jest tend yer sick and leave the prisoners to me. I ain't moving no one. I ain't got scavengers fer all that work. And I ain't got room upstairs for common prisoners who cain't pay their way."

"You have ten private rooms upstairs. Transfer some of the clean prisoners up there. Give the trollops in your cockloft a vacation and use that. This is an emergency, Oglethorpe. You have plenty of space. Use it!"

Oglethorpe gave a laugh that sounded like a short bark. "I run a bus'ness here—a paying bus'ness. I got a paper from the owner. I pay seventeen pounds a year fer this grant."

"You will not have this grant long if an epidemic starts here. If that happens through your negligence, you will find yourself locked up in these dungeons—along with the owner."

Oglethorpe had been watching him with shrewd eyes. Now they suddenly showed a mocking gleam. "They cain't jail the owner, Doc. Him be a high-up churchman."

John's chin came up with a jerk. "A churchman! The owner of this pesthole a churchman? Profiting from human misery? Profiting from a brothel?"

Oglethorpe shrugged. "Lor' Almighty!" The words sounded like a taunt.

"Whoever he is, when news of this pestilence gets out, the frightened citizens of Dorncaster will go screaming to the City Fathers to close down this jail."

Again Oglethorpe shrugged. "Forgit the whole thing, Doc. Worrying 'bout it 'ull do you no good. I ain't the on'y one making money out of this jail."

He turned to go, still smiling his knowing smile, and John found himself suddenly without words.

The City Fathers? No wonder Oglethorpe was able to rule by extortion. No wonder the more comely young women condemned by local courts to transportation overseas were transported upstairs instead. The prison system was one of coercion under pressure of physical pain, of the encouragement of drunkenness and vice to the enrichment of Oglethorpe, the City Fathers, and this "high-up churchman."

And Oglethorpe felt secure. He knew there was no way to fight it.

No way? Well, now . . . John caught up with Oglethorpe midway up the stairs.

"And another thing, Oglethorpe," he said, "that brothel of yours up in the cockloft."

Oglethorpe turned. His eyes sharpened. "What about it?"

"Some of those women. They have venereal disease."

"They have what?"

"The pox."

"That's a lie."

"Your customers will want you to prove that."

"Prove it? Prove so'thing ain't even come up? I 'ud on'y need to prove it if some liar started talk—"

"Exactly!"

Oglethorpe stared hard into John's face. His crafty eyes probed an instant. "This the doc talking?" he asked in seeming disbelief. "And all the time I thought 'ee was an honest man."

"And so I am—occasionally."

"But now it be the thumbscrew? 'Cos that be what I calls it. The thumbscrew."

"Call it what you choose, Oglethorpe, the effect will be the same. When the rumor starts flying that your women are diseased, it will not much matter how it got started. Your brothel will be emptied overnight of paying customers. That means your taproom, too."

Oglethorpe gave a whistle of cynical surprise. "Well, well, I 'ud niver have thought it of 'ee, Doc."

"So long as you understand it, Oglethorpe."

"I do. I do, indeed!" The jailer's suspicions were thoroughly aroused now. "And what, besides? What else 'ee want to cozen me out of?"

"You have heard it all."

"That be all? That be the bargain?" Oglethorpe did not move. He seemed rooted to the stair. He had grown rich by being a shrewd businessman. He knew when to press forward, when to retreat, when the time had come to make terms. But his mind moved slowly, especially when caught off-guard by lack of greed on the part of the opposition. That puzzled and confused him. Now he stood carefully weighing this new development, figuring the cost. The sound of his heavy breathing filled the empty stairway.

At last he shrugged acceptance. "I 'ull cut a shaft, then, in each cell. It cain't be big, mind, but enough to bring in the fresh air 'ee want. I 'ull move the prisoners like 'ee say, but on'y till this thing blows over, quiet-like. Both dungeons 'ull be cleaned. That it?"

John nodded, his mind already grappling with the next problem. He still had to get Billy out of there.

"And one last thing, Oglethorpe." He drew the jailer back in the cell and over to the far wall.

A man hung there, without even a rag to cover his emaciated loins. An iron belt encircled his waist, locked to a rod rooted in the stone wall behind him. On his wrists were iron cuffs attached to chains that held his arms aloft and which in turn were locked to iron rings a foot above his head. Long years of incarceration had armed his fingers with hawk-like talons. Through those years, moved by some deep inner need, he had awed his fellow prisoners with his lonely wolf calls. But he would never howl again. Now his skeletal body hung limp, his chin sunk upon his breast. Flies clustered about his staring eyes and gaping mouth.

"This man," John said, "has been dead at least three days. The body must be removed now—immediately."

Oglethorpe swung on Leo. " 'Ee heard the doc. What be him doing here? A dead man! I want him down at once—now!" He turned to John. "That all, Doc? 'Ee be satisfied now?"

"I am satisfied, Oglethorpe. Thank you."

Oglethorpe nodded curtly and turned and left the cell and John cocked his head and listened, following the jailer's heavy footsteps up the stairs and across the entry to his office. He stepped out into the passage. It was empty. Billy's toes were barely visible as he crouched there, squeezing back as far as possible behind the tubs.

"Get ready, Billy," he whispered.

He returned to the cell and loitered there, watching the turnkey wrestle with the rusty locks and chains. Released at last, the lunatic's body fell to the floor like a sack of bones, and Leo, with a gesture of distaste, picked it up, shouldered it, and started out of the cell. He turned and waited for John to follow him out, then he slammed and locked the clouted door and, with a muttered curse, started up the stairs with his burden.

John followed at his heels, halting in the entry to watch the turnkey exit to the backyard, where the deadhouse was located. He waited till the door to the yard banged shut. He glanced about the empty entry. Only the porter stood guard at the door. He crossed to Oglethorpe's office and peered in. The jailer was sitting at his desk, eating. He returned to the top of the stairs and called softly to Billy.

The porter at the jailhouse door watched John walk toward him. He eyed Billy suspiciously. He was remembering that the doctor had arrived at the jailhouse alone.

"A favor, Jake," John said under his breath. He extended his open hand. On his palm lay a coin. "My young friend here must leave town by noon to visit his uncle in Beaminster. No, I am not asking you to assist his departure, only to take an easy turn down the passage."

Jake's expression was coldly indifferent. He did not even trouble to glance at the coin. "Pish! And what him do? Murder?"

"He is just a boy who stole a pound of bacon. You know him, Jake. He is Billy Davis. His father is missing—unable to help."

The porter turned on John in irritation. "See here, Doc, 'ee kin leave if 'ee want to, but the boy stays. I ain't got orders to pass him. Now, 'ee want me to sound the 'larm?"

"If you wish," John said quietly. "But first, take a look at this."

He raised his hand, forcing Jake's eyes to drop to his palm. Jake looked. His eyes widened and he looked again.

The gold piece gleamed in the lantern light like some princely treasure. Jake gasped. It was more gold than he had seen in his lifetime.

His expression changed. He looked up quickly, straight into John's eyes. "Where be Oglethorpe?"

"In his office—eating his breakfast."

"And Leo?"

"He went out to the deadhouse with a body. He will be gone another few moments."

"And the boy—him 'ull be gitting out of town, 'ee say?"

"Before noon. He will not be around to talk."

The porter's indecision vanished. He snatched the coin from John's hand. Then, without another word, he turned his back and walked away.

It took only a few moments for them to cross the street to the Mermaid, where John arranged with the taverner, Mr. Coots, to bathe, clothe, feed, and hide the boy until a stagecoach arrived to spirit him out of the city under the noses of Kirke's Lambs.

"And me mam?" Billy asked anxiously. "Her 'ull be worrying 'bout me."

"I will drop by and tell her you are safe," John promised. "Here, take this money. It should be enough to get you to your Uncle Stan's. Be a good boy, now. And, Billy, not a word of this to a living soul."

John made a quick visit to the hothouse to bathe away the jail filth. Then he went home to shave and change into his other suit, taking the old one to the hospital to be burned, it now being postulated that infection could be carried on clothing. It was so late that he cut short his morning rounds, visiting only Father Dominic and those other patients who required his continual care. Father Dominic was sinking fast. Strange, that the old man seemed unaware that his dosage was being constantly increased, or that his pain invariably eased after John's visits. But he was still sufficiently alert to look forward to their chats. And young Noah visited him daily, demonstrating his growing skill at "finger talking" and bringing joy into the old man's closing days.

John finally hurried down the stairs to find a groom from Aethelthorpe Manor waiting for him. He listened to the man's message with considerable skepticism.

"Are you sure it was *Lord* Coningsby who sent for me?" he asked.

"His Lordship cum hisself to the stables, sir, an' tole me in his own words."

"Tell me what he said."

"Him says, 'Her ladyship pears to be dying. Go fetch Doctor Toller, an' scramble to it.' "

Still John hesitated. "Are you *sure* that was the message?"

The man gave a vigorous nod. "Ain't no doubt of it a'tall, sir."

"Very well," John said at last. "Ride on ahead and say I will come at once."

His mind was filled with questions as he rode cross-country, urging

Iris up high pathless hills and over boggy grounds, choosing the shortest-possible route to Aethelthorpe. If Agatha died of illegal drugs, he would be required to testify against Coningsby, something, he thought, grinding his teeth, he would do willingly. But that would be too late for Agatha. Her young life would be over. Perhaps, he reflected, suddenly turning his anger on himself, this was one time when he should have disregarded Henry's shrewd advice.

Between the hills he sighted the gabled roof and tall stone chimneys of Aethelthorpe and again he was conscious of a strange foreboding. It was not his custom to indulge in fancies, but this was too compelling to be ignored. As he turned Iris into the long driveway he glanced up at the elms. Those rooks!—they were still there, perched and silent, creating an uneasy stillness.

What waited in that house?

Bradley had been watching for him. He threw open the door even before John knocked.

"Thank God you came, Doctor," he whispered. "Her ladyship—poor thing!" Aloud he said, "His lordship is waiting in the library."

John was expecting Lord Coningsby to offer some apology for his rudeness of the previous day. But, though Coningsby's face appeared strained, he had lost little of his arrogance.

He said, "I want you to take a look at my wife. That terrible woman! She must have been insane. She had been tending Agatha for an hour or so when suddenly she abandoned her and went screaming out of the house."

"What woman? An abortionist?"

Coningsby flinched at the word. "She called herself a midwife, sir. One must accept such terms."

"You fool!" John wheeled and went flying up the stairs to Lady Coningsby's apartments.

A terrified girl opened the door at his knock.

John brushed past her. "Who are you?"

"I be Dora, sir."

"Where is Maggie?"

The girl hesitated, her eyes dropped to the floor. "They say her run off, sir. I don' know—I be on'y—on'y—"

"Well, I am Doctor Toller. Stay with me, Dora. I will need your help."

He crossed quickly to the bed. Lady Coningsby lay on her back, her sleeping robe pushed up to her waist. Her face was gray-white. She appeared to be unconscious. Blood drenched the bed sheet beneath her exposed lower body. The midwife, perhaps because Lord Coningsby had become impatient of the slow-working drugs, had attempted to destroy the unborn child by perforating its skull with sharp instruments but, knowing little of the disposition of the maternal soft parts, had severed tissues indiscriminately. Judging from the hemorrhage he could only guess at the extent of the internal damage. He was suddenly filled with despair. How could he hope to repair such deep lacerations in time to save her life? No wonder the midwife had run screaming from the house. The mother was rapidly bleeding to death and the child, its scalp bearing marks suspiciously like those of attempted embryotomy, lay half-born between its mother's thighs.

He bent anxiously over the bed. "Agatha? Agatha?"

She did not stir. He took her pulse. He listened to her heart. Her breathing was almost imperceptible.

She was slipping away fast.

God damn those abortionists! Somehow he must find a way to stop the hemorrhage.

He turned quickly to Dora. "Go, girl! Run below and fetch hot water. And fetch some older women to assist. Quick, now! Go!"

The girl ran off and John turned to the washbowl and started hurriedly to wash his hands. He was just drying them when Lord Coningsby burst in, pushing the weeping Dora before him.

"I will not have you giving orders in *my* house—to *my* servants," he stormed. "The staff is not to know what is going on up here."

John looked coldly into the dark blazing eyes. "I need women to help me," he said. "Some older women who are experienced in childbirth."

"You have Dora. She must suffice."

John's voice was quiet, but it had a dangerous underlying tautness. "Coningsby, come over here." And when Coningsby approached the bed, John's anger broke in a torrent. "Look at that, you pompous bastard," he said savagely. "See how your wife has been butchered. And on your orders. Your wife is bleeding to death, Coningsby."

Coningsby's unwilling eyes had dropped to the form on the bed and now he stood frozen, staring down in horror. "Oh, my God! My God! I did not mean that. I never gave orders—"

John turned away in disgust. "Oh, stop your blubbering. And get out of here so I can do my work."

He pushed Coningsby roughly aside. The next instant he was running down the corridor to the head of the stairs, shouting loudly for Bradley. "Fetch me some women—the housekeeper—anyone with experience. And hot water. Go on! Do not stand there! Yes, yes, his lordship has changed his mind. Move!"

As he turned back, Lord Coningsby stumbled past him, heading down the stairs. His face was white. He seemed to have shrunk into his skin. He was starting to retch. He pretended not to have heard John's orders or to see Bradley disappearing in the direction of the kitchens to obey them.

Back in the bedroom John moved with all speed.

"Bring those lamps closer, Dora—all of them." He pulled a small table to the bedside and quickly tumbled out forceps, syringes, vaginal specula, compresses, drugs in tiny labeled bottles.

"Hand me these as I call for them."

He bent over the bed and gently drew the child out of its mother, lifted it above the fluid discharges and set it down between its mother's knees. A portion of the membranes covered its face. He quickly removed them and lost a precious instant trying futilely to force the child to breathe. But there was no help for it. The little thing was either dead . . . or it must be left to die, unless one of the women. . . .He sighed unhappily. A physician's first responsibility was to the mother.

He was starting to work when an elderly woman came rushing in. "I be Mrs. Salmon, Doctor—the housekeeper. I 'ull do whatever I kin to help. Janice be jest behind me, bringing the water. Ah! here her be now. Betwixt us, sir, us has eight children—if that be a help."

"A considerable help. Thank you, Mrs. Salmon," John answered, gazing with relief into her kindly face. "Janice, take the child. It is not breathing. Do what you can—clean its mouth, its nostrils. Mrs. Salmon, please stand there on the other side of the bed and hold her legs abducted so that I can try to stop this hemorrhage. Hold tight, now! She is weak—unconscious—but we cannot have an unexpected struggle."

There was no way he could examine the pelvic cavity. The hemorrhage was too severe for that. He started working feverishly, against time, to halt the flow from the internal lacerations, hoping they were not too many, too deep, too vital.

"God damn!" he muttered under his breath. "These ignorant abortionists!"

He inserted the dressings, working with strips of fine white linen, packing deep and firm. He thought suddenly, what had Maggie been talking about? That was no mere embryo of "a few months" he had just taken from its mother. *That* child had reached the eighth month of gestation. Unless the midwife had succeeded in her purpose, the child should be viable.

He called, "Any signs of life yet, Janice?"

"No, sir."

"No mucous matter obstructing the air passages?"

"There be nothing I kin see, sir."

"Try blowing air into its lungs. That has been known to work."

At last the vaginal dressings were in place. He was glad Agatha was still unconscious. So much the better. The pain would come later. But for now she felt nothing.

He glanced down at the gaping perineal tear waiting still to be repaired and saw that the flow of blood was slowing. He was heartened—

Then suddenly he straightened up and stood staring fixedly down into Agatha's face.

She lay serene, her face eased of pain, as pretty and girlish as when he had first seen her. Quickly he bent over her. There was no pulse, no heartbeat, no breathing.

He looked up and met Mrs. Salmon's questioning eyes. "It is no use," he said softly. "She is gone." Then, after a moment, he added, "May I leave her in your care now, Mrs. Salmon?"

He turned, and with a burdening sadness crossed to where Janice sat, the seemingly lifeless newborn across her knees. She had washed it and now was alternately slapping and rubbing it, trying unsuccessfully to rouse it.

"Let me take it," he said.

He carried it over to a table and brushed the ornaments onto the floor, then he started to examine it.

A beautiful child, a boy, the tiny body perfect, the sparse hair fair like its mother's and soft as thistledown. The nails were soft but fully formed, the skin pale as a water lily, a sebaceous deposit beginning to form upon it. What, then? Why was it lifeless? There was no ecchymosis round the neck. He turned quickly to the head. Ah! The abortionist had indeed tried to kill it by perforating the skull while it was still in its mother's uterus. The scalp clearly bore the marks of her cruel implement, but the stabbing blade had glanced off the child and killed the mother instead. The lacerations did not appear to be deep. In the living child they would heal. There was something else, then. . . .

The flattish chest! The unnatural pallor!

A decanter of wine stood upon a table.

"Janice, quick! Some of that wine!"

Janice was shocked. "For the baby, sir?"

"The wine! Quick!"

Carefully he forced a few drops down the baby's throat. After what seemed an endless wait, the baby gave a gasp. A single gasp. It was alive! John's heart turned over. He scarcely dared breathe. Another drop of wine. Another gasp. The baby gave a feeble kick, then let out a faint mewling cry like that of a lost kitten.

John laughed softly.

He slapped the baby's cheek. He forced down another drop of wine. Now the child was responding in anger, opening its tiny mouth to inhale great gulps of air and let them out again in cries of outrage that were growing steadily stronger.

Again John laughed. A strange elation was welling up inside him. All three women had run over and now were standing staring down at the child in astonishment and delight.

Janice crossed herself and invoked the Blessed Virgin.

"Glory be!" Mrs. Salmon murmured. "What a pity his mam cain't see."

The child was crying lustily now, its little chest no longer flattish, but ample and arched, rising and falling as its lungs dilated with each healthy rush of air. Its skin was rapidly losing its unnatural pallor.

For a moment John stood watching it, smiling, so lost in wonder at the power and the anger of this fragile living thing that he was almost insensible to his surroundings. Then he took a fresh towel and wrapped it around the baby and handed it to Mrs. Salmon.

"Take good care of him," he said. "Already the little lad has had to struggle manfully to live. Let us hope it is not a portent. Send at once for a wet-nurse. You know what to do."

As he started down the stairs, he saw through the oriel that the moon had risen. He had been here half the day, then. He was tired. He felt a desperate urge to walk straight out the front door without having to set eyes again upon Coningsby. But he had an obligation to break the news about Agatha. At the foot of the stairs he turned and made his way back to the library.

He found Coningsby sitting by the fire, waiting.

"I am sorry, Coningsby," he said. "There was nothing I could do to save Agatha's life."

Coningsby turned his head and stared. His proud, chiseled face looked almost ashy. "It cannot be true! It is *not* true!"

"Unfortunately, it is quite true," John answered. "Perhaps if you had called me a few hours sooner, I might have stopped the hemorrhage. I do not know. In any case, you had better prepare yourself to face the criminal charge of attempted abortion resulting in a woman's death. I will be making my report in the morning." He paused, carefully choosing his next words. "There is a child upstairs, a newborn infant—a boy—Agatha's son. Legally he is your son, too. He is small and weak, having been forced into this world before his time. But with proper care he will live. In the circumstances, I suggest you would be wise to do right by him, Coningsby."

John had no intention of prolonging this interview beyond its necessary limits. He had said what he had come to say. He turned on his heel and headed for the door. But as he opened it, a faint sound caused him to look back.

Coningsby was slumped in his chair, huddled over, his face in his hands, weeping. "Dear God!" The words came huskily between his sobs. "I did not mean to hurt her . . . I just wanted . . . a child . . . of my own. . . ."

John frowned. He would have felt more comfortable with the man's usual display of arrogance, which excited his detestation, than with this extremity of defenselessness, a proud man broken by grief. Then it came to him, with a degree of astonishment, that Coningsby had actually loved his wife.

Coningsby was weeping for Agatha.

He stood watching the sobbing man, stirred by an unwelcome compassion. Then he came back across the room and placed a comforting hand on his quivering shoulder.

"Pull yourself together, Coningsby," he said, not unkindly. "You are not the only man among us to make a mistake. We all do, you know. We all do." Then, almost reluctantly, he added, "If at any time you should need someone to talk to, send me word. I will come."

He was glad to get out into the fresh night air. The Aethelthorpe groom had taken good care of Iris. She was rested, watered, and fed, and now was in a mood to run. She wanted to be given her head.

He leaned forward and patted her neck. "All right, girl. Let us see how fast you can get us home."

It was a beautiful night, the air so clear that the moonlit fields lay like some housewife's sheets stretched out to be blanched by tomorrow's sun. The lonely farmhouses stood like shadowy shapes rooted in their own stillness. The earth smelled of autumn, the twisted knees and elbows of the apple trees all but bare. How sad the land looked tonight, with the darkness of approaching winter upon it, with the harvest gone and the dead leaves breaking free and flying on the wings of the wind.

Or perhaps the sadness tonight was within himself.

He was suddenly aware of a crushing weariness. He was lonely. He was hungry and wanted his supper. He wanted a warm fire. He wanted to drop onto his bed and sleep until midday tomorrow—

He closed his eyes. He let his head droop, his thoughts drift. . . . Jenny. . . .

Had she noticed, he wondered, that he had not come to visit her today? Had she thought of him at all? Perhaps not. Perhaps her thoughts were only of her lover. Still, he was relieved that there would be no immediate demand to return her to jail. The outbreak of jail fever and the consequent overcrowding would provide a temporary excuse to keep her at Lying-In. For now, at least, she was sheltered and safe, out of that stinking dungeon, out of—

He started with a jolt as Iris halted in front of the cottage and blew softly to let him know she was waiting. He dismounted. Then he opened the door and led her across the threshold.

"It will be the quick curry tonight, my lovely," he apologized. "I promise you more attention in the morning."

They stepped into the interior dimness, for the moon was sliding down the sky behind the cottage. But suddenly Iris checked, then threw up her head and snorted. Her eyes showed white, startled. John put out a hand to steady her and felt the muscles of her neck go tense.

Alert, he glanced around. Off to the left he was vaguely aware of a huge crouching form rising up, a furtive rush of movement. He did not need to see his attacker. His nostrils caught the familiar stench of the unwashed body.

Saul Perkins!

John swung away to avoid the first blow, but it caught him on the side of the head with a force that staggered him. He fell backward against Iris. The mare snorted and shied violently and John went into a stumbling fall, dragging Saul down with him. The next instant Saul had twisted around and lay sprawled across John's body, keeping John rammed against the floor while the blacksmith mustered his appalling animal strength to drive his fists into John's face with brutal, vicious, calculated blows.

But John, whose boyhood experiences had taught him to answer each taunt about his obscure parentage with his fists, had learned a few tricks along the way. He gave Saul a chopping blow to the throat. The blacksmith choked and seemed stunned for a second, one hairy fist clenched and raised, but now forgotten in midair. While Saul collected his wits, John threw him off and with a kicking leap was back on his feet. Saul sprang up at almost the same instant, surprisingly agile for a heavy man, and the two faced each other, fists raised, muscles tense and ready. Then John lunged. His blow glanced off Saul's chin and the two become locked again in a struggle, crashing through the tiny parlor into the bedroom, tumbling over the bed, falling together on the other side, twisting and thrashing on the floor.

The next instant they were up, their arms locked about each other. Saul pulled away, stood for an instant, bull-like, then lashed a kick aimed full at the groin. John had been expecting it. It was Saul's way of fighting. With a twisting movement he took the blow on the inside of his thigh. Saul cursed and came in again, his huge fists dealing their punishing blows till John began to reel. The attack was so savage that there could be no mistaking Saul's deadly purpose. Saul had no intention of letting John live to testify in court as to the cause of Mikey's death.

Somehow they were back in the parlor. For an instant Saul was dimly silhouetted against the night sky in the open doorway, a massive, muscled, wild-haired giant. Then they were under the back window, the moon shining through the glass. John hurled Saul backward, pinning him beneath his own body, driving his clenched fists into Saul's face, pummeling him till he felt the bone in the blacksmith's nose give way and knew it was broken. Saul grunted in pain. His nostrils darkened with a slow trickle of blood and John's hands flew to Saul's throat.

But suddenly Saul, his great muscles straining, threw John aside, twisted quickly out of reach and jumped up, only to stumble over an overturned chair. As he struggled to regain his balance John moved in and hit him with a blow like a sledge hammer. Saul cursed and dropped hard. But as John leapt on him, Saul thrashed over and the next moment he was straddling John's body, clamping one huge, sweaty, splayed hand over John's face, while with the other he took a grip on John's throat.

John struggled, fighting desperately for air. Saul had the advantage now and knew it. The entire weight of his hulking body was holding John trapped and helpless while his strong blacksmith's hands did their work. Saul grinned, triumphant. His eyes narrowed, grew intent, and with a succession of grunting animal noises he continued to tighten his grip, squeezing down harder on John's throat. John tore at the gripping hands. His lungs were bursting. Pain was flooding his body. A great noise roared in his brain. He began to go limp. Thoughts swam unbidden in his head. With crystal clarity he was suddenly and piercingly aware of the sweetness of life in spite of its pain; of Jenny—

Jenny!

His eyes sprang open. The thought of her helplessness without him, her vulnerability roused him to struggle anew and he drove his fists into Saul's face, again . . . again. . . .But his strength was almost gone. Soon he was only clawing futilely at the grinning face, then feebly beating the air. The pain in his lungs was a roaring whirlwind of flame. He knew he was dying. He had so often watched other men die. Now he knew how it was . . . this terrible agony . . . this sense of awareness receding . . . fading into the distance . . . the jagged darkness closing in. . . .

Jenny . . . ah, Jenny. . . .

From somewhere far off he heard Iris give a piercing scream. Saul must have known what was coming, for he let out a cry of horror and broke his stranglehold, raising both hands to ward it off. But there was no way he could save himself from the angry animal. In the dim light John saw the mare's hooves flash and strike, then Saul's hot blood spurted out as the blacksmith fell sideways, a pulpy red mass where his head had been.

John shut his eyes against the nightmarish sight. He gasped for the air that now was flooding his lungs, marveling in a vague and puzzled way that air could be so unearthly sweet. He wanted to lie there forever, breathing, feeling this terrible agony within him drain slowly away. He remembered that only a few moments ago he had been dying. He was not even sure yet that he was still alive. Perhaps, after all, this vast peace he was feeling now was death . . . perhaps he was dead and standing on the distant edges of some far other world. . . .

Then Iris stepped lightly over Saul's body and came and lowered her head and began gently to nuzzle him, her long silky mane brushing his face.

Dorset buzzed with the rumor that John Toller was in love. He had been seen in the tailor shop in South Street, and Mr. Graves, the tailor, when questioned, gave out that the doctor had ordered two new suits to be made up in a hurry. And that, everyone agreed, sounded suspiciously like a man who planned to do some courting.

And the doctor had taken to wearing his Sunday suit on weekdays since, it was rumored, he had actually thrown his old suit into the hospital furnace. The barber reported that the doctor had come in for a haircut and had sat patiently while the work was being done instead of jumping up and rushing off in the middle. And when the haircut was finished, the barber reported, the doctor had taken his time inspecting the result with care, which was not at all like John Toller. So folks began to speculate on who she could be, this woman who had so taken John Toller's fancy that he was giving some thought to his appearance.

The girls of marriageable age were put out by the rumor. If their eyes still lingered on the tall, pensive doctor as he rode by, they now began to find fault, asking why he lived in a humble workman's cottage when everyone knew he had rich patients and could afford a big house. And why did he not buy a large-framed stallion more in keeping with his own size instead of riding that bullheaded, quirky mare? All the same, they began to watch John Toller's comings and goings more closely, reporting to one another what little they gleaned.

John Toller went about his business as usual, unaware of the town's sudden interest in his private life. On the morning following his fight with Saul, he was too immersed in his own thoughts to notice the shocked glances directed at his mauled face as he rode to the hospital. When a pretty woman in a sedan chair, her stylish hat streaming with feathers, leaned from behind the leather curtain to ask what accident had befallen him, he only bowed and rode on, his thoughts reverting instantly to the plight of Cally Perkins and her sickly, scabby brood now that Saul would no longer be there to support them. But perhaps good would come of it. He had just reported Saul's death. Perhaps now, relieved of Saul's threatening presence, Cally could at last be brought to accept help from others, including himself.

On the stairs of the hospital he was met by Andrew Barnes, who halted and stared in amazement.

"Bless me! Look who was out brawling last night. Just look at that black eye. And cuts and bruises everywhere. The staff will not recognize you for our Doctor Toller. They will take you for one of our town rowdies come in to get patched up."

John gave a painful laugh. "And you can do the patching later, Andy. At the moment I am on my way up to see—"

"Oh, yes, they are asking for you in the Men's Ward. It seems Father Dominic is suddenly weaker—"

But John had already anticipated the bad news and was leaping up the stairs three at a time.

As he entered Father Dominic's cubicle the old man lay with closed eyes. His face was deathly white, his lips bloodless, small beads of sweat stood out on his forehead. He did not become aware of John's presence until he felt the fingers on his wrist, taking his pulse.

He opened his eyes. A forced smile twisted his lips. "Ah, it is you, then, my son."

"Yes, Father. How do you feel this morning?"

"Very well, thank you, my son. Very well—"

But John had already seen the white-knuckled hand gripping the crucifix. He had read the pain in the old priest's face. Quickly he mixed a potion, then he raised Father Dominic in his arms and put the cup to his lips.

The old man drank it down like an obedient child. He no longer resisted the daily medication or insisted on being assured it was not a palliative. Perhaps he knew. They never spoke of it. John wiped the priest's mouth and set him back among the pillows, then pretended to busy himself with the now futile examination. But in a little while he saw that the hand loosed its grip on the crucifix. The muscles of the wrinkled face relaxed.

"And you, my son," Father Dominic asked presently. "What have you been doing?"

"The usual, Father—tending my patients. The clinic is always full. So are the wards."

"And your face?"

"That? It is nothing. I was waylaid and suffered a few bruises. In a day or two I will have regained my deceptive air of respectability. But tell me, how is Noah doing with his lessons?"

The old priest did not answer the question. He had been watching John's face, studying it closely. Now he said, with intense concern, "What is it, my son?"

"Father?"

"What is troubling you? These days you are carrying a heavy burden, John. Recently you have changed."

"We all change, Father Dom."

"But this is different. I have seen it. Some new, disturbing element has entered your life."

John gave a short laugh. "You are clairvoyant, Father Dom. I can hide nothing from you."

"Only because I care about your happiness."

John did not answer for a moment. Then he said, trying to make light of it, "Well, you are right. Something new has come into my life."

"A girl, perhaps?"

"Yes."

"And there are problems?"

"Yes."

"She is married?"

"No, Father."

"What, then?"

John hesitated. "I doubt that we can ever marry."

"Does she know you love her?"

"Only if she has guessed."

"Then you have not told her?"

"No."

"And is it not customary, when a young man loves a girl, for him to make known his feelings?"

"Yes."

"Then why do you hold back?"

Again John hesitated. "There are complications, Father."

Father Dominic lay very still, his wise old eyes once more searching John's face. Through the past twenty years the delicate perceptions of the aging priest had enabled him to read on that face the unspoken, tumbling emotions of youth—the grief, the anger, the joy, the sometimes unyielding pride that would admit neither pain nor defeat. The priest had felt privileged to share them all. Now it hurt him to find himself suddenly excluded from this young man's life.

He said with gentle reproach, "Secrets today, John?"

John understood. But he pretended surprise. "Secrets, Father?"

"The reason for those cuts and bruises, that black eye. This girl you love, yet whose name and circumstances you have so carefully withheld."

John was slow to answer. Then he said reluctantly, "Should I tell you, then, that last night the blacksmith waited in the darkness of my cottage to surprise and kill me?"

Father Dominic caught his breath. "Oh, my son! Then you were only trying to spare me."

"And would have succeeded, Father, if you had not been too quick."

"And the girl?"

"There are things there, too, which might only disturb your peace of mind."

The wrinkles in the old man's brow deepened in distress. "Yet I would give much to be able to help you, John." Then, after a moment of thought: "Perhaps we could pray together."

John covered one frail hand with his own strong one.

"Father Dom, you know this religion thing is not for me. But you must be the holiest of men. You must be dearer to God than most of us will ever be. God would listen if you were to pray for us—for her and for me."

"God will listen to your prayers as readily as to mine, John. Why not pray to Him yourself?"

"Because I am a sinner, Father," John said at last. "Because you are closer to God."

But the old priest reached out and stroked John Toller's bent head.

He said tenderly, "I am closer to Eternity, my son. But you are closer to God than you know."

The old man's words stayed with John like a benediction as he moved from bed to bed through the wards. They followed him down the stairs to the clinic.

In the examining room a man lay stretched out on the table. He was slight, wiry, and middle-aged. He ran a small draper's shop on the poor side of town. Now he lay still, in a stupor following an epileptic seizure. Blood mixed with foam was issuing from his mouth and dribbling down his chin. Beside the table, concerned but helpless, stood the two husky sons who had carried him in.

"Again!" John cried angrily, as he set to work to control the bleeding from the bitten tongue. "And where was his wooden block? I have told you boys your father is never to step out onto the street unaccompanied. His convulsions are too severe for him to be left sprawled on the cobbles without someone there to recognize the first signs of a seizure, to clamp that block between his teeth. One of these days he will bite his tongue right off with his gnashing. He has a wife, four strong sons, and three daughters. I want one of you with him at all times. How often must I tell you that?"

The two sons, both in their late teens, looked uncomfortable.

"Him was going but a short way," Edwin muttered. "Who 'ud of thought a fit 'ud cum on him jest a few doors from his own shop?"

"A fit has come on him right in his own bed," John stormed. "And this is not the first time your father has suffered through a seizure alone on the street. He needs someone there at all times to prevent him from fracturing his own bones during these convulsions. Just you boys remember my orders in the future. I do not want them ignored again."

The older son, Davie, was as resentful of John's disapproval as he was of John's angry tone.

"The conjuror over to Waltham said him 'ull cure Pa's fits right off 'stead of him having to come here all time."

John turned on Davie in disgust.

"Yes? And how would he cure him? With superstition? With the blood of a christened cat? With the eyes of a living bird? God's beard! Davie, show some wits. In twenty centuries no cure has been found for epilepsy, and no quack in the world has one. So you boys had better prepare to care for your father as long as he lives. He is a good man. He has a nice little business and has worked hard to support you. So remember! Someone with him every minute of the day and night. Now, it will be a while before his stupor wears off. You boys can carry him into the next room and place him on one of the emergency beds. Stay with him, both of you. I will be in to tell you when you can take him home."

The waiting room was crowded. A case of consumption to be isolated and reported, two cases of whooping cough, a precocious puberty, an aged man bent almost double with rheumatism, a rare case of gargoylism, for which there was neither remedy nor hope.

He found himself hurrying through his cases that morning, suddenly impatient, filled with a disturbing expectancy at the thought of seeing Jenny. Several calls came in, including a pressing one from Dunheved. He sent back word that he would be along later on in the day, then he crossed the street to the Mermaid. A half hour later he was speeding out in the direction of St. Mary's Lying-In.

The door to Jenny's room stood open and he knocked and entered. She was sitting in her chair by the window, sewing. A pile of children's garments lay on the table beside her.

"I see Sister Brigit is keeping you busy," he said.

She turned quickly and he read surprise and delight on her face.

"I was afraid you had given up coming."

"And why would you think a thing like that?"

"You did not come yesterday."

"There was no time, Jenny. It was barely dawn when they called me to the jail. There is an outbreak of fever there. After a stop at the hospital, I had to make an emergency call miles out in the country. It was a complicated case. By the time I turned my mare homeward, the moon was shining." He smiled. "You will agree that Reverend Mother would have disapproved had I set up a banging on the admitting gate at midnight."

He sat down in the chair opposite her and at once her gaze began moving over his battered face in a quiet assessment he had come to expect of her, unhurried, examining each bruise and cut by turn. He waited, amused.

She said, gravely, "He meant to hurt you, then."

John laughed. "Oh, yes. And he did an admirable job, did he not?"

"Why did he do it?"

"He had a grudge."

"What kind of grudge?"

"He had maltreated two of his sons. He was afraid I would testify against him in court."

"And would you?"

"Certainly."

"Then he will try again."

"I doubt it."

She waited for an explanation. When he offered none, she did not persist, but looked down instead and gently touched one of his swollen hands.

"Do they hurt?"

"At least I can still wind a passable bandage. Andy Barnes, our hospital chirurgeon, fixed me up. But now, Jenny, tell me how you are feeling. Less abdominal pain?"

"Much less."

"Is Sister Brigit still giving you your medicine?"

"Yes."

"Are you eating?"

"Sister Brigit is pleased with me." Her rare smile touched her lips. "I think you would be, too."

He reached over and put his fingers on her wrist. Her pulse rate was a little rapid. But then, he reflected, so was his own.

He said, "The fever in the jail means those dungeons had to be emptied. Now work must be done to bring in fresh air, to break through floors and walls and make shafts. All the prisoners had to be transferred, and there'll be considerable overcrowding on the upper floors. That will give us an excuse to keep you here at the convent a while longer. I hope the prospect pleases you?"

Her soft gray eyes were warmly grateful. "How much longer?"

"Perhaps we can stretch it into two weeks. It will depend on the progress of the rebels' trials." He paused thoughtfully. "Are you lonely in here all by yourself?"

"Sometimes."

"You are well enough to be moved, I think. Would you like to be placed in one of the wards with the other women?"

She cried in sudden anguish, "Oh, no! Please! They would ask questions. They would want to know my name—about the baby—what happened—If ever they learned the truth—"

"Hush! Jenny, you will stay here, then. But if you should change your mind, just tell Sister Brigit."

She sighed with relief and took up her sewing again and he watched her, seeing how inexpertly she held the needle and pushed it through the cloth.

He asked, smiling, "Did you never sew before you came here?"

"There was no one to teach me. One day, when I was seven, my father brought home needles and thread from the store and told me to mend. After that I made my own dresses. I used to try very hard, but was never much good at it. Now Sister Brigit is teaching me." She spread out her work and inspected it with frowning dissatisfaction. "Sister Brigit is very kind, very patient, and I do not want to disappoint her, but I still do not think I am much good at it, do you?"

He laughed. "I am no judge of such things, Jenny. One of my neighbors does my mending for me."

She looked up at that. He understood the question that was crossing her mind. He understood, too, that she had too much delicacy to voice it.

"Yes," he said, "I had a wife. But she died."

She thought about that for a moment, her head bent over her work. Then she said softly, "It seems wrong that a man like you should have private sorrow."

"We all have private sorrow, Jenny."

"Yes, but you—I think you probably help others more than you help yourself."

He knew her words were not intended as flattery. Living as she had, she was too unworldly to understand its uses. Besides, it was evident from the manner in which she looked into a person's face and made her candid assessment that there was no artifice in her.

He said, "Jenny, do you remember that I wanted to ask you some important questions?"

"Yes."

"Would you mind if we were to start today?"

"No."

"As I have explained, Attorney Pollexfen will want to talk to you in order to prepare your defense. But first I would like the answers to a few medical questions. Is that all right?"

She laid aside her sewing. "I understand that questions must be asked. I would prefer that they be asked by you."

"Then let us start with the coroner's explanation that the court requires at least one corroborating witness to stillbirth. If you could produce such a witness, Pollexfen would work to get the charges against you dismissed."

"I told the truth in court. I have no witness."

"But what about your father, Jenny? The thing that plagues and puzzles me is that, for a first mother, childbirth is a long and painful process. A woman cries out. The vicarage is a small house. How is it possible that your outcries went unheard by your father during what must have been many hours of labor?"

She said slowly, "My father heard my outcries. But he left the house."

"What do you mean, Jenny?"

She spoke reluctantly, like one unwilling to look back.

"The pains started after breakfast. I climbed the stairs to my room and knelt by my bed, trying to make no sound. But the pains grew worse. Soon, against my will, I was crying out. My father heard. He came halfway up the stairs and stood there, listening. I tried not to scream. I pressed my face into my pillow. But he heard. He left the house. A moment later I heard him playing the organ in the church, blocking out the sounds."

John was staring at her with horrified eyes. "Jenny, surely you are mistaken. Is it not possible he was unaware you were giving birth?"

Slowly she shook her head. "He knew."

"What makes you think he knew?"

"Because an hour later he returned to the house. Again he came and stood halfway up the stairs, listening. Then, when I was writhing on the floor, moaning, he turned and went down to the kitchen. I had never known my father to cook before—he never even entered the kitchen. I had done the cooking since I was eight years old. It was his custom, when the hour for his midday meal drew near, to go to the dining room and take his seat at the table, waiting. But on that particular day he knew I would not be down. He went into the kitchen and I smelled the onions and bacon he was cooking. Later, he saddled his horse and rode away."

"And left you there in the house alone?"

"Yes."

"He knew you were giving birth, yet he did not fetch a midwife?"

"No."

John was silent for a moment, appalled by her chilling revelations. "Then he must have known you were pregnant?"

"He had guessed it weeks before."

"But he never asked about it?"

"No."

"And you told no one—no one at all?"

"I knew no one to tell."

"So you delivered your child in total solitude—alone in the house?"

"Yes."

"Had you ever been present at the birth of another woman's child?'

"No."

"So you had no way of knowing what a newborn looked like—what to expect?"

"No."

"Then how did you know the cord should be cut?"

"As you said in court, country people have opportunities to learn these things. A few winters ago a stray kitten came to my kitchen door. It was just a little thing, starving, and I fed it. I wanted to keep it, but I knew my father would not let me, so I made a warm place for it out in the vegetable shed. I continued to feed it and it stayed. Later, it had kittens of its own. I watched them being born."

"Were there any stillborns among them?"

"I think there was one. The mother carried it away and hid it."

"Now, Jenny, you understand that the fact of your baby being stillborn is a vital point in your defense. We cannot take a chance on being wrong."

"Yes, I understand."

"Would you mind, then, describing how your baby looked—how you knew it was dead?"

The question distressed her. She swallowed hard. "At first I did not know. But in a little while, when it did not breathe, it did not move . . . I began to understand. . . ."

"By what signs did you finally recognize that it was dead?"

Again she struggled for control. "When it was first born, it was warm and limp. But then, I saw its legs and arms were getting stiff . . . and . . . and . . ."

"And that," he suggested gently, "was when you took it out and buried it in Squire Haynes's woods?"

"Yes."

He sat looking down at her, searchingly, troubled by so many still-unanswered questions.

He did not want to ask the next one. He had sworn to himself that he would never ask it. Yet unaccountably, almost harshly, he found himself saying, "And the father of your child?"

Jenny stared up at him, startled, as though he had trespassed on forbidden ground. Until now she had answered his questions with her customary artlessness. But suddenly there was something veiled in her eyes, something defensive in her manner. She looked quickly away, out the window, then down at her hands, twisting them till the fingers showed white. Her silence had an unyielding quality. It was as though a wall of riven rock had fallen between them.

His eyes lingered on her face, looking deeply into it, seeking some clue, but seeing only the soft contours, the shape of her mouth, full and well marked, suggesting strength and passion, yet with sweet, dreaming lines. He loved her almost more than he could bear and was goaded by the thought of this unnamed lover, filled with anger toward him, filled with a savage, grinding jealousy that, although he had abandoned her, although he had left her to face her cruel ordeal alone, she still protected him, still loved him. And he thought sadly, if only we had met at an earlier time, before we both were hurt by life, how different it might have been.

He said quickly, "Forgive me, Jenny. I should not have asked. I will not ask again. Forgive me!" Then, when she remained silent, he added helplessly, "But now I think I have stayed long enough. You must be tired, and I have many miles to ride before nightfall. I have patients to see."

He waited, but still she said nothing. He got to his feet and crossed the room. He had almost reached the door when she said, in a strange, muffled voice, "It is not what you think."

He turned. "No? What is it, then?"

She did not answer. Her hands lay clenched in her lap.

He came back and put his hand under her chin and turned her face up to him, searching it with a close, intent look. He asked very gently, "Were you raped, then?"

For an instant she met his gaze, the gray depths of her eyes so clear he could read in them the pain of the long and lonely struggle he knew was tormenting her. Then, as though some new thought had intruded, they suddenly clouded over, becoming as remote and unfathomable as the waters of twin mountain lakes under a black wind.

He said, "Jenny—Jenny, whatever it is, it makes no difference. I would help you if only you would let me."

She looked down at the floor, but sat tense and silent. It was so quiet in the room he could hear her quickened breathing. He stood a moment gazing down at her bowed head. Then, because there was nothing more to say, he turned and left the room, carrying with him the curious awareness that she had turned, drained and comfortless, to watch his back recede through the open doorway and listen to his footsteps fading down the hall.

As he sped off in the direction of Dunheved, he cursed himself for having so clumsily called back her grief. He had always sensed that there was more to her story than she was willing to tell, things she could not bring herself to confide even to him. Yet he had probed anyway. "It is not what you think," she had said at last in despair.

He swore out loud. "What a fool I was. What a consummate fool!"

And he had done the unforgivable. He had allowed his personal feelings to intrude upon his professional conduct. He had allowed this gnawing jealousy of her lover to infect the delicate relationship a doctor must maintain with his patient. Now by rights he should discharge her. She was well enough for that. Sister Brigit was competent to take over. After that he would be free simply to stay away.

Yet he had just left her feeling alone and frightened. That, too, was unforgivable. He could not abandon her just when she needed him most. From the start she had instinctively turned to him. Now only he could help her through these coming weeks of anguished waiting. She must know he was still there. She must not be left to suffer in lonely uncertainty. She was too young, too tender. And he loved her. He could do nothing to hurt her. He must go on just as before, never allowing her to guess his feelings, keeping tighter control over his turbulent emotions.

His thoughts were interrupted as the towers of Dunheved Castle rose up before him, dwarfing even the lofty elms and oaks of its park. He eyed the great pile with the intensifying sense of desolation and betrayal and loss that these periodic visits invariably aroused, with an almost premonitory awareness that the guarded secrets and painful whispers of the past, until now securely locked away behind those thick stone walls, were being shaped by fate into slowly becoming his own.

As the trees of the park thinned out, he scanned the ancient battlements. Before the moat was filled in, before artillery came into general use in the last century, the castle must indeed have been impregnable. He could still make out a thousand eyes from which to dart the crossbow's bolt, the machicolations for dropping missiles down on the heads of attackers. It was said that in the heart of the four-towered pile was a secret hiding place richly filled with jewels and other treasures, and that directly below it, sunk deep in the earth, was an oubliette into which captured enemies of the proud Tremoignes were lowered to starvation and death by means of a rope. But that was in the long ago. Now Dunheved was silent within and without, a lonely place to which no visitors came, a cold sepulcher to whose fretted face dark lichens clung to suck existence from the stone, from the coigns of whose empty watchtowers, at call of dusk, the great-handed bats swarmed with eerie, piercing cries.

An aged footman opened the portal at his knock.

"Good day, Doctor. His lordship is waiting in the library. Please to follow me, sir."

"No need for you to trouble, Sisley. I know my way."

Passing through the Great Hall, John paused as usual before the portrait of his father. He had only been there a moment when Lord Tremoigne, coming in search of him, drew up beside him and the two stood together, gazing silently up at the strong, remembered face.

"I hope it is not James," John said, turning.

"Unfortunately it is. He must have fallen sick several days ago but, brave lad that he is, he said nothing. Yesterday he would not eat, and when I visited him I saw he had a fever. Today he cannot leave his bed."

"Has anyone else at the castle been sick?"

"The kitchen boy died two days ago of a fever."

"How did they dispose of the body?"

"His mother, a neighborhood farm woman, carted it off last night. I wanted it out of here for fear of contagion."

"I had better go up and see James."

He climbed the tower steps and knocked. There was no reply. He pushed open the heavy oaken door and entered. The stench within the room was overpowering.

"James?" he said softly. "James?"

He crossed to the bed and stood looking down. The leprous youth lay so still he could have been taken for dead except for the throaty gurgle that issued at intervals from his gaping mouth. Sweat glistened around the oozing vesicles of his thickened, grotesque face and on his hairless scalp. His eyes were closed. His head lolled slackly on the stained pillow. Due to the nature of his disease no one could be found to tend him, so he lay filthy and uncaring in his own diarrhetic excrements.

"James?" John said again, louder this time.

Still James did not stir. It was doubtful if he even heard. He was too far gone to be helped, even if a way could be found.

John thought, it is better so. Then he backed away and quietly withdrew, closing the door behind him.

Lord Tremoigne was waiting anxiously at the foot of the stairs.

"Well?"

"I am afraid James has dysentery. It is epidemic at the moment."

Anger flared in Lucas's face. "That damned kitchen boy?" he asked.

"It is possible."

"And James? What now?"

"James is close to death, Lucas. It would be painful to try to revive him, to bring him back to consciousness and suffering. He feels nothing now—no pain, no anguish. Let him go, Lucas."

Lucas's face was shattered with grief. There were tears in his eyes. "So young! Only twenty-five."

"He is still more fortunate than some. At least he had a father who showered love upon him." Then he added gently, "I know, Lucas, you cannot help but grieve for James, but you must regard this as merciful. James was a brave lad, but there is only so much the human spirit can endure."

Lucas had turned his face away, his shoulders heaving. But after a moment he said quietly, "John, will you come and sit with me awhile? I want to talk to you."

In the library Lucas poured two glasses of vintage port, then they sat before the fire, for an autumn chill had crept indoors. John waited, knowing what to expect, comfortable in this atmosphere of rare books and early manuscripts and copies of Dorsetshire genealogies that cast light on the history of the county's most powerful families.

Presently Lucas said, "John, have you given thought to the subject of our little talk? Are you willing to have me clear the way for you to claim these titles and estates at my death?"

John answered with extreme caution. He had indeed considered the matter, but his thoughts had taken a somewhat aberrant turn, a fact he was at present unwilling to have Lucas suspect.

He said, "We would first have to establish that a state of marriage existed between my parents."

"There are ways of doing that."

"I take it, then, you have not yet established that point."

Lucas hesitated an instant too long. "I was intending to instruct my attorneys to do so."

John let the evasion pass. "Tell me about Margaret Bemis. You did know, I believe, that she was your brother's wife?"

"Yes."

"But you said Adam kept his marriage secret. He did not confide the fact of his marriage to you?"

"No."

"And when you heard the rumor that Adam had been secretly married, you did not follow it up to learn the truth of it?"

Lucas's face flushed. "John, I feel as though I am being interrogated."

John gave an apologetic smile. "Forgive me, Lucas. Call it vulgar curiosity. But answer one innocuous question: Why would Margaret Bemis have been considered an unsuitable wife for Adam?"

"My dear John, for one thing they were Catholics. For another, Margaret Bemis did not have a penny to her name."

"And Chérie?"

"Chérie?"

"My mother."

Lucas shifted uneasily. Something furtive crossed his features. "I have told you, I know nothing of Chérie. You will recall, John, it was you first mentioned her name."

"My father never spoke to you of Chérie?"

"Never!"

"And yet you suggested that Chérie and Margaret Bemis might be the same person."

Lucas was starting to sweat. His nostrils dilated as though he needed air. "I was only speculating."

John had been studying Lucas over the rim of his glass, picturing him as he must have looked years ago, slender of form, with a full head of dark hair and a lean face where the jowls now hung. Yes, he thought, with a cruel stab of anguish, he remembered that face. He did not want to remember it, but now he remembered—

He said, in a quiet tone that betrayed none of his sudden perturbation, "Well, Lucas, we will need more than speculation if I am to frustrate the ambitions of your Cousin Sidney and displace him as your heir and eventual successor."

Lucas relaxed before John's sudden mildness. "And you can count on my help, John. It is settled, then. I will instruct my attorneys to start work on the matter immediately."

John took his departure shortly after that. He rode slowly down the drive and turned onto the highway, thinking over his conversation with Lucas. He had been simply lost in abstracted musing as he sat there, studying Lucas over the rim of his glass, picturing him as he must have looked as a young man. But something had happened then that he could not explain.

It had come like the swinging open of a door to reveal scenes long obliterated from his memory. All these years he had forgotten—except for the shapeless black thing ever hovering in the back of his mind. Now that black thing had been prodded back into being by the idle imagining of a young man's face, and with a sense of agonized horror the events of that day twenty-odd years ago all came rushing back: Lucas kneeling in the brook, the water swirling about his knees stained with Adam's blood . . . Lucas bending over the dying Adam, making promises he never meant to keep. . . .Lucas. Even now John felt himself resisting the renewal of memory. But he remembered.

Now he remembered.

And suddenly, almost savagely, he swung Iris off the road and headed down into the Dunheved Forest.

Here the forest was strange to him. He had not roamed this far when he was a child. But after a while he began to recognize certain landmarks: A ravinelike cleft in the side of a hill, a stag-headed oak, an otter's portage, well-patterned from generations of use. Presently he turned into a familiar deer run. It passed through miles of unbroken woodland, bringing him out at a grouping of rocks in whose shadow stood the cabin where he and Chérie had lived their enchanted lives.

He dismounted and approached it on foot. It was in ruins now, its roof fallen in, its shutters hanging on their hinges. The broken door stood ajar. It creaked as he pushed it open. A family of stoats had taken up residence and the brave little mother rushed to protect her young, taking a threatening stance. Birds roosted in the cove roof. Their droppings whitened the rotting furniture. A rusty cook pot hung by the hearth, almost hidden by tall grass tussocks springing from between the cobbles. The door of his own small bedroom hung open. Now a sapling, deep-rooted in the earth beneath the floor, grew out through the roof and seemed to stand marking the passage of the years. Everywhere was the taint of mold, the dank odor of decay. A gust of wind carried through the chinks in the walls, scattering the accumulations of dead brown leaves, sighing as it passed, as though the dim shapes of yesterday were drifting back through these rooms. He could almost feel their presence. He turned quickly and left the cabin, pulling the door shut behind him.

He took Iris by the bridle and led her farther into the depth and mystery of the great woods, among patriarchal oaks of enormous girth, their gnarled limbs thickly hung with ivy and mistletoe and trailing mosses, so tall the sky above was narrowed to bright gaps between the high tops. Even his own footfalls sounded loud in the hushed stillness. Occasionally a squirrel darted across the grass and leapt into a tree, chattering angrily till he had passed. Or a frightened blackbird flew ahead with a shrill alarm cry. Or a deer stopped chewing to watch from behind its maze of cover. But nowhere was there any sign of man—no trail, no footprint. Even the poachers, it seemed, were disinclined to venture into so wild a part of the ancient Dunheved Forest.

The brook.

In the stillness he heard it before he sighted it, gurgling lustily, chafing against the mossy boulders that strewed its channel. From the top of a hillock, he looked down. It was just as he remembered it, except that the old path along the bank had vanished, overgrown now with weeds and stunted bushes. Had he really roamed so far from the cabin on that fateful day? Leaving Iris in the shade of a tree, he moved downhill, halting on the bank, remembering. . . .

They had come riding along the bank by the brook, a party of young men out for a day of stag-hunting, his father in the lead. The child had only just discovered the brook, and he was exploring it, armed with a willow wand for poking around boulders. He looked up when he heard the horsemen and was surprised and happy to see his father. He jumped up and down, shrieking with excitement, waving his willow wand in the air. Then he started running at top speed straight toward the stallion.

His father shouted and waved him away, out of the stallion's path, but the boy only laughed and came on. He was no longer afraid of the great black beast. His father had taught him not to fear it and he had learned his lesson well. Again his father shouted, trying to swerve, struggling fiercely to rein in. But for some reason the stallion had taken fright at the sight of this whooping, streaking object coming straight at him. As the boy drew near, the stallion snorted and half-reared, its ears flat back. His father was still struggling to bring it under control, but suddenly it shied violently sideways, then wheeled, neighed, and went slithering down the bank into the brook, where it stumbled about among the treacherous boulders. In its frantic thrashing of hooves it managed to throw its rider before it lurched on three legs up the far bank where it stood, its flesh quivering, one leg dangling uselessly.

But his father lay motionless on the rocks.

The child stood aghast. His first instinct was to run to his father. But already the huntsmen were dismounting, some of them glancing threateningly in his direction, so he scampered along the bank till he was out of their sight, then zigzagged down to the brook and waded back upstream, waist-high in water.

By the time he came within sight of his father one of the huntsmen was already there, kneeling in the water, bending over him. The boy halted, afraid to approach, so he crouched behind a boulder and peered around it. The man bending over Adam was trying to rouse him. One of the huntsmen on the bank shouted to him, "Lucas, shall we come down?" The man called Lucas waved them away. He said in urgent tones, "Adam! Adam!" Then, when he got no response, he scooped water over Adam's face. Presently Adam opened his eyes. He lay dazed a moment, blood trickling from his mouth.

But it was clear he wanted to speak. He was struggling to tell Lucas something. He raised a hand and took a grip on Lucas's coat, gazing intently up at him. He seemed to be gathering his strength. At last his lips moved, but he spoke so low that only a scattering of words reached the crouching child.

"Take care of Chérie and the boy . . . you know, Coster's cabin . . . Chérie and the boy. . . ." Then his grip on Lucas's coat loosened. His hand fell away. His body went limp.

The huntsmen lined up on the bank watched in numb silence as Lucas bent over and closed Adam's eyes. Then they all raised an angry outcry. "That wild boy did it. The wild boy killed Adam. We all saw him do it. Let us find the wild boy."

The child made himself smaller, trembling like a rabbit, crouching low behind the boulder. He had not meant to do it. He had not meant to kill his father. The awfulness of it was seeping through to him, making him sob, so he stuffed his fist into his mouth so they would not discover his hiding place. But the man called Lucas, who had risen to his feet and now was standing in the middle of the brook, absorbed in thought, suddenly stopped the search, saying the boy must be well away by now. He crossed the brook and put down the injured stallion, then, taking Adam's body, they all mounted up and started in silent procession back the way they had come.

For a long while after they had gone, the child stayed where he was, afraid to come out, crouching there till even the echo of their hoofbeats had faded into the distance. Then he crept out and, sobbing as he went, raced all the way home and burst into the cabin, screaming out to Chérie that he had just killed his father.

The moon was high by the time John found his way back to the highway. He rode home slowly, deep in thought.

So Lucas had known all along about Chérie. Then why did he deny it? What reason could he have had for saying he had never heard her name? What did he have to fear by admitting it? And why was he always evasive when they talked of Adam?

It puzzled John, too, that he himself should have forgotten what happened by the brook. Why had he lived all these years with this sense of cruel betrayal, unable to understand why his father went away one day and never returned, why he had abandoned them? How could he have forgotten that his father was dead? He must have been six years old the day he wandered by the brook, old enough to have remembered that his father died there and how he died and the part he himself had played in his death. He knew that after he and Chérie fled up to the High Moor he used to cry himself to sleep at night, grieving for something half-remembered that was lost. Yet until now he had never remembered the reason for his grief or why he was inconsolable.

Why had he hidden the truth from himself all these years?

A grief too deep to be borne?

Sophocles said, "Not to know is to be happy."

Thirteen

By ten o'clock next morning John was in the coroner's court testifying in the matter of Saul Perkins's death. The hearing was brief. Scores of witnesses had heard Saul's threats and knew Saul's reason for fearing John Toller. The mare's hooves had been examined. The verdict of the coroner's jury was death by misadventure when John Toller's mare killed the intruder in her master's cottage.

Arriving late at the clinic, he tried to focus his attention on his cases. But he was anxious to ride out and mend things with Jenny. By mid-morning his irritability was such that he could stand it no longer, so he sent Mrs. Colley out to tell the rest of the patients that he had to make an emergency call and they should all come back tomorrow.

He was just rushing through the packed waiting room when an anxious little girl, who had been watching for him, darted out from the crowd and placed herself directly in his path. He halted. She said nothing, only tugged vigorously at the corner of his coat. Then she just stood there, looking up into his face with an expression of frightened urgency.

"Why, it is Emmeline," he said. "What is it, child?"

Emmeline did not reply, only tugged again at his coat and John, seeing she had a weighty secret to impart, stooped to listen.

She cupped her hands and whispered excitedly into his ear.

"And how did he get hurt?" John asked in low tones. "On the farm?"

Emmeline silently shook her head.

"Did he get into a brawl?"

Again Emmeline shook her head.

John reflected a moment, then, stooping low, he whispered directly into her ear, "Has your father been away from home lately?"

This time Emmeline gave an emphatic nod.

John smiled reassuringly and, taking a coin from his pocket, pressed it into the child's hand.

"Emmeline, I want you to go next door and get yourself some honey cakes before starting the long walk home." Then, stooping again, he whispered into her ear, "Tell your mother I will be out tonight, after dark."

And Emmeline nodded and scampered away, out through the clinic door and across the courtyard to the bakeshop.

Iris was not in a mood to be hurried and snorted to show her displeasure. But at his nudge she moved obediently into a full gallop. At the convent John ran up the stairs. He met Sister Brigit coming along the corridor. She looked at him in surprise.

"So early today, Doctor?"

Hurriedly he excused himself. "I had an emergency nearby, Sister. I thought I might as well call."

"Well, after you have seen Jenny, would you have time to stop at the nursery? The new baby has a fever. And they keep asking for you downstairs. Some child took a nasty fall. By the way, perhaps you could spare a few moments to have a quiet talk with Jenny. Something is wrong, but she will not say what it is. I declare, Doctor, you seem to be the only one who can bring her out of herself."

He halted as he reached Jenny's door and looked in through the open doorway. She was sitting in her chair by the window, engaged in pairing children's socks from a basket at her feet. He knocked and entered. She looked up quickly and he saw that her lashes were wet.

"Good day, Jenny," he said.

"Good day." Her voice was inexpressive, listless.

He sat down opposite her, searching her face with the long, loving look he was not quite able to conceal.

He said gently, "What is it, Jenny? The baby again?"

She bent her head over her work, but did not answer.

He thought about it for a moment. "Would you like me to ask Sister Brigit to let you sit in the nursery with the babies when the mothers are not there?"

Still she said nothing.

"Jenny, mothers who lose their babies generally feel great pain. But in time, little by little, you will suffer less. You *must* believe me, Jenny."

She seemed to be sunk in her own thoughts. But then she said, "It is not only that."

"No? What is it, then?"

He waited, but she only bent her head lower over her work.

At last he said, "I have been thinking about you, wondering if you are all right."

She spoke without looking up. "Sister Brigit is pleased with me."

"That is not what I meant, Jenny. Yesterday, when I left, you were unhappy. It was my fault and I am sorry—very sorry. I should not have asked you that question. It was an intrusion. I would never hurt you intentionally. Do you believe that?"

She said nothing, only nodded her head.

"I will not be questioning you again. I think we covered all the necessary medical points. There will, of course, be legal questions, but Pollexfen will be out to see you about those—nothing of a personal nature, only facts he will be needing for the trial."

Again she nodded. Her hands seemed to fly at their work.

"You can have confidence in Pollexfen. He did the legal work to get you transferred. And although you probably were not aware of it at the time, it was he who brought you here to the convent."

They sat for a while in silence. He gazed down at her bowed head, his face strained and anxious.

He said softly, "Jenny, do not be angry with me."

She looked up quickly at that. "Oh, I am not. I thought *you* were angry with me."

"I could never be angry with you, Jenny."

She gazed at him long and thoughtfully. "No?"

"Was that why you have been crying?"

"Yes."

He reached over and put his hands on hers.

"Jenny, I am not asking you to explain what went before, or what may come after. I only ask that just for now, while you are alone and your world is dark, you will let me be your friend. Jenny, will you do that? Will you let me be your friend?"

She seemed vaguely perplexed. "But why?"

"Because I want to. Jenny, will you let me?"

There was a long pause. Then slowly she nodded.

"And there will be no more doubts of any kind, no more tears?"

"No."

"I have your promise on that?"

"Yes."

He smiled. "Thank you, Jenny."

She smiled back at him, her slow smile that seemed to illuminate her face from within, the smile that lingered in the currents of his mind even after he had left her presence. Again he felt drawn by the strange, warm beauty of her. Her hair was still in long pigtails—like the ripe wheat, he reflected fancifully, that he had once harvested in Farmer Scopes's grainfield—their ends tied with two odd ribbons, one red and one green.

He said, making an effort to lighten his tone, "Do they have no matching ribbons in this convent?"

She was still smiling. "Sister Brigit had a hard time even finding these."

"Well, matching or not, they look very pretty. Have you been walking about your room?"

"Sister Brigit insists on it."

"Perhaps you have wondered why we do not let you go outdoors, but we are under certain restrictions. We have been ordered to return you to jail just as soon as you are strong enough to stand on your feet."

She said, amused, "I think you know I can already stand on my feet."

"But neither Pollexfen nor I have seen it, so we cannot report it. And with this fever sweeping the jailhouse, no one is counting prisoners. We are hoping it will be a long time before they start. Meanwhile, of course, you are required to remain indoors. I am sorry."

"I do not mind, really. I was never allowed out at the vicarage. Still, I sometimes look out at those strange grassy circles and wish I were free to explore them and find out what they are."

He leaned forward, following the direction of her glance.

"Those? Those are the Cleybury Rings, an amphitheater built by the Romans. What you see as grassy circles are actually seats cut in the chalk for spectators."

"But why is the place always deserted?"

"The local people have their own superstitions, Jenny. They have a predisposition to the arcane and the mysterious and are apt to see things beyond what they see with their eyes. They are largely unschooled, these country folk, yet they can describe the gladiatorial combats with uncanny accuracy, and there is little doubt that there are things they have seen in the Cleybury Rings which they have come to fear—the misty shapes of gladiators fighting to the death, man against wild beast, the excitement of the blood-greedy mob. Down in the arena you can still see remnants of the holding cells cut in the chalk. Those for the gladiators are smaller, since the wild beasts were expected to survive, the gladiators were not."

"Have you ever been there?"

John laughed. "I hid there once when I was a boy and got into trouble at school. I did not want to get caned. I felt I had done nothing to deserve it."

"And did you—get caned, I mean?"

"I did. Doctor Toller came looking for me. He always seemed to know where to find me."

"Did he have to drag you back?"

"No, indeed! Doctor Toller would never have so humiliated me. He simply said, 'John, you go back there and get yourself caned like a man.' "

"Did you?"

"I like to think I did. At least, Doctor Toller said I did."

"Why do you keep calling him 'Doctor Toller'?"

"Because that is what he was to me. He was not my father. He found me when I was little, freezing and starving under a bush one cold autumn night. He took me home and fed me. After that I just went on living with him. He was a widower, with no children of his own. I had no name of my own, so he gave me his, John Toller."

"How fortunate for you both. Is he still alive?"

"He died when I was thirteen."

"Did you never learn your real name?"

"I may be close to learning it now."

"When you do, will you want to use it?"

" 'Want'? Yes, because I remember my parents. But I doubt that I ever shall."

"Why not?"

"There might be obstacles. It might be difficult to use my own name and continue being a doctor."

"And you told me once that being a doctor was the single thing your heart was set upon."

"You remember that, do you?"

"I think I remember everything you ever said to me."

He laughed. "That is a great deal of remembering, Jenny. I talk a lot."

"I know," she said, smiling.

A long stillness hung like a spell upon the air. He found himself searching for words to restore the conversation to the commonplace, but was distracted by the way she was looking up at him, amused by his self-perception, smiling still, her lips slightly parted. The morning light flooded down upon her and it seemed to him, at that moment, that the pure beauty of her face was like something Greek strayed out of time and place, and he had the urge, the overmastering desire, to lean forward and take that face between his hands and kiss those parted lips. The thought made his pulses throb. He sat tense, gazing down at her, scarcely breathing, waging a fierce battle with his emotions.

Then hurriedly he rose to his feet.

"Jenny," he said, surprised by the slight tremor in his voice, "you are getting me into bad habits, sitting here talking when I have patients waiting."

"You usually come in the afternoon. Will you be back later?"

"I doubt there will be time. I have already neglected my morning work. This afternoon I will be making calls all over Dorset and probably will not get home till midnight. I will try to come tomorrow, though."

As he rode away he looked out over the autumn countryside. Summer died differently on the hills than in the hollows, in some places flushed gold and scarlet, in others already brown and withered. A mood of change was in the air. The martins were flocking, readying to fly south. A blackbird was perched in the eaves of an oak, singing his quiet autumnal subsong, not the song of passionate precipitancy he let forth into the mounting light of February, but a song touched with pensiveness, the song he sang only to himself with the fall of the leaf, when the days of mating and nesting were over. John recognized the song. He slowed down and listened as he passed.

He was glad he had mended things with Jenny. She was so alone, so friendless. As Sister Brigit had said, he seemed to be the only one who could rouse her from her own painful thoughts. He had believed in her and had given her hope. Now it was natural that she looked to him. He must never again hurt her, must never again cause her to weep by allowing his own frustrated love to influence his response to her needs. But nor must he ever allow himself to forget that she loved another man, that she had borne this man's child, that even in the face of this man's cowardly desertion she still clung to him, still refused to betray him by revealing his name. All of that he must remember and, remembering it, must still remain her friend, must still—rightly or wrongly—continue to give her hope. Without hope, these dragging days of waiting would be a torment of black despair.

He had reached the crossroads. But here, unaccountably, he drew rein. His next patient lived at Puddle Minster. The road lay straight ahead. Yet, instead of following it, something stopped him, a dark presentiment. Impulsively he turned the mare's head and headed back to the hospital.

In the courtyard he threw the reins to the groom and ran up the steps. Andrew Barnes was passing through the lobby.

"Oh, John," Andy said, "I'm glad you came. I think Father Dominic—"

But John was already taking the stairs three at a time.

He entered the cubicle noiselessly. Father Dom lay as though asleep. His breath was coming in harsh gasps.

"Father Dom?"

The aged priest heard the whispered words and opened his pain-dulled eyes. But at the sight of John the reflection of a smile gathered about his lips.

"Ah, my son," he whispered, "I was hoping—and you came—"

"Yes, Father Dom. I came."

John dropped to his knees beside the bed. There was no time now for a potion. A gray death pallor was on the wrinkled face. The eyes had the faraway look he had so often seen in the eyes of the dying. He bent his head to cover his rush of anguish.

But there was little he had ever been able to hide from Father Dom. The old priest reached out and took his hand.

"No, my son," he said gently, "no need for that. We both know it is time. Besides, there are things I have wanted to say to you. Will you listen?"

John forced himself to raise his head. "I will listen, Father."

For a long, thoughtful moment Father Dominic gazed up into John's face.

"My son," he said at last, "I know you well. It has always been your way to judge yourself too harshly. But you should know by now that a man cannot be other than himself. You must not grieve that you seem to have lost touch with God. He understands the rebellious heart. He will forgive. He will still be with you in all the things that you do. Nor must you grieve for what you see as your own failings. For if you have sinned, that, too, He will forgive. He will have compassion, seeing the compassion you have for others. Above all, be at peace within your troubled heart. Somehow you must find peace, John—my dear, dear John—"

The voice ended in a little sigh. The aged priest lay quite still, one wrinkled hand still clasping John's.

John did not move, only continued to kneel there, gazing down into the loved face, remembering all those times when, as a boy, he had sought Father Dom's company because he was too proud to tell anyone of his private griefs. But with Father Dom there was never any need to talk. Father Dom seemed to understand. Father Dom asked no questions, just offered what quiet companionship a boy seemed to need.

A soft footstep broke in upon John's thoughts, and Andrew Barnes drew up beside him. For a moment the young chirurgeon stood looking down at the bed. Then, without a word, he did what he knew John could not bring himself to do. He bent down and closed the old priest's eyes.

"Strange," he murmured, "you never come to the hospital at this hour. What made you come today?" Then, when he got no reply, he asked gently, "Would you like me to do what is needed now, John?"

John gave a grateful nod. Then, without a word, he left the cubicle.

He started again on his rounds, out of habit, riding from one village or town to the next in his accustomed way. But his distracted thoughts lay elsewhere, sometimes with Father Dom and the years long past, sometimes with Jenny and the troubled years ahead.

He had just left Wotton when suddenly his eyes focused on a ramshackle farmhouse just off the road. Above the door was nailed a freshly cut ash-branch. Every Dorsetman was familiar with the branch and its meaning.

He slowed Iris to a walk.

He knew the farmer. He was young Ken Walsh, married within the past year and struggling energetically to make his small farm pay. But something was clearly wrong. The cows were crowding the gate, still waiting to be milked. The hens were still cooped. And the ash-branch? It was certainly freshly cut. Shrew-ash was believed by the superstitious local folk to have curative powers in cases of "bewitched" infants. Had Ken's expectant wife delivered, then? The infant must be ailing if it needed the ash tree's supposed curative powers.

He moved Iris over to the gate and nudged it open, then rode up the crooked path leading to the farmhouse.

Dismounting, he knocked on the door. After a moment it was opened by a disheveled, worried young man with sleepless eyes.

"Ken, I was passing and saw the ash-branch. Meg has delivered, then?"

"Ah, Doctor John—no, not yit. The babe don' want to git borned, and soon 'twill be too late fer me Meg. Her be in a awful way, Meg be —so weak at times I think her be going from me."

Ken had motioned with his hand and now John entered the small kitchen.

"How long has Meg been in labor?" he asked.

"The babe started to come three days ago and it ain't come yit."

"Is a midwife tending her?"

"Since day before yisterday. 'Ee knows her. Her be a good woman —Fanny Carver."

"The best hereabouts. Would she mind if I took a look at Meg?"

It was a small bedroom, bare-floored and stuffy, furnished only with a few pieces of crude furniture. Meg lay in a wide homemade bed, moaning feebly. A gray-haired woman was bending over her, sponging her forehead with cool water, speaking in soft, encouraging tones.

John knew Fanny Carver well. For thirty years she had delivered the farmers' wives hereabouts. In an age when many an expectant mother went to her grave with her unborn infant still inside her, Fanny showed a rare skill at her calling. Nor, in her gentle hands, were infants indiscriminately mutilated in a difficult birth.

She looked around as John entered and her worried expression turned to one of intense relief.

"Doctor John!" she exclaimed. "Glory be! The Lord Hisself must have sent 'ee. And none too soon. Her be bad, pore Meg. I don' know— this babe jest ain't coming—"

She broke off helplessly and moved aside to allow John to approach the bed.

Meg was bathed in sweat. Her eyes were closed. He shook her and spoke to her gently. She opened eyes that were pools of pain, but she seemed neither to see nor hear him. He took her pulse and listened to her heart. Protracted labor had exhausted her. Her moans were sinking to frail whispers as the last of her strength slowly drained away.

He pushed back the covers and began his examination, using the tips of his fingers to estimate the size of the uterus, the position of the fetus. The tiny creature appeared to be in poor condition. He suspected obstruction of the birth passages. Or possibly disproportion of the fetal head to the maternal pelvis. In any case, there seemed to be small chance of a normal delivery through the natural passages. The unborn infant was weakening. Its brief existence would shortly end, along with that of its mother.

But there was time. This mother he would not lose.

He straightened up quickly and turned. "Fanny, I will be needing your help. How brave are you?"

Fanny's eyes met his without wincing. She was Dorsetshire-born and bred. Her strong face put him in mind of Molly Grimage.

"As brave as 'ee be needing, Doctor John."

"You understand, this will be something new to you. I will have to take the child by cutting through the walls of the abdomen. Are you still willing to help?"

A look of alarm had crossed Fanny's face, but she stood her ground. "No matter, Doctor John. Jest 'ee tell me. I 'ull do it."

"Hurry then. Get hot water. We will start by washing our hands."

He roused Meg sufficiently to administer a potion containing wine of opium, gently overcoming her feeble efforts to push the cup aside. He pulled up a table and laid out his instruments, then he began carefully washing her abdomen.

"Now, Fanny, stand ready."

He began his incisions, cutting through the various layers, one by one, instructing Fanny how to assist, what instruments to pass, when to mop the welling pools of crimson. He worked more slowly as he started the uterine incision, lightening the pressure now to avoid injury to the fetus. Soon he had reached the membranes and was able to rupture them with a few sweeps of his hand to expose the crouched child. At the sight of it a gasp escaped from Fanny. He glanced up. Her face had blanched. She was staring down, her stomach heaving, into the gaping aperture.

He asked quickly, "Can you go on, Fanny?"

She took a deep breath. Her frightened eyes met his. She whispered, "But what 'ull pore Ken do, sir? Him 'ull take it hard to lose her. Him loved that girl so'thing sizable."

"We are not going to lose her, Fanny," John said. "Now, mop, please."

Soon he was able to insert his entire hand into the uterus and seize the infant by the feet. He drew it out slowly, slipping his free hand beneath it to support the large head, which lolled with a seeming lifelessness from the thin neck, fragile, inert.

A moment later, roused by human hands from its lethargy, the infant gave a surprised gasp, followed by a cry, not a robust cry, but with enough spirit to show it was healthy. John and Fanny exchanged quick glances and smiled at one another, then Fanny fetched the swaddle clouts and held them while John laid the newborn safe and warm within its folds.

He said, "Put him in the crib and come back to me, Fanny," and instantly returned his attention to the mother.

He cleansed the abdominal cavity, then began his closing, passing his sutures, drawing them tight, one after another, while Fanny threaded the needles with trembling hands and passed them to him. When the closing was done, he covered the entire area with clean linen, then bandaged it by passing wide strips across the abdomen in crisscross fashion to hold the dressing firmly in place.

At last he stood by the bed. His work was done. Fanny would tend the child. Meg, in her weakened condition, would continue awhile under the influence of the opiate. He could safely leave her. Yet still he did not stir. She had come so close to death. Now something inside him made him want to stand there and just watch her breathe.

After a while he said, "Thank you, Fanny. You are one of the best assistants I have ever had. I will be back to see them tomorrow." Then he turned and left the room.

He found Ken waiting by the empty fireplace, too full of anxiety to have remembered to tend it. The unbearable strain showed on his face. He caught his breath as John appeared, but could not bring himself to ask the question.

"They are both all right, Ken," John assured him. "Meg will need some time to recover, but she is all right. And it is a boy, a healthy boy."

Ken seemed not to have heard this last. His thoughts were only of his young wife. "Meg?" he asked wonderingly. "Her 'ull live? Meg 'ull live?"

"I certainly expect her to. She will have pain when she wakes up. But she will live. I have left some medication with Fanny."

Ken could only stare as the meaning of John's words began to seep through his numbness. Then, with a moan, he sank to his knees, his face buried in his hands. "Thank God!" he sobbed. "Thank God! Oh, thank God . . . thank God! . . ."

John waited, letting the minutes pass. Then he went and tapped Ken on the shoulder.

"There now, my friend, you had better go out and milk those cows. They have already waited overlong. And the chickens, too. Fanny must be hungry. I am sure she would like a fresh egg for supper. So hurry, now! Get your tasks done. You can talk to Meg tomorrow after I have seen her. I will try to come early."

It was dusk by the time he rode away. The moon was rising over the nearby hills. It silvered the sea and the veils of silent, creeping mist that hung over the fields. He looked about him and felt the exhilaration that always swept over him when things went right and lives were saved. This time he could scarcely bear the miracle of it.

He gave a fierce sigh of pure happiness.

When he reached the crossroads he drew rein and looked south toward Dorncaster. The moon was gone now, hidden behind swirls of mist drifting in from the sea. The landscape was disappearing in blurry shapes of gray. The sheep were huddled under the hedgerows and the missel thrush was without an evening orison. Even the mist-wraiths, drifting by on silent feet, were poor company tonight. He thought of his empty cottage. He thought of his cold hearth.

Quickly he turned away and headed north for Wynford Eagle.

He was just below Yeggor Dun when Iris flung up her head and looked toward the hill, nervously pricking her ears. The hill's great bulk rose black against the sky, its summit wreathed in mist. John gazed thoughtfully up at it, waiting to know the cause of Iris's alarm. It was said that myths were rooted in dim folk memories of true events. Perhaps. Certainly the belief persisted that Yeggor Dun had once been a vast tribal acropolis, remote and half-fabulous, until it was crushed under the Roman Eagle. The Romans had been gone now these many centuries, but the old pre-Roman gods endured. The pre-Roman gods still were powerful on Yeggor Dun, and the countryfolk believed the shades of their ancestors, slaughtered by Vespasian, still lingered on the hilltop battleground that held their bones.

Even the Church had failed to break the awesome power of the elder gods, or stop the faithful from climbing to that haunted, blood-stained fastness. The countryfolk were taking no risks. They had a lively dread of the ancient gods, and were in no mind to offend them. Now it was being rumored that Sam Quigley, over to Hexham, had restored his lost virility by waylaying a red-haired vagrant and sacrificing the man's male member to the phallic god here on Yeggor Dun. Such rumors were nothing new. Often, if a red-haired vagrant could not be found, a red-haired puppy served. That such traditions survived was borne out by the fact that a red litter fetched an extravagantly high price in these parts.

Iris was still watching the hill, only now he could feel small nervous tremors running under her skin. Something lingered on that height. The air was thick with it, something freakish, something alien. He reined in and sat, staring fixedly up at the mist-wreathed hilltop, his eyes straining. Then he heard it, a faint crashing sound, followed by what sounded like a sob. After a moment it came again, a crash, followed by a sob that he was now sure was human. Someone was being hurt up there, perhaps being battered to death.

He flung himself off his mare and started running uphill.

When he reached the summit he halted and looked about. The mist was thick up here, hugging the ground, shrouding everything more than four yards off. Presently he made out the slope of the hill fort's turfed wall, worn down now by time and weather. Swiftly he scaled it and leapt down into the vast open space of the inner enclosure.

Here he stood, listening. The unnatural quiet of the hilltop made the sounds seem very near. They came from somewhere off to the left and he ran in that direction, his feet swishing through the crisp heath bells. Presently, black against the sky, he made out the huge bulk of the phallic god, his head thrown back, his cheeks bulging grotesquely with his lascivious grin. The sounds were coming from directly below the idol and here he glimpsed the dim outlines of a man hacking at something in a torrent of rage, bending over, straightening up, bringing all his passion to his savage task, sobbing with every blow. And, etched darkly each time he raised it, the shape of an ax.

"Stop!" John cried, as he ran toward him. "Stop that!"

The man was startled. He straightened up and turned, presenting a tall but indistinct silhouette. Only the pale sphere of his face showed in the mist. He seemed to hesitate. His ax was raised, but he did not swing it. He threw a quick glance into the surrounding dimness as if to make sure John was alone. Then he whirled and, moving with lightning speed, darted off in the opposite direction.

John hurled himself across the narrow space and caught the man from behind and for an instant they were locked together in a scramble of heaving, straining bodies, staggering back and forth over the rugged ground. There had been something vaguely familiar about the man's silhouette, and now John was anxious to glimpse his face. The man was equally anxious not to be recognized. He was strong and wiry, and suddenly, with astonishing speed, he twisted and almost wrenched himself free. John still managed to grasp a handhold on his jacket. He felt the rough surface of wool cloth between his hands, then the man lurched sideways and broke John's grip. The next instant the man had whirled around, his breath rasping hard in his throat, and with a flurry of thudding feet had vanished into the mist.

John made no attempt to follow him. His first thought was for the man's victim, but a search revealed no sign of a body. Then he noticed that the heather about the idol's feet was white with stone dust and chips and, looking higher, he saw with amazement that the victim had been the idol itself. Its penis had been chopped away and only stumps remained of the rest of its exaggerated masculinity. Now the ancient phallic god was a mutilated thing, deprived of its symbolism, unmanned, sexless. Henceforth this dishonored god would wait in vain for offerings formerly due him. Something of his new presence, resentful and unforgiving, could almost be felt on the wet air.

John stood there, wondering why a man would commit such a senseless act of vandalism. What freakish compulsions, what dark sexual urges could have driven him to such a frenzy against a block of stone? Then his eyes fell on something glinting among the stone chips at the god's feet. He stooped and picked it up. It was a key, very large and ornamental, so beautifully wrought that he guessed it must belong to the lock of a door to some castle or manor house. The vandal, then, was not some simple countryman. He was someone of consequence in the neighborhood. He would soon discover his loss and, unaware that he had dropped it on Yeggor Dun, would begin to make inquiries. It would be enlightening to see who came forward to proclaim himself the key's owner.

John smiled with amusement at the thought and slipped it into his pocket. Then he started back down the hill.

By the time he reached Wynford Eagle, Sydenham had already supped and had retired to the library. The doctor was delighted to see him. He hobbled over on his gouty leg and poured John some port, then he rang for Kathleen to bring a supper tray.

"And how is the Sykes case progressing?" he asked, as John sat eating his cold mutton and salad.

"There is nothing new, Tom. I am still awaiting the documents from Van Roonhuyse in Amsterdam. Henry doubts their usefulness, but says that without them we have no defense."

Tom raised a concerned brow. "The papers have not yet arrived?"
"My courier was arrested in London and thrown into Newgate.
The papers were seized. I have hired Joe Fox to attempt another ride."
"Joe Fox? I am surprised you would deal with such a man."
"The situation is now critical, Tom. Joe Fox is the only courier
with the resourcefulness and unscrupulousness to surmount the odds."
"Indeed, he will need all his trickery—and luck besides," Tom said
grimly. "Just this morning I received a smuggled newsletter from London. As you have heard, plots are springing up around the King like
weeds after rain. But now the coffee houses are buzzing with rumors of
a new, more ominous plot to depose him. A formal invitation to William and Mary to succeed James on the throne was reportedly signed by
twelve Whig and Tory lords, headed by the powerful Earl of Danby, at
the same time requiring them to bind themselves, as joint sovereigns, to
maintain the law and liberties of the realm. A reply from Holland is
awaited."
"James has quashed other such plots, Tom."
"But this last has him in a frenzy of apprehension. He has tripled
the agents he has lying in wait all along the coast, watching for couriers
attempting to slip ashore from the Continent. By intercepting William's expected Letter of Consent and accompanying Manifestos, he
hopes to smash this plot at the head. No, my boy, I very much doubt
that even Joe Fox, for all his reputed cunning, can escape this deadly
ambush."
John looked troubled. "I can only trust you are wrong, Tom. So
much hangs on his ability to get through."
"Then you must face it, my boy," Tom said, "the situation is
hardly likely to improve. James has been pursuing a policy of ever-
increasing violence and illegality, chafing under the traditional restraints
placed on the King by Parliament. He claims it is his divinely appointed
birthright to govern without restraint."
"That would only establish an irresponsible despotism."
"Just what James has in mind. He has now commanded Parliament
to furnish him with yearly sums sufficient to maintain a standing army
of thirty thousand men—an army which, at his whim, could be turned
against Parliament, the Church, and the people."
"And?"
"Parliament refused, of course. James met their refusal with the

haughty declaration that he would find the money himself and raise his standing army without Parliamentary sanction."

"How can he do that?" John asked. "The raising of such an army would be illegal. Besides, an army must be paid, and James cannot raise such funds without the consent of Parliament."

"That is how the lawful mind would reason, my boy. But not James. James is determined to dispense with the laws of England and rid himself of control of Parliament. To do that he needs an army obedient to his will. To pay such an army he must have access to a source of foreign money."

"Who would be so reckless as to lend James money?"

"Louis of France."

"Why?"

"It is rumored that James, in return for the money, has pledged himself to kneel as vassal to the King of France."

John stared. "That would bind Englishmen to fight France's ceaseless aggressions against Austria, Italy, Spain, Holland, the German princes. Englishmen will never tolerate subservience to France. There will be another revolution."

"Let us hope not. Let us hope James realizes his folly before we are forced to execute another Stuart. We beheaded his father for less."

John got to his feet and started pacing the library.

"It was an evil day for England when we fell heir to these Stuarts," he said. "Already James has done his best to subvert the courts, advancing lawless judges like Jeffreys—a chief justice who makes such shameless profit from the sale of pardons that he will free a rapist for a thousand pounds. Little wonder James's subjects plot against him. And now this watch upon our coasts so that Englishmen no longer come or go on their free business without the risk of being seized by James's agents and vanishing without a trace. God's body!" he burst out, in an explosion of anger and despair. "God's body! Even the life of one young girl now hangs on the King's misdeeds. For if Joe Fox disappears, what then for Jenny Sykes? Already in her short, unhappy life she has suffered more than her measure of injustice. And now her fate—whether it be given her to live or die—is being made to rest on the political vicissitudes of England."

Sydenham had been watching him, a look of sudden awareness in his wise old eyes. Now he said quietly, "You love her, do you not, John?"

John turned quickly. "Yes, Tom. I love her. I think I loved her the moment I saw her."

A long silence fell in the room.

Then Sydenham said soberly, "And what of this other man? What of the father of her child?"

"She is still silent on that point. She still will not talk of him."

Sydenham nodded thoughtfully. "And have you been honest with yourself in assessing the probable outcome of her trial?"

"Tom, I cannot look to the outcome with the pessimism you and Henry share. And I must be able to convey a feeling of hope to Jenny. I cannot let her suffer through weeks of anguish and despair."

"But this hope you are conveying, is it not perhaps a *false* hope?"

John thought a moment. "You are saying it might have been kinder to leave her to die in jail of puerperal fever?"

"No, I am not saying that. I was not even thinking that. But it might well be true, John."

"Yes, it might well be true. It is a point I have argued with Henry and which I find increasingly worrisome. But let us go back to the morning I found her crouching against the wall of the jail, dying. You know yourself, Tom, that the physician's instinct is to act promptly to save a life."

"The more so, perhaps, because even then you loved her?"

"Perhaps. Or perhaps it was simply because she was so young and innocent of crime."

"But how could you have known, then, that she was innocent of crime?"

"I had examined her child. Remember?"

"Ah, yes. And now, having worked to bring her back to health, do you sometimes have regrets?"

"I have no struggle with my conscience as a physician. It is my conscience as a man that troubles me. I find they make an uneasy pair."

"Benign neglect is something we all practice, John. We physicians may not talk of it. We may pretend it does not exist. But we are all aware that it is an ever-present choice."

"But one so young, so guiltless?"

Sydenham was silent for a moment, his brow creased in perplexity.

"You have raised a difficult question, my boy. Unfortunately you can only know the answer to the right or wrong of it at the end of the girl's trial. If she is found innocent and freed, you will have the satisfaction of knowing you saved a young girl's life. If she is found guilty . . . But, John, that thought appalls me. Your personal anguish will be intense, knowing you saved her from one death only to face a still more terrible death on the gallows. And you know that in cases of concealment there is no appeal. Execution follows swiftly after trial. If she is condemned, there will be nothing you can do to save her. Ah, John, my dear, dear boy, have you faced all that?"

Sydenham's anxious eyes were quick to observe the change of expression his question brought forth—John's look of pain, the tightening of the facial muscles.

"Yes," John said quietly after a moment. "I face it daily."

There was deep emotion now in Sydenham's voice. "John, I had always hoped that one day a woman would enter your life for whom you could feel the kind of love you appear to feel for Jenny. I had hoped you would have a fortunate marriage, a large and happy family. You were meant for that, John. Children are drawn to you. You would make a good father."

John heard the note of desolation and forced a smile. "Come, Tom, do not give up hope. I am a young man. The day will come when you will find yourself playing grandfather to my swarm of children, showing them the mysteries of Wynford Eagle, showing them the secret staircases and passages in the walls you used to delight in showing me when I was a boy."

They sat for a while in silence, content as always to be sharing the same comfortable room, the same fireside. Presently John raised his head and listened to a flock of migrating plovers passing overhead, calling as they went. Then the *laka-laka* of a saddleback on its way to the sea. The sky had momentarily cleared. Through the tall French window Pegasus was flying clear and bright behind the dark boughs of a half-stripped oak. And from the woods came a fox's bark, a young dog-fox trying to copy his sire, but sounding squeaky and ludicrous, like the protest of a disgruntled child. John set aside the empty tray and for a moment closed his eyes. There was a gentle peace at Wynford Eagle that never failed to soothe and refresh his spirit.

Presently he said, "Father Dominic died today."

"I am sorry, my boy. But you were expecting it. And in a doctor's life one day compensates for the last. Today, for instance?"

"Yes—a mother and her child. Young Ken Walsh's wife. How did you guess?"

"I read it on your face when you came in."

"Tom, you know me too well."

Sydenham lapsed into deep thought, his eyes on John's face.

"My boy, I know we have talked of this before and you have given me a negative answer. But a man experiences change as he goes through life. The time may come when you will want to leave Dorset, when you feel you have to start anew elsewhere. If that time comes, will you not reconsider joining me in my practice? You see how crippled I have become by gout. I cannot even return to London at the moment. When I eventually do, it will have to be by hired coach. I can no longer sit a horse. You would be of enormous help to me in London. I would feel content, knowing my patients were in your capable hands. It is a partnership I am offering you, John—an immensely profitable partnership. In time, the practice would be entirely yours. Will you not think it over?"

John smiled affectionately. He understood the thought Tom was trying so touchingly to convey to him.

"I am grateful to you, Tom, and if ever I leave Dorset, it will only be to come to you. But whatever lies ahead, the joy or the pain, I will never leave Dorset. My choice was made long ago. I am a Dorsetman. It is bred in the bone, along with impatience and an unruly temper. I will leave my bones in Dorset."

"If you practiced in London, you would be no less a Dorsetman. And you could still inherit Dunheved."

"It is not Dunheved I have in mind."

"What, then?"

"I am a doctor whose unique terrain reaches from the mansions of the rich, who welcome me for my overpriced professional skills, to the hovels of the poor, who offer me only their trust and a cold turnip for my pains. The care of this hodgepodge of raw, diseased, long-suffering humanity is the sum of my hopes and dreams. I want nothing more."

"Then what will you do when Lucas dies? You will find yourself with a personal conflict you will need to resolve."

"I will never give up the practice of medicine, Tom."

"You mean, you will relinquish the Tremoigne titles and estates to the cousin?"

"It is possible."

"Have you told this to Lucas?"

"No, nor will I. He could hardly be expected to understand."

"Has he mentioned the matter lately?"

"We talked of it only yesterday. I was called to Dunheved to look at James. I found the poor leper dying. He must have contracted dysentery from a kitchen boy whom I suspect had been handling his food trays. James was mercifully unconscious, and it is only a matter of days. It is tragic that one born to such golden prospects should die so young in a tower room, shunned and alone."

"It is tragic for Lucas, too. But he is fortunate to have found his brother's son. What did he say on the matter of your prospects?"

"He asked if I would be willing to let his attorneys search for proof that a state of marriage existed between my parents."

"You think he still does not know that?"

"Oh, he knows. But Lucas has his reasons for concealing more than he tells."

"It would be interesting to know what those reasons are, John. Is there no way to circumvent Lucas and learn the truth for yourself?"

"There may be. Last winter we had a patient at the hospital, an old man named Dan Reeves. Dan was born on the Dunheved estates and spent his entire life as a forester there. At the time I spoke to him, I had no idea my connection with the Tremoigne family was anything but an illicit one. I had seen my father's portrait in the Great Hall and had drawn the natural conclusion that I had been born out of wedlock. But Dunheved had always held for me a curious and powerful attraction, and I can only think it is because I felt my father's roots deep inside me. Perhaps that was why I spent so much time chatting with Dan Reeves about Dunheved and the Tremoignes."

"Did Reeves remember you as a boy?"

"I was careful to keep my personal history out of our conversations. But he did remember Adam, and Adam's little boy, whom he knew was also Chérie's son."

"And you think you were that son?"

"I *know* I was that son. What I do not know is whether, at the time, Adam had a wife whose name was Margaret Bemis. Perhaps Dan Reeves might have the answer. Dan is back in his cottage now, but I plan to visit him one day when I am passing by and have another chat with him."

"But if you do not care about the Tremoigne inheritance, why, at this late date, is it important to you to confirm that you were not born out of wedlock?"

"That is not what I want to find out, Tom. I want to find out about Chérie. I want to know why she was killed on the High Moor. I want to know who killed her."

"Are you suggesting Lucas—"

"No, I am not suggesting Lucas killed Chérie, though I feel sure he knows how she died. But Dan Reeves remembers Chérie. I think he will be able to answer some of my questions." John rose to his feet. "It is getting late, Tom. I promised to call at the Follet farm after dark. Little Emmeline came to fetch me this morning. I suspect her father fought at Sedgemoor."

Sydenham shook his head. "Another rebel, John? It is dangerous work. You will not always succeed in eluding the watch. One of these nights they will burst into a cottage and find you treating some rebel with a pike wound. My boy, you worry me. You take too many chances."

John grinned and patted Tom's shoulder as he passed.

"I will drop by soon again," he promised.

The Follet farm was situated only two miles out of Dorncaster. John slowed Iris to a walk as he approached the lane leading to it. There was still no moon, only the stars and some ragged clouds herded by the wind across the sky. No sign of Kirke's men. He reined in and listened. No sound of hoofbeats. He turned slowly down the lane leading to the farmhouse.

Willy Follet, a stalwart seventeen-year-old, was waiting in the shadows of the house. He came forward as John dismounted.

"Mam be in the kitchen," he said in a low voice. "Her tole me to hide Iris in the woods till 'ee want her."

"Thank you, Willy."

He did not need to knock. Ginnie Follet had been watching for him. As she opened the door he observed an embarrassed look on her face.

" 'Ee be kind to come, Doc. Gil has bin feverish this past month— and gitting worse, I reckon."

"What is it, Ginnie?"

But she quickly turned away, pretending not to have heard his question, and led him down the passage to the bedroom.

He found Gil Follet lying in bed. He had always been a vigorous man, brown and muscled from a lifetime of farming, with high cheekbones and a ready smile. But now his lips were tight with pain. His skin

was ashy, almost bloodless. His bright blue eyes had sunk so far into
their sockets they looked black. They glittered with fever.

As John drew up beside the bed, Gil tried to force a smile.

"I ain't gonna lie to 'ee, Doc. Reckon 'ee 'ud know anyway." He
paused, then added shamefacedly, "I was at Sedgemoor. Doc, please
don' blame me."

"I do not blame you," John retorted angrily. "I blame God. It was
he made you a half-wit. Now, show me your wound."

Gil pushed back the covers and exposed his naked thigh. John
motioned Ginnie to bring the lamp closer, then he bent over the bed
and began to cut away the bloody rags.

He scowled when the wound was exposed. It was angry and swollen, with an odor like rotten meat.

"God damn it, Gil!" he cried, "never do this again. Never wait so
long before calling me. You must have a bullet in there. The entire area
is infected." He turned to Ginnie. "I will want hot water. I have nothing left to blunt the pain. I used it all on my last patient, so I will need
cloth for a gag. What I have to do is going to hurt, and we cannot have
him waking up the younger children. And, Ginnie, get Josh out of bed.
Tell him to go up and watch the road. At first sign of Kirke's men he is
to let me know. Then tell Willy I want to see him."

He was getting out his instruments when Willy came in. He had
always liked Willy. Willy was strong and dependable.

"Will, where are the pigs?"

"In the woods, Doc."

"Good! Keep them there at least a week. Now, I am going to need
your help. I have to extract this bullet, but after it is done we cannot
keep your father here. If they come searching and find him, we will all
hang by the neck. You will have to take him across the river, so get the
farm cart ready—blankets and water—but do not bring the cart back to
the house. No fresh wheel tracks. Take it directly down to the riverbank."

"Then shall I come back, sir?"

"No, I will carry your father down and set him in the cart, then
you will cross over into Squire Dougal's woods. You will find a little
shack near Signal Rock. Keep him there, right in the cart, till I come
tomorrow."

"What of Squire Dougal, sir? Him 'ull not like me trespassing his
land."

"It will be all right, Willy. I will ride by in the morning and have a talk with Squire Dougal. No one will disturb you."

Gil was a brave man, but he writhed in agony against the pain. His gagged screams shuddered and recoiled back down his throat as John probed for the bullet. At last, when the pain became too great, he fainted. John looked up and nodded reassuringly to Ginnie across her husband's body. Then he cleansed the wound and dressed it with clean linen.

At last he picked up the unconscious Gil in his arms. "You know what to do here, Ginnie. A hurried clean-up, please. No signs of this— no soiled bed linens, no bloody rags. I will be back shortly." And he left the house and started down toward the river.

By the time he got back, Josh was waiting.

"They be there, Doc," he said breathlessly.

"Kirke's men?"

"I don' know—but soldiers—two of 'em. They be on the highway, mounted, jest sitting un'er a tree, waiting."

"They are Kirke's, all right. Josh, I am going in to wash. Will you fetch Iris for me?"

He rode slowly up the lane and turned onto the highway just as the horsemen moved forward to block his way. There were four of them now.

"Good evening, gentlemen," he said. He sent a long searching look through the dimness. "It is Colonel Kirke's men, is it not? Sergeant Brickert, is that you? What are you doing out so late? Neighborhood girls?"

"I was just coming down to look for you, sir."

"I was not hard to find. How can I help you?"

"You can tell me what you was doing at the Follet farm."

"I do not see that it is your business, Sergeant, but I know you have your duty to perform, so I will tell you. Emmeline Follet came to my clinic this morning with a belly ache. She had been out in the woods yesterday with her father and had eaten unripe berries. The clinic was crowded and I forgot to give her some medicine to take home with her. Tonight I chanced to be dining with Doctor Sydenham at Wynford Eagle and decided to drop Emmeline's medicine off on my return. Does that answer your question?"

The sergeant thought a moment. "You say the girl was in the woods yesterday with her pa?"

"That is right."

"What was Farmer Follet doing in the woods?"

"Sergeant, if you will come to the point, perhaps I could help you."

"We got a report that Farmer Follet ain's been seen for weeks, that he has been laid up with a wound he got at Sedgemoor."

"And you thought I was treating him for such a wound? God's bones! You must think me a fool, Sergeant. But with such a report, why were you waiting here? Why did you not just go down the lane, knock on the door, and demand to search the farmhouse?"

"Because only two men was on watch. Me and the other only just got here to make the arrests."

"Whom were you planning to arrest?"

"You and Farmer Follet."

"Well, Sergeant, I have been up since dawn, so either go ahead and arrest me or let me go home to bed. But I warn you, if you arrest me, I am going to insist that you prove your charge by returning now to the Follet farm and producing Farmer Follet with a freshly treated battle wound. If you fail to produce him, I will lodge a complaint that Kirke's Lambs are overstepping their authority by recklessly arresting peaceful citizens. Now, go ahead and arrest me, because I will not go back to that farmhouse till you have your shackles on me."

The sergeant was thrown into confusion by the vigor of the attack, and as he wavered, John nudged Iris, pushed in between two troopers, and started, unhurriedly, down the highway toward Dorncaster. He called over his shoulder as he went, "Sergeant, if you are going in my direction, let us ride together. A doctor is so much on the road, he gets deucedly lonely."

The sergeant moved to join him, coming up alongside, but motioning his troopers to fall in behind. He was still uncertain of his position, but John did not leave him any time for reflection.

"Now, let me answer your question," he said pleasantly, resuming their conversation. "You asked what Farmer Follet was doing in the woods yesterday. You see, Sergeant, a farmer lives by the seasons. This Gil Follet has five children, which gives him seven mouths to feed. He has to work hard to do it. His two eldest sons, Will and Josh, are able to take over a lot of farm work, so at this season of the year, after the harvest has been carried, he leaves Will and Josh to do the plowing and sow the winter wheat while he goes off to the woods with his pigs."

"His pigs!" The angry words seemed to explode on the quiet night air. Sergeant Brickert turned and stared at John in utter disbelief. "You trying to tell me Farmer Follet walks his pigs in the woods? You think to have me swallow a lack-brain tale like that?"

John slowly shook his head.

"It is plain to see, my friend, that you know nothing at all about farming. But then, why should you? You are a soldier. Still, I am hurt and offended that you take me for a liar as well as a rogue doctor, so I will have to prove what I say. We will stop at the first farmhouse that shows a light and you can knock on the door and put the question to the farmer himself."

"At this time of night? Knock on a farmhouse door and ask the farmer if he walks his pigs in the woods?"

"You would not put it that way, Sergeant. You would ask if he lets his pigs run free in the woods in search of pannage."

"Pannage? What is that?"

"I take it you are not a Dorsetman, Sergeant. Pannage is mast— the acorns and beechnuts that fall in the autumn. Pigs love it and devour it greedily. They do not know it, of course, but they are getting fattened up for the Christmas market. Ask any man in Dorset."

Sergeant Brickert's wrath had waned. He was thoughtful. "And you think that is where Farmer Follet has been—out in the woods with his pigs?"

"Oh, now you have me understandably timid about answering your questions. But it is easy enough to prove. We can just ride back to Follet's farm and search his pigsty. You will not find a single pig there, of course, but at least you will be satisfied. You probably will not find a single pig on any of the farms around, either. They are all in the woods. But do not take my word, Sergeant. There is a farm yonder, just beyond the trees. The farmer is a patient of mine. He will be glad to let you search his sty. And I will feel better knowing you no longer think so ill of me."

The thought of searching for pigs at midnight did not appeal to Sergeant Brickert. "Do all farmers stay in the woods with their pigs?"

"No, but not all farmers have two fine strapping sons to do their farm work. And Gil Follet lost four of his prime pigs to thieves last year. Now you may not know anything about farming, but as a soldier I am sure you know a lot about crime. You know there are always thieves around with an eye to a good thing. And can you imagine anything easier to steal, my friend, than an untended pig in a wood?"

And he talked amiably on, instructing the sergeant in farming all the way back to Dorncaster.

Back in town he discreetly rid himself of the unwanted company of Kirke's "Lambs," then he rode back through the byways and alleys to the stableyard of the Mermaid to inquire if there was news yet of Joe Fox.

There was none. The other couriers had not even a sighting to report. John rode slowly homeward, comforting himself with the thought that he was being overanxious. The rebel trials would not end for at least another few days.

There was still time.

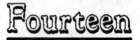

"Well, Clemmy," John said as an old woman shuffled into his office and slid into the chair by his desk, "what seems to be the trouble?"

"I be sick, Doctor John."

"In what way?"

"Well," she said vaguely, "I got these pains."

"Where?"

"All over. I got to come here to the ho'pital, Doc. I got to be took care of."

"Come, then, let me take a look at you."

He led her into the examining room and looked her over. He found no physical ailments other than the ones she had suffered patiently for years.

He brought her back to the office.

"Now, Clemmy," he said, "your arthritis is no worse. Nor is that cataract. You had no reason to come to see me today. I can find nothing wrong with you."

She was full of silent anguish. "But I be real sick, Doctor John. I got to come here to the ho'pital. I got to real bad."

He sat back and looked thoughtfully into the old woman's face. He had known her all his life. She had been widowed young, her husband a sailor lost at sea. She had worked hard to raise her son, going out daily to do cleaning, always neat and independent and full of self-respect. She was still mentally alert, physically healthy. Yet today her clothing was rumpled, her thinning white hair uncombed, her face unwashed.

"Clemmy," he asked, "where did you sleep last night?"

She stiffened her spine and he knew that with the deep breath she had quickly drawn she would deny that she had slept anywhere but in her own bed. He shook his head at her.

"Clemmy," he said gently, "why not tell me about it?"

His sympathetic tone undid her resolve. She began to weep silently. He passed her a piece of linen bandage and waited until her tears had subsided.

He said, "It is your daughter-in-law, is it not? What did she do? Turn you out?"

She could not bear to look at him. "Them don' want me to live with 'em no more. Millie says her don' want an old woman 'round, costing money, taking up space. Her wanted me out of there. Her packed me things and pushed me out."

"How long ago was that?"

"It bin three days now."

"And David?"

She rushed to her son's defense. "Him's a good boy, Doctor John. It be jest hard to stand up to Millie, once her mind be made up."

"And where are you living now, Clemmy?"

She looked down at her boots, ashamed.

"And where are your belongings?"

"Out in the waiting room."

He gave the matter a moment's thought. "Clemmy," he said, "they need a helper down at the almshouse, someone dependable like you, to clean and wash dishes and help with the elderly. They would provide you with room and board in exchange for your work. Would you like to do that?"

She looked uncertain. "But 'ee think—? No one 'ull hire me no more, Doctor John. I be near sixty-eight, 'ee know. The almshouse 'ull say they don' want me no more, neither—that I be too old."

"Too old?" He smiled. "You will be working among men and women much older than you, Clemmy. You will feel like a girl among those people in their nineties. Here, I will give you a note to Mrs.

Songe. Then Mrs. Colley will find a boy to walk you down the street and carry your bundle."

When Clemmy was gone, he treated a vomiting infant, a fracture of the lower jaw, a woman with face and scalp burns caused by an overturned lamp, a shaking palsy victim, numerous local infections, a carbuncle, an abscess of the axilla that had to be opened and evacuated.

Jeff, a boy of ten years, had congenital club foot. He was a fine-looking boy, not handsome in the accepted sense, but with arresting dark eyes and an intelligent face whose sensitive expression showed a hurt awareness of his physical deformity. He wore a special boot the saddler had made at John's directions.

"Well, Jeff, did you come alone today?"

"No, sir. Mam knows the rules. But she could not wait. Me little sister be home ailing."

"Not too badly, I hope. And what is your problem?"

"It be this cough, sir. I cough all night. There be no way I kin stop. No one in the house kin git no sleep."

"Come into the examining room, then. Take off your shirt and let me have a look at you."

The boy's shortened and twisted foot made it difficult for him to climb onto the examining table. John helped him, then, perceiving the deep humiliation the boy felt at his own insufficiency, made a point of talking to him as he proceeded with the examination.

"You go to school, do you not, Jeff?"

"Yes, sir."

"Are you good in school?"

"Yes, sir—I be very good."

"Very good, are you? What do you like best?"

"I like everything. I be learning all I kin now in case I kin go on later."

"Go on? Go on where?"

"To 'nother school where I kin learn more."

John stopped and looked down at him in surprise. "You mean you want to go to university?"

"If I kin. But Mam says I prob'ly cain't 'cos it takes a lot of money."

"Your father owns a stall, does he not?"

"Yes, sir. Us sells vegetables."

"And your grandfather and great-grandfather kept that stall? Do you not want to go into business with your father?"

"I will, but on'y if I cain't go on."

"But why do you want to go to university?"

The boy hesitated. Then he said shyly, "So I kin be a doctor."

John felt a sudden upsurge of emotion. There had been something in the boy's voice, a passionate note that reminded him of his own youthful but seemingly hopeless yearning to be a doctor. He thought of the curious way in which that dream came to be realized. He thought of the two great men who had helped him realize it.

Sometimes a boy needed a man to reach down a hand to him.

"You can put your shirt on now, Jeff. I am going to give you some medicine for that cough. Take it four times a day and stay home for two days."

"Yes, sir."

John turned and stepped to his cabinet, busying himself with his bottles, and the boy, still slipping into his shirt, limped over and watched, his eyes following every move.

"Jeff," John said, "why do you want to be a doctor?"

"I don' know, sir. It be the on'y thing I ever wanted."

"How long have you thought about this?"

"Ever since I was little. Ever since I kin remember."

"And you say you are good in school?"

"Yes, sir. I be very good. No other boy be as good as me."

"And do you know that it takes years and years of hard work to become a doctor? Are you prepared for that?"

"I kin do the hard work, sir. But do you think—" He stopped, looking anxiously up at John, an unspoken question in his dark eyes.

"Your foot, you mean?"

"Yes, sir. 'Ull it matter? Maybe folks 'ull not want a doctor with—"

"Folks will always want a good doctor, Jeff. Folks will not mind about your foot if you can diagnose and cure their ailments."

"But what if Mam be right and us don' have the money?"

John turned and put a firm hand on the boy's shoulder.

"Then we will just have to find the money, Jeff. When you turn twelve, if you have worked hard in school, if you are still as set on being a doctor as you are now, you just come back here to me. I have a lot of rich patients, you know. I will see that the money is found."

The boy said nothing, only stood staring up at him. But there was such a burgeoning of wordless hope in his dark eyes that John felt pained by it.

He thought about Jeff as he rode out to Lying-In to see Jenny.

It was a pity nothing could be done about the boy's deformity, but no surgical technique had been devised to correct club foot. Unfortunately the humble craft of surgery still came nowhere near to taking rank with the older order of physicians. Perhaps, in time, surgeons of originality and genius like Richard Wiseman and Richard Lower would turn their attention to natural deformities. After all, it was the unschooled surgeon Ambroise Paré, formerly a rustic barber's apprentice, who reintroduced the operation for harelip, a technique that had passed out of use since the time of the Arabians.

Sister Brigit smiled a greeting as he hurried down the corridor toward Jenny's room.

"Baby Alice has the snuffles, Doctor," she said. "Later, would you have the time to drop by the nursery and take a look at her?"

Jenny had been listening for his footsteps. She was sitting in her chair by the window. Her face was already turned toward the door as he entered.

"Well, Jenny, how do you feel today?" he asked, taking the seat opposite her.

"Each day I feel stronger, Doctor—that is how Sister Brigit says I must address you. I now move about the room quite easily. I make my bed and wash myself and comb my own hair." She had been gazing steadily at him. "Your face is healing," she said. "The bruises are fading."

"That is a pity," he laughed. "I was beginning to think red and purple spots become me."

Suddenly she leaned forward and with her forefinger gently traced out the length of the scar on his cheek. "I have often wondered—how did you get that?"

The question left him somewhat startled. From early childhood he had been aware that he was not like other people. The mystery of his background had always set him apart. As a boy he had been tall and rugged, good with his fists and ready to use them to punish any reference to his murky parentage. Those experiences had left him reserved on matters relating to his private life, disinclined to talk about them, adept at evasion.

This was not the first time Jenny had penetrated his reserve by asking him a question of a personal nature. For all her erudition and intelligence, her cloistered life had left her understandably naive in matters of conventional decorum, prone to inquire into concerns which the worldly-wise would have hesitated to touch upon. Yet he never had the feeling that Jenny was invading his privacy, and now, as in the past, he was as much surprised by the grace with which she posed her question as he was by the ease and naturalness with which he found himself responding to it.

"I told you I had been married," he said. "Her name was Amy. She died recently in a bedlam."

"A bedlam? What is that?"

"A hospital, Jenny—for the insane."

Her voice was soft, filled with tender feeling. "And Amy cut your cheek?"

"She was not responsible for her actions. I know now that she must have suffered cruelly. I sometimes blame myself for not having understood sooner."

"How long had she been in a bedlam?"

"Four years."

"Did you have children?"

"Two little boys."

"How old are they now?"

He looked across the narrow space into the pool-like clarity of her disturbingly lovely eyes. "They both died," he said.

He felt her spirit move toward him. She asked, "Is that why you work so hard?"

The perceptiveness of her question caught him unprepared. "I think I work hard mostly because I love the practice of medicine. It absorbs my mind and my life."

"But you told me once that you live alone."

"I do."

"And at night, when your work is done and you go back to this home where you live alone, do you never feel alone?"

He smiled. "I have little time to feel alone, Jenny. Last night it was almost dawn when I got home, then I just dropped onto my bed and slept till it was time to get up and go to the hospital."

"That is what I mean."

John's eyebrows lifted. For an instant he was puzzled. "You are suggesting that I keep busy in order not to feel lonely. It is possible, of course. An old teacher of mine, Father Dominic, once made a similar observation with regard to religion. He said I was permitting medicine to substitute for religion because the provable in science offered an excuse to reject the unprovable in religion."

She thought about that. "You are not religious, then?"

"I used to be when I was a boy. I even sang in the choir. Now I am an irreligious brute."

She smiled at that, clearly unconvinced. Then suddenly she said, "You told me once that you remember your mother. Tell me about her."

He sat quite still, his gaze fixed on Jenny's face. Only recently Father Dominic had asked the same question and he had found himself unable to answer it. But there was something about Jenny, something in her presence and acute sensitivity, that seemed to release the springs of memories locked in silence now for year on year, making it possible for him to speak of them.

"Her name was Chérie," he answered. "She was beautiful—all love and laughter and gentleness. She and I lived together in the heart of a great forest, but often my father came to visit us. My mother was all mine until my father came, then suddenly she was all his."

"Did that trouble you?"

"Not at all. It seemed right, the proper order of things. You see, my parents never excluded me, Jenny. I was always a part of their happy secret world."

"What was it like, this 'happy secret world'?"

"My forest? It was beautiful, Jenny, with its dome of yellow-green light under oaks ten centuries old. And stretches of purple foxgloves through which a child could run, singing at the top of his lungs. Or sheets of bluebells that seemed to flow like water under a breeze, and hosts of fairy blue-winged butterflies that would alight without fear on a child's outstretched hand. Or dragonflies like darting needles of red and emerald light. Jenny, there is a silence in a forest, not at all like the silence in a room. It is more a hush, profound, almost religious, broken at times by a blackbird's flutelike notes, or a cuckoo's call, or the laughter of a green woodpecker filling the ancient woods with its wild liberty and gladness. You learn the secret places where, in spring, the cock pheasant sheds his shyness and comes out from cover to stand among the primroses in his nuptial suit of copper and bronze and purple, with his glossy green head and scarlet wattles, rising jubilantly on his feet, crowing and beating his wings. I know now that he did this to please his hen hiding there among the hazel-stubs, but at the time—and I was only six—I thought he was dancing just for me."

She smiled. "Were you never lonely?"

"Jenny, I was as wild as the other young wild things. I played with the fox cubs, who seemed to take me for one of their own. Many a night I missed my supper, forgetting to go home, waiting hidden in a gorse brake for the vixen to leave on her nighttime hunt so the cubs could come out and play with me in the moonlight. Those early years taught me to know and love the night, not to fear it, to stand under the stars and listen for the nighttime sounds, the rhythmic rise and fall of the nightjar's churr, the grunts of badgers at their earth, the lovely long-drawn hoot of the brown owl, snatches of song, lark or ringdove or chaffinch or robin, sung carelessly, without effort, without thought."

"Did you fear nothing?"

"There was nothing to fear."

"Not even the dark places?"

"The dark places were only the thickets and coverts of the denser woods. There was nothing to fear there. Oh, I was certain there were things in the forest beyond what I saw with my eyes—tree-spirits, perhaps, like the dryads of the Greeks. Or goat-men such as lurked in wild places. Often I feared to turn my head too sharply lest, by setting eyes on them, I offend them. But atonement was easy. I would stand and sing to them and they would let me pass unharmed. A child accepts his own vision of the world. And those were days of utmost secret joy."

"Then," she asked thoughtfully, "why did you leave it?"

The question seemed to stab a festering wound deep in the core of his being. His face clouded over.

"Because two events occurred to destroy our world."

"Two events?" Her voice was soft with solicitude. "What were they?"

His brows knotted together in a frown. "I have only recently been able to recall the first of them—my father's death. The other I still cannot recall. It just seems to hang there like a great darkness."

"A darkness?"

"Something that comes only in disjointed flashes of memory—something so terrible I still cannot remember what it was."

"But if you cannot remember, how can you know it was terrible?"

"Because the horror of it has stayed with me. It is with me to this day."

There was a great stillness about her as she carefully considered his words. Her eyes had a puzzled, questioning look.

"You could be wrong," she reasoned. "Perhaps what you remember is not horror at all, but some other emotion."

"Jenny, I remember the look on my mother's face. She seemed to know then that something was gone forever, that everything had changed. All that day she sat by the hearth, holding me in her arms, trying to soothe my inconsolable grief. When nightfall came, she packed some food. Then she took me by the hand, slipped out of the cabin, and fled with me into the deep forest."

"But why?"

"That is what I do not know."

"Did you ever learn what happened?"

"I may be close to learning it now."

"Only now? After all these years?"

"Life sometimes takes a strange turn, Jenny."

She frowned, struggling to understand. "But it must have been only a short time after that terrible last day in the forest that you were found, abandoned, by Doctor Toller. What happened in between—after you and your mother fled the cabin, I mean?"

He turned and looked out the window, out over the Cleybury Rings, staring, seeing nothing. But presently he turned back to her, his face reflecting the anguish of that far-off night.

"The rest is just a snatch of memory, Jenny—a fragment that has stayed in my mind. We must have run for miles, passing through a part of the forest that was strange to me. We were moving sharply uphill, climbing jagged ledges of rock, slipping on the wet humus, panting so we could hardly breathe, our damp clothing cold against our bodies. By now my mother was sobbing. Between her sobs she kept halting to listen. Then suddenly I heard them, men—many men—riding. They sounded on the forest floor like a herd of running deer. They could have been only a short way behind us. I knew then why my mother was sobbing. I knew we were the game the men were hunting. But my mother did not stop. She only tightened her grip on my hand and ran on."

"Yes?"

"Then suddenly she gave a gasp and halted, pulling me against her, wrapping her arms protectively around me. I looked up. Directly in our path stood a man. To me, he was a giant standing there, legs apart. I could see he was a forester, paid to guard the vert and venison. My mother and I waited, pressed together, trembling like trapped creatures awaiting the club of the huntsman. But the man did not move. I saw his face clearly in the moonlight, his weathered skin, his pale eyes. No one spoke. The pounding of oncoming feet was growing louder. The man cocked his head, listening. He, too, knew we were the quarry. For an instant he stood there, gazing thoughtfully down at us. Then, without a word, he turned and melted noiselessly in among the trees and my mother clutched my hand and ran on."

"Did you know the man?"

"Not at the time. But years later I learned who he was."

"How?"

"I was working one day in the clinic, tending my patients, when a man shuffled in. By now he was white and stooped and crippled with disease. But I recognized him at once. His face, his pale eyes had been indelibly etched on my memory."

"Did he recognize you?"

"No, nor did I tell him I was the boy in the forest that night, the boy whose life he had saved. It no longer mattered. By then he was so wasted he could scarcely remember his own name. It turned out he was alone in the world, and destitute. I found a good woman to take him into her cottage and nurse him. I used to visit him there. I cared for him till he died."

"Did your mother never tell you the reason for what happened that night, why she was running from those men, why they were tracking you?"

"Perhaps she would have told me later, but at the time I think she was more anxious to calm the terrible grief that continued to haunt me. She used to hold me in her arms at night, singing softly till I went to sleep."

"She must have loved you."

"Yes, Jenny, she did."

"But where did you go when you left the forest?"

"Up to the High Moor."

She looked perplexed. "What is that—the 'High Moor'?"

"It is an empty moorland some miles out of town, an elevated plateau thought to be the worn-down stump of an ancient volcano. The soil is barren. Nothing will grow there but ling and heather. The coun-tryfolk shun it, so it remains a place of mystery, the cradle of legend and superstition. Perhaps that was why my mother thought we would be safe up there."

"And were you?"

"For a few days. But my mother never ceased to be afraid. She seemed to be waiting until she was sure the men had given up watching for us and it would be safe for us to leave. I used to see her crawl to the edge of the moor and look down, searching its flanks for any sign of movement."

"But the men never came."

For a moment he gazed quietly down into her face.

"Yes, Jenny, they came."

She waited, but he said no more, and Jenny did not press him. She seemed to have a natural art for understanding why things were left unspoken. So they sat in silence. He knew he should be on his way. He knew he had patients waiting. Yet still he sat there, content just to be near her, to feel her presence across the narrow space of the window's width.

He was hardly aware of the sound of Sister Brigit approaching down the corridor. It was not the patter of her hurrying feet nor the clicking of her beads that intruded on his momentary absorption, but the unfamiliar thump of heavy male booted feet that sounded out of place within the quiet convent walls.

"Doctor," she said, entering, "this man says he must see you now —at once. I thought you would want to know. He says there's an emer-gency."

John rose to his feet. "Thank you, Sister. I know the messenger. He is the Aethelthorpe groom. What is it, Saunders?"

"Bradley said to fetch 'ee, Doc. Right 'way, please, 'e said."

"The baby?"

"No, his lordship. Him's took bad, I reckon."

"Thank you, Saunders. I will ride back with you."

They rode hard, taking every possible cross-country short-cut. He had somehow been expecting this. As he told Henry, he had been troubled by this premonition. He recalled Agatha's tragic and unneces-sary death, Coningsby's bitter grief. It seemed that Aethelthorpe had always been an evil-starred house. What was waiting there today? he wondered.

What would he find this time?

Aethelthorpe rose up before them, its gabled roof and tall stone chimneys dark against the pale September sky. Strange, how he always had an eerie feeling riding up this driveway. Why? He looked up and eyed the rooks mistrustfully. They still seemed to be waiting, brooding on some impending tragedy. Rooks were not always funereal birds. What was the matter with these sad, black, seemingly wingless creatures, the rooks of Aethelthorpe?

Saunders led Iris away to the stables and John ran up the steps. Bradley had been watching for him. He flung open the door.

"What is it, Bradley? What happened to Lord Coningsby?"

Bradley spoke in a low voice. "I do not know, Doctor. But I am afraid. His lordship went into the library a while ago. He had an odd look on his face. He came out a short time later, carrying this letter. He told me to send for you and place it in your hands. He said you would know what to do."

John took the letter and quickly opened it. It read:

> To Doctor John Toller.
> I desire to be buried beside my wife, Agatha. You will find my body by the Maesbury Stone. My Last Will is on the library table.
> Coningsby, this seventeenth day of September 1685.

John looked up. "Bradley, where is the Maesbury Stone?"

Bradley looked surprised. "It is right here on the Aethelthorpe grounds, sir—about three miles off to the east, at the foot of the hogback."

"What is the quickest way to get there?"

"I can send a boy with you, sir—"

"No, no, I must go alone. The quickest way?"

"You just follow the traces, sir."

"Traces of what?"

"The old Roman road. There is hardly anything left of it now, only the traces of paving here and there, but you cannot miss them. They run straight through our forest, straight as the crow flies, mostly."

"Iris?"

"Better not, sir. It is easier afoot."

"And the Maesbury Stone?"

"When you sight the hogback, sir, take the deer-trod running east. You will find the stone. Come, I will take you through the side door and point the way."

Out in the forest John started running, picking out the irregular strips of Roman paving with long intervals between, the old stones broken and sunk now, moss-covered and slippery, overgrown with turf, yet making shift to hold in place. The going was so treacherous he was glad he had not risked bringing Iris. On all sides the forest soared, giant oaks ten centuries old, interspersed with clumps of shining hollies and tall ferns forming a mimic wood beneath. The branches of the old trees laced thickly overhead, shutting out the light. The pounding of his feet sounded loud on the silent air. Once, at his approach, the alarm note of a green woodpecker rang out and a doe and her fawn stopped munching to raise their heads, then, uneasy at the unfamiliar sight of man, moved off, silent as ghosts behind the foliage.

John was panting now, but dared not stop. Still following the "traces," he ran on, through shagged glens and dark forest, lost at times in glimmering half-lights. Overhead, between the treetops, he saw that the sun was easing up the sky. A breeze stirred, gentle but cold. The loneliness had an oppressive quality. His eyes kept circling the surrounding woods, but now even the deer were couched. Suddenly the road angled sharply to the south and he halted to wonder if this could be right. But there was no other road. He ran on. He halted again. Dear God! He must surely have covered three miles! Then, in the distance, he saw the steep brow of the hogback, and turned east at the deer-trod and slowed his pace, searching now for the Maesbury Stone.

He sighted it up ahead. It stood in a small clearing, a tall, rough block of granite, scarred and hoary with age, a pagan menhir, hauled up to mark some ancient grave. At first there appeared to be no sign of Coningsby. Then, as he drew nearer, he saw a hand reaching out from behind the menhir, resting on the ground.

Swiftly he rounded the stone. Coningsby sat hunched against it. His eyes were closed. His face was white, his proud mouth set tight. One stocking had been pushed down to the ankle. He had severed an artery in his leg and had done his work well. The blood spurted out with every heartthrob, drenching the earth beneath.

John dropped quickly to one knee. "Coningsby!"

Coningsby opened his eyes and stared quietly up at him. He said weakly, "You came too fast, Toller. It was my body I wanted you to find —not me."

"Uh-huh!"

John had already opened his medical bag and had taken out a tourniquet. Now he began quickly wrapping the fillet around Coningsby's leg.

Coningsby stared in dismay. "You are not thinking of saving my life?"

"I am going to try."

"Good God, man, what for? So I can be tried for the murder of my wife?"

"That will be the business of the court."

"Very righteous of you, Doctor—very professional. But have you considered the consequences of your damned righteousness on the boy's life?"

John had been turning the stick, tightening the fillet. Now he looked up sharply. "What about the boy's life?"

"You did not stop to read the will I left in the library, then?"

"There was no time."

"If you had, my dear Toller, you would have seen that I assigned to the boy all my titles, lands, and wealth—aye, even my ancient and honorable family name."

"You are a good man, Coningsby."

"But now it seems that you, Toller, are going to ruin my plan and wreck the boy's chances."

"How am I going to do that?"

"By saving my life."

John stared at him, puzzled. "And how would saving your life wreck the boy's chances?"

Coningsby gathered his strength. "Because if I live to be brought to trial, I will be compelled to save myself from the gallows by pleading a *crime passionnel.* Such a plea would reduce my offense from murder to manslaughter, but would necessitate the explanation that when Agatha married me she was, unknown to me, already pregnant by another man."

"You bastard!"

"That is the second time you have dishonored my mother, Toller. If I had the strength, I would get up and thrash you."

"However you plead, you will still be guilty in Agatha's death."

"Ah, yes, but if I escape the gallows, I will be committed to prison for life. The Tower of London, probably—being a nobleman, you know —where I would soon bribe the keeper to bring me a knife so I could repeat this performance. I would not choose the life of a prisoner, Toller."

John was gazing thoughtfully away through the trees. "And if you were to succeed in this present suicide attempt, how would that secure the boy's prospects?"

"If I were to die now, by the Maesbury Stone, I would die with my secrets undisclosed. Only you and I know for sure the boy's a bastard. The rest can only speculate. Once you said to me, 'Do right by him, Coningsby.' I did right by him. I assigned everything to my son—you notice I say 'my son,' Toller—not Agatha's son, or Chaworth's son. It is one of life's little tricks, perhaps, that now this unfortunate misbegotten dreg of humankind will be recognized by the world as the scion of an ancient house, the son of my body, my legal heir, when in truth he is neither the son of my body nor my legal heir, but Roger Chaworth's bastard. It is a strange brew we have here, Toller."

"A strange brew, indeed! But why are you doing it? Why are you claiming a son you know is not yours?"

A sad, crooked little smile played over Coningsby's lips. "Toller, have you ever truly loved a woman?"

John caught his breath. "Truly loved?" he repeated. Then, almost to himself, he added, "Aye—but only this once."

"Then you understand. I need explain nothing. Now, are you going to remove that damned tourniquet and let me die?"

John continued to kneel there, considering all the aspects. He looked into the stricken man's eyes and knew he was afraid, not afraid to die like this, but afraid of being nursed back to health only to face a life in prison or the humiliation of being taken by cart to the Tyburn gallows. He had loved Agatha, but—yes, if compelled, he would seek to escape a felon's death by revealing the truth about her son.

And the boy? Unless he was claimed by his maternal grandparents, which was unlikely in a family made sensitive to scandal by the presence of two younger marriageable daughters, the boy would be cast out, quietly committed to a foundling home in some conveniently distant county, nameless, having no clue to the mystery of his origins, left to fight with his fists to defend himself against the taunts every fatherless boy must endure.

John knew about that.

He bent and untied the tourniquet, then continued to kneel there, thoughtfully watching the lifeblood start spurting again, making a little scarlet fountain in the air.

He asked, "Are you in pain?"

"I can tolerate it."

He rose to his feet. "I will not be long, Coningsby. I am going to take a walk. I will be back presently."

He was troubled as he strode in among the trees. It was not often he was guilty of a lawless act, yet there had been times when the defeat and suffering of human existence seemed to outweigh the sacredness of his Hippocratic oath. By English law, the act of suicide was a crime. The failed suicide was often healed, then hanged for his crime. The accessory to a successful suicide was liable to indictment for manslaughter, if not for murder. He had mostly held the laws of England in respect. Yet sometimes a man's own conscience, a man's own sense of right, transcended man-made laws.

A doctor's world was a hard world. It was a world of deep and intricate emotions, of soaring joys and shattered hopes, of a fierce striving to heal despite discouragement and self-doubts, of trying to see tomorrow's promise while the failures of yesterday filled his blighted vision. It was a lonely life, in which a man was left to assess his own decisions, to catalog, dissect, and analyze them, to ask himself where he went wrong; a life of rare unimagined wonder and bleak indefinable despair, at times drawing courage from the courage of the dying, or feeling more concern for his patients than for the law, yet through it all stumbling on, remaining passionate and caring, reverencing life, clinging indomitably to his beloved calling while living with its pain. Yes, there was pain, but there was hope—always hope—boundless hope—

Coningsby was dead by the time he returned to the Maesbury Stone. He laid him on the ground, closed his sagging mouth and tidied him up, as the proud man would have wanted. Then he went back to the house and told Bradley to have his lordship's body fetched and laid out in the chapel. In the library he read Coningsby's will. It had been made out the previous day at the law offices of Pollexfen & Moss. He replaced it on the library table, then he rode into Dorncaster to report Lord Coningsby's death.

An hour later he was sitting in Henry Pollexfen's office.

"Coningsby died this afternoon," he said.

Henry tilted back his chair. His face showed no surprise.

"I supposed yesterday, when I was called into Moss's office, that he had suicide in mind. It was the best way out of his legal difficulties. How did he accomplish it?"

"He opened an artery and bled to death in the ancient Roman manner. It will be listed as accidental."

"A strange turn of events. Strange, indeed! Did you by any chance speak with Coningsby before he died?"

"Briefly."

"Did he mention his new will?"

"He directed me to read it."

"Then you know he acknowledged the boy as his son. That infant is now heir to the Coningsby titles, estates, and wealth."

"Can the next of kin contest?"

"Hardly. Coningsby made it very clear that the boy was his 'beloved son.' And the boy was born in wedlock. I cannot help wondering, though, what induced Coningsby to do such a thing." Henry's eyes leveled in sudden shrewdness. "What do you know of this, John?"

John's face did not change expression. "The last time I was here you advised me not to involve myself in the Coningsby affair. Remember?"

"Quite!" Henry said dryly. "Ah, yes, quite! And how is the infant coming along?"

"He is small and puny, but gaining weight. He has a good wet-nurse, young Sally Both, whose own infant died last week. And Mrs. Salmon and Janice mother him as if he were their own. He is loved."

Henry gave a short, cynical laugh. "With considerably more love to come, I suspect. Now that his affairs have taken an unexpectedly prosperous turn, his maternal grandparents will find time to notice him. The local gossips have it that so far they have not even been over to see him."

"Prudent nonobservance, it is called. They will be sorely perplexed, though, when they learn he is now young Lord Coningsby of Aethelthorpe."

"So will the gossips," Henry said with a certain glee. "This will keep them bustling for a month. Well, now to business. Have you given any more thought to selling the mill land?"

"I have never given thought to it at any time."

"Oh, come now, John, you must have something in mind. I rode by the other day and saw them tearing the old mill down."

"I ordered it torn down."

"May I ask why?"

"That would be pointless."

"In any case, it is not the mill itself my client is interested in. He is interested in the land. He wants to build a house there. He will pay a good price, John."

"It is not for sale."

"Are you planning to build on it yourself?"

"Heaven forbid!"

"Well, then, why not sell it?"

"Damn it, Henry! Because I am going to *give* the land away."

Henry raised his eyebrows in surprise. "Give it away? To whom?"

"Do you never stop probing?"

"It is my business to probe."

John grinned. "It is your nature, too, my boy."

"Agreed!" Henry said, unruffled. "But would it not be more profitable to sell than to give?"

"If you are talking of money, yes."

"Well, what else is there?"

Henry waited, his chair tipped back, his green eyes fixed intently on John's face as if seeking to penetrate his mind. When the minutes passed and he got no reply, he grew impatient.

"Honestly, John," he burst out, "I am curious. Here you are, admittedly the most respected doctor in the county, with a lucrative practice, yet you live in that cottage under the city wall among the poorest 'prentices, draymen, tanners, tailors, bootmakers, and what not. Why? Why not build yourself a mansion on that valuable mill property? Why do you not ride a fine stallion? Why do you not dress extravagantly like the gentleman you are? Why, John, why? What do you do with all that money?"

"What makes you think I have 'all that money'?"

"Because I know who your patients are. I know you are abstemious. I know how you live. What do you do with all your wealth, John?"

But John only grinned. "You seem to know everything else, Henry. I thought you knew that."

Henry shifted his feet and changed the subject. "Any news yet of Joe Fox?"

"Not yet."

"He will be lucky to get through, John," Henry warned. "And Jenny Sykes. I hear this jail fever is abating, that the place has been cleaned out. You will be expected to return her, you know."

"She is not yet well enough to be moved."

Henry said nothing for a moment. He let the minutes pass by while his mind explored the more immediate business at hand.

"This morning," he said, "I rode over to Lying-In and had a talk with Jenny Sykes."

"Good! I told her you would be coming. Did you find her helpful?"

"Helpful? Unfortunately, no. That is an exceptionally intelligent girl, John. I was surprised to find a woman so highly educated. At first this seemed to offer some encouragement, since I felt she would be capable of understanding how vital her co-operation would be in the preparation of her defense. But I got no help at all. I left Lying-In knowing as little about her case as when I arrived. I am certain of only one thing—she is hiding something she is desperately afraid we may uncover."

"I am certain of that, too, but that 'something' is not her own guilt."

"How can you be sure of that?"

"Because I have come to know Jenny."

"Have you questioned her?"

"On several occasions."

"Did she answer your questions?"

"Not always."

"Did you ask if she had been raped?"

"Yes."

"And?"

"I got no answer."

"Did you ask about her lover?"

"There, too, she was unresponsive."

"Precisely! John, this girl simply has no defense. On the surface it looks like the age-old story of an innocent girl seduced, then abandoned, by her lover. If there is more to her story than that, she is not telling, and the only one who knows is the man who impregnated her. The fact is, John, as this case now stands, it is already lost. I do not want you to think I have any hope of an acquittal. I do not. If it were not for your extraordinary interest in the case, I would have washed my hands of it at the start."

"Jenny is not guilty, Henry."

"Not guilty of what? Not guilty of concealment of birth? She is guilty as hell of that!"

"She did not kill her child," John said. "I am hoping this hydrostatic test I told you about can prove her child was stillborn."

Henry swung around and put down his feet. "Tell me about this test."

"I do not yet have all the particulars. But it is based on the fact that the lungs of a stillborn are dense, heavier than water, so when they are placed in a bowl containing water, they sink to the bottom. The lungs of an infant which was born alive, however, by consequence of the admission of air, will float on water once it has breathed. The general conclusions deducible from this hydrostatic test, therefore, are that if the lungs swim, the infant was live-born; if they sink, the infant was deadborn."

"But the trial might not be scheduled for another week—perhaps ten days. What about decomposition in the meantime? Would not decomposition admit air into even the dense lungs of a stillborn?"

"No," John answered. "An infant's lungs are known to be among the last, if not the very last, parts of the body to become putrid. In the case of stillbirth, putrefaction of the lungs has been known to be delayed up to five months."

"And has the validity of this test been confirmed?"

"It has, but I have asked for fuller particulars on that. In the German States the test has already been successfully applied in several legal cases."

Henry shook his head. "My dear John, do not be misled by that. You know Europe has been the leader in this new legal medicine. You know the University of Leipzig is already giving courses in medical jurisprudence, something all but unknown here in England. It will be a hard struggle to get any such new test admitted in an English court of law. If we are fortunate in having a young, alert trial judge and can prevail upon him to admit it, it will still be a pioneer case, and pioneer cases are rarely successful. And even after you have explained the rationale in layman's terms, I doubt that either judge or jurors will feel secure in blindly accepting a process which in England is untried and which they do not fully understand."

John said nothing. His face was grave as he got to his feet and moved over to the window, standing there, gazing down into the street. Henry watched him with a kind of questioning uncertainty.

"John," he asked after a moment, "are you infatuated with this girl?"

"Not infatuated, Henry."

"What, then?"

Henry waited, but John did not answer.

Slowly Henry's inquiring eyes widened. "In love, John? With a girl who, for all our willingness to help, remains deliberately evasive, incomprehensible, an enigma, a girl who, according to law, stands to be hanged within forty-eight hours of her trial?" Henry stared in astonishment. "John, are you drunk?"

"At this hour? Hardly."

Henry was speechless for a moment.

"But this girl has borne a bastard child," he said. "She has a secret lover whom she clearly has no intention of forsaking. She has secrets that will not bear airing. How can you feel anything for her except, perhaps, pity?"

"Henry, I have puzzled over all the points you have made. There is nothing I have not thought of, no argument I have not wrestled with, no unanswered questions I have not asked myself. Yet still I trust her. And—yes, I love her."

"Bless my soul! The human capacity for self-delusion is unfathomable." Henry paused, frowning. "But if you truly love her, John, how are you going to take it when she goes to the gallows?"

John said nothing. His expression was unreadable.

Henry's voice was suddenly gentle, with a depth of compassion he rarely permitted himself to show. "You know, do you not, John, there may be no way we can prevent her execution."

Still John said nothing. His face was hard and grim, his mouth set in so stern a line it might have been chiseled out of granite.

Henry grew uneasy. He said warily, "I hope you are not planning anything rash, John. Infatuated men—even men in love—can at times be irrational. . . ."

But John Toller had no need just then of practical or moral wisdom. He turned without a word and walked slowly out the door.

He still had many calls to make and it was not until late afternoon that he turned homeward through the autumn dusk. It was suppertime and the narrow streets of the working quarter were all but empty, so the measured *clop-clop* of Iris's hooves echoed loudly on the cobblestones. Iris was cantankerous tonight. She resented having been neglected all day, stalled in so many strange stables without John himself to feed and water her and give her his sole attention. A quirky mood was on her and she moved at a laggardly pace to make her displeasure evident.

John leaned forward and patted her neck.

"There, girl, take your own time getting home, then. Tomorrow I will walk to the hospital. I will leave the doors of the cottage open so you can stay in your stall and come over and join me when you are ready."

He settled back and allowed his thoughts to run on.

Henry's somber appraisal of Jenny's chances had left him weary and dispirited. There was much cold logic in Henry's arguments and the outcome would now depend on the trial judge, on his intellectual vitality, on his personal sense of justice and independence—virtues which, under a chief justice who pandered to an increasingly tyrannical king, were hardly to be looked for at the moment. Since this test had already saved innocent lives on the Continent, there was no doubt it would in time come to be recognized by English courts of law. But perhaps Henry was right. Perhaps it would first, as in the German States, have to be evaluated and confirmed by English medical faculties.

He sighed.

But that would be too late for Jenny.

They were nearing the cottage when Iris blew warily. John looked up. The window of his parlor was rosy with the glow of lamplight. Whoever had trespassed his home tonight was making no effort to conceal his presence. A horse was tethered outside.

John dismounted and, leading Iris by the bridle, entered the house.

"Good evening, Vicar," he said.

The vicar had been bending over, looking through John's microscope. He glanced up. "I hope you did not mind me entering, Doctor. You did leave your door unlocked."

"I leave my door unlocked, Vicar, because people do not generally enter in my absence, so there is no need to lock it."

"I apologize, sir. I seem to recall you entered my home once without permission."

"Not in your absence, Vicar. But you are welcome. Just let me stable my mare, then perhaps you will join me in a glass of wine."

The vicar stared uncivilly as the mare paced her way daintily through the parlor. By the time John returned from the yard, however, he had recovered his aplomb and was again bending over the microscope, adjusting the screws for a clearer view.

"What have we here, Doctor?" he asked.

"It is one of the newer, more powerful microscopes. I ordered it two years ago. It only arrived last week."

"And what are you studying?"

"The circulation of the blood. Before his death, our own William Harvey, the great physician-anatomist, had correctly inferred the existence of the capillary circulation, but got no further with the unaided eye. It was not until some four years after Harvey's death that the Italian scientist Malpighi, employing a compound microscope, saw for the first time the blood coursing through a network of small tubes on the surface of the lung and in the distended urinary bladder of a frog. Malpighi, of course, was working with living animals."

The vicar straightened up and turned, a towering, cadaverous figure in his black threadbare garments. His sharp nose was sharper than before, his sallow face disturbingly haggard. The dark, intense eyes glittered strangely from the caverns of his sockets. His fierce, hawklike spirit seemed to fill the room, to turn the atmosphere into a battleground for the raging conflicts of his furious mind. Even his voice had a turbulent quality. He made no effort to conceal the disdain he felt for what, to him, was a fatuous pursuit.

He said, "And it is frogs you are interested in, sir?"

"It is humans I am interested in, Vicar," John replied with scrupulous courtesy. "To understand what goes on in the lower animals is to have a better understanding of what goes on in the human body. But come, tell me what you think of this wine. It comes from a small vinyard in the Côte-d'Or."

The vicar seated himself and sipped his wine, but without apparent interest or enjoyment. He was frowning, as though his brilliant, fanatical mind was having trouble grappling with the practical applications of a science annoyingly unfamiliar to him.

He said with hostile skepticism, "And you actually see a similarity there?"

"Between humans and the lower animals? Indeed, at times there appears to be a startling similarity, one might almost say a uniformity."

"Absurd! The Book of Genesis tells us that only man is made in God's own image and that He created the beasts 'each after its own kind.' Your assumption, sir, is entirely without logic."

"Each man perceives logic through his own eyes, Vicar."

The vicar gave a disparaging smile. "I can see that the logic of doctors, like the logic of kings, is rooted in sophistry. Indeed, sir, I have heard it said that these days all a man needs to be a doctor is a glib tongue."

John was silent for a moment while he mastered his sudden up-surge of anger.

"I can only say, Vicar," he replied at last, "the man who expressed that opinion was exposing abysmal ignorance. These days, with the enactment of harsher measures against treason, with new restrictions on printing presses and the consequent sparsity of medical publications, the physician who exercises only his tongue would soon find himself sunk in a quag of medical stagnation. Rigid censorship has led to the impover-ishment of scientific life, and today's physician must initiate for himself a primitive form of medical journalism—laboriously written by hand, dispatched by courier and exchanged through a webwork of designated corresponding physicians in England and overseas, thereby ensuring the continued circulation of scientific discoveries and experimental trends. This archaic system is all that preserves what would otherwise be lost under the new restrictions—the concerted advancement of medical sci-ence. No, Vicar, in these days of stifled debate, when the printed word is all but outlawed and Milton's dream of liberty of unlicensed printing is yet unrealized, it is not a glib tongue a physician needs so much as an innovative mind."

The vicar dismissed this with an impatient wave of his hand. "And do you study things other than frogs through your microscope?"

"Quite a number of things—the fluids and solids of the human body, the corpuscles of the blood, the spermatozoa in the seminal fluid."

The vicar's dark eyes turned on John disapprovingly, amazingly alive. "That last is indecent, sir—positively ungodly."

"Not to the man who desperately wants a child, but is having trouble impregnating his wife."

"Some women are barren, sir."

"It is doubtful that this woman is barren. She bore her former husband eight healthy children before he was killed in an accident."

Again the vicar made an impatient gesture. He said incredulously, "And you enjoy this profession?"

"I know of no greater satisfaction than to save a life and make it possible for that person to go on living."

The vicar's face seemed to tighten. The veins thickened in his forehead. "But what if a man *wants* to die?"

John gazed thoughtfully into the dark face with its restless, blazing eyes and tormented mouth. The man had changed since that day in the courtroom. His afflictions did not appear to be physical, though he was certainly scourging his body with prolonged starvation. But these other scourgings were more deep-rooted, more complex. He seemed to be suffering from destructive forces at work within him, from recurring spiritual crises, fierce and bloody battles raging on the wild landscape of what religionists would call his soul.

John answered in a quiet voice, "If a man *wants* to die, Vicar, he is likely to die."

"Even if he has a good physician?"

"Seneca said, 'It is part of the cure to wish to be cured.' "

"And in your practice have you found that to be true?"

"In general, yes. But we still know so little. At times it is impossible not to stand in awe before phenomena which seem to defy the laws of nature. I have witnessed two such phenomena recently, a two-year-old boy with a malignant abdominal tumor which cleared spontaneously, and a newborn I delivered from his dying mother only last week. The child, puny, born before his time, seems determined to live. I believe he will live."

The contemptuous insolence was back in the vicar's manner. "Then you also act the midwife, sir?"

"No, Vicar—the obstetrician. These days, qualified physicians concern themselves with pregnancy and childbirth. Even William Harvey, physician extraordinary to the King and one of the great anatomists of our time, had considerable obstetric experience and wrote on the nature of generation. It is necessary to have a knowledge of the anatomy and physiology of the female genital tract, to be familiar with the different positions of the fetus *in utero*, in order to know when cesarean section is the only way to deliver a child and save a woman's life—something no untrained midwife would have the anatomical knowledge to perform."

"Medicine is changing, sir."

"Medicine is advancing, Vicar."

John got up and refilled both glasses, then returned to his chair and waited quietly for the vicar to make known the reason for his visit. He was hoping the vicar would ask to see Jenny, that the natural order of things would take over and the father would seek to help his child.

But the direction of the conversation soon disabused him of that hope.

"Doctor," the vicar began, "the last time we talked you said there was a new test by which my daughter might escape the gallows. I have been wondering how that matter is progressing."

John slowly sipped his wine. Unaccountably he felt his body go tense. He was suddenly on guard.

"That," he replied warily, "is as much a legal matter as it is medical. Henry Pollexfen is preparing her case, though I doubt he would be willing to discuss that particular point at the moment."

"I see. And how soon do you expect Jenny's case to come up?"

"Probably as soon as the rebel trials end and the regular jail delivery commences."

"Has she provided you with any further disclosures?"

Again John sipped his wine. "Disclosures, Vicar? Concerning what?"

"Concerning the circumstances of her—her foul crime?"

"Vicar, what grounds have you for assuming that your daughter is guilty of a foul crime?"

He waited. The silence dragged.

"There, now," the vicar said, rising suddenly to his feet. "I must not keep you. I have enjoyed our little chat. It is rare to find an educated man in these parts."

They shook hands in the open doorway and John stood there, thoughtfully watching the emaciated form ride slowly into the dusk astride his emaciated, spiritless horse.

John wondered what force, conscious or unconscious, had driven the vicar to see him. What was his purpose? What was he searching for? And had he found it?

John stood in the tower room, looking down at James.

He had been dead at least six hours. The distorted features had taken on a brutish look, thickened and swollen into something grotesquely unhuman. A few torpid flies explored the inside of the gaping mouth and buzzed around the sightless eyes and the vesicles of the hairless scalp.

Poor James! Lucas's protective love for his son had only caused the boy more suffering. Perhaps he would have been better off living with the other lepers on the banks of the river near Delft instead of here in this lonely tower room, a sad prison aloof from the world, his days filled with intensifying horror. But Lucas could not face the personal sacrifice of separation from James. Love, at times, could be more cruel than hate.

He turned to Lucas, waiting in the doorway.

"He went peacefully, Lucas," he said. "He is lying in the same position as when I last saw him. I doubt he ever regained consciousness."

Lucas turned away to hide the convulsive workings of his face. He started slowly down the stairs. John took his own handkerchief and dropped it over James's face to keep off the flies. Then he followed.

"As to the disposal of the body," he continued, "no one must handle it, Lucas. It must be covered with a heavy cloth and left where it is. Then this tower room must be sealed forever."

Down in the library they sat before the fire, sipping their port, each man absorbed in his own disturbing thoughts.

Lucas was the first to speak. "You are my heir now, John."

John looked up. "I am not yet prepared to accept that, Lucas."

"Why not?"

"I will not place myself in the position of being a pretender."

"You will have a valid claim."

"How can you know that?"

"My lawyers have assured me."

"How can your lawyers give you any such assurance unless they already have proof of my legitimacy?"

Lucas hesitated. "Presumably they expect to obtain proof."

John sipped his port and contemplated Lucas. It would be interesting to know what game Lucas was playing. His cousin Sidney was within his rights to regard himself as Lucas's heir-at-law after James, and Lucas must be aware that, however much he resisted the idea, he could not hope to substitute a false claimant for a legitimate heir. So what design was he carrying out? What was his scheme of action? Lucas seemed to be a reasonably honest man, but fear of some event he foresaw as calamitous to his own interests was forcing his puzzling behavior. He seemed to be working to conceal some crucial information while revealing just enough to keep his plan moving forward. But Lucas was an uneasy liar. A strong suggestion of conscious guilt tainted his every subterfuge.

On impulse, with sudden insight, John asked, "What did they do with Chérie's body?"

Lucas answered without thought. "They buried her in the forest—" Then he stopped, aghast, realizing he had been surprised into an admission he never intended to make.

"Does her grave have a marker?"

"We did not think to set one up."

"Why not?"

Lucas's eyes shifted, evading John's angry, penetrating gaze. "John, I was distraught. My brother had just been killed in an accident. My father lay dying. I had no thought for markers."

"Why did you not bury Chérie next to Adam?"

"In the Tremoigne family cemetery? John, she was not a Tremoigne. She was not Adam's wife. She was only Adam's—"

"Do not say it, Lucas!" There was a moment of angry silence. Then John asked more quietly, "What makes you think Chérie was not Adam's wife?"

Lucas cleared his throat. "Well, we had no reason to suppose—"

"Then why do you insist that I have a valid claim?"

Lucas's forehead glistened as the perspiration burst out at every pore. "John, you are now delving into matters of which I know very—"

"Why did you tell me you had never heard of Chérie?"

"Well—I was afraid—"

"How was Chérie killed? Who killed her? Were those your men, Lucas?"

Lucas's face was tense. He had never foreseen the possibility of one day being asked to account for a woman's broken body.

He temporized. "I did not say they were my men."

"Are you saying they were *not* your men?"

There was a long pause. Lucas's face had turned ashen. He stared back at John with the supplicating look of a frightened animal caught in a trap.

"Chérie's death was an accident, John," he said evasively. "The men went up to the High Moor to search for Chérie and the boy—only to bring them back—back to their own comfortable cottage. But Chérie seemed obsessed by some irrational fear. She started running. She ran so recklessly that the men thought afterward that she must have been trying to draw them away from the boy's hiding place. She was leaping down the Caistor Rocks. She fell. They found her sprawled at the bottom. Her neck was broken."

John drew a long, hard breath. "But why, Lucas? Why? Why Chérie? Why have you never told me the truth? Why, even now, do you continue to lie to me?"

Lucas had started openly to weep. He hid his face in his hands. "No more today, John," he begged. "No more today. Today I am grieving for my son."

John's voice was cold and hard. "And I," he answered harshly, "have grieved for Chérie these twenty long years."

They sat in silence while John's anger cooled and Lucas recovered his composure. Then John rose to leave.

He came and put a sympathetic hand on Lucas's shoulder. "I am truly sorry about James," he said. "Through his long ordeal he showed himself to be a brave lad—a son of whom you can be proud."

But something smoldered inside him as he headed back toward Dorncaster. Lucas's careless words rebounded through his brain like a series of echoes. *She was not a Tremoigne. She was not Adam's wife. She was only Adam's—*

Again the swell of protective anger rose within him. And all these years Chérie had lain in the forest, without a marker, without a name. By God, that would be changed! Tremoigne or not, he would have her moved. He would have her buried where she belonged, beside Adam.

She was only Adam's—

"God's teeth!" he muttered angrily.

He was skirting the Dunheved Forest when suddenly he reined in.

A cottage stood by the roadside. In the garden an aged woman was hanging out the wash.

"Good day, Effie," he called. "Do you happen to know which trail leads to Dan Reeves's cottage?"

The old woman turned and gave him a toothless smile. "Day to 'ee, Doc." She raised a bony arm and pointed with a knotted finger. "Jest 'ee take that first trail yonder into the Dunheved woods. There be many a trail 'ee 'ull cross 'long the way, mind! But jest 'ee keep heading south till 'ee smells the salt o' the sea. That be where 'tis. 'Bout a mile off the cliffs. 'Ee 'ull find it."

It was quiet in this lonely part of the forest. The poachers worked only at night, at which time they hoped the foresters, whose duty it was to guard the vert and venison, would be in their beds. But they were so audacious that signs of their activities were everywhere: abandoned nets into which they drove the deer to first entangle, then strangle them; tracks of men and dogs; hoofmarks of the horses on which they loaded their kill. It was said the entire countryside maintained itself bountifully on Lord Tremoigne's deer.

After a while the great oaks gave way to light woodland dotted with wind-bitten firs and pines, the blue sky wide above. The sea breeze blew in his face. The trail became sandy. Presently he sighted, above the treetops, the curl of blue wood smoke.

He dismounted and tethered Iris to a tree. Then he crossed to the cottage and knocked on the door.

A white-haired woman greeted him with a delighted smile. "Why, 'tis Doctor John come to see us. Come in—come in, Doctor John, and sit 'ee by our hearth a spell. These autumn days do give the bones a real chill." She went to the foot of the stairs. "Dan. Dan, hurry down. 'Tis Doctor John is here to see us."

Dan Reeves limped in with the aid of his walking stick, his white hair flowing to his shoulders, a wide smile on his face.

"Now, Doctor John, this be a grand surprise—none grander in this house in many a year."

"How are you feeling, Dan?"

"Good! Real good, Doc. 'Ee fixed me up so I be fit and strong as I ever was. I kin hunt again, and chop me own firewood and all. Come, join me in some ale and cheese and some o' Mary's fresh home-baked bread." He turned to his wife. "Hurry 'long, girl, open up the parlor for our guest."

They sat together in the front room as Mary fussed about, first putting tinder to the fire and watching it flare up, then setting out her best china for her guest. But after she had served them, perceiving that some private matter was about to be discussed, she discreetly withdrew and closed the door.

"Dan," John began, "I wonder if you would answer a few questions. While you were in the hospital last winter we talked of an accident in the Dunheved Forest, the one in which young Adam Tremoigne was killed. Do you recall?"

Dan sensed a closer questioning on the subject and a wary expression came into his face. "But us was on'y passing the time, Doc. That acc'dent was all of many years gone by. It is 'most forgot. Why 'ud 'ee be asking 'bout it now?"

"I have an interest in the matter, Dan. But let me say before we begin that whatever we talk about today must go no further."

Dan looked more comfortable. "Seems fair."

"When we talked at the hospital you told me you remembered Adam Tremoigne's death."

"I was not there at the acc'dent, Doc, but it was the big talk at the time."

"And you remembered Chérie and her little son, who was also Adam's son?"

"Aye, I 'member 'em."

"Can you tell me what happened to Chérie?"

Dan's eyes clouded over. "That be so'thing none of us ever talked 'bout much, Doc. I reckon I don' like talking 'bout it now, either."

"I understand. But will you talk about it anyway? Remember, this is just between you and me."

Slowly Dan's hesitation seemed to fade. "Well, then—it was the new Lord Tremoigne."

"You mean Lucas?"

"Aye, Doc—as he was then, the new young Lord Tremoigne. Him sent a party of trackers to find out where the woman and the boy had run off to. The tracks led up to the High Moor, so him sent the trackers back up there to find the woman and the boy and fetch 'em back."

"Why, Dan? Why did he want to fetch them back?"

Dan hesitated. Again he looked uncomfortable. "Doctor John, there was so'thing queer 'bout it all, but none of us foresters was ever able to figure out what 'twas. In the end, though, it made no matter.

The woman was killed. Her little boy dis'peared and was niver heard of again."

"Do you know how Chérie was killed?"

"No, I was not in the tracking party. And those that was in the party 'ud niver talk of it."

"And what do you know of Chérie, Dan? Where did she come from? Was she a Dorncaster girl?"

"Nay, I don' reckon her was from anywheres 'round here. I reckon her must have come from somewheres east of here."

"Why do you reckon that?"

"Because Lord Tremoigne—young Lucas, that is—give her little cabin over to me youngest son, Ben, while him was still a forester here, before him went off to the wars and got hisself kill't. Ben cleaned out the little place 'fore moving in. Him found a prayer book, all black and gold, with some writing in it. Him give it to me to give to her family in case one of 'em come riding 'long the cliffs looking for her."

"Did no one ever come?"

"No, Doc."

"Do you still have the prayer book?"

Dan looked blank and scratched his head. "It was all that long ago," he muttered. "Now, let me see—"

The old man turned and searched the drawers and finally found the prayer book. He dusted it off on the corner of the tablecloth and brought it to John.

John held it between his hands, gazing down at it.

Aye, for some reason Chérie had loved this prayer book.

Slowly he opened it. The writing on the yellowed page was round and girlish and very faded. But he could still read the words.

CHÉRIE. LITTLE CHAPEL IN THE WOODS. A.D. 1656

After a moment he looked up. "Dan, have you ever heard of the Little Chapel in the Woods?"

"Nay, Doc, I niver did. But my Ben said him knowed it. It be a tiny run-down chapel on an old estate somewheres east of here—eastward 'long the cliffs, him said. That be why him thought a brother or someone might come riding 'long the cliffs looking for her."

"Eastward along the cliffs? Thank you, Dan. May I keep the prayer book?"

"Why not, Doc. No one else be wanting it."

"And one more question. Have you ever heard of Margaret Bemis?"

"Margaret Bemis? Nay, Doc. Who was she?"

"That is what I want to find out."

He set off along the track on the edge of the cliffs. The sea sparkled under the blue sky, lacing the beach below. The seabirds soared and mewed above. He was climbing a headland that rose to a rocky peak when, up ahead, he heard the clatter of pots and saw a peddler on a donkey round the bend and start precariously downhill toward him.

He reined in to the side of the narrow trail. "Would you know the Little Chapel in the Woods?" he called.

The peddler seemed afraid to check his lurching animal on this dangerous slope. He swung around in his packsaddle and pointed back the way he had come.

"Keep a-going, sir," he shouted. "The headland . . . a cove . . . some woods . . . to the Little Chapel."

John called his thanks and rode on.

He came upon it suddenly, a quiet, neglected graveyard filled with mossy headstones leaning at grotesque angles, half-hidden by rank grass and weeds, ancient beyond belief. The names on the headstones were obliterated, worn away by centuries of rain, frost, and storm. He could make out only one date—1325 A.D. and, here and there upon some stone, worn and faint, the family crest, a wivern rampant with expanded wings, its barbed tail knotted. Rising tall among the humble hillocks was a mausoleum above whose ruined portal he made out the same worn crest. Once it had been a noble burial chamber, now it was moldering to dust, patterned with emerald moss and white and orange patches of slow-creeping lichen. Where were they all gone, this proud and ancient race represented here by the fabulous wivern rampant?

Did only blind Time walk now in this abandoned place?

"My son, may I help you?"

John turned and looked down at the wizened priest with his wild white hair, his scrawny neck encircled by its frayed collar, the cassock blowing about his thin shanks almost gone to rags.

"Forgive me, Father," he replied. "I was quite lost in reverie. My name is John Toller, physician, from Dorncaster. I have come to ask your help." He drew the prayer book from his pocket and handed it to the priest. "As you will see, Father, there is a name written in this book —'Chérie.' I am hoping you can tell me something about its owner."

The priest took the open book and raised it close to his eyes, looking intently down at it in an effort to make out the inscription. After a moment of scrutiny he nodded. "Ah, yes—Chérie. Yes, yes, my son. I remember Chérie." He peered regretfully up into John's face. "But Chérie disappeared, you know. I cannot tell you what became of her. I do not know. No one knows."

"Then you do know who Chérie was?"

"Of course, my son. I baptized her—right here in the Little Chapel."

"Was Chérie her baptismal name?"

"Dear me, no! Her baptismal name was Margaret Mary. Margaret Mary Bemis. Only her young man ever called her Chérie."

"Do you remember her young man's name?"

Slowly the old priest shook his head. "Ah, no—I do not recall. So long ago! He was not from hereabouts. But such a nice young man. He and Margaret were so much in love. No, I do not recall his name, I am afraid. Too many years! Too many years! But he called her Chérie— always Chérie. I married them myself, you know—right here in the Little Chapel."

John's heart gave a leap. "Then would not his name be in the church register?"

"Why, yes, of course—the church register."

"Would you permit me to look at it, Father?"

"Of course, my son. Come with me."

The old priest led John across the graveyard to a dilapidated chapel with quaint round-headed, double-splayed windows and a squat bell gable. The heavy oak door creaked on rusty hinges as he pushed it open. A stiff sea breeze whipped through the broken window, yet still the taint of mold and decay hung on the air. Weeds sprouted among the pews. Rats had gnawed off Saint Anthony's wooden toes. Yet in the dimness could be glimpsed recumbent effigies carved in alabaster, mutilated but still sublime, of knights reclining in their armor, their unseeing eyes fixed on measureless eternity. Beside them, in peaceful sleep, lay their alabaster ladies, and carved on all the tombs was the family crest, the token of the wivern rampant.

Suddenly the old man halted and began searching about among the pews, frowning in bewilderment.

"Now, I know I put it away," he muttered, "out of the rain—yes, yes, rain was dripping from the roof that day. Yes, I remember that. I brought it out here, where the roof was solid—now, let me see, where did I put it—?"

At last he located the church register, safe and almost dry beneath a pew. He dragged it out and lifted it in his arms and tabled it on a knight's alabaster stomach. Carefully he unrolled the black cloth in which he had wrapped it, an old cassock scarcely less ragged than the one he wore. Then, lovingly, with trembling hands, he began turning the yellowed, rain-spotted pages.

Suddenly he paused. "Ah, yes, yes, here we have it—yes. Yes, yes. Her young man's name, then, was Adam—Adam Ambrose Charles Tremoigne of Dunheved Castle—that might well be somewhere out your way, my son. Now, let me see. Adam married Margaret on June 8, 1656. Yes, that is what it says." He turned. "Would you care to look for yourself, my son?"

John was acutely aware of the quickening of his pulses as he read the words: *Margaret Mary Bemis of Beaumyss.*

He turned to the priest. "Is that where she came from, Father? This place called Beaumyss?"

"Of course, my son. All the Bemises came from Beaumyss. This little chapel was once part of the old Bemis estate. All the tombstones you were looking at in the graveyard—all Bemises. Here in this chapel —all those armed knights carved in alabaster—all Bemises. All were born at Beaumyss."

"Was Chérie born at Beaumyss?"

"Of course."

"But where *is* Beaumyss?"

The old priest peered up at John in surprise. "You do not know Beaumyss? No? Well, it is far gone in ruin now, of course, so perhaps it is not surprising. A backwater. Forgotten by the world, I am afraid. But it is still there, my son. It is still there. Would you have a mind to visit it? It is only three miles up the Oxhill Road." Then, reading the eagerness in John's eyes, he smiled. "Come, my son. I will take you to the edge of the woods and set you on your way."

At the chapel door John stopped to empty his pockets of gold coins and drop them in the church box. The old priest heard the thudding and turned, surprised, and laid a restraining hand on John's arm.

"No, no, my son, you are too generous. God does not expect— here, let me give you some back—"

But John shook his head, apologizing for his insistence. "Forgive me, Father, but this Little Chapel and its memories mean much to me."

"But why, my son? Why? I have wondered at your interest."

It was a moment before John could bring himself to make the admission he had never felt free to make until now. "Because Adam and Chérie were my parents, Father. Because I am their son."

On the Oxhill Road he nudged Iris to a fast trot, eager to set eyes on Beaumyss. "You cannot miss the gates, my son," the old priest had said. "They will lie on your left—big double gates. The name is writ above them."

It would, indeed, have been impossible to miss the gates. They rose majestically between two crumbling stone towers, tall against the sky. He drew rein, gazing upward. The elaborate ironwork was embellished with a profusion of roses, lilies, and pomegranates, interspersed with foliage and birds. Above was the single word B E A U M Y S S, surmounted by three shields bearing the ancestral arms.

The gates were rusted, unused. One of them hung partway open on broken hinges. He rode through the narrow space and started up the drive.

It must have been magnificent once. Now it was long neglected, overgrown with weeds and saplings, untrodden for ages by human foot. "A backwater," the old priest had said. "Forgotten by the world." Where, then, had this abandoned driveway once led? What, indeed, was Beaumyss? He had forgotten to ask. He turned and looked about. Deep woods and turfy glades extended on either side. A few birds called in the high woods. Last year's beech mast crackled under Iris's hooves. But all else was strangely silent, a place of deep enchantment.

At last the woods ended. He came from under their shadow into the sunlight of a spacious outer court.

Then he saw Beaumyss.

It was a gaping ruin, the skeleton of a great castle sunk into decay. Creeping ivy had taken the gutted thing into its deadly embrace, twisting Hydra-like convolutions into the rotting mortar, loosening the stones of battlements and towers. The Norman keep, which for centuries had withstood the wild sea winds whirling round its gray skull, had finally been reduced under the ferocity of a siege train. The lower walls of the west front had been breached in several places, apparently by cannon fire, and the ensuing conflagration had taken what remained of the structure's paneled walls and inner timbering. Now only the granite shell remained, with a single turret stair winding upward to end in forlorn nothingness. The roof was charred. The sky showed through the empty sockets of the windows. No sense of placid repose wrapped this silent ruin. Beaumyss seemed to stand brooding on its fate, resentful and unforgiving.

Irresistibly drawn, he dismounted and tied Iris to a sapling. Then he walked around the castle until, on the east front, he saw where the besiegers had battered down the great portal. He went up the mossy steps. "Is anyone there?" he called, and waited for the echoes to run on from room to room and die.

Inside, he found himself in what appeared to be the great banqueting hall, with armorial ceiling and the one unbroken window displaying the arms of Beaumyss and their quarterings. The paneling of the stately room was charred. A rich arras, moth-eaten now, hung on one wall. The rest of the furnishings had been looted and the place was bare, a pile of age-worn stones deserted even by its ghosts. The music gallery at the far end had been hacked down. Broken columns lay upon the floor. The long gallery and ballroom were a vast cemetery of the past where even death was dead. He wandered on from room to empty room.

He had reached the inner court when he heard a sound behind him like the creaking of a floorboard beneath a stealthy foot. He swung around. He saw no one. But something was there. He could almost hear it breathe. His heart thudded uncomfortably. Nervous prickles raced along his spine. When he came to the next room he stepped behind the doorpost and waited. The minutes stretched out. Presently, when no one overtook him, he decided it must have been the patter of debris falling from the ceiling. He moved on. A sweeping double staircase opened up before him and he started up it, then halted, seeing it led only to a charred and devastated landing. He turned back the way he had come, and after a while, coming to a maze of ruins like tumbled rocks at a cliff's foot, he went out again into the sunshine.

He left the courtyard by the postern gate and wandered down a majestic avenue to the lake. Here the surrounding woods were one great canopy of gold and bronze. The tall willow herbs had burst their long seed pods and smothered themselves with clinging down—along the shore the reeds and sedges were changing from green to darkly amber. They made a crisp, plaintive whining when the wind brushed them. He looked across to the opposite bank and thought of Chérie. How often she must have stood on this spot, gazing off in the direction of distant Dunheved, dreaming of Adam—

He swung around.

Someone was there. Now he was sure of it. He could feel a pair of human eyes upon him. Quickly he glanced about. "Who are you?" No one answered. The air was full of furtive rustlings as the wind stirred the branches and sent the leaf-ghosts pattering down. Nothing else moved. Yet still he knew someone was there, watching him.

Then suddenly, off to his left, a pheasant skirred up from cover, flopping out with a gush of gold and brown feathers, and flew away with quick wingbeats low over the brush. John focused his eyes back toward the place from which it had risen, knowing the bird had been frightened by a human intruder.

At first he saw nothing. Then, as the branches of an oak tree stirred under the wind, he made out a man's face. Even then he was not certain that it was a face, for the flickering lights and shadows dappled the features with deceptive shapes. But he reasoned that whoever he was, his presence was not threatening. He would have had ample opportunity for a surprise attack back in the maze of empty rooms.

He took a few steps forward. Then he halted.

"Sir," he said, "my mother was a Bemis. I have just come from the Little Chapel where she was married. I was told she was born here at Beaumyss."

The reply came only after a moment of cautious reflection. "What you say may or may not be true, but you are trespassing my land."

"Then I apologize, sir. I did not intend to trespass. I only wanted to visit my mother's home."

"Who are you?"

"My adoptive name is John Toller; I am a physician from Dorncaster. My mother was Chérie—that is, Margaret Bemis. My father was Adam Tremoigne."

The man gave a low gasp and limped forward a few paces, then halted and put his hand on the trunk of a tree for support, seemingly so overcome by emotion that he was unable to advance any farther.

After a moment he said, "But how can that be? Margaret's little son is dead."

"No, sir. I am that son. I lived with Chérie in the Dunheved Forest until my father's death. Then we fled up to the High Moor. Chérie died there."

The tone was full of suspicion. "And you?"

"My mother had hidden me under a dolman. The searchers left without discovering my hiding place. A few days later I wandered down from the High Moor. Doctor Toller was making his rounds. He found me. He raised me and gave me his name."

Slowly the man emerged from the checkered shadows and came and stopped a few paces away, and John saw now that he was aged, one leg was crippled, and he walked with the aid of a blackthorn cane. His frame was stooped and frail, but his face was strong still, and weathered as a coign of rock. There was a bitter line to his lips. His fine hair made a silvery nimbus above the intense blue of his eyes which, in their look of haunted quiet, seemed to reflect long years of experience with pain and loss.

For a while he stood there, staring silently up as though seeking to find in John's face something reassuring, something to dissipate his lingering doubts.

At last he said, "You do look like him, though. Yes, you look like Adam. But no—it is impossible! Margaret's little son is dead. He died that winter with his mother up on the High Moor."

"No, sir. I did not die. I survived and was found by Doctor Toller. I am Chérie's son."

Still the old man seemed unable to believe. "If that is true—if what you say is true—then tell me—yes, tell me—by what special name did your mother call you?"

"She called me 'Child.' "

At that the old man let out a great sob and flung himself on John's breast and began to weep as though giving way at last to half a lifetime of pent grief. And John, seeing how it was with him, put his arms around him and held him, afraid the frail old man would fall.

A short while later they were sitting before the fire in Christopher Bemis's cabin, sipping homemade blackberry wine and eating cold pheasant.

It must have been a keeper's lodge at one time, for it was set back from the trails along which the poachers were likely to creep and was built of logs to blend in with the trees. Inside, it consisted of a single room, with a wooden bed at one end and the fireplace at the other, a rustic table, a few chairs, some shelves for cups and dishes. But it was comfortable, with a tight roof and deerskins hanging on the walls.

"I am your mother's elder brother, you know," the old man said,

"—older than Margaret by twenty years. She was just my baby sister, my little pet. I gave her to Adam Tremoigne because he promised to take care of her."

"He could not have foreseen the accident that killed him, Uncle."

"No, he could not have foreseen it. And he loved her. Do you remember your father, Adam?"

The use of the Christian name took John by surprise. "Was that my name, then? Adam?"

"Adam Ambrose Charles, after your father. Did you not know?"

John shook his head, smiling. "I do not recall ever being called that. Perhaps Chérie felt there could only be one Adam in her world. But yes, I remember my father very clearly. And I remember Chérie. Her memory has filled my life with warmth."

"And mine, too, my boy. And mine, too."

They sat for a while in silence, gazing into the flames, each man thinking his separate thoughts of Chérie.

Presently Christopher said. "It grieves me that you did not see your mother's home as it used to be, Adam. Parts of it dated back to the eleventh century, with walls ten feet thick. Beaumyss has been in our family for more than four hundred years."

"What happened, Uncle? The Civil Wars?"

"Aye, Adam. You see, we Bemises—the name was originally Norman, de Beaumyss, but was Anglicized—were ardent Royalists. We felt that, while the Stuart kings exceeded the bounds of their just prerogative, the Roundheads were no better. Cromwell was an arrogant usurper, investing himself with the trappings of royalty, using the royal estates for his personal enjoyment while keeping an ambitious eye fixed on the Crown itself. My father—your grandfather, Adam—was among the first of the great families to rally to the King's standard. But the royal coffers were empty. The King could not keep an army without money to pay it. So we, like all good Cavaliers, offered him everything we had—our jewels, our plate, our horses, our swords, our lives, our honor."

"Then you saw battle?"

"My father died on the battlefield at Naseby. My brother and I fought beside him. I suffered a musket bullet in the leg, which left me with this limp. But once again, the royal coffers were empty, the army so destitute of provisions that the best officers had but a biscuit a day, with only a handful of powder for the entire force. When the battle was lost, my elder brother was captured and taken to London. There he was attainted and beheaded. I was imprisoned. Parliament ordered Beaumyss to be demolished, our goods confiscated. Cromwell sent Fairfax with his heavy guns to breach our walls and reduce the castle to ruins. Having carried out his mission, Fairfax rode away, leaving his troops behind to loot and burn."

"Yet you are still more fortunate than most Cavaliers, Uncle. At least you still live on your own lands."

The bitterness was back about the old man's mouth.

"I do now, Adam. But for years I was turned off these lands and wandered, homeless, working as a groom on the estates of neighboring new-rich Roundheads. It was not until after Cromwell's death—after the Restoration—that the ruined castle was turned back to me, together with a portion of the forest land immediately surrounding it. But all the rest was gone. Cromwell had given our productive farmlands to a Colonel Hawkes and certain other officers by way of satisfaction for arrears in pay. Shortsighted fool! Today those farms stand idle, neglected. Rapacious plunderers do not make good farmers."

"And have you lived here alone all this time?"

"Ever since my wife died five years ago. My two sons quit England and I doubt I shall ever see them again. The older one, Daniel, lives in a place called Boston. The younger one, Randolph, captains a ship in the Caribbean. In leaving England they hoped to leave their bitterness behind. They will never return."

"But why, since the Bemises suffered so greatly, did the Tremoignes come through the Civil Wars unscathed?"

"My boy, old Tremoigne was the most wily of a knot of peers who took the side of the Parliament, yet still refused to align outright with Cromwell and the military. Later, when the tide turned, Tremoigne declared for the Restoration of the monarchy. He was politic, my boy, turning his coat without regard for principles." The old man paused and seemed to lose himself in unquiet thought. But after a moment he roused himself. "But now tell me about yourself, Adam. What are you doing with your young life?"

"My life has been troubled by sorrow, too, Uncle. I lost my wife and my two little sons. But I have found compensation in my professional life, first through Doctor Toller, who nurtured my love for medicine, then through Doctor Sydenham of Wynford Eagle, who educated me. I have a sizable practice."

The intense blue gaze was fixed on John's face for a moment of penetrating study. The question came slowly. "And Dunheved?"

"It seems I have a problem there. Lucas's only son, James, died recently after a long illness. Lucas claims I am his brother's son and therefore his heir. But supporting such a claim would require proof that I was born in wedlock. Until today I had no proof that my parents were even married. I still have no proof of birth."

"And Lucas?"

"Lucas says he is sure proof exists, but it will take time for his attorneys to establish it."

"Ah, yes, you were lost all those years. What name did you say you go by?"

"John Toller."

"And is it in your heart to want Dunheved?"

"Sometime in the future, perhaps."

"Not now?"

"No—not now."

"Why not?"

"Because my practice includes the poor as well as the rich."

"And you feel a viscount could not tend the poor?"

John smiled. "I could tend them, Uncle. The question is, would they permit me to? Would they permit Lord Tremoigne to visit them in their hovels? The poor are intimidated by titles. They tend to avoid them."

"And does the practice of medicine mean more to you than a viscountcy?"

"I would never give up medicine."

"You would prefer to renounce the inheritance?"

"Possibly. But I am hoping Lucas will enjoy a long life and spare me that painful decision till I am too old to sit a horse."

Again the old man was silent. He sat very still and seemed to be staring at something in his own mind.

"Noble birth imposes obligations, Adam," he said at last. "I hope in time you will come to see that. Should you ever wish to claim your inheritance, you will find your birth and baptismal records over in Sandford. You were born there at my cousin's house, Denbigh Hall, to Adam and Margaret Tremoigne on April nineteen. I particularly remember the date since it was also my little Margaret's birth date. The year was fifty-seven."

"Then I was born in wedlock?"

"Did you ever doubt it?"

"Then why did my parents find it necessary to keep their marriage secret?"

"Because old Tremoigne was trying to force Adam into a marriage which would have enriched the family and strengthened its alliances. Just then, however, he suffered a stroke of apoplexy—he was, in fact, thought to be dying—and Adam wanted to spare him on his deathbed. It was only a matter of time, Adam reasoned, before he would be free to announce his marriage to the world. So Adam waited, and old Tremoigne lingered on year after year. Then Adam was killed in that hunting accident."

"But why did Adam hesitate to tell his father the truth?"

"Because old Tremoigne had already forbidden the marriage. In his view Margaret was an unsuitable wife for Adam."

"Why? Because she was Catholic?"

"That, yes. But, my boy, look around you. We Bemises, for all our illustrious past, are now virtual paupers. Margaret had no dowry to take to the Tremoignes, no estates to carry into her marriage. Margaret was penniless."

"Did you ever try to learn what happened to her?"

"I went to Dunheved and demanded to see Lucas. He said that after Adam's death she took her little son and went to live on the High Moor. He said they both died up there, but he knew nothing of the circumstances."

"Did you believe that last?"

"I was disturbed. I was puzzled. I did not know what to think. Yet I was helpless. You must know now, Adam, that there is nothing a poor man can do against a rich and powerful one. I came back here and kept vigil outside the gates, hoping she would find her way back to Beaumyss."

John said very gently, "She could not come back, Uncle. I am certain she died on the High Moor."

"You truly believe that, Adam?"

"Yes."

"Why?"

"Because Chérie loved me. She would never have abandoned me. If she had lived, she would have come back to get me."

It was a moment before the old man spoke again. "Tell me what happened, Adam."

"There was something my mother feared. I do not know what. She took me in the night and fled up to the High Moor. A band of searchers trailed us up there. My mother hid me, then started running. I saw her run toward the Caistor Rocks. Lucas told me this morning that she was crossing those rocks when she fell."

"Then you do not believe he killed her?"

John considered that point. "Lucas is weak, Uncle. He is designing. He is a liar on occasion. But I do not believe he is capable of murder. Murder calls for a ruthlessness his indulgent nature lacks. Yet clearly his conscience is uneasy. This morning I tricked him into making partial admissions. But I am not done yet. I intend to have *all* the truth. I will force him to tell me how Chérie died, who was responsible."

"Do you know where she is buried?"

"Only that she is buried in the forest, on Dunheved land. But I am not done with that, either. Now that I know she was Adam's wife, I will insist that she be moved to the Tremoigne family cemetery. She will lie where she should have lain all these years, next to Adam. Her grave will be marked 'Margaret Bemis Tremoigne, Beloved Wife of Adam.' I will ride over and report to you on that later, Uncle. Perhaps you will come to Dunheved to visit her grave. But now tell me, are you happy living here alone? Would you prefer to come and live near me in Dorncaster?"

The old man's drawn lips relaxed into a grateful smile. "Thank you, my boy, but this is my home. I know every stag and hind, every buck and doe, every bird, every stream, every tree. I live sparingly off the land, taking only what I need to survive."

They talked on after that until the sun was sinking and John rose to go. Then Christopher Bemis went to a corner of his cabin and scraped away the earth and brought out a bundle tied up in deerskin. Unwrapping it, he exposed a two-handled wine cup. He came and placed it in John's hands.

John gazed down at it in amazement. It was wrought of heavy silver, embellished with the graceful forms of dancing nymphs surrounded by flowers and vines heavy with their grapes. The silver was worn from centuries of use, but it could still be seen as a work of beauty and consummate artistry. On the front was engraved the now-familiar wivern rampant. Beneath it was the single word B E A U M Y S S.

He looked up to find Christopher Bemis gazing at him with delight. "It is yours, Adam. Take it, my lad. It is rightly yours."

"No, Uncle," John said quickly. "I cannot accept it. This is something from the old days—something you treasure. No, I cannot—"

But the old man cut him short. "Adam, I want you to have it. You are Margaret's boy. It is yours. Take it for your sweet mother's sake. I can see from the way you talk of her that you treasure her memory."

"But, Uncle, your own two sons—"

The old man sadly shook his head. "My sons care nothing for their family heritage, Adam. But with you it is otherwise." Then suddenly he flung his thin arms about John. "Ah, Adam, you have brought joy back into my life. Come back to see me, Nephew. Come back. Come back."

John had already ridden halfway home when suddenly it came to him.

He had a name of his own.

He was Adam Tremoigne—Adam Ambrose Charles, after his father.

He was twenty-eight years old.

His birthday was April 19.

He was born in 1657.

Strange!

How strange!

And for some reason he threw back his head and laughed up at the sky.

But his joy was dashed an hour later when he stopped at the stableyard of the Mermaid to ask for news of Joe Fox.

The stableman shook his head. "Ain't no news a'tall of Joe Fox, Doc. Not even a sighting. On'y couriers coming through be from north and west and the like. None from east-coast or Kentish ports."

"What about coaches? Have no coaches come through?"

"There be one come in from Gravesend, Doc. The coachman's abed long since, but I could rouse him up if 'ee want a few words with him."

The man came willingly, in bare feet and rumpled shirt, sleepy-eyed, but willing to tell what he knew for a few coins.

"Riders coming through from Holland, sir? None a'tall that I hear'd of. 'Fore I left Gravesend it were all the talk. The King has a tight watch all 'long the coast, guards jest lying low, waiting, so's them couriers is clapped hands on as they come ashore—trapped like weasels, sir."

"What of the Kentish ports, Dover—Folkestone?"

"It be the same there, too, sir. All ports is under watch now, from Berwick down to Kent—and so tight that scarce a man in a rowboat kin sneak ashore. No, sir, it don' look good fer yer rider if him be coming from Amsterdam. The east coast be bunged up tight as a barrel, sir."

John gave the man a few coins, then turned Iris and rode slowly homeward through the falling dusk.

That evening he spent long hours sitting by his fireside, staring despairingly into the flames.

Sixteen

John stood looking down at the comatose child. She could not have been more than six years, with the black hair and dark complexion of the caravan people.

"Who brought her in?" he asked Sister Brigit.

"Old Josh Clemens. He was driving his cart home last night and saw her lying by the roadside. He called around for her folks, thinking perhaps they were hiding in the bushes, afraid to come out. But no one answered. He thought there might still be some life in her, so he put her in his cart and brought her here. And a pitiful sight she was, too, Doctor. A bundle of filthy rags."

"Well, her folks were probably just passing through—on the run, most likely. That could be why they abandoned her, thinking she was dead."

"She is not far from it. Poor lamb!"

"At least she shows no signs of battering."

"What ails her, then, Doctor John?"

"It is hard to say at the moment. I suspect that blemish on her shoulder bears some relation to her condition."

"A rat bite, you think?"

"Not from the blue color and curious design. It looks more like one of their marks, the Gypsies' 'flesh-brands.' In any case, keep her isolated. We do not want a spreader of pest in the convent. And send me word if she shows signs of regaining consciousness."

He turned and started out of the room. "I must drop in and see Jenny," he said.

He found her with a broom in hand, sweeping her room.

"Well, it is nice to see you getting stronger," he said. "Come and sit down. I want to talk to you."

He waited until she had seated herself opposite him by the window and he could study her face.

Then he said, "Jenny, it is about your father. Would you tell me about him?"

She looked surprised. "Why, Doctor?"

"Because he came to see me two nights ago and I am still puzzled by his visit. It must have been important to him or I do not think he would have come. I was hoping you might be able to suggest a motive."

She shook her head. "I never understood my father. I think the only person who ever understood him was my mother. And she was afraid of him. That is why she ran away."

He asked his next question gently, mindful that her unnatural existence in the repressive atmosphere of the vicarage made it difficult for her to share with another human being anything of a deeply emotional nature.

"What happened there, Jenny? Would you care to tell me?"

He saw her flinch. She quickly turned her head and looked out the window, across at the Cleybury Rings, and he thought that now, as had happened so often in those first days, she was going to leave the question unanswered. But he waited quietly and after a moment she turned back to him and her words came slowly, as if she were unburdening herself of painful, sharp-etched memories.

"My mother and father—they were never happy. My mother used to cry when she was alone. Then one day, when my father was out, a man came in a coach and my mother hurried me into it and we all drove away as fast as we could, away from the vicarage, away from my father. We went to a pretty little town. It was by the sea. My mother and I used to walk along the sands and I would collect seashells."

"Yes, Jenny?"

"And then one day my father found us."

She stopped talking and looked away again and John waited, his eyes on her half-turned face.

"It was daytime and Jim—the man in the coach—was out at work. My father burst into the room and picked me up and started to carry me off. I screamed out to my mother. She came running in and began pounding with her fists on my father's chest and arms. But my father did not stop. He carried me out to the street and tried to drag me up onto his horse. I struggled against him, kicking and biting. My mother was holding on to me, fighting to keep me, but my father raised a boot and kicked her in the face. The last thing I saw of my mother was all that splashed blood as she fell backward into the street. I screamed out, 'Mommy, I love you—Mommy, I love you.' But my father spurred his horse and carried me away, leaving my mother lying there—" She stopped, unable to continue.

He said softly, "Poor little Jenny. It is not a happy memory you have of your father, is it?"

She struggled for breath. "I have no happy memories of my father."

"And you have lived all these years in that cold, dark house with that cold, unloving man. Jenny, did you come to hate him?"

"No."

"How did you feel?"

"I think I grieved for him."

His brows went up in surprise. "Grieved for him?"

"For the tragedy of his life."

"Did he not create his own tragedy?"

"I was still afraid of what he might do to himself."

"Suicide? Why?"

"Because he suffers, silently, secretly. His life is one vast emptiness. His mind is one long, unrelieved spasm of pain."

"Why is that?"

"He is driven by bitterness."

"What made him bitter?"

"He was denied the single thing he craved, to be successful in the struggle for Church preferment. With his brilliant mind he should have been a bishop by now. Yet here he is, mired in Little Liscombe, writing sermons for unschooled farmers who can neither perceive nor understand his genius."

"Yet they still seem drawn to his church."

"Not, I think, for reasons which would satisfy his pride or give purpose to a ruined life, not because they see him as their shepherd, their spiritual leader."

"Then why do they come?"

"My father is an entrancing preacher. To these simple countryfolk his sermons, though at times ugly and brutal, are filled with extravagant imagery, with traces of the arcane and the mysterious familiar to them from their popular folktales. He quotes from the Bible, 'Faith is the substance of things hoped for, the evidence of things not seen.' They listen and nod in agreement. 'Things not seen.' Their folklore is filled with tales of invisibility, of magic, of 'things not seen.' "

John thought back to the wedding ceremony he had witnessed in the vicar's church. He remembered the extemporaneous but lurid sermon on the evils of fornication with which, on sighting him there in the back of the church, the vicar had suddenly harangued the bride and groom.

"But do you not think his own behavior might be at least partially responsible for his loss of preferment?"

"Perhaps, but my father would never see it that way. He would look for other causes."

"Such as?"

"Jealousy on the part of his superiors. Persecution."

"Do you think he ever feels remorse for his wrongful actions—for his treatment of your mother, of you?"

"I doubt such thoughts ever trouble him," she said without rancor. "He seems to have spent no time wrestling with his conscience before naming me the mother of the dead infant."

John asked in amazement, "You knew about that?"

"The arresting constable told me."

"Were you shocked?"

"No."

"Why not?"

"I have lived with it for so long."

"How could your father do it, Jenny? His own daughter?"

"I think my father has a reason for everything he does."

"What was his reason this time?"

For a moment her breath came convulsively and he knew she was trying to control her tears. He reached out and put a hand on hers, but he did not try to press her. He understood that she was revealing things that until now had been a part of her private inner world.

"I suspect," she answered presently, "he has learned that my mother is alive. I suspect he has learned she is living somewhere nearby."

"And?"

"And she will hear that I have been hanged."

John stared at her in horror. "What would make him capable of so terrible a vengeance?"

She shook her head, baffled. "I sometimes think of Shakespeare's words, 'Canst thou not minister to a mind diseas'd, Pluck from the memory a rooted sorrow, Raze out the written troubles of the brain. . . . ?' "

"You think your father has 'a mind diseased'?"

"Not that, unfortunately for him."

"Why 'unfortunately for him'?"

"I think—perhaps—because a man with my father's brilliant but tormented mind might conceivably welcome insanity as a blessing."

Again he stared, astonished at her perception.

"And you have lived in the shadow of this human torment all these years? Jenny, Jenny, how did so tender a flower bloom in that poisonous atmosphere?"

"Until recently I had little experience in such things. It is only now that I am beginning to understand how different things can be outside the vicarage."

The sadness in her tone tore at his heart. It racked him to think how her young life, so tragically lived, might now as tragically end if Joe Fox did not return and Henry's predictions held true. And suddenly, yielding to despair, he cast his solemn pledge to her to the winds and determined to try one last time to persuade her to agree to confide to Pollexfen the identity of the one participant in her tragedy whom she had thus far refused to name, but within whose power it was to swear the oath that would save her from the gallows.

He said, "Attorney Pollexfen tells me he came to see you two days ago."

"Yes, we had a long talk."

"He was not very happy with that talk, Jenny."

"Why not?"

"Because you did not answer his questions."

"I told him the truth."

"Not the entire truth."

"Is that what he said?"

"He said you evaded his questions."

"Perhaps he thinks I evaded his questions. Or perhaps he asked questions I could not answer."

"*Could* not answer, Jenny? Or *would* not answer?"

Unintentionally his voice had hardened and she stared up at him, her gaze roving thoughtfully over his face.

She asked, "Why are you suddenly angry with me?"

"I am not angry with you."

"You are. I can feel it."

He leaned forward. "Jenny, I am not angry. But I am anxious. I am wondering if you understand the precariousness of your legal position. When Pollexfen came out to see you, he did not come to exercise his horse. He came to get answers to certain questions which are vital if he is to plan a successful defense."

"I understood that."

"Yet he found you unresponsive."

"I gave him what answers I could."

"Then why did he leave here knowing as little about your case as he knew when he arrived?"

She looked silently down at her hands and he waited, thinking that now, at last, she would begin to reveal those final harrowing, profoundly secret fragments of her story that had so far baffled them.

But in the end she only shook her head. "There is nothing more I can tell you, or him," she said.

Once more a wave of despair flowed over him. He tried again, patiently, to rouse her to an understanding of the stark reality of her position.

"Jenny, I think you know that from the beginning Pollexfen was reluctant to defend you. At no time did he foresee a happy outcome to your trial."

To his surprise she showed no consternation. "I know," she said.

"Then why did you not at least do your part by co-operating with him?"

"I tried. I really tried."

"No, Jenny, you did not try. And perhaps you have not yet realized how fortunate you are to have Henry Pollexfen agree, against his own deep-seated convictions, to defend you. Pollexfen has already proven himself a brilliant barrister and is expected in time to be a brilliant judge. He has successfully defended men and women in circumstances even more challenging than your own. Now your life is in his hands. For this brief time you are utterly dependent on him, on his intelligence, his knowledge of the law. Do you fully understand what that means?"

"Does everything rest with Mr. Pollexfen, then?"

"It does—unless you raise objections to his standing for you, which you are perfectly entitled to do."

"But once you said there might be another way of proving still-birth."

"We are still awaiting details of that test, Jenny. And I am still hoping it will be admitted, but Pollexfen thinks it unlikely. He argues that since such a test has never before been introduced into an English court of law, it will probably be rejected on the first presentation. Or the court may question the degree of reliance to be placed upon it. If Pollexfen is right, we will be left with but one last hope for an acquittal."

There was a deep stillness about her as she sat there carefully following his line of reasoning, waiting, seeming in some mysterious way to anticipate his next words.

He drew a long, almost painful breath. He had a strong urge to leave this next question to Henry, but felt certain she would more readily respond to him, whom she trusted, than to the lawyer's cool logic. Still he hesitated. Once before, driven by jealousy, he had probed the matter of her lover. The outcome of that unhappy incident gnawed at his memory. He would not willingly repeat that blunder. Yet he and Henry were both certain of one thing: that in her answer lay the only sure and certain key to her acquittal.

"Listen to me, Jenny," he began, "we know that at the vicarage you lived a cloistered life and had no opportunity to form friendships with the neighborhood women while under your father's strict surveillance. But it logically follows that somehow you met and consorted with the father of your child. When Pollexfen questioned you on this, he got no answer. But the time has come for you to place some trust in Pollexfen, the more so since, in common with all attorneys, he is bound by a code of confidentiality between himself and his client. If you were to trust Pollexfen to see this young man in private, he could explain to him that in cases like yours at least one witness is the legal requirement for acquittal under the concealment law. Jenny, if the father of your child were to come into court—even now—and swear that he was present at the birth and your child was stillborn, that stringent requirement of the law would be satisfied. His testimony would be accepted. Your acquittal would be ensured."

Her wide-pupilled eyes showed surprise at his words, the disappointment of one who had just lost a cherished illusion. "Then you do not believe me after all, do you?"

Her response so painfully expressed her loss of trust that for a moment he was speechless, stung as much by the reproach as by his own knowledge that it contained more than a kernel of truth. This last seemed to demand justification and be blazed at her, "Jenny, I am a doctor. I know a woman becomes pregnant only through the offices of a male partner."

He saw her flinch and instantly cursed himself for having spoken so harshly to one so vulnerable. When she made no reply, but only sat staring up at him, small and quiet, he leaned forward, taking her hands in both of his, making a passionate appeal in repentant tones.

"Jenny, it is your life I am pleading for. Your dear, dear life."

She said nothing for a moment, only carefully searched his face. Then gently she disengaged her hands, got to her feet and went over and started again to sweep the floor.

He waited uneasily, watching her, sensing that for some reason she needed time to summon all her courage for what she was about to say.

Then presently she came back and reseated herself opposite him.

"You see," she said, "I know how much you have tried to help me, and I am grateful for your concern. But after talking to Mr. Pollexfen I have come to know that the truth—whatever the truth is in my case—will make no difference to the outcome of my trial. I asked Mr. Pollexfen to explain the law to me. He explained it. Now there is no doubt in my mind that in the end, despite this test, or anything else you can do, I will face the gallows."

He was shattered by her words. He asked, "Have you no hope at all?"

She shook her head. "I understand what Mr. Pollexfen so carefully explained to me. He said he hoped to base my defense upon the argument that my baby was not murdered, but was stillborn. But the coroner said that murder was not the charge. The charge, he said, was concealment of birth. And concealment, he said, was a hangable crime."

John drew a quick deep breath. It seemed to sigh out of him. Suddenly he was tired, more tired that he had ever been in his life. That was it, then. It had to be true—quite true—as Henry had said, "She has a secret lover whom she clearly has no intention of forsaking." She would not even save herself by implicating him.

They were silent for a long time before he forced himself to rise to his feet.

He heard his own voice come as if from a distant emptiness. "Very well, Jenny. I will mention it no more. I apologize for having broken my word to you. But I hope you will reconsider. If you do, if you should want Pollexfen to return for a confidential talk, just send me word through Sister Brigit and I will arrange it."

She appeared to dismiss this last.

"And when the time comes for me to go back to jail, will you take me back yourself?" Then she added tremulously, "Like that I will not be so afraid."

He stood gazing down at her, heart and mind resisting the brave finality of her question.

"I always meant to do that," he answered gently. "I will make sure you are lodged upstairs again, with the women. They are rough, perhaps, but they are kindly. They will watch over you."

"And when will I be going back?"

"The trial has not yet been scheduled, but Henry expects it to fall toward the end of this week. In any case, I will leave you here as long as I can. I will come for you only on the morning of the trial."

"Thank you," she said.

He stood another moment, waiting, finding nothing more to say. Then he turned and walked rapidly through the door and down the corridor.

He scarcely noticed the smiles and greetings as he passed. In the courtyard he mounted up and sped through the gate, then he nudged Iris into a furious gallop. All the galling feelings of jealousy and contempt he felt for her lover, so sternly held in check these past weeks, were again roused up, creating within him a raging sea of flames that threatened to consume him.

She must indeed love that cowardly wretch to be willing to die to protect him. And there was nothing anyone could do. Nothing! It had been assumed from the start that she was protecting someone, and that someone was her lover. Now only her lover would have credibility in court. A surrogate? At this late date? That would be dangerous. It was too sensational a case. Besides, Henry would not hear of it. Hope? In his secret, unreachable soul he knew that even if Joe Fox returned, the hydrostatic test might still be rejected. Then Jenny would die. She would die because this faithless lover, this cringing parody of a man would not risk his good name for her. He would stay safe and silent while she walked to the gallows—would see her hanged in the Market Place—and still he would not stir.

And—Jesus God!—she would die loving the wretch.

He was not aware that he had returned to town until he found himself back again in the stableyard of the Mermaid. These days he seemed to haunt the yard, always asking after Joe Fox, so anxious for word of him that the stablemen had become curious, staring at him queerly. They began to answer even before he put the question: "No word yit, Doc. Nothing on Joe Fox." He would throw them a few coins, then turn without a word and ride away.

His oppression continued to hang over him after he reached the hospital and plunged back into work. There were two emergencies waiting, then a vomiting baby, a farmer with a fractured arm, a woman with a circulatory disease, a child suffering from malnutrition. As numerous as sparrows, he told himself for the thousandth time. It was two hours before he was able to go upstairs.

He was visiting the wards when he caught sight of Noah wandering slowly down the corridor. He stopped an orderly.

"That boy—the deaf-mute—does he still come to the hospital?"

" 'Most every day, Doc. I meself has chased him off more'n once. So has others. Us cain't seem to make him un'erstand him should not come here no more. And us cain't question him, so's it be hard to know what him wants."

"I know what he wants," John said.

He caught up with Noah just as the boy was disappearing around a corner.

"Noah," he said, looking him in the face and speaking slowly so the boy, who could scarcely lip-read, could watch his lips and perhaps understand some part of what he said, "come and sit beside me on the stairs. I want to talk to you."

Noah seated himself beside John and gazed quietly up at him. He had changed since John had last seen him. The bright eagerness was gone. His clothing was dirty. His sensitive face was unwashed. His soft flaxen hair was tangled with clods and bits of straw as though, instead of going home, he had been sleeping in the fields. He looked hungry, he was probably foraging for food. There was a startling new expression in his blue eyes, a look of bewildered desolation, of hurt betrayal, and a painful question. It was this question that John was now going to try to answer.

"Noah," he began gently, "it is no use searching these rooms. You will not find Father Dominic. He is no longer in the hospital. Father Dominic was old and sick. He has gone away and will not be coming back. He asked me to say good-bye to you and see that you continue your studies."

But clearly John's words were incomprehensible to Noah. The boy's face failed to register any change. He continued to gaze up at John with an expression of hopeless, passionless grief. Even his hands lay idle on his knees, as though he had lost interest even in the deaf-mute signs he had previously learned with such expectancy and joy.

John took a deep breath and tried again.

"Noah, do you ever pray to God?"

The word "God" seemed to hold some meaning for Noah. He gave a vague nod.

"Well, Father Dominic has gone away to be with God. You and I both loved him. But neither of us will ever see him again."

Noah's face remained blank. He was making no effort to puzzle out the meaning of John's words. He was indifferent now to things around him. John had a feeling of helplessness. He realized that the concept of death had not yet been explained to Noah. He realized, too, that when Father Dominic began instructing him in the deaf-mute signs, he forged a link between the boy's silent inner world and the vital outer world, he opened up a magic door that now must seem to the boy to have been slammed shut, leaving him in darkness more terrible than before.

John's thoughts quickly flew to Sister Teresa at Saint Elizabeth's Convent. He must ride over and have a talk with her tomorrow.

But for the moment there was another language that every boy understood.

He stood up and reached for Noah's hand. "Come, I am going to buy you a big plate of steak and kidney pie." Then, remembering Tom's clever inducement in his own hungry boyhood, he added, almost to himself, "And mashed potatoes to take up the gravy."

He kept Noah with him for the rest of the afternoon. He left the hospital early and, taking Noah up behind him on Iris, set off through the cobbled streets, heading for the poorest quarter of the town.

Mrs. Frazer, Noah's mother, was running frantically before them up the street. She turned at the sound of hoofbeats. When she caught sight of Noah she ran back and threw her arms about him as he slid down from Iris's back.

"Oh, Noah, 'ee be a bad boy to scare me so," she sobbed. "I bin searching the town fer 'ee." She looked up, tears streaming down her cheeks. "Thank 'ee, Doctor John, fer finding him. I cain't un'erstand what come over him this past week. Him dis'ppears the moment me back be turned. This time him has bin gone two days."

"He spends days searching the hospital rooms for Father Dominic."

"What 'ud him do that fer?"

"You did not know, then, that Father Dominic had died?"

Doris Frazer gave a little gasp and drew her son closer. "Nay, I did not know. How could this boy un'erstand death? How could this boy tell me?"

"I should have told you, Doris. I blame myself. Father Dominic was my old teacher, too. I loved him, just as Noah did. Now I condemn myself for having been so absorbed in my own concerns that I failed to recognize Noah's greater need."

"But why 'ud Noah set so much store by Father Dominic?"

"Perhaps because Father Dominic was Noah's link to his family, to you and his brothers and sisters. You were all learning the hand alphabet and starting to communicate with him in the only way he can comprehend. I do not think any of us can understand Noah's sense of loss. But it is important, Doris, that you take him to Saint Elizabeth's without delay and ask Sister Teresa to explain Father Dominic's death to him. You must also arrange for her to continue his instruction so that he does not fall back into isolation."

"I 'ull do it tomorry, Doctor John. On me word, I will."

"Meanwhile, keep him with you this evening. Make much of him. Communicate with him in whatever hand signs you have learned. Do not let him feel alone."

John was disheartened. He started homeward, then changed his mind and turned Iris in the direction of Wynford Eagle.

Dusk was falling. In the west, feathery pink cloudlets still floated amid the sun's amber afterglow, but in the east a rising moon was fringing the trees with a glow like molten metal behind a film of dross; a hunter's moon, when the barn owl, pallid as a ghost-bird, set out to wing its silent way above the stubbles, hunting the frightened mice and young rabbits who had lost their beneficent cover. A wild barking came out of the sky. John glanced up. The brant geese were in flight, massed in a dense black phalanx, tailing off into long skeins, making for the open sea. "Hell hounds," the countryfolk still called them, awed from time immemorial by the strange aerial voices that sounded to them like a pack of barking dogs overhead. All sounds seemed strangely loud on the damp evening air. John was acutely aware of the leisurely *clip-clop* of Iris's hooves, of the call of the coveys, of the sound of nuts dropping with a precise tap from their green baskets. Already the yellowing grasses by the roadside were glittering with dew, creating their own brief autumnal world of unearthly light. "Hath the rain a father? or who hath begotten the drops of dew?" Job had asked.

He drew a long, deep breath. Few times of the year were more beautiful, or, under a hunter's moon, more cruel than an autumn dusk.

He passed through the shadows of Yeggor Dun and approached Little Liscombe. As he drew near he saw that someone was at work boarding up the church door, nailing planks of wood across it. A moment later he was surprised to recognize the tall, lean outlines of the vicar.

He edged Iris over to the lych-gate and reined in, sitting there, watching. The vicar was working furiously. He appeared to be in a rage.

"Good evening, Vicar," he called. "I hope this does not mean you are about to leave us."

The vicar turned, heaving from his labors. For a moment he peered belligerently through the dusk. Then, recognizing John, he put down his tools and came over to the gate.

"No, Doctor, I am not leaving the parish—not just yet. It is God's will that I endure this ordeal awhile longer. But these parishioners of Little Liscombe are an odious lot. The offscourings of humanity, sir, is what they are—a thieving, knavish, lawless rabble."

"You surprise me, Vicar. Why do you say a thing like that?"

"Because recently I lost the key to my church and now can no longer lock the door. These miserable rustics have a nose for loot. In no time they were sneaking into the church at night to steal whatever was not locked up—prayer books, Bibles, sacred vestments, everything. Disgraceful! Stealing from the Lord's House. But God's wrath burns against them. Have no doubt of it. Hell opens its flaming mouth to receive them. Amen."

"And this lost key, Vicar. What did it look like?"

The vicar slid John a sharp look. "A large key, sir—very ornamental, very beautiful—the only beautiful thing about the unsightly edifice you see behind me. I must have lost it while visiting some parishioner—probably slipped out of my pocket as I was bending over his bed. But the finder will not return it. Church property is salable and these rustics have a niggardly eye to a penny. A contemptible lot!"

John put his hand in his pocket and drew out the key he had found on Yeggor Dun. "Vicar, could this be your lost key?"

The vicar reached for the key and looked down at it. There was a curious pause. "Yes," he said, "this is my key. Where did you find it?"

Even though the conversation had prepared John for it, the vicar's admission still caught him unprepared, glad that the dusk hid the amazement he knew must be showing on his face. Then, too, the question, "Where did you find it?" He peered into the proud, hawklike face and knew this man could not bear to hear the truth. "I found it not far from here," he said evasively, "just off the highway."

The vicar smiled his thin smile. "I am most grateful to you. Now I can lock my church once again." He hesitated, obviously out of practice at proffering invitations. "Doctor, would you care to come into my library and share a glass of port with me?"

John shook his head. "Another time, Vicar. But now I am on my way to Wynford Eagle to dine with Doctor Sydenham. He was my mentor, you know. Good night." And he bowed courteously and rode on.

When John arrived at Wynford Eagle, Doctor Sydenham was just sitting down to dine.

"Ah, John, what a pleasure. But you look tired. Here, my boy, have a glass of this fine Bordeaux. That is what you need. Drink up, my boy. Drink up."

John sipped his wine. "Tom, how is the gout?"

"Worse than ever, I am afraid. These acute attacks continue. No relief. John, for all our learning, what do we physicians know? We suffer just as other men. We cannot heal ourselves. Gout? 'An atony of the digestive system which causes vicarious congestion of the joints.' Stuff and nonsense! Small wonder these canny countryfolk still cling to their charms."

John laughed. "These canny countryfolk still call a physician when their charms fail. But tell me, Tom, how soon will you be returning to London?"

"I should have been there a week ago. But such a trip would be agony with this leg, even traveling by private coach. Perhaps next week, if the leg improves."

So the conversation proceeded during dinner, for the doctor's new waiting maid was a gossipy village girl. But later, when they were settled in the library with their port, the conversation turned to more private matters.

"And now, John," Sydenham began, "tell me what happened. You had a most curious expression on your face when you came in."

John smiled at Sydenham's unerring perception. "I had just come from a strange encounter with the vicar. You recall the last time I was here I told you of finding a key on Yeggor Dun among fresh chips of granite and of seeing a man racing off into the dusk. Just now, as I was riding through Little Liscombe, I saw the vicar boarding up his church door and stopped to inquire what it meant. He explained that his parishioners had been stealing church property ever since he lost the key to his church door. I showed him the key I found on Yeggor Dun. He claimed it as his lost key."

"Bless me! Then the man you saw so furiously chopping off the pagan god's symbols of masculinity must have been our vicar."

"At least, the vicar claimed the key."

"Extraordinary! That man is an interesting case, John. He certainly suffers from some mental derangement. On the surface he is a religious fanatic, yet the few details we have of his private life show him to be a wholly irreligious man. The Bible teaches, "God is love," yet this ecclesiastic, this minister of the Church, seems to indulge in orgies of hate which for some reason are focused on the phallus. He seems to find it morally offensive. I told you how he tried to emasculate himself and almost bled to death. And now he has turned his fury on the age-old phallic figure on the hill."

"Perhaps he does not see it merely as the forgotten god of a forgotten people, but as a lecherous representation of the mythological Priapus."

"However he sees it, his mania becomes dangerous when he turns it upon his errant daughter. I am beginning to understand your sympathy for the girl. Has he ever inquired about her?"

"Only in general terms. A few nights ago I came home to find him in my cottage. He gave no reason for his call and after he left I found myself troubled as to his purpose. I am convinced he came in search of information."

"Did he show no concern for his daughter's plight? No remorse for having denounced her?"

"I doubt if the vicar is capable of a normal sense of guilt."

"Which brings up an interesting point," Sydenham said, after a thoughtful moment. "It is now being said that throughout history many professional torturers, men who were otherwise loving husbands and fathers, could mentally adjust to the brutality of their work and remain aloof from the screams of their victims by the simple act of self-persuasion that these poor wretches—even the young and innocent—were deserving of punishment. Is it not possible that the vicar, too, is justifying his inhumane treatment of his daughter by picturing himself as the righteous instrument of his own stern God?"

"I am beginning to think the vicar has a shrewder, more sinister motive for what he did."

"John! You shock me!"

"I know him better than you do, Tom. I have had more opportunity to study him."

"It is a horrifying thought, all the same. How does his daughter feel about him?"

"She feels neither love nor hate. She grieves for him."

"Grieves? Did she say that?"

"Yes."

"Why does she grieve for him?"

"She feels he lives in a world of private torment."

Sydenham raised his brows. "That observation suggests rare acuteness of mind. Does she know he denounced her?"

"The arresting constable told her."

"And she still does not hate him?"

"We talked of it only this morning. She replied by quoting Macbeth's plea to his wife's physician."

"Did she, indeed? Remarkable! Quite remarkable!" Sydenham paused. "John, are you still in love with this girl?"

"I am, Tom—more than ever." John gazed abstractedly into the fire. "It is strange, I have rarely been conscious of loneliness. I have always felt fortunate at having so full and rich a life. But now, since knowing Jenny, I find I am often lonely, lonely because she is not beside me, lonely because she is not there at the cottage when I get home at night. Whatever I am doing, she is in my thoughts."

"Under more fortunate circumstances, then, would you have considered marrying her?"

"Without a question—if she would have me."

"I am sorry, my boy. What a pity! What a tragedy for you!"

Sydenham gazed anxiously at John. Their affection had always been of the unspoken kind, never demonstrated, but keenly felt.

Presently he asked, "And what of the father of her child? Does she still love him?"

"I must assume that she does. She still will not talk of him."

"Then she is still protecting him?"

"That is Henry's assumption. And mine, too. Yet I continue to be mystified by this curious feeling—a feeling that her story has not yet been told."

"Will it ever be told?"

"I have no way of knowing."

"Is Pollexfen still pessimistic?"

"He has always said her case is lost before it even goes to trial. Our one slender hope seems to lie now in this hydrostatic test. But even that—"

"Have you heard yet from Joe Fox?"

"Not a word—not even a sighting." Then John added somberly, "I am beginning to consider the possibility that Joe Fox will never return."

Sydenham studied John's face as the younger man got up restlessly and threw more wood on the fire, then refilled both glasses before returning to his chair.

"John," he asked, anxious to turn the conversation away from Jenny Sykes, "what about this new rumor? It is being said there was a death at Dunheved. Is there any truth to it?"

"Unfortunately the rumor is true. James died yesterday. It was a sad and unattended death . . . a terrible death."

"Then I take it he died hidden away at Dunheved?"

"He did."

"Poor Lucas! How is he taking it?"

"Lucas is grief-stricken. James was his entire world, the only person Lucas deeply loved. My anger has often been turned on Lucas for his foolish lies and evasions, but now I feel truly sorry for him. A man bereft —alone in that great pile of granite with its long silences and memories and ghosts. A man from whom everything has been taken—the young wife he adored, and now his only child."

"It is pitiful! Pitiful!" Sydenham reflected on his next question. "And what of your own prospects, John? Has Lucas spoken again about helping establish your possible legitimacy?"

"I no longer need his help in that, Tom. I have finally stumbled on the truth. Did you ever hear of Beaumyss Castle?"

Sydenham frowned, his thoughts flowing backward through the years. "But that was all long, long ago. I seem to recall that Beaumyss was caught up in the Civil War and was left nothing more than a burned-out ruin. Why do you ask?"

"Because yesterday I went there." And John briefly related the details of his last conversation with Lucas, which had led up to his visit to Beaumyss and his meeting with Uncle Christopher.

When he finished his story Sydenham sat looking intently at him, an expression of astonished enlightenment on his face.

He said, "Then, John, that explains everything."

"What does it explain, Tom?"

"You say your parents were legally married, which makes you young Adam's legitimate son."

"Yes."

"And therefore his legal heir."

"Yes."

"That your baptismal name is Adam Ambrose Charles Tremoigne."

"Yes."

"And of course you could not know that in the Tremoigne family it is traditional for all elder sons to bear the name 'Adam.' "

"No, I did not know—" John broke off and stared as suddenly

everything fell into place. "So that is it! That is what Lucas has been trying so desperately to hide."

"Without a doubt. I would have told you this years ago except that, like you, I did not think your parents were married."

"Which of course is what Lucas was depending on. And that is what has been troubling his conscience—he knew the truth and was concealing it. But why did he do it, Tom? Lucas is not an avaricious man. He is not an evil man. Weak, perhaps, but not evil. So why would a decent man like Lucas steal his brother's small son's inheritance?"

"I think the answer to that lies far in the past," Tom answered. "You see, when Lucas was a young man, he fell deeply in love with the daughter of the Earl of Kingford, the Lady Sabrina Draycott. He was desperately anxious to marry her, but his lack of prospects made him unacceptable to her father. You know what primogeniture does to England's younger sons. Lucas, apart from the usual family pittance, had virtually nothing. He suffered his hopeless, passionate love in silence. Then Adam was killed in that accident and suddenly, as the future Viscount Tremoigne and heir to Dunheved, Lucas became instantly eligible. His engagement to the Lady Sabrina was announced. So you see, even if he was in fact aware of your parents' secret marriage, the temptation to do what he did must have been irresistible."

"And all these years he must have lived in fear that I would turn up. Now, with James gone, he is glad I am here and is looking for ways to return what he took. The irony of it!"

"What will you do, John? You are now, and always have been, the rightful Lord Tremoigne. Not Lucas. Now that you have proof of it, will you claim your inheritance?"

"In time, perhaps. For now, my chosen path lies in my profession. Later, if I have sons, I will go to Lucas and make arrangements to protect their inheritance. But even though I will pose no threat to Lucas now, I still plan to confront him. There are still questions I must ask and he must answer."

"What questions, John?"

"I am still troubled by many aspects of the matter. Why, for instance, did Lucas halt the search for the 'wild boy' only to press a search for him three nights later by sending a tracking party up to the High Moor? Why was he anxious to capture us in secret? Was Chérie a threat to him because she could prove her son legitimate? And what would he have done had he succeeded in taking us alive? Would he have cast us down into Dunheved's ill-famed dungeons, hidden away from the world till we grew old and died?"

Sydenham frowned. "Troubling questions, indeed, John. And do you really believe now that Chérie's death was accidental?"

"Yes, Tom, I believe that. They could not have known of her rash habit of leaping the Caistor Rocks. But I knew. I had too often seen her leaping the Rocks, hunting for leverets."

"Leverets?"

"Baby hares which are born in every season of the year and which were our main source of food. Chérie knew the rocks well. She leapt them with ease. But this time it was different. This time she was thinking of me, afraid for my safety. She was drawing the trackers off from my hiding place. In her anxiety she might have slipped."

"Possibly. And what other questions do you have for Lucas?"

"He obviously knew about the marriage record at the Little Chapel. Why did he never destroy it? Did he feel, after Chérie died and her son disappeared, that the risk was unnecessary? But there are other questions, Tom, which I shall never ask. For instance, in these twenty intervening years, was Lucas haunted by the fact that the boy's body was never found? Did he wait uneasily for the boy to reappear? Did he scan the face of every boy in Dorncaster as he rode through? And how did he feel when, under the name of John Toller, summoned by him to Dunheved to attend his only son, I came back into his life? Did he look for ways to be rid of me forever? Or did he, even then, see me as a possible welcome replacement for the hated Cousin Sidney?"

Sydenham nodded. "Yours is a strange story, John," he murmured. "Poor Lucas! Tragedy has indeed been his bedfellow. His life has been a succession of disappointments and blighted hopes. But tell me, my boy, knowing what you know now, do you feel no malice toward Lucas?"

John took a moment to reflect on this.

"Looking at it broadly," he answered, "why should I? It is true that Lucas caused me to lose much that I loved. Most particularly I grieve for Chérie. But fate brought me under old Doctor Toller's loving tutelage. Then it brought me under yours. You gave me the one thing in this world I truly wanted—to be a physician, to practice medicine. And you know better than anyone, Tom, that was all I ever really wanted—until Jenny came into my life."

He rode home under the red glare of the hunter's moon. Its luminous mist made the scents of earth seem stronger, more intimate. The bases of the trees were wrapped in smoky ribbons of vapor. The deep silence of night lay over the land, broken now and then by a careless snatch of bird song.

It was strange, he reflected, how easy it was to talk to Jenny, to open the door to childhood ghosts that he had always kept tightly shut. There was an atmosphere about her, the way she would sit gazing up at him, seeming to know intuitively that these treasured green things of his memory were being unshrouded only for her. At such times her eyes had a grave, penetrating look, as though she were seeking to reach into his inmost thoughts, as he at times sought to reach into hers. A rare invisible filament seemed to bind them.

There was something unique in her naturalness. The isolation of her life had left her without the usual inhibitions in the company of men that most girls grew up with. He remembered the day she had leaned forward and with her forefinger traced out the scar on his cheek and asked how he got it. He never failed to be surprised by her concerned directness. Her remarkable intellectual gifts gave her a command of thought and language that was remote from the flighty, superficial chatter of most women. No, it was not just her singular, mysterious beauty that drew him. It was her total grace, her candor, the sweetness of her voice, the lack of self-consciousness with which she bore her extraordinary erudition.

He knew he was spending too much time with her. He had excused himself to Sister Brigit, saying that Jenny was too much alone, she needed someone to talk to. But Sister Brigit knew it was more than that. He loved to sit there, watching the changing expressions on her face, aware of feelings he had never before known for a woman. Her pearl-pale skin seemed to exhale a freshness that lay upon her like dew, a freshness he wanted to touch, to caress, to kiss. Yet for all her softness, he sensed in her a certain fortitude, the inner strength that was sustaining her now as these last agonizing days of waiting drew to a close.

It was inevitable that no woman would ever again so fill his life. Yet always, skulking in the background, was the misty figure of her lover, a reminder that, whatever the outcome of her trial, he must lose her in the end.

He sighed, racked by sudden anguish. Chief Justice Jeffreys was due to leave tomorrow evening. The rebel trials would be over. The general jail delivery would commence. Jenny would be brought to trial and then—

But Henry could be wrong—

Perhaps, if Joe Fox got through—

He looked up. The rooftops of Dorncaster were coming into view. He gave Iris a nudge.

In town he rode directly to the Mermaid. The innyard was empty at this late hour. The night hostler shuffled out of the stable.

He knew whom John was looking for.

"Not yit, Doc," he said. "Not a sign o' Joe Fox. No other rider's caught a sight o' him on the road, neither. Mebbe tomorry."

John turned slowly homeward. Perhaps this time Joe Fox's vaunted ingeniousness had failed him. Perhaps this time he had come ashore unaware that in his absence the King's agents had extended their watch to the entire east and Kentish coasts. Joe Fox had always been an adventurer, a gambler, wagering his life for gold, supremely confident in his own cunning, in his ability to sense the waiting danger. He seemed to relish unequal odds, facing them with his insolent grin.

And now, not even a bell would toll for him. Perhaps only his dogs would miss him.

John was nearing his cottage when Iris gave a snort. He peered into the darkness. Someone was standing on his doorstep. He could make out only a dim silhouette.

"Who's there?" he called softly.

Joe Fox stepped out into the moonlight and came toward him. In his hand he gripped a satchel.

"It be here, Doc," he said. "What 'ee wanted. On'y 'tis gonna cost 'ee more'n the twenty golds us come up with."

This last was spoken in defiant, menacing tones, but John scarcely noticed. His attention was on the satchel. He dismounted and pushed open his door, then he led Iris inside and beckoned Joe Fox.

He left Iris standing and quickly lit a lamp.

"The satchel, please."

Joe Fox cautiously hesitated. But only for an instant. He handed it over. John swept aside the clutter on the table and tipped out the satchel's contents. He riffled hurriedly through the papers. It was here! All here! The procedure for the hydrostatic test, described, sketched to the last detail.

For an instant he felt almost light-headed.

Then he turned. "You said this would cost more than we agreed upon. How much more?"

Joe Fox looked him unashamedly in the eye. "One hundred golds," he answered.

But if Joe Fox judged the price excessive, John judged his purchase beyond price.

"You shall have it," he said. He went to his desk, scribbled a note and signed it. "Take this to the goldsmith's in the morning. He will pay you." Then he added with some curiosity, "How did you evade the watch?"

For once Joe Fox lost his menacing air. He seemed to be gloating over his recollections.

"I listened to the talk in them Amsterdam mughouses. Seems our English James be fidgety, waiting fer Dutch William to sail fer England to snatch the crown off his very head. Me? I figured the sea in them parts were not safe jest then, not with all that ado, so I rode down through Flanders looking fer a way. Turned out that were not safe, neither. Seems the French army was all drawed up and camped fer miles, jest waiting fer Dutch William to sail off to England 'fore marching in to grab his Dutch lands. So I bided till one night the rack hung low, and a fall mist clung to the ground like a babe to his mam's teat, and the Frenchmen's campfires was all lit up and them close-huddled 'round 'em. Then I stoled a French horse, and I stoled some French food, and I slipped through the French lines and come down by back roads through Normandy to Honfleur. There I bribed a small fishing-boat crew to carry me 'cross to Devon. I come ashore at Torbay." Joe Fox paused a moment and grinned. "Figured there were no danger on the south coast. Fidgety James 'ud still be looking east."

Despite his disapproval of Joe Fox, John found himself smiling at his daring. "You did admirably," he said.

He saw Joe Fox to the door and watched him stride off into the night, a man who took danger as it came; who lived with death, yet did not seek it; who must at times foreglimpse for himself a violent end, yet did not retreat before it. One could almost admire the spirit that drove him. A pity he was a scoundrel.

Iris had followed John to the door, out of patience with his neglect. So he took her out and stabled her and saw to her comfort. Then he came back, lit his reading lamp, and picked up the Van Roonhuyse papers.

Seventeen

John was late leaving for the clinic next morning, and when he arrived the waiting room was already full. He treated a crooked, defeated man who had tried to commit suicide by slashing one wrist with a sickle. A cripple who dragged himself along the ground on little hand crutches. A hydrocephalic, doomed to an early death. A small girl with rickets.

A ragged scarecrow of a woman, wild-haired, brown and furrowed as the bark of a dwarf oak from aimlessly wandering the countryside, her idiot son tied to a rope looped around her arm.

John scolded her gently. "I have told you, Nelly, the boy needs shelter in this chilly weather. He is not as strong as most boys. He is frail. His lungs are delicate. He will always get these terrible coughs unless you let me arrange for the two of you to lodge in the almshouse every winter. Only in winter, Nelly. Later, when the weather turns warm, you can take him and go wandering again. What do you say?"

She looked up at him, troubled and irresolute. " 'Ee don' reckon they 'ull try to holt 'um cum seedtime?"

"No, come seedtime, Nelly, you will be allowed to leave and wander as you choose. But the boy cannot go on like this. I will give him something for that cough, but he needs more than that. At the moment he needs warm clothing, a roof, a bed, nourishing meals. They will take good care of you both at the almshouse. I will come by to make sure they do. What do you say, Nelly? Will you go?"

The woman turned and looked down at her son. He was lolling on the floor at her feet, his eyes vacant, his nose running, the sparse hairs of his unshaven chin wet and raddled. She took the hem of her tattered petticoat and patiently wiped the dribble from his nose and mouth. Then she continued to stand looking down at him, struggling to clear up the confusion in her mind as she wrestled with this momentous decision.

As John waited, Mrs. Colley came in noiselessly and said in an undertone, "A lady is asking to see 'ee, Doctor. Not a patient, her says.

Not even from Dorncaster. But her begs 'ee to see her. Her 'ull not give her name. But her wrote so'thing on this paper."

John took the paper and unfolded it. On it was written the brief message: "I am Jenny Sykes's mother."

John looked up quickly, surprise on his face. "Tell the lady not to leave—I will see her at once. Make sure she stays, Mrs. Colley. I do want to talk to her."

A few moments later Nelly had given in to John's urging. He went to a window and beckoned to an urchin who often ran errands for him. He gave him a penny to conduct Nelly and her son to the almshouse. Then he asked Mrs. Colley to bring in his visitor.

She was small of stature, neat and well-groomed, though her plain black cloak was worn along the edges and her gloves had been neatly darned. Looking at her tugged at his heart for, like Jenny, she was fair of hair and skin, with something of Jenny in her features. Once she had been pretty. Now she was worn by the hardships of life.

He welcomed her and offered her a chair.

"Doctor," she began, "I must thank you for seeing me."

"Indeed, I am glad you came. You say you are Jenny's mother?"

"Yes, my name is Elizabeth Lundy. I no longer go by the name of Sykes, but by the name of"—she hesitated—"by the name of my second husband."

John appeared not to have noticed the hesitation. "And who suggested that you come to me, Mrs. Lundy?"

"Last night I stayed at the Mermaid. I asked Mr. Coots, the landlord, for news of the Sykes case. I did not tell him I was Jenny's mother because, after Jim Lundy died, I found employment as housekeeper at a girls' school in Morcombe and was afraid of losing my position. Instead, I explained my interest in Jenny's case by saying she was the daughter of a distant cousin. Mr. Coots suggested that my cousin might be better served if I were to come to you for news instead of talking to the jailer."

"Excellent advice. As it happens, Jenny is no longer in the jailhouse. She developed puerperal fever, so in my capacity as town doctor I had her transferred to a convent hospital. She has been receiving proper care and is much improved."

Mrs. Lundy nodded and appeared to be hesitating. A soft pink flush, perhaps of embarrassment, had risen in her cheeks.

"I find myself in a difficult position," she confessed at last. "I would like to visit my daughter, but frankly do not know if such a visit would be advisable. She has not seen me since she was five and I am not sure how she remembers me. I long to go to her, but in the present circumstances such a visit might be upsetting. I am in a dilemma, Doctor."

John sat back in his chair, his face in the shadows. The flush had said more than Mrs. Lundy's words. She was aware, then, that her visit would give rise to incalculable problems. It could not be kept secret, not in Dorncaster. The local people would still remember that Mrs. Sykes, as she was then known, had abandoned her husband and run off with a player in some obscure theatrical company. What Mrs. Lundy would not have foreseen, however, was that with the excited speculation as to the identity of Jenny's lover, with unabated whisperings of her wild nights on Yeggor Dun, the mother's unfortunate reputation would cast a still more cruel light upon the daughter. Henry was already troubled by the chancy factor of public opinion in Jenny's case, particularly by the unlikelihood of finding twelve jurors who had not already prejudged her, from listening to the gossips. Mrs. Lundy's presence in town could not help but have a calamitous effect upon a case whose chances of a happy outcome were already dim.

He said, "Are you asking my advice, Mrs. Lundy?"

"I am, Doctor—if I may."

"Then I must agree with you. We expect Jenny to go to trial within the next few days. She is, as you suggest, under great emotional strain. I strongly urge that you delay your visit until after the trial."

"But will there be time, then, Doctor—afterward?"

Her meaning roused up the sense of desolation he had come to live with daily.

"If the decision goes against us? Morcombe is just a few miles along the coast, and by law execution does not take place until the day next but one after trial and sentencing. Yes, there will be time. You will see Jenny, I promise. If you leave your address with Mrs. Colley, I will send you word after the trial. And it should comfort you to know that Jenny remembers you with love. You are one of her happy memories."

He waited quietly, watching the torturous flow of thought reflected on her face. Another problem, then? Clearly, at the moment she was racked by indecision. He said gently, "Come, Mrs. Lundy, I have the feeling there is something more."

"You are right, Doctor. There is something more."

Mrs. Lundy remained silent for a moment, looking down at her folded hands. When she looked up again her eyes were filled with tears.

"Doctor Toller, a strange thing happened in Little Liscombe recently. Occasionally, through the years, I have gone over there for Sunday service, standing unobserved in the back of the church. In that way I was able to at least see Jenny from a distance without either Jenny or the vicar being aware of my presence. The last time I went, I was disturbed to find her absent from her usual seat. Perhaps in my anxiety I craned too far because during the sermon, from his pulpit, the vicar chanced to look up and see me." She paused and frowned. "Something happened then, Doctor, that was so unnatural it has weighed on my heart ever since."

"Yes, Mrs. Lundy?"

"On seeing me, Jude abruptly halted his sermon. He gave a sharp little gasp, then stood silent, his mouth open, his eyes wide, staring straight at me. He was so startled he seemed to forget he was in church, even that he was preaching. When next he spoke, his mind had wandered from the text and he was talking of things quite extraneous from the service, things which apparently lay heavy on his mind. He seemed to be reciting some lines of poetry."

"Why did you find that so disturbing?"

"Because I knew intuitively that those lines had a singular meaning. Because seeing me there threw Jude's mind into such confusion that, all unconsciously, he began speaking words he had no intention of ever speaking, revealing things he never intended to reveal. His face was blanched and drawn with fear. It was the first time I had ever known Jude Sykes to be afraid."

"The vicar? Afraid? Why?"

"Because on the instant of seeing me he realized with horror something he had not realized before: that I am the one person who knows him well enough to read that dissimulating mind, to perceive his guile."

John sat quiet for a moment, puzzled. "I am afraid I still do not understand, Mrs. Lundy. Are you suggesting that the words the vicar spoke from the pulpit have some bearing on Jenny's case?"

"I am certain of it, Doctor. I am certain that his words, obscure as they at first appear to be, hold the key to Jenny's plight."

"Do you remember those words?"

"I am not much of a scholar, Doctor. I cannot identify their source, but I believe they must be a quotation from one of Jude's scholarly books. The phrase that particularly struck me—that haunts me still and makes me shudder—was 'This borrowed likeness of shrunk death.' I recall that phrase quite clearly. A few lines later he said something about 'two-and-forty hours.' "

"That was all?"

"That is all I remember."

"And in those few enigmatic words you perceive a clue?"

"I know him too well to be deceived. The sight of me caused him extreme distress. His nostrils quivered. His eyes glittered strangely. Then, after a moment, his fear left him and he seemed to be swept up by some kind of exultation, something horribly gloating, jubilant. I did not understand what was happening, but I knew that in some way it concerned Jenny." Suddenly she stopped. "Doctor, I can see you do not believe me."

"On the contrary, Mrs. Lundy, I have reason to believe the vicar quite capable of such a digression. I will think over what you have told me. I will try to make some sense of it."

"I am sorry, Doctor. Perhaps it was foolish of me to have taken up your time. But the matter has troubled me so that I have not slept. That is why I came to Dorncaster."

"You did the right thing. I am grateful to you for coming."

"And, Doctor, I brought some money." Mrs. Lundy opened her purse. "It is all I have at the moment, but I will bring more."

John quickly interrupted. "No need, Mrs. Lundy. The Sisters make no charge for their services. Now, if you will leave your address with Mrs. Colley, I will get in touch with you after the trial and arrange for you and Jenny to meet. I know nothing would make her happier."

They shook hands and he watched her leave. He did not immediately call for his next patient, but instead sat thinking over what Mrs. Lundy had told him.

He repeated the words, slowly, thoughtfully, half-aloud. " 'This borrowed likeness of shrunk death.' " And then, again, " 'Two-and-forty hours.' " That certainly sounded like Shakespeare. Nor could there be any doubt that the vicar had actually spoken those words, or Mrs. Lundy, who did not recognize them, would not have known them. But those particular words suggested something so horrifying, so sinister, so evil that—

Suddenly he tensed in his chair. A glacial chill ran through his body. Jesus Lord! So that was it!

That was it!

He called loudly for Mrs. Colley. "I find I must leave the clinic early today. I will see only emergencies now. The rest must return tomorrow."

A short while later he was in the dining room of the Mermaid. He ordered a pot of ale and was just starting, with small interest, on a dish of beef and dumplings when Henry came in and dropped into an empty chair at his table.

"I thought I would find you here," Henry said. He gave the waiter his order, then turned back to John. "I came looking for you because the rebel trials were completed this morning. The Sykes trial has been scheduled for Thursday. Old Bassenthwaite will be the presiding judge."

John's heart stopped beating for a moment. A great sickness filled him and suddenly the smell of his meal was offensive to him. "Old Bassenthwaite! But he is a fool! He is asleep on the bench more than he is awake. He will never understand the complexity of this case. And if the judge fails to understand the case, what can we expect of the jury? You know yourself that these days the judge has even more control than the jury over the course and outcome of a trial."

"Old Bassenthwaite knows the law, John."

"The law be damned!"

Henry glanced at him swiftly. "I am sorry, John. But we have all known this trial was coming. And everyone but you seems to know how it will end."

John said angrily, "Have you read the papers from Amsterdam I left at your office this morning?"

"Steady, my friend! Steady! Yes, I read them. I read them right away. You know I would not keep you waiting, John. I know what this means to you." Then he added soothingly, "Can you come back to the office with me so we can talk?"

Back in the law offices of Pollexfen & Moss, Henry slouched in his chair and put his feet on his desk, preparing to face the clash he knew was coming.

John said abruptly, "Henry, your opinion, please."

"Well," Henry began carefully, "those papers are very interesting, John. I now see your point. This hydrostatic test, once it is generally accepted, can be expected to save countless innocent lives."

"Spare me, Henry! The future can wait. It is Jenny's innocent life I am interested in saving."

"Very well, let us commence with the case of the fifteen-year-old German peasant girl. Like Sykes, she bore her child in secret and, like Sykes, she was brought to trial."

"And would have been hanged had not the defense introduced this hydrostatic test into the courtroom."

"Very true! But it must be borne in mind that the defense, in addressing the court for the purpose of explaining the usefulness of the test, was able to note that its author was the famed Dutch anatomist Jan Swammerdam, already a revered name in the German States. The defense was able to note that the German medical community, always forward-looking in medico-legal matters, had confirmed the validity of the test, ruling that it was an infallible criterion for determining still-birth and that it could be applied in every questionable case with almost unerring success."

John was silent. He saw where Henry was heading and he was appalled.

"You know better than I do, John," Henry continued, "that such has never been the case in England—"

"The medical argument is as valid here as it is in Europe," John interrupted angrily. "The fact that a dead infant is born in secret to an unwed mother should not of itself be taken as proof of murder. The German court recognized the logic of that. The test proved the child deadborn. The girl was acquitted."

"True again!" Henry understood John's anguish. His habitual aggressiveness was under tight control. His sympathy and concern were undisguised. "But if our medical faculties have knowledge of this hydrostatic test, they have remained strangely silent. Apparently our English medical writers have not yet taken cognizance of it. How, then, can we introduce into an English courtroom a test which thus far is unheard-of and unrecognized and expect it to be given credence?"

"Are you telling me that even if this test proves Jenny's baby was stillborn—and it was!—that she can still be hanged for concealment?"

"What I am telling you is that the court may not accept this test, John. I know the reluctance of our courts to accept any new methods, and I very much doubt that any English judge would countenance a verdict of innocent based on such a novel procedure. We will not be dealing with searching, independent minds here, but with an old man who is too rigid in his views to do other than hold to the law as it is written, and with twelve men who, being summoned to sit in judgment on a girl who has unquestionably enjoyed the sin of fornication, must go home and get into bed with their moralistic wives."

John leapt to his feet and strode about the room. "But this old law is iniquitous. Every lawyer in England knows it."

"It is indeed iniquitous, and perhaps someday it will be changed. But it has stood for decades and it is still the law by which Jenny Sykes will be judged and sentenced."

"Then still another innocent girl will be condemned under this law?"

"We do not know that Sykes is innocent, John. You are the only one who maintains a belief in her innocence—and a man does not need to have cut his wisdom teeth to see that your judgment stems from emotion, not from any special knowledge of the facts."

"Jenny did not kill her child, Henry."

"Whether she did or not is immaterial. The fact remains that still-birth is not the prime issue in this case. The charge is concealment."

"But old Bassenthwaite! Have we no grounds for a postponement?"

"You know better than that, John. Trials for concealment do not even come under the ordinary rules of evidence."

John was silent for a moment. "And if Jenny is found guilty, how soon will they schedule her execution?"

"Her trial is set for Thursday. She will be hanged on Saturday."

Again John was silent. Henry watched him, his astute green eyes studying his friend's face in an effort to read his thoughts. He recalled that only a few days ago they had sat together in this room discussing the probability that Jenny would shortly face the gallows. At the time he had felt something tenuous in the air, something he did not comprehend, but which left him with a deep stirring of uneasiness. He felt it now again, only more pronounced. He continued to search John's face, yet still he gleaned nothing. The circumstances of John Toller's life had prepared him for the occasional need to master his facial expression.

Henry cleared his throat. He said anxiously, "You know, John, you will be required now to return Jenny to jail."

"I know that."

"You will have to do it soon."

"I know that, too."

There was another troubled pause.

Henry asked, "How is the girl taking it?"

"On the surface she appears to be surprisingly self-possessed. I think she is determined to face her ordeal with courage. Yet I know that when she was first admitted to Lying-In, her fevered moments were haunted by the mental image of the hangman's noose waiting for her, dangling black against the sky. Sister Brigit used to tell me how Jenny cried out in terror in the night. I am certain that her solitary moments are still haunted by that terror. Henry, right now I would gladly face the gallows myself to be able to protect her from her own thoughts."

"Dismiss such tender feelings, John. Consider rather where you stand in her affections. Whoever her seducer is, she must love him to protect him with her own life. She will return to him if she can, so whether she is freed or hanged, you stand to gain nothing. You will have wasted your love, added nothing to your reputation, and done nothing to improve the human condition."

Henry waited, but John made no answer. He seemed suddenly far away, remote from the scene.

"We all fall in love," Henry continued. "We all feel she is the *one* girl—the only girl we will ever love. But we get over her. We recover. We fall in love again." The lawyer paused, searching for words of comfort. "It is hard for you, John, I know. Why not go away right after the trial? Go up to London. A little gaiety will be good for you. I will attend to Jenny. I will walk with her to the gallows, if you wish. I will stay with her to the end."

But John appeared not even to have heard. He had arisen and moved over to the window and now was looking out over the city.

He said, "I may have some new evidence."

Henry was taken by surprise. "Oh?"

"I heard a curious story this morning."

"From whom?"

"From Jenny's mother."

"I thought she was dead."

"She is living over in Morcombe under the name of Lundy—the name of the man she ran away with."

"Well?"

"There is certainly some truth to her story. How significant it is, what bearing it will have upon our case, I do not know. I am planning to get to August Winn's after closing."

"The pharmacologist? Why after closing?"

"To have a private conversation with him."

"Why must it be private?"

"I want some information."

The lawyer's green eyes narrowed. "Not something from his books, John. There are laws, you know. Pharmacologists operate under separate charter."

"Which is why I am telling you nothing that would trouble your fastidious legal mind. And now I must go. I am late for my rounds. I have to ride all the way to Pilbeacon."

"John, listen! You cannot always ignore—"

But already John was out the door and running down the stairs.

A short while later he was heading out of town, absorbed in somber thought. He was sorely troubled by his conversation with Henry, by Henry's continued gloomy assessment of the outcome of Jenny's trial. Even with the hydrostatic test, Henry still held forth no hope at all for Jenny.

Suddenly John was roused from his musing by angry shouts and, looking up, found himself edging into a throng in the Market Place, a route he had been avoiding lately. Vaguely he wondered what had drawn so large a crowd. The rebel trials had ended, but three rebel corpses still hung from gallows made to serve six. Presently the hangman would cut them down and proceed with the tarring of heads and limbs for distribution throughout the country. But that had now become commonplace. There had to be another reason for this angry, surging mob.

He was trying to turn Iris toward one of the side streets when a piercing shriek split the air. He swung around. A woman was being dragged by the assistant hangman, Pascher Rose, up the ladder to the scaffold. John knew the woman. She had been accused of stealing two silver spoons. She could only have been tried that morning. A cursory trial, then off to the gallows. Only money bought the rights prescribed by law. "God Almighty!" John's heart gave a jerk as his thoughts flew to Jenny. The horror of what he was witnessing wrenched the deepest part of him. He wanted to turn away, but some overpowering compulsion forced him to draw rein and sit there, watching.

The woman was vigorously resisting Pascher Rose. She shrieked, then shrieked again, and kicked, and flung herself down on her knees before him, pleading, clinging desperately to the rungs, hysterical with fear. The crowd fell silent, moved to pity. One man roared, "Fer two sil'er spoons?" But Pascher Rose was impervious to the rage of the crowd, or to the woman's terror. He raised his clenched fist and brought it down hard on the hand gripping the rung. She gave a sharp yelp and her hand fell away, maimed by the blow. Then Pascher Rose picked her up, tossed her over his shoulder, and continued his climb up the ladder.

On the scaffold, in the shadow of the three rebel corpses, the hangman, Jack Ketch, waited. The woman caught sight of him and again her struggles started, so frantic this time that Pascher Rose stumbled and dropped her. Somehow she scrambled to her feet and was about to hurl herself down into the crowd, but Pascher Rose caught her and dragged her back. The woman was crazed with terror at the sight of Jack Ketch, the noose ready in his hands. She sprang at him to smash him in the face with her manacles. When he stepped out of reach, she uttered a long, wavering, high-pitched bellow and sank down on her haunches, sobbing wretchedly, and the hangman moved in and slipped the noose over her head. Then Pascher Rose jerked her to her feet and drove his knee into her spine, holding her powerless while the hangman adjusted the noose to his professional satisfaction.

An instant later her booted feet kicked in the empty air, her cries stilled, her twitching body gyrating slowly in the September sun.

For a moment John sat there, staring up at the ghastly sight. Then he turned Iris toward the side street, fought his way through the mob, and rode swiftly out of town.

The memory of the woman's abject terror stayed in his mind. He could think of nothing else. He forgot his rounds. He gave Iris her head, letting her go wherever her fancy might take her. She chose open country, going first at a canter, then quickly lengthening into a carefree gallop.

John paid no heed to her direction. Now his harrowing thoughts were all of Jenny.

He would never let her suffer as that other woman had suffered. He would never let her go to the gallows. He would not let the haunted visions of her fevered delirium become reality. "I will give no deadly medicine—" The Hippocratic oath. All his professional life he had striven to live by that code of medical ethics, violating it only rarely, only to alleviate human suffering. But now? Jenny . . . a fatal dose . . . a peaceful drifting into sleep, without pain, without fear. She knew so little of the stringency of the law, was too unworldly to comprehend the magnitude of the crime he would be committing or the enormity of the price he would pay for committing it. Briefly it troubled him to think of his patients standing in silent awe in the Market Place, watching the doctor they once trusted walking in chains to the gallows. How could he explain to them? How could he make them understand? He only knew that he could not let Jenny be given over into the brutal hands of Jack Ketch and Pascher Rose—not that tender flower with the magical beauty and luminous mind.

Several hours later he shivered, suddenly aware that he was cold. He raised his head. Iris had halted and was standing still, scenting danger ahead, waiting for human guidance. John looked about. The sky was black. A storm was driving in from the sea. Already it was raining hard, the large scattered drops that flew before a Dorsetshire "wilder." The drops made a lonely drumming on Iris's harness.

He had no idea where he was. He thought he knew every inch of the country around Dorncaster, but this empty landscape was strange to him. Morose, inhospitable, remote from all human habitations, it might have come down savage and untouched from the beginning of the world. Nothing stood out on the flatland except one starved tree blown to rags and bones by the pitiless wind. The soil was a saturated peaty agglomeration of ancient vegetation, too sour and wet to nourish any crops. Only a few clumps of heather and wiry grass sprouted among the mossy bog pools and here some scraggy sheep sought shelter, looking as tattered and lichenous as the rest of the landscape. Where there were sheep, there was usually a shepherd. But nowhere was there any sign of a shepherd or his hut.

John rode slowly forward, seeking refuge from the storm. Presently, through the driving rain, he sighted a low turf cot tucked away in a hollow beside a slimy bog pool. He reined in. By now the distances were closing in fast. It would be dangerous to try to find his way among the treacherous bogs. He dismounted and took Iris by the bridle. Then he knocked on the door of the hut.

It was opened by an aged man. When he saw the rain-sodden traveler and his mare, he gave a wide toothless smile. Then he quickly shuffled his feet and pulled the door wide.

"Thee be welcum, Doc," he said. "Bring in thy mare. Her kin stand i' the dry an' git warm."

John was surprised at the recognition. "You know me?" he asked, as he entered.

Again the old man smiled. "I be Asa Pook, Doc. Thee took care o' me wife at the hosp'tal coupla winters back. But her wuz real bad. Her's gone now, course. But thee wuz good to her while her needed it. Lor' guide us, thee be wet clear to the skin. I 'ull git the beast took care of while thee slips off them sopping clothes and puts on this lambskin kiver. Then thee kin sit by the fire an' warm thy bones."

Asa quickly unsaddled Iris and rubbed her down. He brought her feed and water, then came and kneeled before the fire, throwing on fresh peat to bring up a rosy glow.

"Me scads be cut fr' me own peat-bed," he ran on with pride. "Dried i' me own sunshine. There be nuthing like good bog peat to fill a man full o' God's peace. Eh! Thy clothes kin dry nice there. Now, Doc, is thee warmer i' that kiver? Cum sit i' this chair, then. I 'ull bring thee so'thing to warm thy inners."

He shuffled over to the cupboard, returning with a mug of home-made bog-heather ale and a slab of mutton that he set on a stool beside John.

"Eat up, Doc. Thee be near starved, by the look o' thee." He went and sat on the other side of the fireplace. "A'ways taking care o' other folks, like thee is, must feel topsy-turned, now, someone else taking care o' thee. Good thing thee found me cot. I declare, the Lord Hisself must'a guided thy feet. Could'a wandered clear off into the bog an' niver agin be see'd by mortal eyes."

John nodded in rueful agreement. "You are right, Asa. I confess I was not watching where I was going. My mind was preoccupied with something else."

He took a long draft of ale and started listlessly on the mutton and Asa watched him, compassion and benign concern in the wise old eyes.

"Ay. I wuz wondering 'bout that," Asa said after a moment. "I wuz asking meself, how cum a knowing man like the doc cud git hisself caught i' the middle o' the bogland wi' dark an' storm cuming on?" He paused, sitting quiet, letting a thoughtful moment pass. "What is't, Doc? Thee got heavy cares to fill thy thinking?"

"Yes, Asa—heavy, painful cares."

Asa's tone was almost tender. "Ay, I kin see it, lad. Thee is sore tormented an' it shows i' thy eyes. But has thee thought to ask fer help?"

John was puzzled. "Help? From whom?"

"From Him. It be plain this hurt lies heavy on thee. Time has cum now to ask God fer help. Him 'ull know what to do, lad. Him 'ull know."

John spoke almost angrily. "This is not a matter for God, Asa."

"No?" The question was gently put. "An' how kin thee tell a thing like that?"

John drew a sigh of annoyed frustration. How could he explain what the trouble was in words the old man could understand? And how could he explain that out of religious disenchantment he had not uttered a prayer in many long years? Even his brief invocation recently in the hospital chapel had been merely the fulfillment of his promise to Father Dominic. It could hardly be called a prayer.

He frowned and gazed thoughtfully across at the old man. There was about him something otherworldly, something fey in the peaceful blue eyes and wispy coronal of hair as white and fleecy as the bogland cotton grass. His skin was weathered from digging his peat and tending his wandering sheep, but his limbs were wiry still. There were no religious symbols in his one-room cot. Perhaps the old man carried his faith in his heart. No doubt he, like so many countrymen, lived with a sense of oneness with God, seeing the Creator's handiwork in each spring's renewal, in the sight of a tired ewe licking her newborn twins, in the laugh of a green woodpecker ringing from the copses in April, in the pipings of new life filling the grass-cup nests of the red-shanks. How could such a man understand the lost faith of one who daily witnessed the unending procession of the maimed and deformed and diseased to which a doctor must somehow grow hardened, but whose brute reality, over time, tended to crush his faith and leave him spiritually rudderless?

John was silent so long that Asa misunderstood.

"What is it, lad?" he asked gently. "Has thee forgot how to pray? Is that it?"

John curbed his impatience. "Asa, religion is not for me."

But Asa only smiled. "Lad, thee is young yit. Thee has to learn, is all. As fer the praying, that be easy. Thee jest kneels there an' tells Him what the trouble is. Jest talk to him natural. Him 'ull listen." He rose to his feet. "I got that sick lamb yonder. Her lost her mam. I got to feed her ev'ry little while, else her 'ull die. Fer thee, Doc, ain't nuthing thee kin do till the storm blows out an' thy clothes be dry. So jest sit there by the fire an' rest the while."

The old man went over to the corner, picked up the lamb and

started tending it, speaking in muted tones, feeding it by letting it lick pap off his fingers.

"Ay, thee be grieving fer thy mam, little one. But no matter. Thee has Asa to mamma thee. Thee 'ull grow big an' strong like the rest. So niver thee mind, now. Niver thee mind."

John finished his meal and pushed aside his plate and mug. He sat back. It was strangely restful in this tiny bogman's cot, with the sea wind screaming around it and rain drumming like hoofbeats on the thatch. He inhaled deeply. The aroma of peat filled his lungs with balm. The scads had settled into a rosy glow and above them a purple aureola danced, as though fire had freed some joyous little bog peri long entombed within.

He felt desperately tired. He closed his eyes.

The recurrent memory of Jenny . . . as he had first seen her standing in the coroner's court, shackled, in her loose gray ill-fitting dress and outsize boots. Even then he had been drawn by something in her face, something he still could not name, something he still loved. From that day she had filled his soul with anguish and delight—

Farewell, thou art too dear for my possessing—

So young to die . . . barely eighteen . . . barely eighteen. . . .

He stirred, vaguely conscious of the old man's continued murmuring, of Iris's steady munching close behind him.

And the odd-colored ribbons, one red and one green, with which she had tied her hair that day—

Time will come and take my love away—

"Ah, Jenny—"

He had spoken her name aloud and his own voice awakened him.

He opened his eyes to find the old man standing there, watching him. "A woman, is't?" he asked gently. "Ay, lad, 'tis hard being young."

John started to his feet. What was he doing, sleeping here by the bogman's fireside? What about his patients? He had neglected them all. And he still had to visit Augie Winn's after closing if he was to learn the answer to Mrs. Lundy's riddle.

He gathered up his clothes and began hurriedly to dress. "I hope there is a moon," he said.

"Ay, a goodly moon, lad. An' thy beast be rested. Thee kin go on thy way, if thee has a mind."

John thanked Asa for his kindness. He went to leave some coins on the table, but the old man quickly waved them away.

" 'Twas nought," he said. "Like I said, there be times us ordin'ry folks mus' took care o' thee, Doc. Now, jest look to the sea. Thee 'ull find the way clear now. Jest look to the sea."

John took Iris and stepped out into the night. The storm was spent and the brown peat bog stretched away into the distance, riven like floes of ice. The moon was halfway up the sky. Its orange light made shining ribbons of gold out of the dark, stagnant waters of the peat-tyes. Above the sedgy pools the will-o'-the-wisps danced their fitful nighttime dance.

He followed the bogman's directions and soon found himself on a rough trail running perilously along the cliffs. The coastline ahead faded into the distance, one spectral headland after another looming dark against the moonlit sea. From far below came the quiet surge of breakers on the beach. A gull drifted ghostlike above.

The peace and stillness of night lay all around, but John felt none of it, for now he was plagued by yet another troubling thought.

What of Tom in all this? It would break Tom's heart to learn that John had sacrificed everything—his medical career, even his life—for love of a woman. Tom was getting old, increasingly alone, increasingly crippled by gout. Tom needed him now—

Yet he could not abandon Jenny.

A towering rush of anguish filled him.

"But has thee thought to ask fer help?"

"This is not a matter for God, Asa."

"No? An' how kin thee tell a thing like that?"

Angrily John brushed all memory of Asa's words aside. He was briefly comforted by the thought that Henry was without a doubt the most able criminal lawyer in the county. Henry could be trusted to do his best. Ah, yes, but even Henry had maintained from the start that all his professional skills would not be enough to save Jenny's life. Only that morning Henry had said, "Her trial is set for Thursday. She will be hanged on Saturday."

Suddenly a great rage filled him. There was nothing, then. No justice on earth. No God who cared. There was no hope anywhere, only this paralyzing revulsion, this deep sense of betrayal. He found himself shouting aloud into the empty spaces of the night. His angry, impotent utterances rang among the rocks and cliffs.

"Time has cum now to ask God for help. Him 'ull know what to do, lad. Him 'ull know. . . ."

He had passed it countless times, a tall stone cross standing on the

promontory of St. Gowan's Head just outside Dorncaster. Rarely had he
given it more than a glance. But now his gaze remained fixed on it as he
passed. Suddenly he reined in, on impulse, not knowing why, not knowing yet what he was going to do. For a long while he sat there, gazing
back at it over his shoulder. Then he dismounted, left Iris by the way-
side, and walked back.

It fronted boldly on the Channel from its awesome, windswept
height. Far below, foaming seas and wild tide-races crashed over rocks
on whose sharp pinnacles many a fine ship had died. Some long-forgot-
ten Samaritan had set up the cross as a warning to sailors far out at sea
and had topped it with a cresset from which, on dark nights, a torch of
resinous wood sent out a warning flare to homing fishing boats.

Standing there, his back to the cliff's edge, John saw the cross
consciously for the first time. It must have stood there for centuries,
hewn from a huge block of native stone. Wind and rain had almost
effaced the cryptic writings carved on its extended arms. Its lower shaft
was dark with slow-creeping lichen, but above, as the moon's light fell
aslant its face, he could make out half-obliterated religious scenes carved
by a skilled craftsman: Christ preaching to the multitude; Christ afflicted by a crown of thorns; Christ stumbling under the weight of the
cross; Christ approaching the Place of the Skull; Christ hanging crucified between the thieves on Calvary.

For a long while he stood gazing up at the crucified Christ, seeing
in his despair that a Saviour who could not prevail against the evil wills
of men was no Saviour at all; yet, even against the arguments of his
reasoning mind, even against his rooted unbelief he was yearning in his
tempest-torn but unsubmissive spirit to believe once again in a loving
and just and merciful God, to know again the assurance of his childhood's pure and unquestioning faith.

Slowly he dropped to his knees and bowed his head. Then, falter-
ing at first, unaccustomed, he groped for words to shape his prayer.

The city was asleep by the time he got back. The shops were
closed. Even the alleys were empty. He rode down the West High
Street and reined in before August Winn's pharmacy.

The shop was dark. He looked up at the upper floor where August
Winn and his wife had their living quarters. A lamp still burned. John
dismounted and threw a few pebbles up at the windowpane. After a

moment Winn himself opened the window and thrust out his white head.

"Who is it? Why, Doctor John? At this hour?"

"Open up, please, Augie. I must talk to you."

They sat together in the comfortable back room of Augie's shop, surrounded by cabinets filled with colorful apothecary jars and caskets of costly drugs from distant lands. The air smelled of aromatic spices. Winn had earned wide fame as a pharmacologist. He had spent three years in the Orient studying local drugs and diseases and had introduced into English medicine many hitherto-unknown plants. Books on *materia medica* crammed the shelves at one end of the room and stood in piles on the floor. His special secret remedies had a way of producing beneficial results. They were much sought after, even by London physicians, and had made him a rich man.

He poured them each a glass of wine.

"Drink up, John," he said. "It is not like you to look so spent. Come, tell me what is troubling you. What brings you here so late at night?"

"I wanted to have a private talk with you, Augie."

Augie's wrinkled face broke into a smile. "So I assume. I also assume you want me to talk about something you know I should not talk about."

John laughed. "We both know it would not be the first time we had exchanged confidences."

"Continue."

"You are known to have an intimate knowledge of the history of pharmacology. Are there any known records of a girl having been impregnated without her knowledge?"

Augie looked closely at John. "Since you alluded to pharmacology, and since you know that a nonvirginal female can be impregnated during natural sleep, you must have a virgin in mind."

"I have."

"Then what you are suggesting is probably the covert and criminal use of Dioscorides's potion."

"But Dioscorides lived in the first century."

"His potion has never fallen into complete disuse."

"And what effect would Dioscorides's potion have on the innocent victim? Would it produce, say, 'This borrowed likeness of shrunk death'?"

"More or less."

"I cannot place that quotation, Augie. Can you?"

"It comes from *Romeo and Juliet*. The words are spoken by the Friar when he gives Juliet the potion which will cause her to fall into a deathlike sleep."

"Can you recall his exact words?"

"I think so. They run:

> *"Take thou this vial, being then in bed,*
> *And this distilled liquor drink thou off;*
> *When presently through all thy veins shall run*
> *A cold and drowsy humour. . . .*
> *And in this borrow'd likeness of shrunk death*
> *Thou shalt continue two-and-forty hours,*
> *And then awake as from a pleasant sleep."*

"And do you believe the potion Shakespeare referred to was the potion prescribed by Dioscorides?"

"It is generally assumed to be."

"But Dioscorides wrote in Greek. How would Shakespeare have had knowledge of his works?"

"Dioscorides was translated into French and Italian, two languages in which Shakespeare is said to have had considerable facility."

"But the Friar's potion was intended specifically to simulate death. Are there any records of such a potion being used for more sinister purposes?"

"To impregnate a virgin without her knowledge?"

"Yes."

"In the last century," Augie answered, "a French pharmacologist made a note in his journal. The event occurred, he said, during the horrors of the Saint Bartholomew Massacre. A Catholic soldier came to him and said he had a young cousin, a sixteen-year-old Huguenot girl, whom he was trying to save from the slaughter. He wished to form a funeral cortege and transport her out of town in a coffin, ostensibly for burial, but was afraid she might grow frightened and cry out, thereby alarming the guards. The pharmacologist mixed up a vial of Dioscorides's potion. Only later did he learn the soldier's cruel plan. The soldier and his companions had taken the girl to an abandoned house and held her for three days. After the massacre, she managed to escape.

She remembered nothing of her captivity. But nine months later, still claiming to be a virgin, she gave birth. The story is interesting in that it answers your question."

"Then the ingredients of this potion must be among the narcotics?"

"They are."

"And you stock them?"

"Aye."

"If a customer came into your shop and asked for Dioscorides's potion by name, would you put it up for him?"

"No."

"But supposing a customer were sufficiently knowledgeable, could he buy the separate ingredients on two or more occasions and mix them himself?"

"He probably could. But he would need to have had access to the ancient medical classics. He would need to be an exceptional scholar."

"I am speaking of an exceptional scholar."

Augie raised his brows. "The vicar of Little Liscombe?" He paused, astonished. "John, have we been talking of the Sykes girl?"

"Has it never crossed your mind, Augie, that the Reverend Sykes is capable of a criminal act?"

"A *criminal* act?" Augie reflected on this a moment. "I suspect he has secrets which at times seem about to betray him."

"Such as?"

"One time a commonplace question left him so shaken he turned and rushed out of my shop without his change. That puzzled me. The vicar is not a man to lightly forget his change."

"What question did you ask him?"

"I inquired about his nephew, Jonathan."

"His nephew? I always supposed he had no kin."

"So did I, until Jonathan came into my shop."

"Tell me about that."

"It happened late one night, after the shop was closed. I had not yet gone upstairs when this young man came banging on the door. An emergency, he called out, the vicar of Little Liscombe was taken ill with chills and fever. I glanced out at the street. Sure enough, there was the vicar's pitiful rattlebone horse. I let the young man in and he handed me a list. I recognized the vicar's handwriting. I told him to wait while I went inside and dispensed the drugs. When I returned, something was missing from the counter—you remember it, the miniature pharmacy jar that stood there for years, crafted in Italy, hand-painted. It was still on the counter when I closed the shop. Only Jonathan could have taken it. It was small enough to slip in his pocket. That was why, as I was wrapping the drugs, I casually asked him about himself. He said he was the vicar's nephew—Jonathan something—that his mother was the vicar's sister."

"Did you ask him about the jar?"

"It was late at night, John. I was alone in the shop and I already had good reason to distrust this young man. The jar itself was of no great value. Besides," Augie added with an impish smile, "the compound inside would act on him like a purgative."

"And you say the vicar seemed shaken when you mentioned Jonathan's name?"

"Very shaken. It was as if I had raised a ghost."

"How long ago was this?"

"About two years, perhaps three."

"Have you seen Jonathan since?"

"No."

"Well, the vicar must have expected Jonathan to play the anonymous messenger. That of itself raises interesting questions. But tell me, Augie, have you reason to believe the vicar has more than a superficial knowledge of the various drugs and their uses?"

"As a matter of fact, I know him to be exceptionally well-informed on the subject."

"Why do you say that?"

Augie thoughtfully sipped his wine. "A few years ago I heard a curious tale. You recall the old surgeon who used to live out Little Liscombe way?"

"Old Mr. Crawford? Yes, I recall him. He is dead now, but he was a good surgeon in his day."

"It was old Crawford who told me. He said that one winter, with snow and ice on the ground, a local farmer named Preston was thrown from his horse just outside the vicarage. His two sons were with him, and the boys, seeing their father in pain and wanting to get him out of the cold, carried him into the vicarage; then one of them ran to fetch the surgeon while the other stayed with his father. But it seems the vicar, who likes quiet, became irritated by Preston's moaning, so he went into his library and came back with something which he made

Preston drink. A short while later Preston was in a deep sleep. When old Crawford arrived he was amazed. He was able to tend the broken leg without awakening the patient. Crawford asked the vicar what he had used. The vicar refused to tell him."

"Has the vicar ever bought drugs separately which, when combined, could produce the effect of Dioscorides's potion?"

"Aye, but until this past year I never gave it much thought."

"What happened this past year?"

"One day last autumn the vicar came into my shop. He gave me a list of drugs. I put them up and as usual entered them in my ledger. I thought no more about it. A month later the vicar again appeared. Again he handed me a list, and again I put up the drugs and entered them. But all unawares, something must have been troubling me because one night, some time later, I awakened from sleep with a heavy feeling. I got up and came downstairs and went to my ledger and began to study the vicar's combined drug lists. Among them were the drugs required for Dioscorides's potion."

"And that was last autumn, you say? Can you recall the precise months?"

"Due to my concern over the matter, the months have stuck in my memory. They were November and December of last year."

"And his daughter's baby was born the following September."

A faint groan escaped from Augie Winn. He pulled himself out of his chair and began to shuffle about the room, his worn carpet slippers dragging rhythmically on the polished floor. He moved down the rows of pharmacy jars, taking off the lid of each in turn and sniffing its contents. He picked up large pestles and mortars, carefully inspecting them, but he did it all absentmindedly, as though his thoughts were somewhere other than in this room.

Then suddenly he returned to his chair. He drew a long, hard breath. His eyes were filled with horror, as though already he felt himself burdened by the weight of the crime that sickened him, but for which he felt himself somehow answerable.

"John—please! What you have suggested—this terrible thing. . . . You do not really believe it, do you?"

John's voice was harsh. "I believe it, Augie. Jesus God, I believe it! Perhaps the law can prove nothing. Perhaps the law will shilly-shally, seeing he is of the cloth. Perhaps he is clever enough to evade the law.

But I am not as punctilious as the law. And Jude Sykes will now have to reckon with me."

Augie asked, surprised, "But what can you do, John? If you were to make any such accusation against the vicar, you would not be believed."

"I know that."

"So it is hard to see how, lacking proof of any kind, such information can be useful."

"I know that, too. Besides, I am obligated to keep your confidence. But an open accusation may not be the best way to deal with this foul, perverted priest of God."

"How, then?"

"I do not think you would care to hear, Augie."

Augie gave a start. He sucked in his breath.

"No," he agreed hastily. "I do not think I would."

John was already halfway home when it came to him. He reined in sharply, sitting there motionless, staring down at the cobblestones with their ordered patterns.

Then Jenny never had a lover!

The realization brought him a moment of soaring elation. Then suddenly he frowned, puzzled by yet another unanswered question.

If Jenny never had a lover, then why had she maintained her silence?

Eighteen

If the clinic was even more crowded than usual the next morning, John for once was unaware of it. He had already ridden over to Little Liscombe, only to find that the vicar was not at home. He had walked up and down for an hour, then, seeing there was still no sign of the man, decided to leave and return about noon. Now, in the clinic, he was trying to concentrate on work, but his thoughts were not on his patients. They were still grappling with the shocking nature of Augie's disclosures and with how best to use those disclosures when he finally confronted the vicar later on that day.

Meanwhile he was struggling, though none too successfully, to bring his dangerously explosive passion of rage under control.

The knave! The blackguard! Jesus God! A hypocritical churchman who knew nothing of charity or forgiveness. A churchman with a vindictive drive, with a festering need to avenge himself on a runaway wife. Was that really it, though? Was that all there was here? No, there was something more. In his bones John knew there was something more. The vicar was a strange and complex man. Simple revenge did not quite fit the picture. Some more rigid and terrible purpose lay behind what he was doing to Jenny. . . .

"Yes, Mrs. O'Reilly, the baby is much better today. He is coming along nicely. Just continue his present treatment. Yes, that is right. Good-bye."

. . . Some girls were lucky. A lover stood by, swearing he was present at the birth and the infant was deadborn. Or a mother or woman friend went into court as witness. Thousands of girls were saved each year by a simple lie. The courts knew it. But it satisfied the law. Jenny, though, had been kept so isolated that when she needed a woman friend there was no one there to help her, no one to lie for her, no one even to advise her. Jenny had been caught in the maelstrom of her own vulnerability. . . .

"Yes, young man, that finger is infected. I will have to lance it to get out the splinter. Hold still! Well, you surprise me. You are too big to cry. How old are you? Six years? All of six years? Soon you will be as big as your pa. There now, that is over. You see, it did not really hurt."

. . . Even Clay Reynolds, whose daughter was motherless. Clay was known to have been five miles away at the time, yet he came into court and placed his hand on the Book and swore he was present at the birth. If the judge knew otherwise, he said nothing. Fathers protected their daughters. But the vicar? A man of God? No! An inhuman monster who played the organ while Jenny was suffering the agonies of childbirth. Jenny left alone to give birth in an empty house. God, to think of it! The man should be thrashed till he screamed for mercy, then strangled till his worthless life was squeezed out of him. . . .

John looked up, exasperated. "Yes, Mrs. Colley? What is it?"

Mrs. Colley spoke in a whisper. "This just came for you, Doctor."

The note was brief. There was nothing to indicate the identity of the sender. But the message made that clear to John.

The one of whom we talked last night. Word just reached me that he has requested and is likely to receive immediate transfer. Reason cited for request: Girl's immorality and likelihood that she will be publicly hanged, making it impossible for him to continue to carry out his ministerial labors within his present parish.

John sat motionless as the meaning of the message became clear to him. This explained everything. The vicar had shown himself to be astute, resourceful. Once the body of Jenny's infant was discovered in the woods, he quickly reasoned that by turning it over to the authorities himself he would not only thwart any accusations that Jenny might bring, but the fact of Jenny's trial and expected public execution would serve to ensure his immediate transfer out of the hated backwater of Little Liscombe.

John swore angrily.

He took the note and carefully burned it. He finished with his patient, saw him to the door, and called for the next one.

The trouble was that even now there were no legal grounds on which to charge the vicar. Nothing was really known about him. He was an enigma, a man who moved in his own twilight, half-glimpsed by the world. He left no traces, had no known companions, save perhaps this equally shadowy Jonathan. Yet such a man must have his secrets. Such a man, once those secrets were penetrated, could be intimidated into playing the role of Jenny's single required witness. Even Henry could hardly question a father's change of heart. And his testimony would be accepted by the court. Blackmail? An ugly word, but a potent weapon against the guilty. Yet blackmail called for a threat of exposure. Exposure of what? When confronted by the unsupported accusation that he had drugged Jenny, the vicar might remain coolly defiant, denying everything. Without proof, there would be no threat. Then there was the question of who had actually raped the girl. The vicar? Recalling the vicar's puritanical nature, it was conceivable that he had used an accomplice. Jonathan? Jonathan so far was only a name. Who was Jonathan? Where could he be found? Once found, was he bribable? Could Jonathan's revelations be used to force the vicar to change his testimony and swear in court that Jenny's child was stillborn?

John turned to his patient. "Dave, you must stay in the hospital. Mr. Barnes must operate on that fistula. No, don't argue. We've tried everything else. And you will be in good hands. Mr. Barnes is the best chirurgeon in Dorset. Yes, yes, I will be up to see you later."

. . . Blackmailing the vicar was a long chance—a very long chance. Yet if the court ruled the hydrostatic test inadmissible, it might be their *only* chance. The one link to the vicar's secret life was Jonathan. And where should he start the search for Jonathan? Augie had seen him only that once. Augie did not even recall his surname. But if Augie had seen Jonathan, then others might have seen him—sometime —somewhere—with the vicar. . . .

"By Heaven's Light! Of course—"

He called out, "Mrs. Colley, in here, please. I have an important call to make, one which cannot wait. I may not have time to make all my other calls. Which are the most urgent? No, no, speak to Mr. Barnes about that—"

John was on his way within minutes, riding westward along the coast. He rode at full speed, eager at last to find the answer to the questions that still baffled him. From Windy Head he had a sudden uninterrupted view of Morcombe, its harbor filled with ships, some riding at anchor awaiting the tide, others already berthed. The quay was busy with the comings and goings of sailors in worsted caps, their belts stuffed with knives and pistols and the deadly curved swords they called hangers. Everywhere exotic goods were being unloaded—bales from Spain and the Levant and Africa and the far-off Indies.

He rode downhill and entered the town by the rambling High Street paved with uncouth cobblestones. The street was narrow and the projecting upper stories almost touched above, shutting out the light, while the ancient timber beams supporting them creaked ominously as Iris ambled by. The shops were low and dark. On either side a plexus of lanes and alleys ran off, crowded with squalid huts and ragged urchins and scrawny scavenging animals.

At last he sighted an open court ahead and found himself before an old hostelry. A groom was lounging against the wall of the stableyard, waiting for business.

John drew rein. "I am looking for a girls' school," he said. "Do you know of any such in Morcombe?"

The groom stepped forward and tipped his cap. "There be on'y the one, sir, and that 'ud be the Allingham Semin'ry fer Young Ladies."

"And where would I find it?"

The groom turned and pointed down toward the beach. "Westward 'long the seafront, sir—the swell part o' town. First 'ee 'ull come to the Harbor Office. Cain't miss it. The Semin'ry be jest nearaways after that."

"And may I stall my mare with you? There will be sixpence in it if you feed and water her well."

He strode swiftly along the quay, passing the Harbor Office before reaching the wealthier part of Morcombe. Here, rich with carved-door porches and fanlights and forbidding gates, stood the mansions of the owners whose sailing ships plied the seas. Beyond those he sighted the seminary, a large building set apart from the rest behind a forbidding iron fence.

He stationed himself across the street and waited. It was several hours before the girls began to leave, accompanied by their mothers or governesses. One by one the lights throughout the building were extinguished. Presently the staff began to emerge.

He recognized Mrs. Lundy at once. He crossed the street toward her.

"Good day," he said. "I am John Toller. I wonder if I may speak to you for a few moments?"

She looked startled. "Oh, Doctor! It is Jenny! What's happened?"

"Jenny is all right, Mrs. Lundy," he answered. "That is not why I came. It is about another matter, a question of some importance to her trial. Where can we talk? Is there a coffeehouse nearby?"

"There is, but though the mothers of our students frequent it, it would be misunderstood for someone in my position. Nor can I invite you to my home. Being a widow, you understand. . . . We could walk back along the quay, though. It is quite open. No one could raise a brow."

They turned and started slowly back the way he had come, past the ships moored along the quay wall, their palisades of masts making a lattice against the early evening sky. By now all activity had ceased. The sailors had already headed for the pothouses. Here and there a lone figure could be seen standing guard upon a deck. The peaceful air was heavy with the smell of the sea, of rotting timbers and sodden ropes and the jettisoned litter of the harbor side.

He said, "Mrs. Lundy, would you mind if I were to ask you a few questions?"

"I am waiting, Doctor. I have already assumed that is why you came."

"Then would you tell me what you know of Jonathan?"

She gave a little start. "Jonathan? How does Jonathan come into this?"

"Ah, then you do know him."

"Jonathan was Jude's son."

"Jenny has a brother? She never mentioned it."

"I would be surprised if she had."

"Why?"

"Because at the vicarage Jonathan was never a subject for discussion. I doubt if Jenny ever heard of him."

John frowned. "Are you saying the vicar was married previously?"

"No. Jonathan was illegitimate."

"Would you mind telling me about that?"

They walked on a way in silence. He did not hurry her. He could see her face was suddenly pale and wrung with anguish.

"Doctor Toller," she said at last, "I know you very slightly, but I judge you to be a man of honorable character. That is why you may find yourself shocked by what I am about to tell you."

His tone was matter-of-fact. "Very little can shock me these days, dear lady."

"Well," she began, "after we were married, Jude became the vicar of Stovington, in the northern part of the county. A few months later he fell in love with—no, not love—developed an infatuation, a besotted passion, for a woman commonly referred to in the neighborhood as—you will forgive me, Doctor—as a slut. Against his own fastidious instincts, Jude used to visit her hovel outside town. Sometimes he would get up in the night and leave the vicarage. He would come back hours later reeking of her. There was no mistaking the odor. Jonathan was the result of that liaison."

She paused and looked thoughtfully across the bay at the fishing boats heading for shore.

"There was something strange in Jude's compulsion. Her name was Doris Grimes and Jude had always despised everything she was—the filth, the slovenliness, the vulgarity of her language, the degradation of her life. It is incomprehensible that a man like Jude—an intellectual, a man of genius, a theologian—could crave the lewdness this woman personified."

"We are often surprised by life, Mrs. Lundy."

"But this was unnatural, Doctor. Sometimes I would see her on the street, unwashed, her clothing torn and filthy, her hair disheveled, screaming bawdy epithets at passersby. Yet Jude was driven to her. He could not stay away. When the child was born, he seemed to develop the same fanatical obsession for the boy. Jonathan grew up a spoiled, unmanageable youth, as depraved as his mother. Even when he was little, if he needed money, he would creep into the vicarage and steal from Jude. Yet still Jude doted on him."

"Did the vicar speak openly of this?"

"He never spoke of it at all. At first, while we were still at Stovington, he used to bring the boy to the house. Then one day Doris Grimes came—right into the vicarage! Without knocking! I was busy in the kitchen. Jude was home. He took her into the library and shut the door. But I heard her screaming at him, threatening him. Somehow he pacified her. He must have given her money, because abruptly she quieted down and left."

"Did she ever come back?"

"Not that I know of. But Jude continued to visit her in her hovel. Then Jude was transferred to Crampton, ten miles away, and as Jonathan grew older he would come to the Crampton vicarage alone. Jude would see him in private, in the library, with the doors closed. Apparently Jonathan always got what he came for because he never stayed long."

"And when the vicar was transferred to Little Liscombe, did he continue to see the boy?"

"Yes, but by then things had changed. Perhaps Jude was afraid the Stovington scandal would follow him to Little Liscombe as it had to Crampton. Perhaps the scandal was the reason for his rapid transfers. Perhaps he had been reprimanded by his superiors. I never knew. In any case, at Little Liscombe, Jude suddenly became abnormally secretive—especially about Jonathan. The boy, who by then was about fourteen, began to come to the vicarage only in secret and only at night."

"Did you see and talk to him on those occasions?"

"On those occasions I only glimpsed him from a distance. You see, my bedroom was just above the library and I would see him running through the dusk, crossing the fields at the back of the house. A moment later I would hear his customary *tap-tap-tap* on the library window and Jude would let him in. Occasionally, though, I was surprised to find him inside the vicarage by daylight, always while Jude was out, looking for things to steal. But he was fast on his legs. Before I could catch my breath, he was out the window and gone."

"Did you tell the vicar the boy was stealing?"

"There was no need. Jude knew. He would find things missing, but he never asked about them. He knew who had taken them."

"Yet he did nothing?"

"What could he do? Open a discussion on the one thing he was trying to conceal? Besides, he had a curious weakness for the boy."

"And what of Doris Grimes?"

"She died suddenly while we were still at Crampton. According to neighborhood gossip, she was killed by one of her lovers in a tavern brawl."

"How did the vicar take that?"

"He suffered in secret. While Doris Grimes lived, his obsession for her filled his life. Even though he was disgusted by his own compulsion, even though he lived in self-loathing, yet still he felt a perpetual need for her. After her death he continued to feel that need. I witnessed his torment, but was unable to help him. I would only feel pity for him. Pity and fear."

"Fear of what?"

"I do not know, Doctor. Fear of the man inside Jude. Fear of something almost inhuman. In any case, it was shortly after Doris Grimes's death that he was transferred to Little Liscombe. At first I was relieved. I thought the change would restore him. But no. He began to wander the countryside at night. He appeared increasingly distraught. He began to watch me resentfully, a curious waiting expression in his eyes. He watched Jenny the same way. At last I could endure the horror of life at the vicarage no longer."

"And that was when you took Jenny and left?"

"Yes."

"And Jonathan, how old would you judge him to be now?"

"Jonathan is dead, Doctor. He was murdered one night in his bed."

"By whom?"

"No one knows. He had many enemies."

"How long ago was that?"

"It will be three years ago this Christmas."

John was silent for a moment. His eyes were carefully averted from her face, fixed thoughtfully on the ancient sundial of the Harbor Office as his mind tangled with a new and heartsickening speculation.

"Mrs. Lundy, most men are protective of their daughters. Can you suggest a reason why the vicar should not have been charged with this same tenderly protective love for Jenny?"

She hesitated, unable to bring herself to put it into words. "Doctor, I can see you have already guessed the answer to that question."

"That Jenny is not the vicar's child?"

"Jenny is Jim Lundy's child."

"And the vicar knew?"

"Jude and I had been estranged since our wedding night."

"Yet being born within wedlock, he was able to claim her."

"Do you find that cruel?"

"Too cruel to contemplate."

Her voice was suddenly broken with tears. "Down through the years I had often wondered why he wanted her. Now I know. He was brooding, the betrayed husband, plotting his revenge, waiting. Now his moment is come."

John laid a quick hand on her arm. "Do not lose hope just yet, Mrs. Lundy. I can promise nothing, of course, but you have my word that I will do all that a man can to save Jenny's life."

Impulsively she reached up on tiptoe and kissed his cheek. "Whatever happens, Doctor, God bless you for trying."

Then she turned quickly and left him.

He rode slowly back along the coast. He needed time to think, time to bring order to his thoughts before his confrontation with the vicar. Certainly in its opening stages that confrontation would be unpleasant. He would need a cool head to counter the vicar's vituperative tongue and bring a vein of reason to the conversation.

It was unfortunate that Jonathan was dead. Impecunious thief that he was, he might have proved a useful tool. But the vicar could still be forced into compliance. John felt certain now the vicar himself was the father of Jenny's child. But whether he was or not, he could not permit such an allegation to come before his bishop, especially in view of the testimony Farmer Preston and his sons could provide as to his knowledge of drugs and their uses. The vicar's reputation must already be an embarrassment to his superiors: the fact of his two previous transfers, the unsavory reasons behind them, his recent request for a new transfer on the grounds of his daughter's immorality, and now this allegation of the criminal use of narcotic drugs to commit rape upon that same daughter. Perhaps all these accusations could not be proved, but there was enough here to alarm the Church.

As for Henry, there was nothing to be gained by taking this new information to him. Even if a crime could be proved against the vicar, it would have no bearing on Jenny's case. The vicar's disgrace was not the objective here, the vicar's cooperation was. Odious as it might be, the time had come to deal with the vicar on the vicar's own unscrupulous terms: the threat of exposure, followed by a bargain—John Toller's silence in exchange for the vicar's appearance in court as witness for Jenny.

John swore a vigorous oath. This time the vicar would find himself caught in a trap. This time, to save himself, he must first save Jenny.

Suddenly impatient, suddenly eager to face the vicar, John turned off the coast road and struck off cross-country, heading over grassy, sheep-dotted hills that would carry him directly down into Little Liscombe. Yes, by God! Jenny would have the single credible witness the law required—the vicar himself.

And the vicar would act the part of the devoted father as convincingly as he had acted the injured one. The court might raise an eyebrow at the vicar's sudden change of testimony, but his word would be accepted.

And Jenny would be acquitted.

A flaming sunset reddened the desolate slopes of Yeggor Dun by the time he rode into Little Liscombe. He dismounted in front of the vicarage and tied Iris to the fence. Then he pushed open the gate and entered the sad, neglected garden.

There was something ominously quiet about the vicarage. Nothing stirred, not a squirrel, not a bird. He was acutely conscious of the plaintive rustle of dead leaves underfoot as he started up the path, of something undefinable that seemed at once to clutch at him. At the door he halted and knocked. There was no answer. The same, he reflected, as last time. He pushed the door open and entered. In the hallway he stood a moment listening to the eerie silence of the house. "Vicar?" His voice seemed to cut the air with the incisiveness of a scalpel cutting flesh. He glanced at the empty rooms to left and right. Then he headed down toward the library.

The door was shut. He paused and listened. "Vicar?" No answer came from within. He opened the door. The room was dark and empty. For a moment he stood there, disturbed by an uncanny sense of finality, of something ended, something abandoned. Then he backed out and shut the door behind him.

He started up the stairs. The silence here seemed breathless in its intensity. On the landing he paused and looked around. An open door seemed to invite intrusion. He moved toward it. The vicar's bedroom was spare and cold as the vicar himself. For some reason he was overwhelmed by a singular aversion and quickly turned and left the room. On the landing he paused, standing there, listening to what the silence seemed to be telling him. Something in his deepest self wanted to turn and leave. Yet now he knew he must continue his search. At a second door he paused and knocked, then he opened it and glanced in. Empty, its dimness relieved only by the chinks in its closed shutters. At the end of the passage was a third door. Somehow he knew this would be Jenny's room.

He trod softly there.

She must have been arrested and taken at once, for the bed was still unmade. This, then, had been her girlhood room. A basin on a stand still held the water in which she had washed her newborn. He looked around, loving the room even in its sadness. A few garments hung upon a peg, an old dress, a pair of black stockings, a petticoat. That was all. Her life had indeed been stark. On her bedside table lay a volume bound in deerskin. He glanced at it. Giraldus Cambrensis. Her world had been contained between the covers of her father's books.

He was glad to shut the front door behind him. Perhaps the vicar was out visiting a sick parishioner. He went around to the stable to see if his horse was gone. But the poor, rawboned beast was still in his stall. He had no feed, no water. John pitched him some hay, then brought in a pail of fresh water. The vicar could not have gone far, then, without his horse. The church, perhaps.

He started out across the graveyard, skirting the weedy tombs, heading for the front of the church. On the squat ivied tower the metal face of the sundial flamed red in the sunset. From a nearby fir came an owl's long, unearthly shriek. No wonder, he thought, that white owls on the twilight hunt, with their luminous eyes and great round faces, were seen by primitive men as ghosts in flight. He found the church door ajar and through it a dissolute family of geese were excitedly invading the holy place. He shooed them out and shut the door against them. Then he turned into the silent dimness of the church.

There was no sign of the vicar. He started down the aisle between the high pews. "Vicar?" The echoes of his voice ran through the empty spaces, rising up to die among the beams of the high-pitched roof. The last rays of the setting sun lighted the colored panes. They flung a dark shadow down on the stone flags of the aisle, the shadow of a man hanging by the neck from a rope.

John halted and looked up.

"God Almighty!"

The vicar was hanging from a roof beam, his long, cadaverous body turning slowly. For an instant John stared up in horror at the thing that was hanging there. Then he turned and raced up the stairs to the choir loft. At the railing he leaned over, took a grip on the beam and swung out onto it. Then he edged slowly out to the body. When he reached it he leaned down and placed his hand against the vicar's neck. He was quite dead. He had probably been dead since yesterday.

Back in the aisle, he stood looking up at the dangling thing still twisting on its rope.

Why?

Jude Sykes had so meticulously carried out his considered plan. So why this? Had his petition for transfer already been denied? Was he being chastised for past transgressions by being left to suffer continuing stagnation here in Little Liscombe? And was his suicide here in this holy place his final malicious gesture of defiance—a final desecration of the Church?

Whatever the answer, there was nothing more to do. John turned and left, first locking the door from the inside, leaving through the vestry. Then he went to report the vicar's death and the fact that his horse had been left shut up in the stable and needed care.

John rode home slowly, deep in thought. Suicide. Poor tormented man. He who could describe Hell's fiery ordeal with such verbal skill and intense imagery, who could condemn human weakness with such ecstatic fervor, had in the end been driven by the tyranny of paradoxical inner forces to end his own life. Perhaps now he had found peace.

But Jenny's ordeal still lay ahead.

Despair washed over him. His heart hurt. The only hope now lay in the hydrostatic test. But if Henry proved to be right and the test was ruled inadmissible in a court of law, what then for Jenny?

What then for Jenny?

He raised his face to the stars. What secrets had the priests of Assyria and Babylonia thought to read there? The fortunes of men and nations? The fate of kings? From early times the stars had fascinated man with their supposed dominance over human destiny, with their inscrutable patterns, their ordered seasons, blooming like fields of flowers in pink and blue and topaz. "Canst thou bind the sweet influences of Pleiades, or loose the bands of Orion?" the voice from the whirlwind had challenged Job. "Canst thou bring forth Mazzaroth in his season? Canst thou guide Arcturus with his sons?" No, even the ancients believed that man's destiny was not his own to guide, that some giant hand moved the stars in the slowly changing sky. Man might claim that he alone of all living creatures was an end to himself, yet still, in some mysterious way, his little world seemed bound forever to that remote and glittering wheel.

He was not even aware that he had reached his cottage until Iris blew softly to let him know. He looked up to see a man waiting at his door.

"Well, good evening, Constable," he said. "What brings you out so late at night? Not sickness in your family, I hope?"

"No, Doc, not that." The constable stepped closer. "Doc," he said, lowering his voice, "I thought 'ee 'ud want to know. The girl has 'scaped."

"The girl?"

"The Sykes girl, sir."

John was silent for a moment. "What happened, Constable?"

"Sir, seems Mr. Oglethorpe wanted the girl picked up and returned to jail—her trial cuming up and all. Him sent some jailers to Lying-In to fetch her. There was a long talk with the Reverend Mother, who said the girl could not go without your say-so. But the jailers won. They had a paper. By the time they got up to the girl's room, though, her was gone. Flown the coop, so to speak. Her room was empty."

"Then what happened?"

"The jailers went back and told Oglethorpe and he sent out a posse to search for her. They brung bloodhounds, sir. Her 'ull not git far. But bloodhounds on a young girl, sir. And one that be sick, at that. I jest thought 'ee 'ud want to know, sir."

John was already turning his mare. "You have been very kind, Constable. Thank you. I will get out there at once. Good night."

He rode swiftly through the narrow, cobbled streets and started out in the direction of St. Mary's Lying-In. The moon was rising now. Veils of slow-moving clouds were drifting across its face, flinging fitful, wavering gleams across the folded ridges of the hills. But most of the countryside still lay dark under the stars, the great bulk of the Whittleby Woods standing black on the horizon. The scattered farmhouses lay wrapped in sleep. Man and beast retired early in this farming country.

He was nearing the convent when suddenly, up ahead, he glimpsed a lighted lantern swinging up over a hill, followed by a line of men with several bloodhounds on leash. The posse! He slowed Iris to a walk, watching. The posse halted. For a few moments the men waited while the hounds sniffed the earth, casting about as though they had lost the scent on the stony track. Seeing the hounds still uncertain, the men converged for a hurried conference, then separated up to work the hounds in teams in an apparent effort to circle about and strike the new trail. Across the cornfields John caught their voices as they set off in different directions, harshly urging the hounds to hunt down the quarry.

His heart was beating with frantic, fearful jerks as he pulled Iris to a halt. The posse had searched the convent, then, and found her gone, so they reasoned she must be out here in open country. But there was very little stony ground in these farmlands. And soft, damp earth held the scent well. The hounds would soon run her down—unless he found her first.

But where should he look? How would her mind have worked? Someone—Sister Brigit, perhaps—had warned her that Oglethorpe's men were downstairs. She had panicked, of course. But she did not have the strength to go far. Besides, he had promised to come for her himself. She would have remembered that and would have run off somewhere to wait for him, somewhere she knew he would find her. But she did not know the countryside. It would have to be a place they had talked about, a place he had told her about—

Suddenly he swung Iris around and started back the way he had come, slowly, lest the sound of hooves thudding on the earth warn the posse of his presence. Soon he turned into an ancient packsaddle track which, screened between two high earth banks, wound without pattern through the placid pasturelands. Here, lying low on Iris's neck to avoid the whipping branches, he felt it safe at last to quicken his pace. The mossy way was soft under the mare's hooves.

A short time later he was urging Iris up the back of a hill. At the top he reined in and listened. He could hear the baying of the bloodhounds and knew they had recovered her scent. They were only a mile off. But the dogs were on leash. They would not travel faster than their keepers. He had easily outstripped them. He swung around and looked down into the mysterious spaces of the Cleybury Rings.

He leaned forward and patted Iris's neck. "All right, girl," he said softly. "Down we go. Easy, now."

Iris started down, surefooted, hesitating here and there as the sloping pathway dropped steeply and her forehooves slid in the long, damp grasses. Once she tried to swerve, but the deceptive smoothness of the rings of the amphitheater, cupped in tier on tier, made the descent too dangerous and he turned her away. "Easy, girl." She checked a moment and her ears went back. Then she started down again, stumbling, slithering, recovering her footing when he spoke to her softly.

She reached the bottom and started out across the wide arena. Abandoned for nearly two thousand years, the vast space was a mass of weeds and bushes. It was said the Cleybury Rings were haunted, that the spectacles of slaves being torn by wild beasts were still played out by men long dead, and so firm was that belief that even the most derisive schoolboys no longer ventured there. Mysteries deeper far than those young minds spun in shadows still troubled this silent, bloodstained place.

The clouds were clearing from the moon's face and across the arena he was able to make out the arched entrance to the chalk caves used by the Romans as slave pens. He moved toward them, slowing Iris as he drew near so that the sound of her hoofbeats would not alarm the already frightened girl. Outside the caves he dismounted and threw Iris's reins over a bush. Then he moved in under the archway, pausing in the dimness just inside.

"Jenny?" he called softly. "Jenny?"

He heard her little gasp of joy. The next instant she was rushing into his arms.

"I had to run away," she wept, her face against his breast. "They were going to take me back without you being there—without you knowing—without me ever seeing you again. I was waiting. I was afraid you would not find me—"

His lips were in her hair. "But I did find you, my Jenny. I came as soon as I heard. Ah, no, my heart's darling, do not cry. Do not cry."

He waited, giving her time to weep away the accumulated fears and tensions of her wild run. Sheltering her there in his arms, he became acutely aware of the feel of her body pressed against him. The warm fresh scent of her was sweet to his sharpened senses. It roused the unsatisfied hunger he had fought so hard to confine. He gazed down at her, taken unawares by the emotions that were sweeping him. In her flight she had lost her ribbons. Now her long hair tumbled loose over her shoulders, catching the moonlight reflected off the chalky walls. Its soft shimmer made him catch his breath. He raised a hand to touch it. It felt alive to his touch and he stroked its silky softness, again and again, with trembling hands. He buried his face in it. "Jenny— Jenny—" One hand moved down to caress her and a passionate desire filled him. He raised her chin to kiss her. But when he saw how blanched her face was, and taut, with undried tears still on her cheeks, his strong protective love seemed to flow out from him to encompass her.

"There, my Jenny," he murmured, his voice tender now, and restrained. "There, little one. Do not be afraid. I will take care of you. I will take care of you." And he gathered her gently to him and pressed her head to his heart.

But after a moment, when she had stopped trembling, he took her face and raised it to his.

He said, "You know they are tracking you."

A shudder shook her small frame. "The dogs? I heard them as I reached the top of the hill."

"That is where they lost your scent. But they soon recovered it. They will be here in a few moments. Do not let them frighten you, though. I will not let them come near you."

Now the sound of distant baying reached them on the wind and she leaned against him, shaking anew as all the terrors of those days in jail came rushing back, the days before he came down to the dungeon and found her. Gone, suddenly, were the defenses she had so carefully erected, the composure she had maintained at Lying-In. Now she buried her face in the rough fabric of his coat. "I am afraid," she confessed. "I do not know anymore if I can . . . I do not know anymore if I can be brave. . . ."

His heart seemed to twist painfully inside him. His arms tightened about her.

"Hush, love," he said. "Hush, my Jenny. You must not be afraid. I will never let them hurt you. I will never let you go to the gallows."

He could feel the surprise run through her. She looked up and in the dimness her startled eyes searched his face. "But what can you do? If I am found guilty, how can you prevent it?"

He did not answer immediately. He was thinking again of the woman in the Market Place, of her long agony of mindless terror before she was noosed and cast off. He answered evasively, "There is little time now to talk of these things, love. But whatever happens, no one will hurt you. That I promise."

Still she was puzzled. "Do you think, then—?" She broke off.

"Nothing is impossible, my Jenny. We must not lose hope, that is all."

"But Mr. Pollexfen said—"

He looked down into her tortured eyes and pale drawn face. "Pollexfen could be wrong," he interrupted quickly. "Lawyers are often wrong. In jury trials surprise is ever present. Often the verdict contradicts the evidence. There is no telling, love. Simply no telling. Behind each legal question there are human beings. And I might have patients on that jury."

The baying was closer now, echoing loudly in the vast hollow spaces as the hounds raced across the arena, the harsh voices of their keepers urging them on.

But now a new thought came to torment her. It made her catch her breath. "I will never see you again, will I?"

The awful finality of her words seemed to lacerate his soul. But still he forced himself to mask his own uncertainties and speak reassuringly. "You will see me, love. I will come to you immediately after the trial."

"But suppose they will not let you in?"

"Love, I am the city doctor. I come and go as I please."

"But suppose Mr. Oglethorpe forbids it?"

He smiled, recalling Oglethorpe's propensity for gold. "There are a hundred ways into that jail, my heart. I think I know them all." He caressed her cheek. "Trust me, my Jenny. I will come. And do not be afraid of returning to jail. You will not be put back in that dungeon. I will see that you are placed in the upstairs room with the women. They are not without sin, but they are good-hearted. And they know the ways of jail life. They will take care of you. Now, the searchers are almost here, love. Are you ready? Shall we go out and meet them?"

She gasped with horror at the thought. "The dogs will leap on me."

Quickly he soothed her. "Be still, then, my sweet. Be still." But he was torn by private grief, knowing that though he could protect her now, he could not always protect her from what was to come. He drew her back into his arms, looking down into her face, seeing it more clearly now that his eyes were accustomed to the dimness. He had watched it so often, loved it so well, could call it to mind on an instant, by night or by day, by his fireside or on his long rides, wherever he chanced to be. Now, as though by some irresistible inner compulsion, he took it between his hands and lovingly, tenderly, put his mouth on hers, holding there for a long moment. "We will wait, then, beloved," he said softly at last. "They will not bring the dogs in here."

She stood tight and trembling after that, her eyes squeezed shut against his coat, listening to the baying draw closer, finally reaching a pitch of excitement as the hounds reached the archway leading to the slave pens and scented the nearness of the quarry. The voices of the keepers rasped out sharp commands and the hounds' exulting cries dwindled to a chorus of disappointed whimpers. Then came the crunch of feet on the loose rubble underneath the archway.

The footsteps halted uncertainly at the maze of passages running off from the darkness of the tunnel.

" 'Ee be somewheres in here, Doc?"

"Yes, Quigley, I am here."

"Thought 'ee must be, with Iris out here waiting and all. Dogs think the girl be somewheres in these pens, too. Has 'ee found her, Doc?"

"Yes, I have found her."

Now Quigley himself appeared, a raised lantern in one hand, irons for legs and wrists in the other. Some of his men trailed along behind.

"Well," Quigley said, "I knowed if 'ee was here, Doc, there 'ud be no need to set the hounds on her."

"Quite right, Quigley. That was considerate of you."

"I 'ull jest git them irons on her, though, so's me men kin git her on the horse."

John's voice was suddenly hard as stone. "There will be no need for irons, Quigley. The prisoner is my patient. She is in no condition to wear irons. I came looking for her because she is also my responsibility. I intend taking her back to jail myself."

Quigley hesitated, confused. "Well, sir, I don' know 'bout that. My orders is—"

"And my orders come directly from Sir Colin Petre, who gave permission for her transfer in the first place. I will be taking her back on Iris, so if it makes you feel easier, you can follow along behind until I have her safely back in jail."

And without a further word he lifted Jenny in his arms and carried her from the cave.

It was after midnight when he rode out of town, heading north. He did not even glance at the moonlit countryside he loved so well. Deep in thought, he let Iris slow to a walk and rode with his eyes on the ground. The sounds of night were all about him, but for once they passed unnoticed—the grunts and squeals of badgers at their earth, a vixen's scream, the strange churring of a nightjar that gave vibrancy to the air and made the darkness of a nearby wood seem haunted as if by some spirit of the night. Then a plover called, free and wild and far-reaching, from the lonely heights of Yeggor Dun. Yet still he did not raise his eyes.

He left the highway and turned into the winding lane leading down to the cottage by the river. He dismounted, as he always did, a short distance from the cabin and led Iris noiselessly along the grassy border to the lean-to. Then he went around and tapped on the bedroom window.

Minnie awakened and saw him standing there. She rose and ran through the kitchen and opened the door to him.

Even in the slanting moonlight she saw at once that his face held something new, a starkness she had never seen before. He said nothing, but went straight into the bedroom and dropped onto the bed, fully clothed. She followed, took off her nightdress, and lay beside him, waiting. But he made no motion to come to her. Instead, he continued to lie there, staring up at the rafters, so alone in his thoughts that he seemed far away from her, too far for her to reach, as far from her as the polestar. She laid a hand against his cheek. He seemed unaware of her touch.

She had often held and comforted her children in their griefs. But now, in some dimly felt way, she understood that here was a grief far deeper than any she could assuage with kisses and soft words, a sadness so overwhelming that he had come tonight not for lovemaking, but only to feel the mute sympathy of a loving human being. So she stayed quietly beside him, an island of separateness, fearing to speak, fearing even to move.

Some time later she felt him stir beside her. When he arose, she hurriedly slipped on her nightdress and ran after him through the kitchen. He was waiting at the cottage door. He turned and took her in his arms, not kissing her, but holding her gently, his mind far away still. "You have been good to me," he said as if in farewell, and held her another moment. Then he fetched Iris from the lean-to and led her noiselessly away.

She watched man and horse disappear beyond the moonlit bend in the lane, uneasy about something she did not want to name; a premonition, something her reasoning mind was resisting, but which her woman's heart had always known: that although he came often to her bed, she had never truly been the object of his love, but only as the shadow to the tree; that someday, when he gave his love wholly to another woman, he would come to her no more.

She closed the door and out of habit went to the kitchen table. Then she stood staring down in amazement, for not only silver lay there, but gold as well, a sizable pile of golden coins. She had never before held gold in her hands and could not even guess at its value, so she crossed to the hearth, prized up a stone, and took out a lambskin bag. This she opened, tipping its contents onto the table, pouring out the hoard of silver coins he had left her through the years, mixing the old coins with the new. Then she tried to count them. But her simple mind was baffled by so great a task, so at last she put all the coins together into the bag and replaced it under the hearthstone.

When she arose from her knees she stood a moment, deep in thought, both hands covering her belly. She had known for some weeks that she was carrying his child. Since she had always thought such a complication in his life would trouble him, she had already gone out into the fields and woods to gather herbs to make her usual abortifacient.

But now she knew she would not use the herbs. She would throw them away. She would keep his child. It was all she would have of him now. The boy would grow up to be like his father, strong and kind. And when he was old enough she would use the gold and silver money to send him to school. The son would be a book-taught man, like his father.

And "John" was an ordinary name. No one would remark on it if she called him "John."

Nineteen

It was barely dawn when John rode slowly up the driveway of Thrushgrove Manor, the ancestral home of Henry Pollexfen. A light rain had fallen during the night, leaving a gloss on the laurels and the leathery leaves of the holly thickets. Overhead a stiff wind was coming off the sea, rousing the sullen, low-hanging clouds from their resting places on the treetops, harrying the lattice of bare boughs silhouetted against the gray. But below, where the underwood foreshadowed the darkness of approaching winter, the leaves of the brier were as red as a robin's breast.

John knew Thrushgrove well. He had visited there often when he and Henry were schoolboys. He knew every trail of its fine old woods, every secret of the ancient mansion, from the ghost-child who burned a tallow candle at midnight in one of the closed rooms, to the secret subterranean vault where the exploring boys found a skeleton lying on a granite slab, in an antique coat of mail, the hand that held the rusty sword still thinly clothed with flesh like the scrapings of tanned leather. Other secrets, too, the boys had shared, for they had always been fast friends. Henry's mother had died giving him birth. The elder Henry Pollexfen had been a renowned barrister, later elevated to the bench, and many famous cases came before him until the very day of his untimely death. It was generally expected that the younger Henry would follow in his famous father's footsteps.

John raised his head as he neared the house and thoughtfully surveyed it. The servants were only just beginning to stir. He could see the first thin plume of smoke curling up from a chimney in the rear of the building where the kitchens were located. But in the front all was quiet. Henry and his family were sleeping still.

John leaned forward and patted Iris's neck. "There, my pretty, straight to the stables with you. Feed and water and rest is what you need. And a bit of currying, too, I would say."

Within a short while he was back in front of the house, leaning against a great oak, waiting. He stood so still that the deer forgot he was there and began moving noiselessly among the yellowing bracken that grew breast-high beneath the trees. The birds hopped out from cover to peck at the holly berries. Deep in the woods a ringdove called.

Something moved just outside his range of vision. He turned his head. Henry was standing at an upper-floor window in his nightshirt, beckoning. A moment later Henry himself, clad in a dressing gown against the morning cold, had thrown open the front door.

"Come in, my friend—come in. It must have been chilly standing out there. Into the library, now. I will have a fire started in just a moment. Alice and the children are still asleep, but I think some of the servants must be up. They will serve us breakfast before the hearth— coffee and fresh eggs and home-cured bacon. Then you can tell me what is amiss and why you have come to see me at this hour."

He rang the bell and ordered breakfast, then quickly turned his attention to the fire, raking over last night's ashes till he roused a spark, adding dry moss and faggots and blowing up a flame with the bellows before finally throwing on the logs.

He talked with seeming heedlessness as he worked. "I hear there has been a death at Dunheved, that the other day there was a funeral in the Tremoigne family vault attended only by close family members." He straightened up and turned. "Were you there, John?" he asked casually.

John looked into Henry's face. The lawyer's mouth was asking one question, but the cool green eyes were asking quite another question, probing a secret he suspected had lain hidden for years among the Tremoigne family skeletons.

John knew that only an empty coffin was buried in the family vault. But he said, "Lucas sent me word. I could not attend."

"Then it follows that Lord Tremoigne counts you 'a close family member.' " Henry waited, curiously intent, for John's reply. When John remained silent, he turned back to the fire. "Who died, John? Young James?"

"God's belly! Henry, do you never stop prying?"

"I try not to. Was it James?"

Again John swore. "You do not expect me to answer that question."

"No, but I knew I would learn something just by asking it." Henry threw down the bellows and dropped into an armchair on the opposite side of the fireplace. "You see, my friend, to a lawyer this 'prying,' as you so inaptly term it, has its uses. Consider, for instance, my aged paternal grandmother. You remember her. She still lives in this house—up in the east wing, where she has her own apartments. She is reclusive, bedridden, crotchety, but to spend an hour with her talking over county affairs of the past fifty years is to get an exhaustive account of family pedigrees, together with every baton sinister that ever saw the Dorsetshire sun. The other evening, when I went up to visit her, we chanced to touch upon the Tremoignes. It seems that before she became old and bedridden there was not the smallest detail of county scandal she did not make it her business to ferret out—"

"Then meddling in the concerns of others runs in Pollexfen blood," John snapped.

Henry grinned. "You might fairly say so. You might also be interested to know, John, what my grandmother had to say about the Tremoignes—"

"No interest at all."

"From which I take it, then, you already know that Lucas—"

"God's sake, Henry," John broke in angrily, "you know damn well I did not come here to talk about the Tremoignes. You know damn well that at six o'clock in the morning I have something more important on my mind."

Henry's voice was unruffled. "If that is a question, John, I think you already know the answer to it. I am talking about the Tremoignes because they are now central to your life. It is no small thing when a young man with a borrowed name finds himself in position of becoming Lord Tremoigne of Dunheved Castle. Within the next twelve hours the Sykes trial will be over and you will have to turn your thoughts back to your own life, your own prospects, your own profession, to some other woman you will find and love and marry. This trial is something you must suffer through, but Jenny Sykes's fate is out of your hands."

At that moment there was a knock on the door and two menservants entered, each carrying a tray. Henry turned the conversation to his prize rhododendrons, the tenant farmers tilling his land, the poachers fishing his streams, until such time as breakfast had been set before them and they were once again alone.

"Now, John," Henry said as they began to eat, "what was it you came to tell me?"

"That Vicar Sykes will not be testifying against Jenny at the trial. Vicar Sykes is dead."

Henry gulped, put down his cup and stared. "Lord Almighty! What happened?"

"To all appearances he hanged himself."

"Where?"

"From a beam in his own church. I found him there last evening. He had been dead at least twenty-four hours."

Henry frowned. He said slowly, "You went over to Little Liscombe, John? Why?"

"To talk to the vicar."

"What about?"

"To blackmail him."

Henry shook his head in dismay. "I was hoping you were not going to say that."

"Then you should not have asked the question."

"You know the law."

"And you know that at times I have small respect for the law."

"You cannot always live by your own personal code, John."

"Rubbish! I reverence justice, not the kind of ragged law our courts dispense in concealment cases."

Henry was silent for a moment. He picked up some bacon in his fingers and chewed it with reflective thoroughness. "I take it," he said at last, "that you hoped to induce the vicar to alter his testimony."

"I did."

"And what were you expecting to use as an inducement?"

"The threat of exposure."

"Exposure? Of what?"

"That he drugged and raped the unconscious Jenny—who is not his daughter, by the way—and got her pregnant."

Henry looked up. "John, those allegations stun the mind. They are horrible! Shocking! Even if he were guilty, the vicar would hardly have acknowledged so heinous a crime."

"I would not have asked him to acknowledge it, only to agree to my proposal."

"Or?"

"Or I would have taken my story to his bishop."

"What evidence do you have to support such allegations?"

"Ample evidence, Henry. But my source is confidential."

"But if you could not name your source and therefore could not threaten to accuse him openly, why should not the vicar have simply laughed in your face?"

"Because, knowing my accusations were true, he could not have risked a visit by me to his bishop. And because I could produce witnesses to his proficiency with drugs."

"Witnesses? Without naming your source?"

"Yes—Farmer Preston and his two sons. The vicar drugged Preston once when he broke his leg and was in great pain."

Henry reflected a moment. "And you believe the vicar himself was the father of Jenny's child?"

"I am reasonably certain of it."

"And you believe he committed suicide?"

"There appears no doubt of it."

"But with his plan working so well, why would he end his own life?"

"Henry, the vicar was a very complex man. One night he came to my cottage and we sat and talked. He asked me a strange question: 'But what if a man *wants* to die?' And I looked into those tormented eyes and felt a cold chill run through me. At that moment I knew there was an unnatural darkness in the man, yet even then I came nowhere close to recognizing the truth. Now I know that behind that fanatical religious zeal was a monster of sexual depravity, a man who craved the company of women as depraved as himself, a man who used his preaching orgies on the evils of fornication for the vicarious gratification of his own ferocious lusts."

"Well, it is a pity you did not reach him in time. Reluctant as I am to admit it, if you could have persuaded him to change his testimony, to swear he was present at the birth and the child was stillborn, the law would have been satisfied and the charge of concealment repelled."

"But even now, if I could persuade my informant to come forward with his corroborative evidence that the vicar drugged Jenny, could that not be made to influence the outcome of this trial?"

"You know better than that, John. The manner in which the defendant was impregnated has never been the prime issue. The charge is concealment against the mother. Only proof of the fact of stillbirth can repel that charge."

John pushed aside his unfinished breakfast and began moving restlessly about the room, picking up objects here and there, then laying them down. But his mind was clearly elsewhere.

Henry watched him, creasing his brow.

"John, I am curious," he said after a moment. "In spite of all opinions to the contrary, you were always convinced of the girl's integrity. Why was that?"

"Perhaps because I loved her from the moment I saw her in the coroner's court. Even then, frightened, half-starved, jail-mucked, there was about her something that I loved and trusted." Suddenly he gave vent to a terrible burst of anger. "All this!" he cried. "All this!—and she never even had a lover."

Henry's eyelids flickered uneasily and a pained expression crossed his face. But he was too pragmatical to allow emotion to sway him for long.

"I hope you are not still nurturing any empty expectations," he said quickly. "You must not, you know. I have warned you about that. I agreed to take this case only out of friendship, only because I knew no other barrister in Dorset would take it. You must prepare yourself for the worst, John. Even the defendant admitted her guilt."

At that John swung around and faced his friend.

"Guilt? The defendant admitted no guilt. She simply spoke the truth. When she told no one of her pregnancy, it was because she knew no one to tell. When she took her stillborn infant out and buried it, that was not done in defiance of the law. That was a tender maternal act done in ignorance of the law. And there was no attempt at concealment. She wrapped the child in her own shawl. Remember? Henry, Jenny has lived as cloistered as a Carmelite at that vicarage. She is unacquainted with the law and its pitfalls. Concealment of birth? Jesus God! That does not violate the Ten Commandments. It is not counted among the seven deadly sins. How can it be a crime under the law?"

"Well, it is useless to argue the justice of a statute we cannot change, John. What must concern you now is your need to turn your back on this unhappy business and take up your life as it was before this girl came into it. Many a young man would envy you your professional reputation, your family connections, your remarkable prospects—"

"Henry, do not read me a lesson in lawyer's logic. Once you said, 'No man can live another man's life.' That is as true now as when you said it. You also said, 'English law enshrines the principle of protection of the innocent.' I wonder if you are as sure today as you were then of the scrupulosity of English law."

The ready-tongued lawyer opened his mouth to retort, then

changed his mind. Instead, he said quietly, "John, this girl—I can see you love her passionately. But in time you will find that—"

"No, Henry, time will not change the way I feel. Yes, I love her. If she could only live to be my wife, I would spend my days striving to make up for what she has suffered, striving to make her happy. She is all of life to me. She is my world. Without her, there is nothing."

Henry frowned, wondering silently how, unperceived, this tender romanticism had managed to combine all these years with the schist-hard realism that seemed so much a part of John Toller. But he said nothing. And presently, when John rose to go, Henry walked with him out to the driveway and stood beside him, silent still, waiting for Iris to be brought from the stables.

But as John was about to mount, Henry put a hand on his arm. "John," he said, his cool unemotionalism for once torn to shreds, "you are my best friend—the only true friend I ever had. I do not want anything to happen to you. I could not bear to lose you."

John stood there, gazing back at Henry for a long time. Then, with a sad, fond little smile, he turned, mounted his horse, and rode slowly down the drive.

The Sykes trial was scheduled for two o'clock, but long before that hour crowds thronged the courtroom—fashionable men affecting earrings and muffs, fashionable women with painted faces and hats perched atop elaborate periwigs, simple townsfolk, all titillated by the still-unresolved mystery surrounding the paternity of Jenny Sykes's baby. It was said she still had not named her lover. Nor had her lover as yet chosen to reveal his identity. It was the continuing mystery surrounding the entire affair that intrigued rich and poor alike.

John had been hoping that old Judge Bassenthwaite, who had long been tortured by the stone, would find himself too incapacitated that day to preside and that his place on the bench would be taken by a younger, more open-minded judge. That is what happened, but not at all in the way John had wished. At eleven o'clock the jurymen were assembled in the morgue to witness the hydrostatic test, but Bassenthwaite and the lawyers failed to appear. Eleven-thirty passed. It was almost noon before the door opened and Henry came in, accompanied by five or six other men.

He came directly over to John and drew him aside. "Old Bassenthwaite is indisposed," he whispered. "His place is being taken by Lord Dowden, the smallish man in the group."

John glanced at the tight-lipped, inexpressive face. His heart did a heavy turn. He asked quickly, "What of his reputation?"

But Henry only had time to shrug, for already the witnesses to the test were seating themselves and it was time for John to commence the demonstration.

Judge and jurors were strangely silent both during the test and after it was finished. Only Gordon Grade, the prosecuting counsel, asked a few questions and those were designed to cast an unfavorable light on the test and the purpose to which it was applied. There was silence again as they all arose, filed out of the morgue and departed.

The test had taken up so much time that there was only a brief interval before the trial was due to start. John and Henry met at the Mermaid.

John was clearly uneasy. "Now, Henry, what about Lord Dowden?"

Henry took a long draft of ale. "From what I could learn, he is tough and independent-minded. And he knows his law."

"Is that good for us, or bad?"

"I cannot answer that, John. I honestly do not know too much about him. He has been on the Oxford Circuit. But I watched him closely during the test and he seemed attentive. Not once during the dissection, which I am sure most of us found hard to watch, did he turn his eyes away, which suggests a strong stomach. In his case, though, that was perhaps not surprising."

"Why?"

"Because his father was the famous pathologist who, on the late King's order, performed the postmortem examination on the body of Samuel Silcox, who died at the reputed age of one hundred forty-four. It was a great disappointment to the elder Dowden, I am told, when his son rejected medicine and turned instead to law."

"Hm! What else?"

"He will not be easy, John. He has a tenacious and retentive mind that grapples with the hard issues. He was a distinguished barrister of Lincoln's Inn and, I am told, was equally brilliant at the bar as on the bench. He made a tremendous reputation as a cross-examiner."

"Is he a hard judge?"

"Hard, but fair—unpopular with his brother judges."

"Why unpopular?"

"Personality, I should think. You saw him—cold, reserved, and wary, exhibiting a frigid pride."

"Is he one of James's creatures?"

"I know nothing of his politics."

"Has a case like this ever come before him?"

"Only once that I could find out."

"What happened to her?"

Henry hesitated. "She was hanged."

There was silence as John toyed disconsolately with the meat on his plate. Henry watched him anxiously for a moment.

"John," he said, "we will not be calling the defendant, you know."

"Why not?"

"These jurymen have heard the gossips. I would rather they were asked to sit in judgment on the facts than on the girl." Then, when John made no reply, he swallowed down the rest of his ale. "Come, it is time we were getting to court."

But John laid a hand on his friend's arm. "Henry, a favor, please. After the trial, will you send word to Mrs. Lundy? She will be waiting and anxious. I myself may be unable to do it. Jenny will need me."

By the time the trial was about to start the spectators stood four deep behind the seating area, squeezed so tightly they could scarcely breathe. John looked around and saw that Tom was there, his gouty foot bandaged and raised upon a stool. Dear Tom! Despite his pain he was determined to be present in case the verdict went against them and John needed him. Dear, dear Tom!

There was an expectant murmur in the court as the defendant was brought in. She walked free, for John had bribed Oglethorpe to let her be tried out of irons on the grounds of her recent illness. Now heads craned, curiosity evident on the part of the men, restrained hostility on the part of the women, who covertly envied her the whispered debauchery of her secret life, her rumored succession of lovers, her wild nights on Yeggor Dun. But the girl's modest appearance surprised and baffled them. She looked frail, her face ashen, her eyes downcast, and John, permitting himself one brief glance, found his heart aching for her.

Suddenly there was a stir as the judge swept in, somehow imposing in his wig and fur-trimmed robe despite his diminutive stature. His head was large, strikingly out of proportion to his frame. His eyes were pale, with a piercing quality suggestive of a cold and penetrating intelligence combined with an arrogant disregard for the opinions of others. His face, seen now as the sunlight from the window fell upon it, was sharp, controlled, passionless. And this was the man, John reflected somberly, in whose hands Jenny's life now rested.

The proceedings were opened by Gordon Grade, the counsel for the prosecution, in a speech that indicated the nature of the charge. He regretted, he said, the unexplained absence of the prime witness, the Reverend Jude Sykes, but the other witnesses were present. He then called the poachers, who described how their pup scratched up the infant's body in Squire Haynes's woods. They identified the shawl. They were followed by the constable, to whom the Reverend Mr. Sykes had confided the care of the tiny corpse, then by the midwife Hetty Crome, who had examined the defendant for signs of recent delivery.

During these preliminaries Henry Pollexfen had sat in a state of controlled impatience. Now he rose quickly to his feet.

"My lord, gentlemen of the jury, the defense will not waste the court's time seeking to dispute the evidence. The defendant has already admitted giving birth to the infant in question—not in secret, as is alleged, but admittedly in solitude, it being, except for herself, a womanless house. Bearing in mind these previously frank admissions, she will not be called. My lord, this morning you and the members of the jury visited the city morgue where you witnessed a test performed by Doctor John Toller, a test known to the medical world as the hydrostatic test. The purpose of the test, as Doctor Toller informed you at the time, was to show that the infant in question was not murdered at birth as is the presumption under the law in the case of an unwed woman, but was actually deadborn—"

At that Gordon Grade leapt to his feet. "My lord, we have already shown admirable patience in sitting through that trying hour at the morgue. Can it be that my esteemed colleague has forgotten that the defendant is not charged with child-murder, but with the separate offense of concealment of birth?"

Henry Pollexfen coolly stood his ground. "We are not in dispute on that point, my lord. Concealment is indeed the charge. It is the wording of the law to which I wish to draw attention—"

The judge's voice was curt. "I am familiar with the wording of the law, Mr. Pollexfen."

"Your lordship's reputation as a legal scholar is recognized. But the

gentlemen of the jury understandably lack your background. I beg you
to bear with me while I cite the law for their benefit since—"

"Very well, Mr. Pollexfen—if you see it as material."

"Thank you, my lord." Henry turned to the jury. "Gentlemen, by a
law passed in the twenty-first year of the reign of King James the First,
it was enacted that concealment of the birth of a child which, if born
alive, would have been a bastard, was to be accounted satisfactory proof
of murder against the mother—"

At that Gordon Grade again jumped to his feet. "My lord, I have
already cited the law governing concealment. It is clear that by a slight
alteration in the wording of the law my colleague is trying to create
confusion in the minds of the jurors."

"In purporting to explain the law, my lord," Henry responded
quickly, "my colleague neglected to explain the law in its entirety. I beg
leave to cite it now for the benefit of the jury."

"On what grounds, Mr. Pollexfen?"

"On the grounds that its omission would work disadvantage to the
defendant."

"But, my lord—"

"Mr. Grade, be seated. Mr. Pollexfen, make your point—if you
have one."

"Thank you, my lord. My point is clear under the law. The concealment act serves to protect the fatherless unborn from destruction at
the hands of the distraught unwed mother. But the law also seeks to
protect the unwed mother from false accusations of child-murder in
cases of stillbirth." Henry paused, looking hard at the jury. "Because,
gentlemen, that portion of the law so carefully omitted by the prosecution specifies: UNLESS THE WOMAN CAN PROVE HER CHILD WAS
DEADBORN—"

Again Gordon Grade leapt to his feet. "My lord, my colleague's
argument is clearly superfluous. The record shows the defendant has
already testified that she delivered her child in solitude. The defendant
has testified there were no witnesses to prove stillbirth. That being so,
the defendant's own testimony clearly brings her within the statute."

Henry turned sharply to the judge. "My lord, I must protest my
friend's unpardonable behavior. Scarcely once in this courtroom today
have I been allowed to close my mouth of my own volition, but have
been constantly interrupted—"

"Mr. Grade," the judge said sternly, "I will not repeat it. Sit down and wait your turn. As for you, Mr. Pollexfen, I should add that I, too, am aware of the record and bear in mind the defendant's previous admissions. Now, you may continue."

"Thank you, my lord." Henry again turned to the jury. "Now, gentlemen, it is these last words which I beg you to bear in mind: UNLESS THE WOMAN CAN PROVE HER CHILD WAS DEADBORN. That, gentlemen, is the essence of the law. It is vital to this case. The point at issue, then, is this: Was Jenny Sykes's infant deadborn? If so, can she prove it? As I have stated, the defendant lived in a womanless house. She had no way of gaining assistance when the birth pains came upon her. Hence, there was no witness to the birth of her deadborn infant— no human witness, that is. But now medical science has brought us a silent witness to aid and assist the work of justice. My lord, gentlemen of the jury, we intend to show that Jenny Sykes's child was born dead. We intend to show, therefore, that Jenny Sykes is not within the statute."

Henry paused and glanced at the judge to gauge the effect of his words. But Lord Dowden's face was expressionless, his pale, kestrel-sharp eyes bent upon Henry with their unsettling, penetrating gaze.

Henry passed hurriedly on. "My lord, gentlemen of the jury, you were all present this morning at the morgue when the test was made upon the infant's body. At the time the purpose of the test was explained to you in brief. I now intend to clarify certain points which must be troubling you. My lord, with your permission, I will now call my only witness, Doctor John Toller."

Gordon Grade was up again. "Any such testimony would be irrelevant, my lord. The test at the morgue was, by the doctor's own admission, aimed at the detection of child-murder, but at the risk of being repetitious, I beg to remind the court that the charge against the defendant is strictly concealment of birth, not child-murder—"

"My lord," Henry interrupted angrily, "we all know that 'concealment of birth' is but the covering term for the real charge in these cases —suspicion of child-murder. As evidence of this, be it noted that the statute covering concealment of birth does not make a new offense, it only makes concealment on the part of an unwed woman evidence of child-murder in cases where the crime itself cannot be proved. The term 'concealment of birth' is therefore a pernicious one, for in such cases the court is not required to prove the child was born alive. It is not required to find signs of violence upon the body. It is not even required to find the body. No, once that pernicious term attaches to an unwed woman, it is undeniably taken that the child was born alive and murdered by its mother. So let us not grapple with legal shadows today, my lord. Let us speak plainly. Jenny Sykes, an unwed woman, is here charged with concealment of birth, the penalty for which is death upon the gallows. Under the law, then, the presumption is that Jenny Sykes is guilty of child-murder because the birth she concealed was that of a live-born child. My lord, gentlemen of the jury, we intend to prove that Jenny Sykes cannot be guilty as charged for the reason that Jenny Sykes's child was born dead."

Lord Dowden had listened patiently to this explosion of anger. Now he took an unhurried sip of water.

"Mr. Pollexfen," he said coolly, "in view of the fact that trials for concealment do not come under the ordinary rules of evidence, I am giving you uncommon latitude. I am giving you every opportunity to present an argument which will save the defendant's life. But the prosecution's objections are well taken. If you have an argument showing the defendant is not within the statute, do the court the favor of presenting it."

Henry bowed. "My lord, my point will shortly be made clear. May I proceed?"

The judge waved an acquiescent hand and Gordon Grade, with a surly look in Henry's direction, slowly reseated himself.

Henry turned. "I call Doctor John Toller."

After a brief pause, during which the requisite formalities were completed, John faced the court from the witness-box.

"Doctor Toller," Henry began, "this morning at the morgue you performed a test described as the hydrostatic test. Would you please explain to the court the medico-legal aspects of this test and the purpose for which it was devised?"

"The hydrostatic test is an important step in the proper recognition of child-murder since it answers the fundamental question of whether the child was live- or deadborn. It is aimed at saving the lives of those innocent women who are unjustly accused of this crime."

"By 'unjustly accused' you mean those unwed women who, without the benefit of witnesses to the birth, are delivered of stillborn infants?"

"Yes."

"And you feel that description applies in the case of Jenny Sykes?"

"I do."

"On what grounds have you formed this opinion, Doctor?"

"A few weeks ago I was called upon to examine the body of the Sykes baby after it was brought in. Upon examination I concluded that this was a case of stillbirth, that the infant had in fact never drawn a single breath of life."

"Did you examine the body for possible violence?"

"I examined for all common causes of death by commission."

"Such as?"

"Blows to the head causing fracture and other injuries, wounds to the throat, puncture of the fontanels, nucha, orbit, ear, or heart; drowning; suffocation by strangling with the hand or a cord, or by cutting the frenum linguae and rolling the tongue back into the throat with a view to choking the infant in such a way it would appear deadborn. All these are common forms of child-murder."

"And you found no indication that the child had in fact been murdered?"

"None at all. All indications were that it was deadborn."

"And this examination was of an external nature, I take it?"

"Up until now such an examination has been customary in these cases."

"When you say 'up until now,' you are referring of course to the introduction of this new hydrostatic test?"

"Yes."

"In the past, then, has medical science been unable to determine the guilt or innocence of the unwed mother in cases of suspected child-murder?"

"Until recently, no test has existed for making such a determination."

"So that in the absence of such a test, under our present law, the unwed mother of a stillborn child must either provide evidence of stillbirth in the form of a reliable witness, or be hanged for child-murder under cover of concealment of birth. Is that correct?"

"Unfortunately, yes."

"Now, Doctor, most of us present in this courtroom today are laymen. I am sure it is difficult for a layman to understand how, in the absence of the necessary witness to the birth, a medical procedure can determine the guilt or innocence of an unwed mother presumed to have killed her child. Would you please explain the rationale of this hydro-static test?"

John glanced anxiously at Jenny. She sat quietly, her eyes upon him. He wanted to jump up and run to her and put protecting arms about her. Instead, he turned helplessly back.

"The test is based upon the observed fact that the lungs of a live-born infant, being filled with air by the process of breathing, are buoy-ant and float readily when placed in a vessel filled with water. The lungs of the stillborn infant, however, having no indrawn air to give them buoyancy, remain instead dense and compact, heavier than water, and sink to the bottom when placed in the vessel."

"And it was this latter that you demonstrated at the morgue this morning."

"It was."

"So that those of us who were present at the morgue, including his lordship and the gentlemen of the jury, were all witness to the fact that the lungs of the Sykes infant sank to the bottom when you placed them in water?"

"Yes."

"And what medical conclusion should be drawn from that?"

"That the Sykes infant was born dead. There was no air in its lungs. It had never breathed."

"I take it this test can properly be made only once?"

"Yes, since it necessitates removal and dissection of the fetal lungs."

"And that is why the demonstration had to wait until his lordship and the gentlemen of the jury were assembled to witness it?"

"Yes."

"Now, Doctor, you have said this is a *new* test. To your knowledge has it ever been introduced into a court of law before today?"

"It has."

"Under what circumstances?"

"Three years ago Doctor Schreyer, of Zeitz in Saxony, first applied the test in the case of a fifteen-year-old peasant girl accused of child-murder."

"With what result?"

"The infant was determined to have been stillborn."

"And the defendant?"

"The defendant was acquitted."

"Then this hydrostatic test has in fact already been accepted by European courts of law?"

"Yes."

"On what terms was it given acceptance?"

"Several European medical faculties confirmed its validity."

"Thank you, Doctor. That will be all. Mr. Grade."

Gordon Grade was a tall, broad-shouldered man in his prime, with bushy brown hair and brows, and thin lips. Now he stood a moment, moving some papers back and forth as if searching for something on his table. But John, noting the tension of his facial muscles, knew he was preparing to swing around and press in with the savagery of a mastiff on the line of a wild boar.

He felt his own muscles go tense and glanced quickly at the judge, then at the row of faces in the jury box, studying the expression of each in turn, trying to peer into their minds. He knew each by name. Three were his patients. But they would need considerable powers of divination to be able to grasp the untouched areas of this case—

"Doctor Toller." John turned quickly and faced Gordon Grade. "You have told the court that this hydrostatic test has been accepted by at least one foreign court of law. But has it ever been accepted by a court of law in England?"

"Not that I am aware of."

"And why do you suppose England would be remiss in this respect, Doctor—if indeed, as you say, the validity of the test has been confirmed?"

"Because, sir, it is an unfortunate fact that in this country medico-legal science has so far been little appreciated or recognized."

"Well, now, Doctor, some of us might have difficulty giving credence to that statement. We all know that the excellence of English justice and the impartiality of its administration stir the admiration of the world. England is known to set standards which other legal systems vainly strive to emulate. Yet now—if I understand you—you would have this court sanction the questionable decision of some minor foreign law court by giving instant acceptance to this unknown theory?"

At that Henry leapt to his feet, his robe and wig flapping. But then he saw a faint flush rise to John's cheek and slowly he reseated himself.

"It is hardly unknown, Mr. Grade," John said. "The phenomenon was known to Galen."

"To whom?"

"To Galen, sir—Claudius Galen, the celebrated second-century physician. Within our own century, the Danish anatomist Thomas Bartholinus noticed the comparative fact that the lungs of a fetus sink, while those of an adult swim in water. A few years later Karl Rayger, a German, proposed this comparative experiment as a means of determining stillbirth. The Dutch anatomist Swammerdam, pursuing the same track of inquiry, explained its rationale. Now, as I have just stated, Doctor Schreyer has for the first time made the test available for purposes of justice. But it should further be said—"

"Thank you, Doctor, I think we have—"

"It should further be said that here in England, and anticipating Rayger by some twenty years, it was our own illustrious Harvey—to whom we must credit the then novel doctrine of the circulation of the blood and who was called 'crack-brained' for his pains—who first envisaged the possibility of legal medicine as a science in its own right by suggesting that Galen's observation be applied to the elucidation of cases of alleged infanticide. After Harvey's death, unfortunately, the English medical community failed to treat the subject scientifically, and it was left to the European physicians to become pioneers in the new legal medicine. No, Mr. Grade, this hydrostatic test is certainly not 'unknown' and could only be so considered by one who sets himself up as a judge of matters with which he is totally unacquainted."

Gordon Grade had been trying unsuccessfully to interrupt this flow of words. Now he turned heatedly to the judge. "I implore your lordship to instruct the witness to limit his responses to the question."

The judge tapped his gavel to quiet the laughter in the court.

"Well, now, Mr. Grade," he said, unruffled, "it would seem the witness saw you were laboring under a grave misapprehension. He was merely enlightening you as to the true facts and, I thought, with admirable clarity and thoroughness. However, your objection has merit. Doctor, please favor the court by keeping your responses brief and to the point."

"I will, my lord."

Gordon Grade's face was still red when he turned back to John. "Now, Doctor, you testified that the lungs of a stillborn infant will sink in water. Is that correct?"

"Yes."

"Now I ask you, are there any circumstances in which this hydrostatic test could be proved to be in error?"

"In what way, sir?"

"You have said the lungs of a live-born infant, being buoyant with air, would float. But is it possible, under certain circumstances, for the lungs of a live-born infant to *sink* in a water-filled vessel?"

The man was clever, John reflected. He knew the tricks of probing for answers he himself did not have. He knew how to try turning a witness for the defense into a witness for the prosecution.

"Perhaps you would make your meaning clearer," he suggested guardedly.

"Is it not possible that a live-born child could die and, although it had actually breathed for an hour or two, its lungs would sink in water?"

"It is conceivable."

"And conversely, would it not be possible for the lungs of a still-born child, which had never lived outside its mother, to float?"

"That, too, is conceivable."

"Under what circumstances would that be likely to happen, Doctor?"

"If the unborn infant had been afflicted with an emphysematous condition, for instance. Or in the rare event that it had breathed in the womb—or in the maternal passages."

"And if the child had indeed breathed in the womb, yet perished before birth, that child would be legally stillborn, would it not?"

"Yes."

"Yet the lungs of that particular stillborn child would float, would they not?"

"In all probability."

"On the other hand, a child can be live-born, yet its lungs could sink. You have testified to that, have you not?"

"I do not believe I so testified."

"What did you say, Doctor?"

"I said that such a thing was conceivable."

"Under what circumstances is it conceivable?"

"Certain diseases which caused the newborn child to die might cause the lungs to sink."

"So that in such a case the hydrostatic test would then give a false reading?"

"No, Mr. Grade."

"No? Explain that, Doctor."

"The hydrostatic test is not concerned with the detection of disease, but with the detection of innocence and the conviction of guilt. In foreign medical circles the test is viewed solely as a means of applying the knowledge of medicine to the requirements of the law."

"And would not the requirements of the law be obstructed if, for example, a mother were to have recourse to artificial respiration by blowing air into her stillborn infant's mouth, thus dilating its lungs? Such lungs would swim, though the infant was stillborn. Could the hydrostatic test detect natural from artificial respiration in that case?"

"Probably not. But I doubt that such an operation would serve to obstruct the law."

"Why?"

"Because artificial respiration would only be attempted for the purpose of restoring an apparently deadborn infant to life, whereas it would clearly be the object of the *guilty* mother to leave the child in its dead state."

Gordon Grade gave some thought to this. He took a turn around his table, then swung back on John.

"But you do agree, Doctor, that a child may be born alive, yet be criminally destroyed *before* it has breathed?"

"Yes."

"And that a child may die by the purposeful prevention of respiration during delivery?"

"Yes."

"And that the lungs of a child that has *lived* may sink owing to the fact that disease may have rendered them heavier than water?"

"Yes."

"Yet in each case the hydrostatic test would be unable to discriminate between the lungs of these children who died through a criminal act and the ones who died of natural causes in the struggle to be born?"

"Yes."

"Then it follows that, since it cannot differentiate between death by natural causes and deliberate child-murder, this hydrostatic test is deficient as a test for stillbirth in that the mere sinking of the lungs is not decisive proof of a child's having been born dead."

"It is not surprising that it appears so to the lay mind, sir. The question of stillbirth is overlaid with refined subtleties which at times escape even the trained medical mind."

"Explain that to the court, please."

"For instance, an infant may breathe after expulsion of the head, yet die before complete expulsion. In such a case, even though the child had breathed, it would be legally stillborn."

"And are you claiming this hydrostatic test can make such subtle distinctions?"

"No, sir."

"No, Doctor? Then what are you claiming?"

"That the test can determine only if a child has breathed."

There was a moment of puzzled silence. Then Gordon Grade asked, "Is that not the same?"

"Not to the medical man. As we saw earlier, a child can be stillborn for different reasons. In the three instances you yourself cited, while in each case the child may not have breathed, a medical examination of the body would reveal signs of murder in the first two, disease in the third. But in the case of the Sykes infant, medical examination of the body showed no signs of either murder or disease. The test showed only that the child had not breathed. That, coupled with the absence of any marks of violence on the body, affords strong evidence that the infant had, in fact, died of natural causes prior to or during birth. The Sykes infant was, in a strict medical point of view, stillborn."

Gordon Grade ignored this last. He spent a moment studying his papers, then abruptly changed his line of questioning.

"Now, Doctor, at the coroner's inquest you testified that the Sykes infant was fully mature, did you not?"

"Yes."

"Which means that the child had been born at or near the full term of its mother's pregnancy?"

"Yes."

"So that, from the strictly legal viewpoint, there can be no doubt that the Sykes infant was viable—"

Henry was on his feet. "Objection, my lord. The witness has already testified that in his medical opinion the child was *not* viable—"

The judge turned his strange, pale gaze on Henry. "Mr. Pollexfen, you should know that when a charge of concealment arises, it is not necessary to prove that the child either was or was not viable."

"I am indeed aware of it, my lord, and my respected colleague is likewise aware of it, and his present line of questioning is a deceptive attempt to influence the minds of the jury by—"

"Mr. Pollexfen, I perceive his purpose. Please sit down."

"But, my lord—"

"Mr. Pollexfen, sit down and be silent. Mr. Grade, proceed."

Gordon Grade bowed to the bench. "As your lordship judiciously points out, in cases of this sort it is not required that the prosecution prove viability. Therefore I withdraw the question." He turned back to John. "Now, Doctor, as a physician you must have appeared at countless trials for infanticide, have you not?"

"I have."

"And in such cases have you ever before performed this hydrostatic test?"

"No, for the obvious reason that—"

"For the obvious reason"—Gordon Grade's voice suddenly thundered through the courtroom as he looked squarely at the jury—"for the obvious reason that in all such trials, where witnesses to the actual birth are required by law, such witnesses have in the past always been living witnesses—*living witnesses* to come and stand before the court and place their hands—"

"My lord, my lord!" Henry was shouting, "once more the prosecution is attempting—"

The judge silenced Henry with a gesture. "Mr. Grade," he said, "it is customary for the presiding judge to direct the jury on the law."

Gordon Grade yielded courteously. "I beg the court's pardon. Once more, I withdraw the question." He stood a moment, a half-smile on his lips, satisfied that he had driven home his major point. Then he turned back to John. "Thank you, Doctor," he said pleasantly. "That is all."

John was about to leave the witness-box when Lord Dowden detained him.

"A few questions, if you please, Doctor."

"My lord?"

"Firstly, I am at a loss to understand the degree of reliance to be placed on this test. To the layman's ears portions of your testimony sounded somewhat conflicting."

"There was nothing conflicting, my lord. But some of the questions posed by the prosecution were irrelevant to this trial and were of such a nature as to make it appear so."

"But did you not say that a child might be murdered by the purposeful prevention of respiration during delivery, yet the test would be unable to detect it?"

"I did, my lord, the reason being that the test is new and there are still some unanswerable questions. But despite any present deficiencies, the test is material to the Sykes case in that it can answer the one question fundamental to the case: WAS THE CHILD BORN DEAD? To that question the test was able to give an unequivocal answer. The child had never breathed. Stillbirth, my lord, is the only reasonable conclusion."

For a moment the judge appeared to study this argument and John stirred uncomfortably under the prolonged gaze. The cold, pale eyes seemed to possess a disturbingly penetrative quality.

"Now," the judge continued, "in murder trials it is often found that putrefaction is a consideration. This morning at the morgue you demonstrated that the lungs of the Sykes infant sank in water. Yet the infant had been dead for several weeks. If one considers the likelihood that air had been introduced into the lungs through putrefaction, they should rightly have floated. How do you answer that, Doctor?"

"My lord, in this instance putrefaction was not a factor."

"Why not?"

"The lungs of a fetus are known to be among the last organs to undergo putrefaction. The lungs of a fetus which has never breathed are in a state of condensation and can remain in that condition for up to five months. It is only with the first gasp of air that a newborn's lungs start to expand."

"Only with the first gasp?"

"That is correct, my lord. Only with the first gasp."

"Thank you, Doctor. That is all."

Lord Dowden listened attentively to the two final speeches. But John, watching him, began to feel his apprehensions rise and a cold dread seep into his very bones. If, before the trial, he had felt any small stirring of hope, it vanished now as he studied the judge's impassive face. The legal profession had at times been accused of misplaced humanity. But surely not this man. This judge had as yet scarcely shown enough interest in the defendant to glance in her direction. His fame and achievement might lie in the domain of pure intellect, but it was not hard to conjecture that his soul had become so shriveled by an unhappy private life that he was incapable of being swayed either by the youth of the defendant or the unusual circumstances of her life.

He turned and looked anxiously at Jenny. She sat quite still, her hands folded in her lap. But he knew the strain was telling on her. Her face was deathly pale. The sight of it made his heart contract, filling him with an almost unbearable anguish.

The courtroom grew hushed as the judge finished studying his notes. Now, turning to the jury, he began his summation in crisp, deliberate tones, repeating the known evidence.

Then he paused, sipped some water, and reflected a moment before pressing on.

"The statute covering concealment of birth is based upon the assumption that the woman who is pregnant with a bastard child may conceal her condition for the single purpose of killing that child at birth. Now, in a trial for concealment you must understand that the burden of proof is thrown—not upon the prosecution, as in other crimes —but solely upon the mother. She is presumed to be guilty of killing her child unless she can prove her child was born dead. The defendant, Jenny Sykes, claims her child was born dead, yet she cannot produce the required proof. That omission would seem to bring her within the statute."

At that a ripple of excitement broke from the spectators as their minds leapt ahead to grasp the ominous meaning of the judge's words. John drew a sharp, painful breath. Suddenly he felt stifled by the overcharged atmosphere of the courtroom. Again he looked at Jenny. She had understood. Her tormented eyes were upon him, her white face straining toward him. He felt a rush of black despair. Dear God, what have I done! he thought. Henry was right. It would have been kinder to have left her to die in jail of puerperal fever. An agony of fear of what was to come created an icy void within him.

The judge was rapping his gavel.

"The prosecution has argued," he continued, "that in trials for concealment it is customary, when seeking to repel the charge, for the defense to produce at least one witness to the actual birth to attest that he or she was present and the child was stillborn. The prosecution is correct on that point. We shall return to it shortly.

"Now, gentlemen, our medical witness, Doctor Toller, has testified that no marks of violence were found upon the infant's body. How, then, did the infant die? In cases of concealment the law does not require the prosecution to determine the cause of death, or even to produce the infant's body. Proof of recent birth on the woman's person is sufficient to prove the woman's guilt. We have proof of recent birth.

"However, the defense makes the unusual argument that when Jenny Sykes delivered her child, she was not within the statute for the reason that she had already ceased to be pregnant with a living fetus. To support this argument they have presented what they allege to be presumptive evidence that, in fact, the infant did not live to be given birth and therefore never drew one single breath of air. They argue that the lungs of an infant that has breathed, being buoyant with air, will rise to the top and float when placed in water. But the lungs of a deadborn infant will sink, a fact assigned to their compact structure previous to respiration. This morning at the morgue we all witnessed how the lungs of the Sykes infant sank to the bottom.

"Why is this argument compelling? It is not an entirely new concept. It is universally known that the body of a drowned person sinks at first, then rises and floats when putrefaction has generated air and rendered it lighter than water. Therefore the mind must follow the logical argument that whatever is filled with air will float, while that which lacks air will sink. If one follows that line, and since no signs of violence were found upon the body, the conclusion is irresistible that in fact the Sykes infant never breathed."

The judge paused. He spent a moment studying the papers before him. By now the courtroom buzzed with excited whispers as speculation rose as to the direction the judicial guidance was taking.

Then suddenly a deep hush fell.

"Gentlemen," the judge continued, looking up, "to aid you in reaching a fair and just verdict, it is my duty to direct you in the law as it applies to this case. The statute covering the crime of concealment reads:

> "If any woman be delivered of any issue of her body, male
> or female, which, being born alive, should by the laws of
> this realm be a bastard, and she endeavour privately, either
> by drowning, or secret burying thereof, or any other way,
> either by herself, or the procuring of others, so to conceal
> the death thereof, as that it may not come to light whether
> it were born alive or not, but be concealed, she shall suffer
> death as in the case of murder, except she can prove by one
> witness at the least, that the child was born dead."

The judge looked up. "That, gentlemen of the jury, is the statute by which the defendant, Jenny Sykes, must be judged. The essence of the law is clear. Concealment of the birth of a child by an unwed woman is held to be conclusive evidence of said child having been murdered by its mother. Now, as the prosecution has pointed out, in cases where the defendant alleges her child was stillborn, the statute does indeed require 'one witness at the least.' But I draw your attention to the fact that nowhere does the statute stipulate, as the prosecution claims, that this one witness must be a *living* witness. It stipulates only 'one witness at the least.' Perhaps the original intent was a *living* witness. But that is not what the statute says. So the question must be asked: Can a witness be other than a *living* witness? The Bible tells us that it can. 'And Joshua said unto all the people, Behold, this stone shall be a witness unto us.' So now we are confronted by a knotty position where, under the law, the defendant is clearly guilty of concealment of birth, punishable by death upon the gallows, while at the same time our silent witness, this hydrostatic test, gives presumptive evidence that the child whose birth the defendant concealed could not, as is premised under the law, have been murdered by her since it was already lifeless when she brought it forth.

"Where proof can be sustained that the child was dead-born, the criminal charge of concealment of birth with its presumption of child-murder cannot be tolerated by the laws of a civilized country. Where a degree of uncertainty favors the defendant, the verdict of guilty cannot be received. Gentlemen of the jury, in the face of strong presumptive evidence of stillbirth presented to this court, it would seem to be legally and morally improper to convict in this case. That is my opinion. You are not bound by it. Each man must follow his own conscience. You may retire now to consider your verdict, if you see the necessity."

But the jury did not see the necessity to retire. Judicial guidance was never more explicit. They needed only a brief conference among themselves to bring in their verdict: "Not guilty."

John sat for one dazed moment, his heart pounding, watching the judge step down from the dais and swiftly disappear, a solitary, slope-shouldered, large-headed little figure, oblivious to those around him, immersed in his own private world of law and justice. As the door closed behind him the tension in the courtroom broke and, with the casual inconstancy of trial spectators, wild cheers rose up to the beamed ceiling. People leapt from their seats and rushed down to encircle John and Henry, clamoring to shake their hands, effusive in congratulations and praise for their unlooked-for legal triumph. Even Gordon Grade had a few gracious words to add as they were mobbed by friends, patients, clients, people from neighboring towns whom they scarcely knew.

But for John there was only one person in that courtroom. He swung around and pushed roughly through the throng and hurried over to the girl who now sat alone, sobbing into her hands.

Iris walked at a leisurely pace along the highway leading back to the convent, and John did not hurry her. Jenny sat sideways in the saddle before him, his arms about her. He had quickly paid the jailer's discharge fees and spirited her out of the courtroom by a side door a half hour ago, away from the staring crowds, and had stopped along the way to buy her some refreshment. But she was weeping too hard to eat. The strain of the past weeks, the strain that had given her strength, had become too heavy once the need to endure was removed. Now her face was buried in his shirt. The fabric was wet with her tears.

He bent and kissed the top of her head. "Jenny, my love" he said tenderly, "you have been brave for so long, it is natural to cry now that it is over. And the memory will fade. Our human griefs do have a way of self-healing."

But by the time they arrived at the convent, she was still weeping. He pulled to a halt in front of the gate and sat looking down at her with a troubled expression.

He said, "And if I let you go now, dear one, what will you do? Will you cry your heart out all night long?" Then, when she did not reply, he raised her wet face and thoughtfully studied it. "And I wanted so much to see you smile, my Jenny—the smile that has haunted me since ever I first saw it."

Still he got no answer. Her body shook with her sobs and it seemed she had not even heard him. He glanced up at the sky. It still wanted an hour to sundown. He nudged Iris and the mare took off again.

He rode up through a pine wood, coming out on a headland overlooking the sea, a lofty solitude, home to a few wild white goats that scrambled among the rocks. The heather was a glory of purple blooming beyond its time. It filled the air with its honey scent. Sea gulls mewed above, their wings gleaming white as they wheeled in the sun, then plunged to float on the blue sea like constellations of little stars. The estuary made a band of silver in the distance.

He rode slowly along the brow of the cliff, leaving the rocks and goats behind. Presently, when he came to a level summit, he reined in and dismounted and lifted her down.

"Come, love," he said.

They strolled along the cliff-edge, his arm protectively about her. He watched her anxiously as they walked. The fresh sea breeze blew in her face and played with her long hair. And presently, sensing the serenity all about her, she lifted her head.

There was something soothing in the changelessness of the sea, in the eternal ebb and flow of the tides, the sky ever full of the wind's voice and the raucous cries of gulls. Down by the water's edge a lone man, dwarfed to bird size by the distance, moved with a basket, probing for mussels in the ooze. Flocks of waders roamed the shore, using their long bills to hunt stranded marine animals among the wrack and scattered bones of driftwood. The yellow-horned poppies were still in bloom, springing like a miracle from the shingle banks of Clowe. She watched the slow changing of the light upon them and, as she watched, almost imperceptibly, her sobbing eased.

Presently she asked, wondering, "Why did you bring me here?"

"Are you not glad I did?"

"Yes."

"That was my reason."

"Have you been here before, then?"

"Many times, love. I come when I am troubled. It is a place to find peace."

He stooped and kissed her cheek, tasting the salt of her tears on his lips. He drew his handkerchief and dried her tear-wet face.

"No more crying, my Jenny," he said tenderly. "Those lovely eyes must never again be red with weeping. You must start to be happy now. You are free. Free! You have nothing more to fear. Do you really understand what that means? Do you really understand that you are free?"

"I am trying. But it is hard—and strange."

"The strangeness will pass with the days. You will come to know that this nightmare is over. You will find safe shelter with the Sisters for as long as you wish to stay."

"Will they not mind?"

He smiled down at her. "Sister Brigit will welcome it. She has grown fond of you. For the present you can help her in the Infirmary, if you wish—or in Lying-In. Or you could help in the classrooms with the children. Later, after you regain your strength, you can consider what to do with your life. But for now you will be safe and untroubled with the Sisters. Does that thought comfort you, my Jenny?"

For an instant she seemed about to smile. Then abruptly the pleasure vanished and the old look of fear he had first encountered in the dungeon came back into her face.

He asked quickly, "What is it, love?"

"My father—when he finds out where I am, will he not come to the convent to fetch me—to take me back to the vicarage, I mean?"

He took her arm and they strolled on as he considered this point. He had seen her briefly in the jail before the trial, but had been careful to say nothing that might undermine her fragile control.

But now her words made it clear the time had come to tell her.

He said, "You need no longer fear the vicar, Jenny. The vicar is dead."

She looked up quickly, a question on her lips. But she did not ask it, perhaps because she had always known it would happen that way.

Then suddenly, through the silence, something communicated itself to him. He was caught unawares. "Jenny, is that why you kept silent?"

Her chest heaved with a surprised intake of breath. But she did not answer his question.

He said, "You realized the vicar was the father of your child?"

Still she did not answer.

"Jenny, did you have reason for believing that?"

Her troubled eyes came up to his face. "No. No reason at all."

"Then why?"

"There was no other explanation. Oh, don't you see?"

He took her hands and held them against his heart. "Hush, love, yes, I see. I see, my Jenny. But why did you not tell me this when I asked?"

The tears were back in her voice. "Because I had no way of knowing. Because I was afraid of what suspicion would cause my father to do. He was a bitter man. And the matter of paternity would have made no difference to the outcome of my trial. I questioned Mr. Pollexfen closely on that point."

John almost smiled at that. Yes, he might have known that Jenny had examined the matter of her position before the law with her usual honesty and intelligence. She had already demonstrated an exceptional insight into the vicar's complex mind. She was a scholar, familiar with the works of Shakespeare. She had guessed something of the truth. But not all of it. Perhaps she need never know the depths of the vicar's immorality, but for her peace of mind she should know the vicar was not her father. So delicate a matter, though, was best left to Mrs. Lundy. No need now to go into it. Now was the time to help her look forward with hope to tomorrow.

He put his arm around her waist and continued guiding her slowly along the cliff. The vast bowl of the sky held the luminous peace of sunset. The sea stirred lazily, glittering with crimson sequins.

He said, "Jenny, you once told me about your mother. You spoke of her with love. Would you like to see her again?"

She looked out to where the gulls were following the herring shoals, marking and dipping and quarreling as they dived for the tiny fish.

"You see," she said wistfully, "I do not know where to find her."

"But I do, love. Your mother came to the clinic a few days ago to inquire about you. She would have liked to visit you then, but with the trial coming up it seemed unwise to put you through the added emotional strain of a meeting after all these years. She is hoping to see you as soon as you feel up to it."

Jenny had turned and was staring up at him, her eyes bright with eagerness. "You think she will come back if I ask her?"

Her unmistakable delight at the thought of a reunion with her mother made his heart shake with desolation to think how soon he might have to lose her. But still he answered, "That is all she is waiting for, my Jenny—just for you to ask."

"Is she living nearby, then?"

"Over in Morcombe, a few miles along the coast."

"Could I write her a letter?"

"She would like that. I will send it by courier, if you wish, to make sure she receives it. He can wait and bring her answer back to you."

"Oh, yes, thank you. I will write her tomorrow—" Then suddenly she broke off and her face reflected still another harrowing thought.

"But can my mother take me away?"

"Away from the convent, you mean? From Dorncaster?"

"From you."

It was a moment before he could find the voice to answer that question. Then he asked softly, "Would you be unhappy to leave me then, Jenny?"

"Yes."

He caught a quick breath. He had not meant to press her so soon after the ordeal of her trial, while she was still under the stress of turbulent emotions.

But now he asked, "Will you marry me then?"

She stood silent, her brow creased in an unhappy frown.

He said quickly, "Come, love. What is it now?"

"But have you thought what they would say?"

"What who would say?"

"Everyone—your patients—the townsfolk."

"I care nothing for what the townsfolk will say. As for my patients, they learned long ago to take me as I am."

"Still, you saw the crowds in the courtroom. The people of Dorncaster are not likely to forget the reason I was brought there. Of what I was accused."

"But for you and me, beloved, nothing of the past matters. Nor ever will."

"You might come to regret it—when people start to talk."

He put his strong hands on her shoulders and held her firmly. "Gossip will hardly touch our lives, my Jenny. I love you. You have filled my heart from the moment I saw you. I could not bear to face life now without you. You are everything to me—all that I love. I want you for my wife. But only if you could be happy with me. Only if you could love me."

At that her arms went slowly up around his neck. There was a quiver in her voice when she answered.

"That first day—the day you came down into the dungeon looking for me. I opened my eyes and saw you kneeling there, the lamplight on your face. I loved you then. I love you now. I will always love you."

"Ah, then, my heart," he cried, but now he was overcome by such a torrent of joy that he could think of none of the things he would have wanted to say to her. "Ah, then, my heart," he cried again, and suddenly, almost fiercely, he swept her into his arms and kissed her. Her lips were sweet under his. He kissed her again, lingering, letting the moments pass.

"I will build you a house, my Jenny," he told her presently. "You shall plan it yourself. It will be everything you want our home to be."

"But this cottage you once told me of. Could we not live there?"

He gave a happy laugh. "It has only two small rooms, my love, and Iris must pass through one of those to get to her stable."

"But would you not be happy there?"

A great tenderness engulfed him. "I would be happy anywhere with you, my Jenny—my only love."

He drew her back into his arms and looked deep into her eyes. They were a soft crystal-gray in the fading light. Their beauty made him breathless. But now all trace of uncertainty was gone. Now they were looking up at him with love and trust, shining with the reflection of an inner joy whose meaning set his heart to a wild pounding.

"I love you, Jenny," he said. "I love you." And he took her face between his hands and covered her mouth with his.

It was the sound of the vesper bells ringing faintly across the estuary that roused him. He looked up. The sun had sunk behind the western hills and its orange afterglow lighted the sky, turning the sea a delicate opal. The chines of distant Applecross were folded in dusk. The heather had set up a ghostly rustle under the sweep of the night breeze. Jenny shivered in her thin dress and he opened up his coat and took her inside, holding her sheltered and warm against him.

"I should take you back to the convent, love," he said. "The Sisters will be anxious."

Yet still they stood together on the cliff, aware only of each other, while the twilight deepened and the landmarks loomed faint and intangible. The tranquil sea flowed as though asleep. Veils of mist drifted across it, pearl-pale, illusive. Sounds were clearer now, more distinct and separate by dark than by day: a flock of plovers crying like lost wanderers as they flighted to the uplands; redshanks noising in the saltings, their wild, haunting cries half challenge, half lament; the lovely long-drawn whistling note of the curlew trilling on the wind.

"I should take you back," he said again.

But he only stroked her hair, and kissed her, and drew her closer, unwilling to let her go.

Afterword

The hydrostatic test finally won recognition by the British medical community as a test for stillbirth, thereby providing a way for the courts to save countless innocent unwed mothers from the gallows. Opposition to the test, however, was fierce, and the many controversies to which it gave rise lasted well into the next century.

But even before the law was repealed, some of the more courageous English judges, troubled by the number of unwed mothers of stillborn infants they were routinely sending to the gallows, began to look for ways to circumvent the harsh directive of the statute. That they were surprisingly successful is made clear by the renowned eighteenth-century jurist Sir William Blackstone who, speaking of the concealment law in his *Commentaries*, says:

> But I apprehend it has of late years been usual for us in England, upon trials for this offense, to require some sort of presumptive evidence that the child was born alive, before the other constrained presumption (that the child whose death is concealed was therefore killed by its parent) is admitted to convict the prisoner.

EARLY FORMS OF SURGICAL ANESTHESIA

Early man was quick to make three momentous discoveries: fornication, alcohol, and the narcotic drugs. That narcotics were known to Stone Age man has been suggested by medical historians who discovered evidence of surgical operations performed on the living subject in prehistoric Europe. These operations took the form of trephining the patient's skull and removing a small segment of bone, possibly to cure epilepsy or to conjure mad or evil spirits out through the hole. Arturo Castiglioni, recognized as one of the world's leading medical historians, tells us that "the patient was usually, perhaps always, dulled or made unconscious with soporific potions." That many of these patients survived is shown by partial healing of the edges through the regeneration of newly formed bone.

The Talmud speaks of a stupefying substance to deaden the pain of an operation. The Greeks used opium, belladonna, and mandragora. In ancient Persia, according to the Sha Namah, the patient was bemused with "wine" to make her "all unconscious." For the same purpose Indian hemp (cannabis indica) was used in India by inhalation of the fumes. Hindu surgery records that in the year 927 A.D. an operation was performed on King Bhoja of Dhar, who was suffering from a brain tumor. Anesthesia was given by means of the drug Samohini, and after trepanation of the skull, removal of the tumor and closing of the wound, the king was revived by application of the drug Sanjivani.

In western Europe, in the early Middle Ages the famous Salernitan physicians produced sleep during an operation by means of a sponge drenched with narcotics such as opium, jusquiamus, mandragora, which was then applied to the nose of the patient, who was instructed to breathe deeply. The operation was not begun until he had gone to sleep. The thirteenth-century surgeon Hugh of Lucca perfected a method of general anesthesia using similar narcotics. And it is recorded that in the sixteenth-century, Hans von Gersdorff of Strasbourg performed some two hundred amputations for gangrene employing opium, gradually given, which caused sleep, after which he awakened the patient by making him inhale vinegar. That at least one such recipe for surgical anesthesia was successful was demonstrated by Sir Benjamin Ward Richardson in the late-nineteenth century. (Brit. and For. Med.-Chir. Rev., London 1874, liii).

CAESAREAN SECTION IN THE ANCIENT
WORLD

The basic text for early Indian medicine is that of the physician Susruta (circa sixth century B.C.), who practiced caesarean section and described it systematically in his writings. Caesarean was known to Roman surgery. Numa Pompilius, the second king of Rome (715–672 B.C.), issued the so-called *Lex Regia* directing that the abdomen of every deceased gravida be opened to save the life of the fetus. Children thus born were called Caesi, Caesones, or Caesari, and the operation was named secio caesarea. According to the *Mishna*, compiled circa 140 B.C., the Jews performed caesarean section of *the living mother*. The Talmud contains two types of caesarean operation: delivery through the flank, and the classical caesarean section. Firdausi, the eminent Persian poet completed his magnificent epic poem *Shah Namah* in 999 A.D. It is believed that the poet, in relating the legends of his people, adhered faithfully to the records of antiquity and that his work contains some valuable traditions of early Persian medicine. He gives a legendary account of the birth of the hero, Rustum, by caesarean section, describing how "a skillful Mobed arrived and intoxicated Rondabeh, the moon-faced beauty. Then he ripped open her side without her feeling it, and turning the child's head toward the opening, brought it forth without harming the mother. She slept for a day and a night. When she awakened and saw the child she said, 'I am delivered and my pains are finished.' "

Thereafter the records of caesarean section appear to fail. But in the year 1500 A.D. an illiterate Swiss sow-gelder named Jacob Nufer unknowingly revived the lost operation by performing caesarean section on his own wife, who was dying of obstructed labor. She lived to be seventy-seven years and bore him other children. According to the Dutch physician Johann Weyer (1515–1588), still another sow-gelder performed a double ovariotomy on his own daughter. This curious lay excursion into operative gynecology was followed professionally in western Europe by other caesarean operations. It appears to have been practiced successfully on the living by Cristoforo Maini (1540), followed by Bain (1540), and Dirlewang (1549), until we find François Rousset recording as many as fifteen successful cases in 1581. In the next century the renowned Amsterdam obstetrician Hendrik van Roonhuyse (1625–1672) championed caesarean section in difficult cases. His excellent work on operative gynecology, *Heelkonstige Aanmerkkingen* (which has been described as the first work on the subject in the modern sense) is illustrated with unique copper plates showing his mode of incision.

A word concerning the widespread belief that the operation known as "caesarean section" derives its name from Julius Caesar. As has been noted above, the operation by which the fetus is taken from the mother's abdomen was being performed by Roman surgeons as early as the seventh century B.C., at which time it was already known by the name of secio caesarea. Julius Caesar was not born until the year 100 B.C.

Bibliography

Ackernecht, Erwin. *Early History of Legal Medicine* (Vol. II). Summit, N.J.: Ciba Symposia, 1950.

Bartley, O. W. *Treatise on Forensic Medicine.* Bristol: Barry & Son, 1815.

Beard, Charles D. *The Office of the Justice of the Peace in England* (Vol. XX). London: P. S. King & Son, 1904.

Blackstone, Sir William. *Commentaries on the Laws of England.* Oxford: Clarendon Press, 1766–69.

Burn, Richard. *The Justice of the Peace.* London: T. Cadell, 1770.

Castiglioni, Arturo. *A History of Medicine.* New York: Alfred A. Knopf, 1947.

Chalmers, Sir M. D. *Local Government.* London: Macmillan & Co., 1883.

Cummin, William. *The Proofs of Infanticide Considered.* London: Longman, 1836.

David, A. H. *Medico-Legal Proofs of Infanticide.* Edinburgh: Neill & Co., 1835.

De Mahon, Paul Augustin. *An Essay on the Signs of Murder in New-born Children.* Christopher Johnson, trans. Lancaster: Longman & Co., 1813.

Edinburgh Medical and Surgical Journal (Vol. XIX). Edinburgh: A. Constable & Co., 1805.

Garrison, Fielding D. *History of Medicine.* Philadelphia: W. B. Saunders, 1917.

Gradwohl, R. B. H. *Legal Medicine.* St. Louis: C. V. Mosby & Co., 1954.

Guy, William A. *Principles of Forensic Medicine.* New York: Harper & Bros., 1845.

Howard, John. *The State of the Prisons in England and Wales.* Warrington: W. Eyres, 1780.

Leonardo, Richard A. *A History of Surgery.* New York: Froben Press, 1943.

Maitland, Sir. M. D. *Justice and Police.* London: Macmillan & Co., 1885.

Neild, James. *State of the Prisons in England, Scotland and Wales.* London: J. Nichols & Son, 1812.

Ogston, Francis. *Lectures on Medical Jurisprudence.* London: J & H Churchill, 1878.

Reese, John James. *Live Birth in its Medico-Legal Relations.* Philadelphia: 1887.

Ryan, William Burke. *Infanticide, Its Law, Prevalence, Prevention and History.* London: J. Churchill, 1862.

Smith, John Gordon. *The Principles of Forensic Medicine.* London: J & G Underwood, 1821.

Taylor, Alfred S. *Principles and Practice of Medical Jurisprudence.* London: J & H Churchill, 1957–57.

Webb, Sidney and Beatrice (Passfield). *English Local Government.* London: Longman, Green & Co., 1927.

————*English Prisons Under Local Government.* London: Longman, Green & Co., 1922.

Wigram, William Knox. *The Justice's Note Book.* London: Stevens & Sons, 1881.